STILL FALLING

BY MARTIN WILSEY

Jeff,

Enjoy!!

Still Falling

Cover Art by Duncan Long

ISBN-13: 978-1507802380
ISBN-10: 1507802382

For more information:

Blog: http://wilseymc.blogspot.com/

Web: http://www.hell-labs.com/

Email: info@hell-labs.com

THE SOLSTICE 31 SAGA:

STILL FALLING (2015)

THE BROKEN CAGE (2015)

BLOOD OF THE SCARECROW (2016)

FOR BRENDA

THE ONLY ONE THAT SAW ALL MY PAIN

FOR ERIC

BECAUSE YOU NEVER GOT TO READ IT

STILL FALLING

CHAPTER ONE

The Fall Begins

"The Ventura was a deep space survey ship, with a crew of over 2000 men and women. When we entered the orbit of the planet Baytirus that day, we never expected the Ventura to be immediately destroyed. We didn't know we weren't the first people to find that planet. But someone knew."

--Solstice 31 Incident Investigation Testimony Transcript: Logs of Master Engineer Wes Hagan, senior surviving engineering member of the Ventura's crew. Recorded on 26291010 over three decades ago and stored in the data being analyzed.

<<<>>>

Barcus crashed back into consciousness when his face smashed into the inside of his helmet.

He was in a three axis tumble. He knew the feeling. All inertial dampening was off. His maintenance suit was powered up, docked in place, but off-line.

He coughed and could feel blood spray into his helmet. Great! His nose was probably broken. Again.

Then he began to remember.

His mind was coming back on-line.

"Status! Visual!" His helmet systems came alive. Temperature and pressure were normal. He confirmed it was a freefall spin. Wherever he was, it was pitch black.

"Lights!" The suit's work lights all activated.

He saw immediately that he was locked into the suit dock on the bridge of Chen's shuttle. Chen was strapped into the command chair. Her flight suit didn't have her helmet, and her arms swayed with her neck in the tumble. The shuttle seemed dead.

The shuttle bridge was all white in the suit's harsh work lights. It was a perfect oval dome around them like they were on the inside of a huge egg. The command chair was in front left. Two support stations were behind that and the four passenger seats.

He hammered the EXIT control in the suit causing its helmet

chest plate to hinge open and back. He pounded the restraint release in the center of his chest, and the straps retracted smoothly, freeing him.

In the chaos of the tumble, he slammed first into the ceiling and then into the seats, but he managed to cross the compartment to grasp Chen's belt. As he felt for her pulse, her eyes fluttered open.

She blinked for a moment and focused by force of will, saying, "Display Delta" to the air, as something impacted the exterior of the shuttle. Suddenly, it was like they were in a convertible, the dome turning into an exterior display. They were in a gut-churning three axis, high-speed spin with no control. Debris tossed all around them. Some more chunks crashed into them, slowing the spin along one axis. The suit was locked into place in the dock. Otherwise, the heavy armor thing would have killed them by now, crashing about loose.

Barcus could see life pods and other shuttles that had managed to get aloft from other bays, but they were destroyed by plasma cannon fire.

"Chen. Don't stabilize." Suddenly a giant explosion destroyed what was left of the main ship. The shock wave crashed more debris into the shuttle.

"Display, Baker," Chen said weakly. It changed to a 3D rendering of the ship tumbling with massive chunks of debris. The display showed the expected path of the shuttle to its crash to the planet.

"Chen, I have no idea what happened, but we have to let the ship tumble towards the planet as debris. I don't see any enemy ships at all. There has got to be some kind of automated defense system that is shooting down anything that looks like it's under power and has people in it."

"Barcus...I'm bleeding...bad." He could see the blood splattered on her neck, flowing up from inside her pressure suit.

"Is the cabin holding pressure? Do we have a breach?" Barcus asked.

"Yes, it's holding, but we can't get you out of your flight suit until we stop the tumble. If we stop, we're dead."

"Slow the tumble with manual thrusters," Barcus said. Chen did until the ship was just turning gently.

Chen's eyes fluttered again. "Shrapnel in my guts, man. It's bad. Listen..." She fell unconscious again.

"Display Delta," Barcus said. Nothing happened. "Damage Report." Nothing. He then saw on one of the log display windows: "Unauthorized Command Attempts 2."

"Status Report!" The count moved to three.

"Chen, wake up. I can't fly this thing." Her faced winced in severe pain. Then her eyes opened.

"Stu. Activate AI, Emergency. (Gasp) Pilot injured...grant full master control authority to Roland Barcus. Present. All systems." She winced and fell silent, except for the occasional gasp. Barcus had to hold tight in the weightlessness.

"Stu. Follow this same trajectory and passive scan the potential crash site. The tactical screen indicates that orbital decay will be in about three orbits. Give me stats on this planet."

"Mr. Barcus, it's an E7 class world. It seems to be sparsely populated by humans, with .89 gravity." He had heard Stu's voice before. "Temperate climate. If we maintain the present course, we will land in a very rocky mountainous region."

"Population there?" Barcus asked, looking at the tactical map display.

"Unable to tell with passive scans only. Little to no population expected. Harsh climate and terrain in that region. Cold temperatures. Estimate, -4 Celsius," Stu reported.

"We need to continue to look like debris as we descend. Grav-foils only until we need the engines and even then, thrusters only. Can we wait until we are well within the atmosphere?" Barcus asked the AI.

"Yes, sir. Our Polycarbon hull can withstand unpowered re-entry temps easily." The computer was calm.

"Find a nice ledge in those mountains and set us down, Stu. Grav-foils only." He began unstrapping Chen.

"Chen." He said. She winced as Barcus moved her. "This shuttle has a med bay. Stu. Stop all tumble. I need free fall in here." Moments later, the tumble sense was gone. He drifted gently down to the lower level and into the infirmary with Chen. The med bay was the dominant feature at this end to the front of the hold.

The door slid closed behind them as Barcus set her on the scanning table still in her spacesuit. Drops of blood drifted everywhere. A vacuum sound began emitting from the table and the floor while a fluids-elimination unit kicked on. The blood was sucked down to collectors. The midsection of Chen's suit was shredded. The unit scanned her and confirmed that her injuries were beyond the abilities of the auto-doc.

Barcus felt his weight begin to return as the Grav-foils activated in preparation for landing when the ship entered the atmosphere.

If they were being tracked, now was when their deceleration would be noticed.

"Chen. Wake up. What do I do?"

Her eyes fluttered open. "Stu. Status?"

"We will be landing in three minutes. I have found a wide, isolated shelf that is clear. I do not detect any active scans. It is heavily overcast, visibility less than two kilometers. Temperature is minus 11 Celsius. No population present."

"Stu... auto-doc, go." The system whirred to life. A bar light swept over her once and returned to her belly for a more detailed slow scan. The monitor read, "Spleen, liver, stomach, large and small intestines, all severely damaged. Medical Nanites deployed will be insufficient. Injury fatal." She squeezed Barcus's hand, holding it as if they were about to arm wrestle again or she was going to pull herself up.

"Stu..." She coughed up a little blood as she struggled to speak. "Activate EM. Emergency Module... Survival mode, hostile environment, Full AI."

"Barcus, listen. They will come. Put on your suit, take the Emergency Module and run. Use Escape and Evasion mode. EM, can you hear me?"

"Yes, sir." Barcus heard the EM inside his head. It spoke directly to his wetware, his internal deep brain systems. A new window opened in his vision via his advanced HUD implants. It was the Emergency Module's operation status window.

Chen gasped to the EM, "Say hello to Barcus. It is now your job to keep him alive. He's got full admin control. Bring his suit down here via remote." Her eyes looked to Barcus.

"Take me outside with you when we land. We will have to hurry."

The suit descended via its lift just as they felt the soft settling of their landing. The forward ramp began to lower.

"I'm sorry, Barcus."

Barcus couldn't speak.

"EM. Where are you?" Chen whispered. HUD systems didn't require volume.

"Right here, sir." The voice transmission was still coming from his HUD, not his ears.

A giant black spider rounded the side of the ship. Its skin was the same as the ship and the suit. Somehow it seemed like it was watching them even though it had no visible eyes. Closely watching. Its body was the size of a large van-type, ground transport.

"That's your souped-up Model 66 EM, isn't it?" Barcus asked, wearing a forced smile as he carried her to the wall and knelt with her in his arms. She was so light. Was the planet's gravity so low?

"Yeah, it is. You're gonna love it. Finally, get to test all the mods," she said.

"We'll have fun running it. Like that time last year. We got in so much trouble," Barcus said.

"I want to go outside," Chen whispered. "I want to breathe real air."

Barcus lifted her tiny frame from the bloody table and walked down the still opening ramp into the cold. They descended to find a sun about to set. It blazed in a gap between the clouds and the horizon. It was cold and windy.

Chen showed an honest but weak smile. Med-bay painkillers were settling in. "No need to bullshit me, man. I know I'm done. I want you to leave me here. Stu will watch over me. You have to. They probably tracked us on our descent down."

Barcus carried her out.

"Stu... Standby mode. Settle," She whispered to the Shuttle Transport Unit.

The ramp closed. The landing legs retracted. The ship's belly settled to the ground. Barcus had always thought it looked like a turtle with all its limbs withdrawn.

"The last orbital rotation indicated that an atmospheric ship of some kind was diverting this way. It's screaming with transmissions. It's not in passive scanning range yet." She coughed more blood.

"What happened?" Barcus asked. He didn't know what to say. He knew he would not let her die alone, whatever the cost.

"Hyper-missiles, nukes, no warning. We had just entered orbit. No warning, no 'go the fuck away' message. Just boom. Point blank." She was fading now. "You had just gone into dock the maintenance suit. I was waiting on the ramp for the rest of the morning crew for our day. The first strike explosion filled my guts with shrapnel." She coughed again, choking on blood. "I made it to the command chair." She was fading. "Barcus, you need to know, the EM is more, it's not what you think, the mods... it's AI, listen..."

"Barcus..." She stiffened in his arms, eyes locked. Then, slowly, Chen went limp. He watched the light disappear from her open eyes.

"We must go, sir. Now. They are coming," the spider said inside his head.

CHAPTER TWO

Escape and Evasion

"Barcus was in shock. This narrative sheds a whole new light on the Solstice 31 Incident. It is clear that he did not destroy the Ventura. Please note: The new hostile environment survival modules in this highly customized AI had never been tested."

--*Solstice 31 Incident Investigation Testimony Transcript: Emergency Module Digital Forensics Report. Independent Tech Analysis Team. 26630113*

<<<>>>

"Mr. Barcus, sir. We must go. Now." The spider AI woke him from his shock and despair. It had an edge of urgency in its voice.

The sun was almost down, and the freezing wind was picking up. It just occurred to him that it was way below freezing. In his standard coveralls that he wore inside the maintenance suit, he'd die of **exposure** soon.

Maybe he'd just stay. Here with her.

He lowered Chen to the ground beneath an overhang of shale and began to pile rocks around her and finally upon her. He closed her eyes and gently kissed her forehead before he covered her face. Finished, he finally stepped back. Tears were freezing on his face.

"Sir, please. We must go." The suit had already docked inside the EM. It had lowered its belly and slid open the hatch. It was positioning directly above Barcus as he began to stand. When he was fully on his feet, it lowered directly over him, through the hatch, like lowering a jar onto a beetle. All he had to do was step up and in. He hesitated. The maintenance suit was like a huge black robot that the Emergency Module's artificial intelligence program could control. It was already secured inside.

The six seats in the EM made it feel like the van his parents had when he was a kid. The interior was completely white - until the HD3D-Display activated. Then it seemed like he was in a convertible with the top down - virtual displays in every direction.

The EM was already moving as the hatch closed. The relatively smooth movement over such rocky terrain was impressive for a ground-based transport. He watched the Shuttle Transport Unit fade into the mountain.

Barcus slumped into the driver seat as more displays activated. He held his face in his hands as the full impact of what has happened sank in. Despair filled him as the adrenaline faded from his blood. The Emergency Module moved easily across the jagged ridge. The lights inside the module had dimmed while he sobbed.

The night sky was full of unfamiliar stars as the clouds thinned. He leaned back and strapped in without thinking. The module was equipped with a full 5-point harness. The cliff to his right convinced him it was a good idea. The EM picked up the pace as soon as he was strapped in. Not as smooth now, but moving at a breakneck speed.

"Barcus?" It was a young woman's voice. She sounded upset. Afraid. "Are you okay?"

"Who are you? Where are you?" Barcus began scanning the displays, looking for comm traffic geolocation. "Where are you?"

"Barcus, it's me, Em." Slowly he realized that it was the AI in the Emergency Module, Em. "I'm worried about you, Barcus. Are you injured? There's so much blood. Inside the STU, we didn't give you a med-scan. Was any of the blood yours?"

Barcus slammed his hand down on the console and screamed, "NO!" He was unaware if he was answering Em's question or venting because he knew he was still alone. The voice seemed so real. So human. So much emotion. "No. It fucking wasn't mine. It was Chen's. I had on the fucking EVA maintenance suit. It's like armor..." He saw bits of debris burning down from the sky above. "They're all dead, okay? I was in the damned suit..." He looked at the sky, debris burning in.

"Barcus, I'm so sorry." She genuinely sounded sad, sincerely sorry for him.

"Look, Em. I know you are in survival mode. I know you are designed to help me in every way, even mentally. But seriously? You sound like... Fuck it." He turned the chair back toward the main console. "Em, I need a status. Anything you got. Start with the terrain. Where the hell are we going?"

Immediately, the display enhanced, augmented with night vision, thermal overlay, planned path indicator trail and many other visuals. The night sky had annotations in the display regarding SAT positions and functions. It showed they were weapons platforms as well as comm-SATs and weather monitors.

A smaller 3D map of the local area showed where they were going. There was a cave on the next peak with a direct line of sight to the Shuttle Transport Unit where they could hide and observe. They could get there reasonably quick.

"Barcus, I didn't mean to offend you. Based on your profile, I thought that this persona would be the easiest for you to live with...in the long run."

Barcus stilled. The meaning of her words sank in.

"We are on our own. I have no indications of other survivors. But if they are smart, they will maintain radio silence and only perform passive scans. Like us." Barcus could have sworn she was about to start crying.

"Why the hell did we leave the shuttle? It could still fly," Barcus said.

"I believe they tracked it down and might find it. Our best chance of survival, long-term, is to evacuate from here and monitor. Chen is dead." The EM sounded upset, and then continued.

"There is a ship coming this way. ETA is four minutes. Hang on." Just then, Em jumped into a deep ravine. Its long legs absorbed most of the impact. She backed under a slight overhang and settled, not moving. Only a small strip of the sky was visible above.

Passive sensors were on full high speed and recording as the ship flashed over them.

Barcus found himself holding his breath.

"Is there any way to tell if they have seen us?" he asked in a hushed tone.

"I don't believe they have seen us or the Shuttle Transport Unit." Em paused, "Barcus, do you mind if I call him Stu? I usually call him Stu."

Barcus barked in laughter. The question was so unexpected. And then he strangled on a sob, covering his mouth. He remembered that

Chen called it Stu as well. "Yes, Em. Let's call him Stu." He knew he was losing it. He put his face in his hands again.

"They are coming back around," Em said with concern in her voice. The display showed a 3D terrain map indicating their position in the ravine and the STU's position on the ledge. The ship was loud, hovering now, but not directly visible.

"There isn't enough room on the ledge for them to land." Search lights scanned the cliffs.

Suddenly, the HUD presented a view in a window as if it were flying up along the cliff face and rising fast.

"Em, what am I seeing here? We are not moving," Barcus asked, pointing at the window.

"I have deployed a remote BUG. A Briggs, Udvar, Green surveillance drone. It will provide video and audio surveillance. It cannot move too quickly. BUGs are only the size of a tiny insect and almost impossible to detect, even with active scans," Em, explained.

It seemed to take forever to clear the edge of the ravine. Search lights were scanning back and forth on the rocks. The lights scanned a few meters away from Chen's cairn. The search light never touched it. There was already a little snow drift obscuring the pile. All tracks and signs of their passing were gone.

The ship's engines began to roar again, and it moved off. The BUG watched it go. It had clear markings - PT-137.

"Colonists?" Barcus asked.

"It appears so," Em replied.

CHAPTER THREE

To Fall or Not to Fall

"Forensic analysis indicates that this Emergency Module was in possession of some very highly classified Briggs, Udvar, Green, surveillance drones. Commonly known as BUGs. None of these units were recovered. No hardware provenance is available."

--Solstice 31 Incident Investigation Testimony Transcript: Emergency Module Digital Forensics Report. Independent Tech Analysis Team.

<<<>>>

Em stayed in the ravine for another hour.

"Barcus, I think we should leave some surveillance BUGs behind and move." Em began to rise from her hiding place. The EM switched to the local view. Barcus had fallen silent. The display had been focused on the Chen's cairn for the last hour.

"Em, should I just leave her there?"

"For now. We have to go," Em replied.

The EM's display came alive with windows of the BUG's views, RF monitors, 3D maps, systems statuses and passive scan screens. They begin to distract Barcus as Em slowly climbed out.

"Em? This one looks like an old style GPS." He pointed to a specific screen.

Em replied, "Yes, Barcus, their SATs supply Global Positioning System location information, which I can use passively. I am currently attempting to correlate positioning with maps I created based on images collected during our orbit and descent. There is also a lot of comm traffic, but it is encrypted... Once I get enough BUGs deployed, we may be able to triangulate passively transmission sources. I will have to find out if they can sense our Radio Frequency if I try to communicate with the BUGs before we risk it."

"How many SATs do they have? Can you tell?" Barcus was studying another display. He looked up as they cleared the edge of the ravine on the other side. The display sky showed markers and other meta-data regarding the SATs in his night sky. "Do you think it's a risk, moving within view of the SATs?"

"My external temperature is the same as the rock around us. No thermal signatures. There is heavy cloud cover now. Perhaps a storm front." Em was all business as she continued to brief Barcus on the information she had. She was in Escape and Evasion mode now. Before dawn, they would reach a cavern one peak over from where they were, in which they could hole up and reassess.

"Em, I am looking at the specs of your BUGs. Impressive. How many do we have?" The view screen had an image of the tiny insect-like device in a large window.

"We have 1,600 total, but they are usually deployed in pairs. They take about three to seven hours to recharge fully in the sun. So they can swap duty to recharge. All 1,600 fit in a container the size of a deck of cards. They were Chen's idea. She was a survival specialist." Em sounded sad. "Chen made a hobby of modifications. She replaced all my leg joints with the new plasteel. They never get hot. Many upgrades improved my abilities greatly. My overland speed has been increased by 85%. Chen did lots of software upgrades as well. The latest AI with custom modules. More comm strength. Less power consumption. Better lens optics. Even better survival rations."

"Do we have any weapons?" Barcus knew weapons were supposed to be kept in the armory, but many of the best, most experienced pilots always kept some checked out

"Yes. We have a Colt AR-79 rifle and a Glock 93 handgun. There are 10 mags of caseless for each. Also, over the last two years, she installed an embedded, 10mm BMG caseless long range projectile weapon. It's forward facing and good to about 5,000 meters. Auto-fed with 1,000 rounds in inventory. I also have two standard 5mm caseless auto feeders that are sound suppressed and have 5,000 rounds each. Ammo is compatible with the AR-79."

They finally reached the mouth of the cavern. The opening was low and wide. The cavern was dry and had a high ceiling. Em backed into the darkness and settled down with a view of the shelf where the STU crouched, barely visible, blending into the mountain.

Snow began falling heavier before the sun rose. Em reported a cold front coming through and severe weather behind it. In three hours, the snow had already begun to drift and fill the spaces behind and beside the STU. Chen's cairn had disappeared completely shrouded in snow.

Barcus fell asleep, oblivious to the snow that blew sideways. Em slowly reclined the command chair beneath him. She watched the STU. More BUGs were deployed to occupy two other peaks.

Night fell as the blizzard continued. Barcus continued to sleep.

"Barcus. Wake Up." The sound of Em's voice was urgent. His seat had returned to upright from its earlier reclined position. The HUD was showing the view from one of the BUGs that were stationed on the opposite ledge near the STU.

Barcus was still shaking off the grog. "How long have I been asleep?"

"Six hours and 47 minutes. I was worried."

"Barcus, I don't think they have seen the STU, even though he is right there. With the snow, he looks like part of the mountain."

The snow continued to fall. Without the wind this time.

"Em, are we going to be able to get off this mountain?"

"Yes, we will."

You sound awfully certain of yourself, Barcus thought.

"We will wait a few hours and go. I have a course planned for moving south," Em said.

"Open the hatch, Em," Barcus ordered.

"Why? It's -11 Celsius out there." Em sounded concerned.

"Just fucking open it," he barked.

The hatch opened, and he dropped through to the uneven ground.

He could feel the cold now. The wind cut through his clothes like they were not there.

He walked to the mouth of the cave and stood at the edge of the precipice.

Just another step and it would be over.

"What are we going to do, Em?" The realization and despair were back in his voice.

Em took it as an actual question and replied. "Initially, we need to get away from the landing site. I am sure they will be searching for it when the weather clears. We will begin, as we have, with standard escape and evasion. We will find a secluded spot to hide for a while as we collect more data. We still have no idea what happened. We need to know."

"We need to know who these people are." Barcus saw in his HUD a list appear labeled "Priority Tasks" where these items appeared.

"Barcus?" Em's voice was very serious.

"Yes, Em."

"I'll do everything in my power to keep you safe. I promise."

Barcus smiled. *Chen did a great job on this AI.*

"Thanks, Em. I know you will."

Barcus looked deep into the ravine before him.

It would be so easy.

"They're all dead, Em. Over 2,000 people. All dead. All my friends, everyone I know or care about. Gone..."

So easy.

"Barcus, I'd like to brief you on our current inventory and priority needs, starting with warmer clothes," Em said.

His hands and feet were already numb. He began to turn toward the EM when he slipped on the icy rocks. He started to pitch over the edge.

Something clamped down hard on his flailing arm before he could fall to his death. Turning his head, he looked into black so dark that it was like a hole in reality.

It was his maintenance suit.

Em must have brought it out on remote.

Barcus knew it had saved him. But he didn't mention it as he was set down farther back from the edge. The suit positioned itself between him and oblivion. It seemed to be a living thing just then, a powerful predator almost.

Then the suit opened without a pause, and the tool returned. The feeling was gone. Realizing how cold he was, he climbed in.

CHAPTER FOUR

The Long Slide Down

"The hostile environment protocols in this AI were so advanced that even now, 34 years later, in 2663, they are under consideration for new Emergency Modules. Even after all that happened."

--Solstice 31 Incident Investigation Testimony Transcript: Emergency Module Digital Forensics Report. Independent Tech Analysis Team.

<<<>>>

Em wanted to wait until nightfall to exit the cave. It was standard ENE protocol. While they were waiting, Barcus explored the cave with some of the BUGs. Em showed Barcus the capabilities of the devices. They had full, high-definition audio and video. They could function as tiny local comm relays, and they were self-powered on minimal light.

They then spent a few hours going over the full inventory of the Emergency Module, the range of capabilities of both its hardware and software. Barcus also configured his internal retinal HUD to remote access the systems within Em. Barcus had a basic maintenance retinal HUD implant. It didn't have any local onboard specialty hardware except the basic 3D vid and short range comms. With a full-time link to Em, his personal HUD was greatly enhanced. It was past nightfall when they were done.

The descent itself from the mountain was harrowing for Barcus initially. It did, however, keep his mind off Chen and the rest of his friends.

"What if this was all just a mistake? What if it was an accident? Should we issue a distress call? "

"Barcus, they were targeting the life pods as they launched." Em began playback of the descent. Adjusting out the pitch and yaw, Barcus could clearly see that high energy particle beams from the weapons platforms were destroying the life pods.

"Do we know anything about the PT-137 craft we saw? It was so loud."

Em brought up several high definition images of the ship and ran video loops in other windows.

"From the markings, it was a PT-137, which was the largest of the Personal Transport PT class vehicles at the time of their manufacture. It held four passengers and was mainly designed as a utility transport shuttle for people. But that was 232 years ago. The war stopped their manufacture when the factory was destroyed."

The images changed to a second, larger craft. "This second one, which I detected on our free fall, I believe was a C-1138a of the same vintage. It was a civilian version of the C-1138 – with no weapons trays. It was used for the transport of large amounts of cargo and personnel. The cargo bay was not pressurized, and they were notorious for not maintaining hull seal in space."

Barcus asked, "Any theories on how they got here?"

Em paused before answering. "Wartime, unregistered, colonists is the most likely answer."

"What? That was over 200 years ago."

"Two hundred twenty-seven years ago. But before and during the war, there were masses of people fleeing from Earth. Most were sponsored by wealthy nations. Most did not survive." Em was sounding now like the other AI systems Barcus interacted with - facts, and lots of them.

"Registered colonies became hostages in the war. Nearly two billion people died in the colonies before the Contraction. Private colony ships would depart and never arrive at their designated planet. It was always assumed that their ships didn't survive, that they were either intercepted or destroyed. Some were rumored to have simply gone to an alternate planet to avoid destruction or any further involvement in the war."

"I heard that. But they always gave themselves away - setting up communications," Barcus added.

A big slide sent Em far too close to a major fall over a cliff. The conversation silenced, they recovered and selected an alternate route. They continued down and south.

Once they cleared the cloud layer, Barcus could see the valley below. Tall pine forests led to deciduous trees farther down the valley. It was clear that autumn was just beginning in this region of the planet.

Em skidded to a halt without notice, making Barcus glad he had his harness on. "What's wrong, Em?"

"It's a distress signal from another Emergency Module." Em sounded shocked.

"I thought you said it was a bad idea to send a distress call," Barcus stated, realizing the implications. "Where is it coming from?"

"It's about 1,620 kilometers south-east from here." EM moved quickly to the top of a near peak.

"Wouldn't that Emergency Module know to keep radio silence?" Barcus asked.

"Only in Hostile Environment Survival mode. I think its user is unaware that the environment is hostile. It is an automated rescue beacon," Em explained as she reached the peak, hoping for a better signal.

Just then, the signal stopped.

Barcus was watching the status display when it ceased.

"It was destroyed." Em paused. "Rescue beacons never stop midstream. They always complete the automatic cycle. And when deactivated, they broadcast reason for deactivation. This one didn't."

"How could they get there so fast? I mean...maybe..." He fell silent.

Em said resignedly, "It was too far away for us to do anything."

"How long would it take BUGs to get there in autonomous mode?"

"It depends on the weather. But I estimate 190 days."

"Too far, too long. Can you think of anything else we can do?"

"No, sir," Em replied.

"Why doesn't the BUGs' RF give them away?"

"They were specifically designed as clandestine surveillance drones. They use encrypted low bandwidth comms that are designed to look and sound like solar radiation noise. Audio, video, command control and relay only. No local storage."

"Where the hell would Chen get something like that?" Barcus asked.

"She had friends on the third shift command crew, like

Worthington. And many friends in security that were former military."

It hit Barcus again. They were all dead. Even the best officers he had ever met in the fleet. Worthington, Lewis, Cook, Metzler, Adams, LaRochelle, all of them. They were the only command crew that would come to the Ventura's best pub, Pecks Halfway, on a regular basis. Peck was dead too, that busted-down, alcoholic, gay, son of a bitch, barkeep... friend.

Barcus covered his face with his hands again. Silently, his shoulders shook.

When he took his hands away, sniffing, his face was wet, and the muscles in his jaw began to work as he clenched and ground his teeth.

A long slide down a slope covered in black shale distracted him for a few minutes, but only a few. His thoughts returned to the 2,067 people that were murdered.

I will make them pay.

CHAPTER FIVE

The Stone Cauldron

"The AI known as Em was collecting data at an incredible rate using the Briggs, Udvar, Green drones. Only a fraction of this data was shared with Barcus. Specifically to ensure his safety."

--Solstice 31 Incident Investigation Testimony Transcript: Emergency Module Digital Forensics Report. Independent Tech Analysis Team.

For seven days, Em and Barcus moved south, out of the mountains and into the forests. The trees were very old growth, very much like redwoods, but thinner. They had trunks that were a meter or two across and were over thirty meters tall. The canopy above consumed virtually all the light. Clearings occurred where the rocks reached the surface like exposed bones. Oddest of all, there seemed to be hardly any tree fall. None of these trees seemed to have ever died. There was no evidence of them having burned, either. On two occasions, Barcus found evidence of the undergrowth burning completely off, but the trees were just a bit charred.

They moved at night following rivers, with Em walking in the water. Hundreds of BUGs fanned out from their position to survey and map the area. Infrequently, they would discover forest roads. The BUGs discovered roads that lead to small settlements.

The first of these settlements was little more than a crossroads village at the edge of a giant freshwater lake. It consisted of a tavern, a blacksmith, a trading post and what looked like a primitive meetinghouse. Em quickly cataloged all the people in the village. There were thirty-six adults and nineteen children out and about. They looked happy and productive and prosperous.

Barcus watched them, an observer. Their lives were primitive, medieval even, but reasonably comfortable. Em convinced him he needed to learn the language. This would be a good way. So they left some BUGs there.

They were making good time, even though Barcus had no idea where they were going. One day, he asked Em to stop.

They were on a bluff that overlooked a wide river.

"Em, where the hell are we going?"

"South."

Is she being a smartass?

"Where? Why? Specifically?" There was a pause. "I know I have checked out a bit. But I'm back now."

"I wanted to let you mourn. So many lost." She sounded like she was going to cry. Barcus wanted to comfort her. *Chen, how the hell did you manage this?*

He had been mourning. He had spent endless hours, zoned out, watching happy people drink ale in a tavern. Watching because they laughed. It was the same everywhere. Sounded just like the Peck's Halfway, back on the Ventura, his favorite place to relax after shift. Peck had actual beer and good bourbon. And there were friends. It was the closest pub to the outer rings. All the "heavies" drank there. It was a "One G Joint."

Goddammit, Chen.

"So what's the plan, Em? An AI as smart as you must have a plan."

There was a pause before she said, "Survive. Gather information. Hide. Be safe. Act on what we discover. Survive."

"That sounds like a plan." He was looking at the view. The trees had a hint of fall color here. "I think we have evaded any physical pursuit. We need to find somewhere we can hold up. Maybe for the whole winter." Barcus was looking at the leaves, wondering to himself how he could think about beauty when all these people were dead.

"I think you're right. We need somewhere secluded. I don't think the locals would like me." Her voice was amused. "There is an abandoned village 30 clicks from here. We surveyed it and moved on." Em replayed a fly-by the BUGs had captured. It looked long abandoned. Almost haunted.

"Okay. Let's go. I want to wear the suit though today. I feel like a run."

Barcus climbed out of Em to find the suit already waiting for him. It was kneeling, sitting on its heels with its hands behind its back so he could use them to climb up and in. It rose as he did in precise motion that allowed Barcus to easily slide his legs into the lower half. As he leaned forward into the harness, the back closed behind him. The suit stood just over three meters tall.

The suit had a full HUD built into the inner torso dome. To Barcus, it looked like he was walking around in an open top exoskeleton. Nothing could have been further from the truth. As the gel expanded around him to secure and protect him and to sense his movements, the internal HUD came up. The dome was not a helmet, really. There were no visors or transparent ports of any kind. The internal surface was about a uniform 30 centimeters from his face, but it seemed like it wasn't there at all. It displayed the surrounding area in ultra-high definition with brightness and contrast control. It was hyper-real. The Augmented Reality Overlay System Environment (AROSE) showed any data as well, based on the user's needs - infrared, sound direction and distance, chem scans, radio traffic and many others. Status windows seemed to float a few feet away, reporting everything from the weather, to maps, to tool availability.

"Em, show me where that abandoned village is." And before Barcus finished his sentence, it was on his HUD with a proposed route indicated on the map and a seeming trail of translucent mist before him.

Barcus didn't want to think. He wanted to run. So he did. He already missed the 2G gravity of the outer rings. The weight of it made him strong. Made him feel more alive.

Em was expecting his move and was away and running an instant after he began, but quickly pulled ahead. Barcus marveled at how gracefully Em moved, so naturally, like a living thing. He was also amazed by how little she disturbed the ground. He was literally tearing the forest up as he ran. The footpads had automatically optimized for maximum traction. Each footfall was about ten meters apart and left great gaping holes in the turf.

"Barcus, this isn't very stealthy."

Was she being a smartass again?

"Do you think anyone is near enough to see us? The BUGs have not seen a person within 50 clicks of here. That village is definitely abandoned. Besides I need this..." So they ran, in broad daylight, faster than any animal on this planet could run, crashing through the forest like a train.

The two Trackers, a man, and a woman heard them coming from more than a kilometer away. They saw a giant, black spider being chased by a black demon with no face. They had been Trackers their whole lives, an effective team. They had heard the tales of demons from the north but always thought they were just stories to frighten children. Barcus never knew they were there. He never knew that moment had made all the difference.

It only took about 40 minutes to reach the abandoned village. It was large for being so remote. Em released over a hundred BUGs to quickly explore. The images they returned to the dozen windows in the HUD were haunting. It was like the people just disappeared. Pots, thick with dust, hung over cold hearths, tables were set for evening meals, mugs sat on the bar and tables in the inn.

To an observer, it looked like the spider and the demon just stood in the overgrown crossroad. Waiting.

Then one of the BUGs found the stone quarry.

As Barcus looked around, he could tell that this was a village of stone cutters and masons. The vine covered buildings were all made of stone. The roofs were slate. Even the interiors had stone arches instead of wood beams. Built to last.

The quarry that provided the materials was deep but still dry. As he approached, his HUD reported that here it was 51 meters down to the floor. The HUD reported that the distance down was an easy jump for the suit. He vaulted forward because he wanted to land past the mountain of bones at the bottom.

The suit landed with a practiced motion. Barcus had done that a thousand times before. He stood up straight pausing for a moment before he turned.

There were hundreds of skeletons of men, women and even children. He walked to the edge, careful not to step on any bones. The demon knelt, extending delicate looking hands with two opposable thumbs on each side to reach down and lift a little girl's skull that had rolled down the pile at the impact of his landing.

The skull still had bits of long dried skin attached to the face, as well as most of the scalp, with its long blond hair still ribboned into a ponytail. There was a gash where some kind of ax had entered the orbit of her eye, diagonally down through her nose, the roof of her mouth and into her brain.

Gently, the delicate hands replaced the head. Horrific carnage had been perpetrated on these people.

"Em, what do you make of this?" Barcus asked. He did not need to see her to know she was there. Her BUGs were her eyes.

"They were rounded up and murdered. Some few were kept alive to collect and throw the bodies down here, and then even they were pushed in alive to be broken and die slowly. I estimate that there just over 300 people here. Sixty-eight are children." She sounded upset. "Who would do this? Why?"

"It was a long time ago?" Barcus asked.

"At least fifteen or twenty years. And no one has ever returned to this village. The forest is taking it back already." Em showed Barcus a BUG's eye view of an area where a road once was that was now scattered with tall grasses and saplings, some as big as six inches in diameter. Haunting.

Still being careful not to disturb the dead, Barcus climbed out. The far side had a serpentine road that wound up and out and around. The exposed gray stone of the walls was beautiful in its way.

He found Em in the center crossroads in town. About 200 feet in each direction had cobblestone. Weeds and moss grew between some of the cracks. But, for the most part, the roads here were clean, only occasional autumn leaves blowing around.

"We will stay here tonight if you are sure no one is about," Barcus said as he began exit procedures in the suit. The suit knelt as the back opened and the sense gel shrank away. He climbed out into the chill breeze of a quiet late autumn afternoon. There was a hush here. The suit closed and stood up. Barcus turned and walked to the gate at the back of the largest building in the village. It was the inn. He suddenly realized he could read the carved sign on the gate post.

The Stone Cauldron.

The actual gate, one of the few things here made of wood, had fallen in the weather. The suit followed him into the courtyard in the back. There were stables and even a few wagons still intact because they were parked under cover. Em stepped over the walls and settled into the middle of the courtyard.

Barcus hugged himself. His one piece coverall was not warm enough. It was designed to be durable and easy to clean with very little care, but not to be warm.

He climbed the steps onto the back porch of the inn. This was the kitchen entrance. The door opened easily. There was enough light in the room to tell it was a kitchen. The high windows had leaded glass, and they were all intact. The dust was very thick and undisturbed, except for what looked like very old mice tracks. Mice and rats must have scurried away with the last crumb from here decades ago.

He moved through double doors to a large main room where there was a bar made of stone, intricately carved and deep in dust. A huge fireplace dominated the room. Even the tables, booths, and benches were made of stone. Shadows were deep here.

"Barcus, on the second floor at the far end of the hall are the innkeeper's rooms. There is less dust there and a bed."

"Does it have blankets? If it gets much colder, I will need to sleep in the suit."

"There are blankets on the bed. And there are several chests."

Barcus found the room. The door was made of stone and fit so perfectly in the casement, a piece of paper would have been hard pressed to fit.

The heavy drapes were drawn. He opened them. There were some old dust webs, but not a lot. The light showed that the room was about eight meters square and had a large fireplace, a large wood four post bed, two overstuffed chairs. There was also a wash basin, a pitcher and a half a dozen chests and cabinets.

There was even firewood made ready for a light.

"Em, is the chimney clear?"

"Yes, but the flue is closed."

It took him only a moment to figure out the mechanism for the flue. He drew out a mini torch from a calf pocket and lit the fire.

The wood was dry and caught quickly. The chimney drew the

smoke out beautifully. As twilight fell, Barcus lit candles that he found all around the room.

Only the top quilt had any dust. He carefully folded it up to minimize disturbing it.

He found more quilts in a cedar chest at the foot of the bed. In other chests, he found women's clothes of various sizes and styles. Finally, he found a man's clothes in two chests. He must have been as big in the shoulders and chest as Barcus but not as tall. Some heavy belted tunics and hooded cloaks would be a good start. Unfortunately, his boots were far too small for Barcus.

All of this had Barcus thinking.

"Em, should we stay here? We only have a few weeks to figure out how we will get through the winter."

We? I'm alone, he reminded himself. Chen, you brilliant bitch. Memories punched him in the guts once, and suddenly, holding his face in his hands, he was sobbing again.

CHAPTER SIX

Peck's Halfway

"This AI, in hostile environment mode, could sense the best way to distract Barcus. It was a brilliant survival sub-routine."

--Solstice 31 Incident Investigation Testimony Transcript: Emergency Module Digital Forensics Report. Independent Tech Analysis Team.

<<<>>>

"Barcus..." Em said.

He still had his face in his hands, awash in despair.

"Barcus?" Em actually sounded worried again. This made him think of Chen even more, dropping him to his knees.

"Barcus, please. We need to talk. We found something."

Barcus realized that there was a faint image of a small woman sitting cross-legged before him with deep concern on her face. She was like a ghost in the darkness of his eyelids. He opened his eyes, and she was still there apparently sitting on the floor in front of him. She actually sighed before speaking.

"I am so sorry. About everything." Her eyes lowered as if she was reluctant to continue. "I know you don't like avatars, but Chen programmed me to convey additional analog emphasis while communicating - more than just tone. And this is important."

The image stood up, with the clear expectation that Barcus should get up as well.

"I have discovered signs people have been here. Recently." She clearly wanted him to follow her out. By the time he reached the top of the stairs, she was at the bottom, waving for him to follow. She even had a cloak like his on.

This is un-fucking-real, Chen.

She was running ahead of him, guiding the way. He had seen avatars like this for his internal HUD. He even had a training program back on the ship that would run with him, and there was that dumb personal assistant guy that reminded you of your calendar. But nothing like this.

She turned near the end of the cobbles and entered into a small building. It looked like a blacksmith shop, which was quickly confirmed by the stone sign carved beautifully into the door. It was a hammer and anvil.

The shop and associated stable was clean and dust free. Hundreds of well-oiled tools hung from the walls. Obviously used recently. Em stood by the forge holding her virtual hand over it like she was sensing heat.

"No one has been here for weeks, but there is a food cache in the loft above where the blacksmith and his family would have lived. The well out back has been maintained." She could have just shown him the BUG video via window. This was better though.

"There is also a clear path that leads out from the back. BUGs are following it now and searching more closely for other paths." She was standing near him now, still see-through, like a ghost video.

"Why do you look like that?" Barcus asked.

She seemed taken aback by the question. She looked down at herself. "You know what? I have no idea. Why do you look like that?" She pointed right at his face.

He suddenly laughed out loud, snorting, "Fucking Chen." He laughed until he was doubled over, holding his belly, with tears running down his face.

Every time he would look up at Em, she had a puzzled look like she was about to laugh and say, "What?" with a little shake of her head, holding her hands up while Barcus was racked with another wave of laughter.

Looking up this last time, he saw she was standing with her arms crossed over her chest, a stern look on her face.

More laughs, but not as deep.

Finally, Barcus said, "Okay, okay, okay, I'm done." Looking up at the avatar, he continued, "I know you're not really there. I know if anyone saw me right now, they would think I was completely insane talking to someone who they could not see. Look, maybe I am kind of going insane here, for real. I actually know that I am alone and that your function is to keep me safe and sane. But I have to say, I'm impressed."

"Do me a favor though. If we meet any of these people. Don't make me look insane. Okay? Because it's not far from the truth right now."

Her face actually looked relieved. "Okay, I promise."

Barcus believed her.

It was almost dark now. The sun set quickly. Barcus pulled out a small multi-tool and activated the powerful utility flashlight.

He made his way back to the inn. Em followed. The room had warmed with the fire, and he piled on some more logs to keep the heat going. He sat in one of the overstuffed chairs after he covered it with a clean quilt from one of the chests. It was almost unnerving to see Em "sit" in the other chair.

"I know you have continuously been with me since the crash, Em. Are you going to always haunt me now?"

She gave a wry smile before answering, "I was going to try a little at first. Just let me know anytime if it's too much."

A thought occurred to him. "Did you do this with Chen?"

Her eyes darkened. She swallowed and didn't answer right away, but finally she said, "Yes. We talked every day, for hours." She sounded like she was about to cry. "Chen hid it well, but she was very lonely. I think she was also afraid of something. All the time. Something awful happened to her long ago. It made her strong but sad." She was staring down at her virtual hands.

"She loved you very much you know. Chen, I mean."

Em might have just as well punched him in the gut.

"She moved to the outer rings to be away from the rest of them. But mostly because you were there. She talked about you a lot."

She paused, noticing his distress. "She said you treated her the way everyone should treat everyone. Respect, kindness, friendship with no expectations. I always wondered..."

She looked up as if she just realized that she said that out loud.

"What?" Barcus said.

"Well...if she would ever have the courage to jump you."

It was her turn to wonder at his reaction. "What?" Em said.

Can Em read my mind?

"Look. We talked a lot. All the time. There was an awful time in her life when she swore she'd never let another man touch her again, ever. But that was before she met you. The fire needs another log." She pointed and wrapped her cloak around her closer like it was cooler. Then he realized it was cooler.

He got up and added more wood. It gave him time to think. And time to marvel at this AI. This was the first conversation he'd had like this in years. He wanted to tell her why he was in the outer rings as well.

Barcus continued as he poked at the fire, "What happened to Chen? She never said. She was very shy when we met. We only really became friends because we were both heavies living in the 2G outer ring."

"Do you remember the night at Peck's Halfway, when that maintenance crew was trying to figure out why all you guys would choose to live on the outermost 2G ring?"

Barcus smiled and said, "Oh yes. Chen stood on a chair, unzipped her pants and pulled her shirt up so high you could almost see her nipples saying 'for this!' Her abs looked like they were cut from stone. She looked at me and raised her eyebrow like she used to, and I stood up and showed mine too. Rand was next, but she had been there at the bar longer, several drinks ahead, and was wearing a one piece jumpsuit that she unzipped all the way down, spreading it wide open to show her eight pack as well as the fine black lace bra she was wearing."

Barcus was laughing lost in the joy of the memory.

"You never heard a bar get so quiet so fast. And Chen broke the silence by saying, 'Nice tits Nancy!'

"I had never laughed so hard in my life," Barcus said.

Em continued, "Chen said that two more people moved to the outer ring the next day. She also said that she was really showing her abs to you. She didn't care about the rest. And even though Rand gave her shit about it from then on, they became friends."

The thought of the death of Rand was sobering. In a more serious tone he said, "We never knew her first name was Nancy before that night. Chen was...I miss her. She saved me." He swallowed hard a few times in silence.

They sat quietly, listening to the fire for a few minutes.

"Do you think there is anything safe to drink in this tavern?"

Both of Em's eyebrows went up, and her eye went side to side like she was thinking. "I think we may be in luck." She got up and began moving to the door, where she waited for him to open it. He followed down to the main level naturally.

They went past the bar, which he noticed was suspiciously devoid of any bottles, casks or jars. They continued into the kitchen where she pointed at a trap door, which suddenly seemed so obviously visible. With considerable effort, Barcus opened it. Through a great cloud of dust appeared stairs that went into the darkness of the basement.

There were many dusty shelves and wine racks with bottles.

"Em. Can you scan these?"

"Sure, just grab two and bring them outside. We can actually put them in the bio scanner I have on board."

He made his selection based on what looked like the finest glass bottles. The corks came free easily with his ever-handy multi-tool. He poured them both into his two liter Thermos and set it on the table inside the EM. The scan returned a safe score, and by the time he got back up to his fire, he knew the wine would be cold. Anything he put in his thermos was the perfect temp in about two minutes. Hot or cold. He just told it what he wanted.

Sitting in front of the roaring fire, he drank right from the container.

"How is it?" Em asked, looking as if she wished she could have a taste.

"Oh my god... This is so good. This is by far the best wine I have ever tasted. And I have to drink alone, dammit."

"No, you don't." He looked up, and Em was raising a glass in a toast. "To lost friends."

It wasn't long before the wine was gone. Em had left quietly at some point. Barcus put some more wood on the fire and crawled into bed fully dressed and slept hard.

During the night, Em found other paths. More BUGs were deployed. Map definition improved.

Barcus slept twelve hours and was awakened by a full bladder.

He was already dressed, so he made his way down the hall and found the midden. He peed for a long time, thinking about food. He had been running on survival rations, 2,000 calorie bars, and he was already tired of all but the peanut butter flavor.

"Em, what's our status?"

"Good morning, Barcus. Or rather, good afternoon. I'm glad you slept." The avatar fell into step beside him as he was moving down the hall to the stairs. "All the wooden buildings in the town were burned to the ground more than a decade ago. The forest has reclaimed those places like they were never there. Only the foundations remain."

Windows opened in his HUD, showing images of what Em was describing.

They entered the common room of the Tavern as she continued. "I found other indications of paths, but none has been used recently. Following them, I discovered six other burned villages. The last one burned only about a year ago."

They exited the tavern and moved toward the spider. It rose up as they approached, granting access to the belly hatch. He climbed in.

The wind was blowing leaves in a mini tornado. The leaves seemed to be falling faster.

"There are no other villages to the north from here, so far. But I did find a possible candidate location."

Em showed the live image of the place in the HUD window. The BUG was flying around an outer wall that was about ten meters high. One section was collapsed, and a hill of rubble ramped up the wall there. Rounding the wall, there was a tower in evidence and gates at twelve o'clock and six o'clock. One large and one small. The road that once led to these gates was now overgrown, moss covered and unused. Returning around the wall to the rubble, it looked like the structure was about 100 meters across and perfectly round. The mapping software filled in the details as it went.

"What's inside the walls?" Barcus indicated on the display. It looked like the EM could walk right over the collapsed section.

The BUG ascended to begin an aerial survey of the fortress. There were multiple sections divided by inner walls. It looked like there had once been a cathedral central to the fortress, but it had fallen to ruin decades ago. The tower remained, but the roof of the main sanctuary had collapsed through the floor into the basements and probably to the crypts farther below that were now flooded with water.

"Barcus, it looks like an Abbey. It has stables and a gatehouse there. Some kind of barracks over there. A great hall of sorts there. Still mostly intact, but fallen into disrepair. These were once inner gardens, I'd wager. All the inner doors have been torn from their hinges."

Barcus studied the images as they moved. "How long will it take to get there?" A map popped up with a route plotted.

"If we continue at this pace, we will be there in about fourteen hours. None of the footpaths we discovered led there. This site is very secluded, and there is very good hunting game available."

One of the BUGs was ascending to a greater altitude to get a bird's eye view of the area around what they started calling The Abbey. It was dense forest near foothills at the base of a small mountain range. A large area looked too organized to be regular forest and must have been orchards. Another higher section held acres of overgrown vineyards and scattered outbuildings.

Straight down The Abbey was a perfect circle, almost invisible because of the color of the slate that covered the roofs and capped the walls and walkways all the way around. It was broken up further by the trees growing inside and outside The Abbey. It almost looked intentionally camouflaged.

The BUG was very high now. The status in the window indicated that it was a calm, cool, dry and exceptionally clear day over The Abbey that allowed a view of hundreds of kilometers in every direction.

"Em, what is that?" Barcus indicated smoke on the horizon to the southeast.

"Maximum magnification," Barcus ordered, but 10x was the best optical zoom on the BUG. Another 100x via digital zoom provided no addition information.

"Can you estimate where that is Em?"

A map popped up on the HUD, showing the basic location of where the fires were.

"Do you have any BUGs near there?" Barcus asked.

"I have some close but still a couple hours away, depending on conditions."

"Redirect them there, please. We need to know what's going on here. And also move in that direction. Just in case we want to redirect there."

"Barcus..."

An image came up of a village burned to the ground and still smoldering.

"I thought you said they were a few hours out."

"This is a different village. One on the way to the smoke."

The BUG flew closer to the largest ruin. The ashes were full of skeletons and charred remains.

They were herded into there and then burned.

"Head for the smoke, best possible speed." His voice was flat.

Anger was building.

CHAPTER SEVEN

Fire and Monsters

"Barcus was acting counter to the Emergency Modules (EM) primary mission objectives. It was able to adapt."

--Solstice 31 Incident Investigation Testimony Transcript: Emergency Module Digital Forensics Report. Independent Tech Analysis Team.

<<<>>>

Em was moving fast, not taking the time to be stealthy. She wasn't trying to hide their tracks. Every step tore great wounds in the forest floor. The constant rhythmic pounding of her feet was like ground thunder.

More BUGs spread out as they ran. Six more freshly burned villages were discovered that day. Each time it was the same, people corralled or piled inside a barn or hall that had been burned.

"There were signs these last two villages fought back - makeshift fortifications and weapons. I think some of the burned remains were of the attackers." Em was all business. It was unlike her.

"Why are we doing this, Barcus? It's not safe. What will we do if we catch up to them?"

"We will kill them all." It had been barely a whisper.

"Barcus."

The main HUD showed a small village under attack. Fires were already burning. Men on horses surrounded the town. They were armed with drawn swords and crossbows. An elderly couple, still in their nightshirts, was being dragged to the crossroads by their hair. None of the villagers were armed in any way. Not even an ax or kitchen knife.

A signal was given, and the people were forced into the blacksmith's barn on the opposite corner from the Inn at the crossroad. After the villagers were all inside, the doors were nailed shut.

"Em, what is our ETA?"

"Two hours at full speed."

Fuck.

He clenched his teeth as the barn began to burn.

"Prep the suit, Em. Stop one kilometer out."

After the barn was fully engulfed, the horsemen started a house-to-house detailed search. Valuables were collected, as well as wagonloads of supplies. It looked like they were planning to bed down there for the night. The barn fire had jumped to the thatched roof of the next building and then on to the next one, downing that section of the village.

It was almost dusk when Em and Barcus stopped and Barcus moved to the suit. As he climbed in he asked, "How many are there?"

Em replied, "I have counted 57 so far."

"I want them all dead. I don't care how. All. Is that clear, Em?"

"Yes, sir."

His suit's HUD had a tactical display of the village and indicated that hundreds of BUGs had already been deployed, and several followed each of the men.

"None of them will survive. There are 59 in total. For now." Em was chilling in her declaration.

It was full dark, except for the fires when the monsters descended on them. Barcus loomed out of the darkness to grab two men by the necks. In the suit, he was over three meters tall. He lifted them from the ground and got exactly the reaction he wanted. The rest drew their swords and attacked.

The claw-like tools he had selected for this work were effective. He snipped off their heads and tore through the rest of the men. Swords shattered or deflected off his suit. It was better than any armor ever invented for the task. A dozen fell, with missing or crushed heads before they began to run. The suit was faster than any man or even a horse. His feet crushed them to jelly without even missing a stride. They could not hide, either, because the un-noticed BUGs followed them with seemingly supernatural ease.

Barcus saw Em taking them easily. Her two front legs were crushing skulls with ease, keeping them contained in the village. Barcus crashed into the tavern, The Archers Dog, ripping the door off its hinges, and was met by six drunken men in the common room. They all died before they got their swords out of their sheaths. The HUD indicated that three more were in the room above.

The stairs would not have held his weight. Sharp tools protruding at right angles from his forearms gouged into the walls as he climbed, taking some of his weight.

There, more drunken men were desperately trying to put on their clothes and draw weapons. The monster Barcus froze. They had been about to rape a girl on the innkeeper's bed. She was now balled into a fetal position, eyes wide, staring at the blank black space where his face should have been. There was a plea for help in her eyes. A plea sent to a monster covered in blood and gore already.

The men were all dead an instant later.

Not knowing what to do then, he did nothing, just loomed there over her.

She looked at him and he thought she said in a trembling whispered, "Thank you..." in English.

His HUD said there were six of them left, scattering in all directions. Em was after the three heading roughly the same way. In a single motion, he crashed out the upper story front wall of the tavern and landed lightly on the street, running after the other three. They heard him coming and tried to hide. The first hid under a wagon loaded with supplies. Barcus crushed his head with the same foot that kicked the cart into splinters with one blow. The second climbed a tree. Barcus jumped into the air ten meters, grabbing the man, tossing him down, then landing directly on the man.

The last one was hiding inside a wooden outhouse. With one swing of his tool-bristling arm, he destroyed the outhouse, nearly cutting the man in half.

Barcus paused over the devastation he had created, longing for more targets to be found in his HUD. His thirst for vengeance was not yet quenched. But none appeared. He ordered a full thermal scan of the village and surrounding areas to ensure they didn't miss anyone.

"Barcus. There is one at your feet," Em said. There was a bit of sadness in her voice.

Barcus looked down, and there was a thermal image of someone below the outhouse floor. He swept the wood aside with a single stroke revealing the midden pit, dug below the outhouse.

There was a boy in the foul wet pool, up to his armpits in fecal matter, shivering.

Barcus knew he must look like a horror backlit by the fire from the village burning behind him, covered in blood and gore. He ordered all the tools in his forearms to retract, large chunks of flesh falling away as they did.

He deployed the fine work hand, one of the suits tools, from the end of his right arm. Slowly he dropped to a knee and then extended that hand to the boy who shrank from it at first, until Barcus made the universal open palm "come here, I won't rip your head off" gesture. With the delicate robot fingers held out to him, the boy placed not one, but both hands in it.

He was easily lifted from the muck and set on clear ground, shaking.

Barcus stood to full height and the boy cringed.

"Barcus. They are all dead. There are just the two survivors. We should go. They have seen too much already." Em was walking up behind Barcus. The boy's eyes got wider. Em was also covered in blood, walking easily on six legs. Her two front legs were still held up in an attack ready position, scalps still clinging to them. The utility arms that extended from beneath the front of the Emergency Module were dripping black blood.

They turned in unison and moved away.

"Em, we need to clean up. Is there a lake or river near here?"

They found a waterfall by a mill a few minutes away. It was perfect for cleaning up.

After the suit had most of the blood cleaned, Barcus got out.

"Look, Em. I need to make sure the survivors are okay."

"They are both together in the courtyard behind the tavern." A window opened in his HUD. The boy was sobbing uncontrollably as the woman cleaned him with rags and buckets of water from the well.

They didn't see or hear him as he approached from the darkness. The boy was still sobbing as he got dressed. They were both so thin, their skin as thin as paper over bones.

With the fires at his back, he stopped close enough to speak.

"Are you all right? Can I help you?" His hands were open, palms up. He was trying not to frighten them.

They were startled, fear in their eyes.

They fell to their knees and cast their eyes down as if in complete supplication. He was surprised by their reaction.

"My Lord. I know just a little of the high speech. And he none at all," the woman spoke hesitantly.

"You are safe now. The murderers are all gone," Barcus said. They remained on their knee with their faces almost on the ground.

"My name is Barcus. You should leave this place. There is another village a day's ride to the east. They need to be warned of these evil men. There might be more. I have seen many burned villages of late."

The boy blurted out a series of words Barcus could not understand. When he was done, the woman said, "Olias says there are more, not just men. Horrible monsters. Demons that killed them all. Ate their heads."

"Olias?" Barcus asked. He stopped babbling.

"Tell him they are gone too. Please, get up." They were on their knees this whole time.

Em interjected into his head, *"We need to go."*

"Will you be able to get there on your own? Or should I take you there?" Barcus asked.

"Barcus. I don't like this."

"We. Will. Manage." She was reaching for words.

"Take what you need from here, but be gone by morning."

"Barcus..." Em insisted.

The barn that was ablaze behind Barcus began to collapse slowly. As it did, the suit stepped out of the inferno. It had been burning off all the organic matter that the waterfall could not remove. It stood and seemed to stay there as if watching Barcus for a few moments. It slowly turned and walked away.

"I must go," Barcus said. "You will be safe as you travel. But hurry. Do you understand?"

"Yes, my Lord."

He turned and began to walk away and then turned back.

"What is your name?" Barcus asked.

"Po, my Lord." The girl replied.

"Goodbye, Po. Goodbye, Olias."

He walked into the night.

***

Barcus returned to Em with the suit following on remote. He got in the spider and sat in the driver seat. Em's avatar was in the other one.

"Are you all right, Barcus? You were...lost."

"I am fine. I need a tactical update," he said flatly.

The display in the spider filled with annotated maps and status information. The maps were much more detailed than the last time they were up. Twelve hundred BUGs had been busy.

"I want to keep an eye on Po and Olias." They appeared in two windows and as new annotations on the maps. They had already gotten cleaned up, dressed and saddled up two horses and had begun to rig a third, a pack horse. Olias was running from body to body, checking pockets and collecting purses. He freed all the animals in the stables. They ran in panic as soon as the doors and gates were opened. Olias was almost run down by the cows he freed from a barn on the edge of town. There, he also found the raiding party's horses in their picket lines. They were all saddled and calm, even as the fires burned closer.

He started going through the saddle bags but stopped. There were about 50 horses here. Trained, calm, beautiful horses with no brands. Olias had obviously seen this kind of picket before. A long rope, secured only at one end, with loops every six feet, and the horses tied by their reins, alternating on each side.

Olias walked to the post where the rope was tied with a beautiful knot that came free with a simple tug at the right spot. As he began to walk, the horses calmly followed, as if they had done this a thousand times before.

"He is a smart one, Barcus. They will be fine," Em said.

"Em, where is the suit?" An icon appeared on the map. It was just outside the village. "I want to have it shadow them, but not too close. But first, I want it to ask something of Po while she is still alone."

Olias was walking the horses back to the center of the village. They all remained calm, despite the fact the fires were so big and so close.

The suit walked directly out of the shadows and paused, facing Po. The fires were so loud now with collapsing timbers, she didn't hear it approach. She almost walked directly into the suit. It was so black, it reflected almost no light. She stumbled back and almost fell but didn't run.

Barcus ordered, "Em, disguise the voice. I don't want her to know it's me."

"I will not harm you," the suit said via its external PA system, in a deep rumbling voice like a cinder block being dragged over cement. At the moment she froze he had a good look at her again. She was not as young as he thought at first. She was about 30 years old he decided and far too thin.

She fell to her knees, visibly trembling.

"Who were these evil men?" the thing asked.

"They are from the Citadel. They carry no livery or other signs." She was choking the words out. "But I have seen them before. These weapons..." She paused again. "It's death to carry them if you are not from the Citadel."

"It's death to carry them if you are." The suit turned to walk back into the shadows.

"Wait. What is your name?" The suit stopped but didn't turn around.

The suit seemed to pause and consider the question. "I have no name." And it was gone, fading into the deeper black.

A minute later, Olias was there with the horses. They spoke rapidly in a language that sounded familiar, but Barcus could not understand. Po pointed into the darkness where the suit had gone. He understood a single phrase as she talked: "the demon with no face and no name."

Just then, another barn collapsed, but this time it fell across the road into the buildings on the opposite side. Olias looped the rope over the pommel of the horse Po held for him, and they left the village, Po towing the single pack horse and Olias with two rows of well-disciplined horses. If they rode all night, they would be there by noon the next day.

"What will they tell them?" Em asked.

"The truth," Barcus replied.

***

Barcus and Em began to move once again into the forest. The tactical display showed them moving away from the ruined village north as Po and Olias moved east.

The tactical display showed they were moving to the point they had called The Abbey.

Without prompting, Em said, "I think the BUGs have found a good place to shelter."

It also showed the village where the survivors were headed.

"By horseback, it would be about seven days from that village to The Abbey. Even then, there are no direct routes."

"Are we officially calling it 'The Abbey' then?"

"You started it."

Is she teasing me?

"Real names are easier to remember," Em said.

Barcus could feel himself crashing. So much adrenaline followed by nothing but burning coals of anger.

"Em, What do we know about this Citadel?" Barcus asked.

"Nothing at this time," she replied coldly.

"Make it a priority to find out." His anger was bleeding though.

"What are you planning?" Concern was hinting in her voice.

"I don't know, just do it," Barcus barked at Em.

The tactical display became transparent as they resumed a stealthy pace toward the point called The Abbey. They walked for almost the entire night in a creek that flowed shallow now but had indications it flowed fast and hard in the spring.

The beast with no name shadowed the survivors a half a kilometer into the forest on the north side the entire night. There was no need to get any closer. BUGs fed info back to Em, who was driving the suit herself via remote.

It wasn't long before the adrenaline crash finally came. Barcus slept deeply for the second night in a row. Em kept the ride smooth. As Barcus slept, Em closed the windows that followed Po and Olias but left their icons on the tactical to show that they had gotten safely to the eastern village. She didn't show how the southern portion of the village eventually burned to the foundations. She didn't show what Po told the elders of that village. She didn't show that Trackers were dispatched that found the story to be true. They also found the tracks of the "Faceless Beast" and followed them back to an overlook above their own village.

Em had the suit turn to climb into the mountains to lose the Trackers. These Trackers were good. It took the beast much longer to evade them than he thought. It eventually required some chasm leaps and waterfall drops and river runs to lose them. They were brave and relentless.

They didn't follow the spider tracks. Em didn't know if they simply didn't recognize them or if their bravery only went so far.

CHAPTER EIGHT

The Abbey

"This is where the data shows that Em began to know far more than she conveyed. The hostile environment module has complex higher functions. It sorted and used the data at an amazing rate."

--Solstice 31 Incident Investigation Testimony Transcript: Emergency Module Digital Forensics Report. Independent Tech Analysis Team.

After Barcus had waked, they stopped by a long, narrow scenic lake.

Barcus decided that he'd had enough power bars and set up a camp kitchen to make some real food. "Real" may have been the wrong term. He still used survival rations but kicked it up a notch. He decided on eggs with onions and cheese with potatoes, toast, fruit, coffee and orange juice.

Em supplied the water, already boiling hot, and soon Barcus was perched on a camp stool eating a hearty breakfast overlooking a beautiful lake.

Em's image had not been in evidence this morning until Barcus asked her, "Did Po and Olias make out okay?"

She seemed to walk from behind a rock as she said, "Yes. They were welcomed and taken in immediately. Po, by the inn keeper's wife, Olias by the blacksmith. Olias was apparently already a blacksmith apprentice. Bringing the horses was a really good idea."

"For some reason, neither of them mentioned you. I will keep an eye on them. It will be useful. I have learned several things already."

"Oh, like what?"

"There is a complex caste system in place here. What you do, how you act, your entire role in society is based on your place in that system. There are many 'ladders' in the system as well. I hope to refine my understanding of it as time passes. This was not evident in that first small,

remote, forest village we encountered."

"Why could she understand me?"

"Standard English is known as the High Tongue here. Only the highest castes use it. Not everyone speaks it, but they all recognize it. The lower castes don't speak it at all. The language they are using is a derivation of English which has become so colloquial and accented that it bears little resemblance to English and is quite difficult to understand."

Their conversation paused a moment.

"Do you understand them yet?"

"I'm getting close. In a few more days, I will have a basic understanding, so if we encounter anyone else, I can translate for you."

Barcus finished his breakfast as Em gave him this update.

"I have had the BUGs exploring The Abbey in great detail. I believe that it will be perfect for our long-term needs. Oh, and I have discovered something new about The Abbey."

"Anything unusual?" Barcus sipped his coffee, trying to focus.

"Yes, actually. The outer wall is too perfect to be made by hand. I believe it is actually a Colony Redoubt structure. The outer wall is exactly 91.44 meters in diameter and doesn't vary even a centimeter except where the wall was destroyed."

"What does that mean? I vaguely remember something about Colony Redoubts from elementary school."

"Early Colony ships were equipped with large machines called Makers - single function AI Bots that built Redoubts. One of the standard Redoubt Designs was 100 yards in diameter. We will know more when we get there. The BUGs can only go so many places."

"Didn't Makers use local materials, like sand and water and fibers to make foamcrete buildings? That and the volcano were the most popular science fair projects. I made a Maker myself."

Em's shoulders were shaking as if she were laughing.

"What?" Barcus said over a mouthful of toast.

"Elementary school? You built a Maker?"

"Never mind that. What else did you find out about The Abbey?"

Em shook her head and sat on a rock. A translucent ghost in the full sun.

"It has not been occupied for decades. The road that once led to it

was reclaimed by the forest. It's about a week away from the nearest populated town or village, and no one goes there ever. Not even Trackers or hunters."

"Trackers? Hunters?"

"They are the only ones, as far as I can tell, that wander and use abandoned villages or other places."

***

Barcus finished his coffee, cleaned up after his meal and headed out. It took them a few more days to reach the ruins because they went slowly so as to leave less of a trail.

The suit had rendezvoused with them the day before they reached the Abbey. It was noticeably cooler there. The elevation was higher. The leaves were in full autumn glory.

They made their initial approach to The Abbey from the side where the wall was destroyed. Then, they circumnavigated the fortress. The walls were bleached white upward for the first ten meters. Above that there was gray cut block for another two meters and then battlements above that. As they continued around, they found there was a huge main gate and tower with a bridge on the north end. There wasn't a moat there, just a deep ditch with a sharp rocky bottom. Water might flow there in the rainy season, but it was currently dry. The portcullis and huge doors were closed. If the gates had been opened, two carts could cross the bridge at the same time, four horses abreast. It quietly amused Barcus that he used that as his mental measurement.

"This bridge seems also to be an aqueduct," Em said, indicating on the HUD the path the aqueduct followed from the north for just over one kilometer to a mountain river. It was running even now in what Em believed the driest part of the year. "The intake is about 90 meters higher than we are at this point, supplying water to The Abbey year round. Clever." She indicated the bridge on the HUD.

"We need to test the wood decking before we use it. The door works have also been destroyed from the inside. They must have been trying to keep someone out."

"Shitload of good it did them," Barcus said as they rounded the last turn again to the broken wall and rubble.

The stony ditch had prevented some but not all of the forest from encroaching. It continued almost all the way around. A few small, brave trees tried to find purchase there.

The spider climbed the rubble easily. The wall had been breached about halfway up. Barcus had Em pause at the top so he could have a look. The wall itself was about two and a half meters thick. At the top, where the materials changed, it looked like there had been a square, meter-sized tunnel going in both directions, surrounded by gray block. The one on his left side was dry, but the one on the right side had water running in a steady stream out of it that got lost in the rubble.

"I think that water is coming from the aqueduct. Before the wall was destroyed, this probably held water for the entire Abbey."

"I estimate that the Abbey itself, in its prime, housed about 300 people, Barcus. There were stables, kitchens, barracks and a hall."

"What the hell happened?"

From their vantage on the wall, they could see that the main sanctuary of the cathedral had suffered massive damage.

"It looks like an explosion just to the side here." The HUD rendered a roof where it might have stood, then performed a slow-motion simulation of what Em thought would have caused this amount of destruction.

"The roofs of the perimeter buildings were impacted by flying debris, here, here and here." The HUD indicated the damage. "The buildings on the southernmost part of The Abbey were least affected."

"There must have been an assault of some kind after the explosion. All but a few inner doors have been destroyed. The rest are burned or torn from the hinges."

Em slowly began to descend the ramp of rubble, which continued right to the foundations of the cathedral and down further into the basement and even the crypts below. Water was running here, and a pool filled the lowest part. The floor of half of the cathedral was still there, creating an overhang above rubble and deep shadows. Em walked directly in, her legs neatly straddling the large pool of water. As Barcus was walking into the darkness, his personal HUD automatically used light amplification. The far end of the cathedral was evenly cast with rubble and debris. The flat of the flooring could be sensed below the layer of stone rubble. At the far end, a staircase climbed up into the base of the tower that was still standing straight.

"This will make an excellent garage for the spider, Em."

"Maybe after we tidy up a bit," Em quipped.

Barcus looked over at the other seat to see that she was smiling at him.

"I want to get out." Barcus had stood before Em replied. The spider rotated so that the front of the module aimed out toward the opening. Only the far collapsed wall was visible, touched by a corner of sunlight.

Barcus stepped out of the hatch and the spider rose, leaving him standing on the debris-strewn floor. He moved toward the steps that were also scattered in rubble until he reached the first landing. He looked up and could see more winding stairs that climbed far into the shadows. They were each about a meter wide and had no railing at all. He climbed the way to the top, emerging in the belfry quietly and the sunlight. The massive bell lay on its side in the corner opposite the stairs opening. The view was spectacular.

To the south, Barcus could see an overgrown willow tree in a courtyard at the exact opposite end of The Abbey. It was higher than the wall and completely filled the courtyard; it had seen better days.

The buildings to either side of it looked in very good condition. "Em, have you assessed those buildings?"

"Yes. I believe they are our best bet for long-term shelter."

Barcus could see to his right that one of the courtyards had a great mountain of ash and charcoal. He made a mental note of that and after looking around in all directions began his descent.

At ground level the tower made up one side of the main gate. If enemies entered the main gate, they were forced to do so directly below the tower, and they were funneled around to the left, exposed to battlements above on both sides. It was a classic kill zone.

He began to explore the desolate, abandoned place. It felt so empty.

The main hall was above a reception courtyard. A wide staircase ran up about two meters to enter the hall - another obvious line of defense. Visitors could be both welcomed with hospitality and easily contained. The roof here was damaged. Inside, decades of rain and bird habitation had taken their toll. The far end had a dais and a stone throne. Doors behind the dais were off their hinges.

Inner courtyards were segregated by beautifully crafted stone walls. All the courtyards were overgrown with trees. All the gates and doors between these spaces were off the hinges.

Finally, Barcus made it the willow tree. It stood in the center of a dry fountain in the middle of this courtyard at the south end of the keep. The courtyard was paved with large flat slate flagstones, fit together expertly like a puzzle, and only two saplings had found purchase between the slabs of paving stones.

The back gate remained on its hinges but stood ajar. There was just enough room to squeeze through. The black iron hinges were frozen. Without prompting, Em spoke.

"I think the doors and gates that were not destroyed were open at the time of the attack 50 or 60 years ago."

This gate and its archway through the wall, was big enough for a single cart to enter and drive around the fountain. To the left of the open gate, an archway showed where the stables had been. To the right was the gatekeeper's guard house through another arch. The door was closed.

Barcus tried the latch, and it opened easily. There were two rooms about five meters square and a loft over the room in the back. Each room had a hearth and fireplace. The windows in the back room were gone. Leaves had collected in all the corners as the wind blew in the window and down the spiral stairway in the corner of the back room.

The door slammed suddenly.

Barcus jumped. Em quickly chimed in. "That must be why the door stayed closed."

He went up the spiral stairs to find an entrance to the loft that was thick with old bird droppings. Up another level, and another open but functional door led to the battlements. The last level went up to the gate tower. This tower was much smaller than the north tower.

A mirrored stair led down on the other side to barracks above the stables and the tack room below. The open balcony all along the inside had let in a lot more weather and evidence of animals.

Crossing the courtyard, he returned to the gatehouse. Em was leaning against the mantel. She said, "Welcome home."

Barcus spent the rest of the day exploring The Abbey. The gatehouse remained the best option for a residence. Most of the furniture had been removed or destroyed decades ago. The large pile of ash and charcoal was mostly furniture, tools, materials and sadly, there was also evidence of books. Whoever did this wanted to render this place difficult to occupy again. There were even signs that they had attempted to burn the only wood in the structure - the heavy wood beams for the roofs.

He found a strong three-legged stool and a narrow cot, and he made a table out of a door and two empty ruined casks. His favorite find was a straw broom.

In short order, the cobwebs, dust, and leaves were swept out of the gatehouse. Barcus knew it would need a good scrub later, but there would be plenty of time for that.

With the help of the suit, in the back room, he covered the broken window with a door on the outside.

"Barcus, these windows are standard sizes. I think we could move a window from elsewhere in The Abbey to make this weather tight."

The suit was assigned the job of collecting firewood and stockpiling it in the cooking pavilion that was just to the left of the gatehouse on the opposite side of the courtyard from the stables. To facilitate that work, Barcus took time and repaired the south gate door. The suit had solvents and lubricants on board that allowed him to get the gate door working smoothly. The drop bar was gone, but they could fabricate one later as time allowed.

Soon after the gate door was open, the suit was easily walking back and forth carrying logs, more trunks than logs in that they were five or even ten meters long. One of the claw cutters made quick work of cutting perfect fireplace sized logs.

The suit soon had multiple cords neatly stacked. The remains of the broken furniture was also collected and broken up for perfect kindling.

As night fell, Barcus had fires burning in both fireplaces to heat both rooms. Stew was heating up inside the two liter camp pot.

"Em, let's make a list of things we need to salvage or make. Things like basic furniture, pots and pans, utensils, tools, and damn, I wish I had snagged a couple cases of wine at The Stone Cauldron." Anger flared. He choked it back.

Em seemed to walk out of the other room and look around. As if to prove the point about furniture, she ended up sitting cross-legged on the floor in front of the fire. "I have had the BUGs doing a detailed survey in all directions. They can inventory as they go. There are so many abandoned farms and villages within 100 clicks that we should be able to collect whatever you need before the snow flies. After a few days' work around here to secure this site, I will head out for a salvage run."

"Do you know how to use a cauldron? There are six big ones in the cook's pavilion," Barcus said.

"Actually, yes. But there is no need. They were used when The Abbey was fully populated. They are only here now because they were too heavy to move and too strong to break, like the anvils in the stables."

"This camp pot is great. It can bring two liters of liquid to a boil in no time. No fire required. How long will it continue to work?"

"We can recharge it every month in the spider. It will last for years. Don't forget the Thermos. It can heat or cool liquids."

"Dammit. Wish I had that wine..." Barcus sat on the three legged stool and stared at the fire.

CHAPTER NINE

Autumn Rest

"The Emergency Module turned to long-term survival. The narrative, if accurate, seems to indicate that Barcus was not the psychopath that earlier analysis indicated."

--Solstice 31 Incident Investigation Testimony Transcript: Emergency Module Digital Forensics Report. Independent Tech Analysis Team.

<<<>>>

Even though the cot was narrow, musty and uncomfortable, Barcus soon fell asleep and didn't awake for a full ten hours, and even then he was slow and quiet. The energy of the previous day was just as gone as the heat from ashes of the cold hearth that he stared at.

Barcus was sitting on the sagging edge of the cot with his elbows on his knees, his chin supported on his fists, staring at the floor. He had remained like that, unmoving, for a few minutes before Em spoke to him.

"Good morning, Barcus. What's the plan for the day?"

He looked up to see her sitting on the floor, cross-legged again. His answer was a long sigh.

"I think we should replace that window and explore this place some more. I have a few places I'd like to show you," Em chirped, trying to encourage him.

He made no reply.

"You should eat some breakfast."

He stood and walked out without a word, out of the gatehouse, out south gate, and straight into the woods.

"Barcus, where are you going?" She looked like she was running to catch up.

"I just need to take a piss for god's sake!" he snapped.

She appeared to skid to a stop and let him go.

"Add that to the fucking list. I am not coming out here when the snow starts to fly," Barcus yelled over his shoulder.

When he returned, he made some instant coffee in the Thermos. After quaffing two cups, he took the third with him. He spent the morning first removing an intact window from a ruined section of the barracks that had somehow not been broken in the blast, and then installing it in the gatehouse.

Both of the gatehouse windows faced the inner courtyards. One was in the willow yard. The other was on the opposite side of the wall on the kitchen side. Both were under a roof that created a walkway so if it was raining, they could move about undercover.

When he was done, he spoke aloud, knowing Em would hear him. "I want to explore now. I'm not going to do this all via HUD." He heard the rocks tumbling as the spider emerged from the garage.

"We will leave Faceless here to work via remote while we explore."

"Faceless?" Barcus asked.

"I am trying names out. So far 'the Suit,' 'Beast' and 'Elvis' don't seem right."

"Elvis?" Barcus raised an eyebrow.

"What? You like Elvis?"

"No!" Barcus snapped.

"I will keep trying. I could give it a complete persona if you like. It would be just another me though," Em offered.

"Don't bother. I already know I am alone and you are simply programmed to keep me sane," Barcus complained.

"I am cut to the quick, sir. To be simplified so."

"It's true."

"Just get in, grumpy. Hey, we could call the suit 'Grumpy!' It looks the part," Em said cheerfully.

"'Scary' is more like it. They were not built for beauty," Barcus observed.

"Get in, dammit." Em seemed to be calling from inside.

The spider moved smoothly over the rubble to exit The Abbey. She followed the wall all the way around to the west side before moving away. There had once been a road here. It wound through the trees, following the contours of the land instead of a straight cut through. They were four meters high, tall enough that the saplings in the road constantly brushed the belly of the EM. Soon they came to a small set of stone outbuildings.

"This is where the beekeepers lived and worked. The hives are all still full and active," Em shared.

Barcus could see them - domes scattered twenty meters apart. Clouds of bees flying about their business. Soon the cool weather would bring them all into the hives.

"Know anything about beekeeping, Em?"

"Enough, I think," her avatar replied from one of the seats.

They walked past the hives and over a hill to what was obviously an orchard. At their approach, a herd of about twenty deer looked up from eating fallen apples. They didn't run only flicked ears and tails.

They moved through the massive orchard to the far end near the encroaching forest. There was another stone building, but this one was much larger. It was long and narrow and had a long sink-like trough that went the entire length of the building.

"It's a sugar shack," Em stated.

"What the hell is that?"

"It's where they boil down maple sap into maple syrup or maple sugar, an occupation of early spring."

"One thing at a time, dammit," he barked.

Barcus did notice a sturdy table and chairs there.

They continued their tour to find grape vineyards gone wild. Instead of neat rows of grape hedges, there were simply acres of grounds overrun with grape vine. Trees had been covered and some of them had even been killed. Buildings that would support a vineyard were easily located.

They found fields gone fallow. And more abandoned buildings.

Barcus got out and went into a small house that had an intact roof and almost all the windows unbroken. It even had some decent furniture.

"Maybe we should move in here?" It was a question and a statement.

"The gatehouse is a little bigger and water is better there. Plus once we fix things, it will be better hidden and defensible," was her instant reply, followed by, "Barcus, can you climb up and stand on the stone mantel? I have found something."

He looked up to see Em sitting on a rafter. She was pointing to a spot he couldn't see.

He climbed to the mantel with ease. He had become used to the light gravity. His head peeked just above the rafter where he could see that Em was looking at an old leather bound book.

He grabbed it and leapt down easily.

Blowing the dust off, he could see it was a well-made book in good condition. As he opened it, he noted that the pages were not dry or brittle and turned easily.

It was in English.

Barcus learned quickly that it was a book about beekeeping. It covered how to establish a hive, keep it, harvest the honey, and there was even a section on making honey mead. Without thinking, he was smiling wide.

"Em, have the BUGs look for more books."

Their tour continued north for several hours until they stopped for dinner at the edge of a large fresh water lake. This was the northern most point that they would explore today. The BUGs had found a stone cottage with a domed grass covered roof near the edge of the lake. It was dry but empty inside.

"We should cache supplies here once we get established." Em was looking around the circular room. "In case something happens and we have to run, this would be a good remote place to hide."

She paused. "I could hide the spider and the beast in the lake if we needed to."

"Is there anything further north from here?"

"Only where we left Chen."

"Did they ever come back?"

"I don't know. We are out of range. I don't dare risk detection by communicating with Stu from here."

Barcus stormed out the door and toward the water. The beach was all rounded stones. He picked one up and threw it as hard as he could with a grunt. He was amazed at how far it went.

"Who did this to us, Em?" he said through clenched teeth.

"I don't know. Not yet."

Barcus was about to throw another rock and stopped.

"You have been trying to find out?"

"Of course. It's the best thing I can do to protect you. That's my job."

"What have you discovered so far?"

"Well, the satellite network supports comm traffic. The traffic is probably voice, video, and data. I believe I know the encryption type, but it will take a long time to break it."

Barcus was toying with his growing beard while he was thinking, a new habit he had acquired.

"I have located all the SATs and all of the ground stations on this side of the planet. We are 800 kilometers from the nearest ground station, which is good. I am doing all I can to analyze passively the traffic. I don't want them to find us the very same way I located them."

"But aren't you broadcasting now to me? To the BUGs?"

"Yes, but that is local, low power, directional and has high contemporary entropy encryption. We sound like background radiation. We are not using the SATs. Just point to point."

"I want you to tag and monitor this site. Name it 'The Northern Cache' for now. Let's head back. I have some things to think about. I want you to include this site and any updates regarding Stu in the daily status display."

They rode back another way so they could see more of the surrounding area. It was after dark when they reached the broken wall.

On the outside of the wall, half the rubble was now gone. The spider could still easily climb over the damaged saddle in the wall, but a man on foot would be hard pressed to do so.

"Faceless has been busy," Barcus said as he exited the spider and it retreated into the shadows of the lower levels.

The area in front of the garage had also been cleared. All the saplings were gone. It was no longer a struggle to move through the inner spaces. The broken doors had all been removed to somewhere. As he rounded the arch to the gatehouse, he could see a warm glow from inside.

When he opened the door, the first thing he noticed was that the flagstone floor was covered with a large rug of deep reds and blues. Then he saw two overstuffed leather chairs which faced the fire. A finely carved, dark oak table and four chairs were under the window. A small table between the overstuffed chairs matched them.

There were candles in jars on all the tables and the mantel. There was also a long, heavy, wool blanket tied to hooks so that it separated the front room from the back.

Drawing it aside, he saw another fire in that hearth, a large ornately carved bed against the wall, a side table with more candles and a smaller area rug of mostly deep green.

Looking back, he saw Em standing there smiling.

"Do you like it?"

"Thank you. I don't know what to say. Why two overstuffed chairs?"

"I hate sitting on the floor." Em's avatar sat in the farthest chair and drew her feet up under her.

Barcus looked around everywhere now, even up to the rafters. "How the hell did you get it so clean?"

"The suit has an onboard power washer. You know that. The tank is only 30 liters, but it made quick work of this space. It took longer to dry than to clean."

"Where did the furniture come from?" Barcus was amazed.

"We collected it last night while you were sleeping. There is an estate not far to the southeast. The main manor building was destroyed, but a small servant cottage remained."

"Why didn't you tell me?"

"And ruin my fun?"

"We also found the closest midden." A map of The Abbey appeared in a HUD window. It was a six-holer, just around the corner, off the kitchen pavilion. "There is also a chamber pot under that table in the bedroom."

"So now I have a pot to piss in and a window to throw it out of." Barcus was thoughtful, a touch of sadness in his voice.

"We found something else." Em gestured to a small chest he had not seen before. She obviously wanted him to open it. He did.

There were four more books in there.

They were all leather bound like the beekeeping book. The first two he opened looked like Student textbooks. One was a text on remedial reading and the other grammar. The third looked like a reference on forging steel. The last was a small, beautifully hand-written book of poems.

Looking up at Em, he could see she was still smiling.

"Thank you, Em." He paused. "For everything."

"We will watch for books wherever we go. I guess we should find a bookcase. What else?"

"Blankets and sheets and towels and more clothes." Barcus started ticking things off. "...and some boots for winter." He looked at his shoes. They were his on-ship footwear, like climbing shoes. "And tools of all kinds. Rope. Nails...glasses, cups, and plates. Maybe a small desk." Barcus was running out of steam.

He sat at the table and looked at the clean surface and said, "Keyboard." It was not part of the list, but a command word. A virtual keyboard appeared as a projection on the table. The standard 312 keys.

His fingers flew over the keyboard. Anyone watching him might have thought he was just tapping the table rhythmically. He was doing research. He was studying the layout of The Abbey.

After searching the archives for a few hours, he finally spoke.

"Em, I think this Abbey may have been one of the original Redoubts from the first wave of the colonists. Tomorrow we will find out."

"I think you are right. The measurements and materials analysis support the idea."

"If so, this may tell something about whom we are dealing with."

Barcus blew out the candles and added a few more logs to the fires.

"Em, add a pitcher and washbasin to the list."

Barcus completely undressed and climbed into the bed. The sheets were scratchy and coarse. But the bed was warm and dry and clean.

Where the hell did she find pillows? He wondered.

Barcus could not see the sky out the window, but he knew the moon was full because its light filled the courtyard. It was very much like the moon from back home, but maybe just a bit smaller. Like Earth's moon, the same side always faced the planet. It looked like a face as well. A horrible, angry, disfigured face.

A line of clouds had crossed over the moon before he fell asleep.

By the time he heard the rain begin, he could barely see the window's outline, it was so dark.

Barcus woke up just after dawn the next morning. As he drank his instant coffee, he stepped outside the gatehouse door under the slate roof that covered the walkway. It was leaking badly. Looking back inside at the gatehouse's vaulted stone ceiling, he saw no leaks there. A large amount of firewood was neatly stacked there, just below the window outside, under the eaves that covered the walkway.

Walking counter-clockwise through the doorway, which ran along toward the kitchen side, he saw the roof there had several leaks as well.

Outside, he could see that the overgrowth had been cut back. Any plant that had managed to grow in between the flagstones in the various inner courtyards had been expertly removed. The area that was once the kitchen garden was now clear of small trees. It wasn't mowed or tilled. It was trampled flat. It looked much better.

There was a neatly stacked pile of poles against one wall. They were the former saplings and trees with their branches stripped, standing by for future use. The debris that must have been cleared was nowhere to be seen.

There were gutters at the roof line, guiding the water down large storm drains. Engrossed in the very effective design, he walked directly into a steady drip of water.

He found the public midden easily. The door hinges were very rusty. The midden was stone with a wooden top that was dried and cracked. There were six keyhole shaped seats to choose from, all with the lids down.

Opening a lid, he could hear water rushing by far below. Pulling out his multi-tool, he switched on the light and shined it down. Water rushed by three meters below. It must be storm sewers and the rain doing it. But what about dry spells?

It was a smart setup.

He had a seat and started to read about beekeeping.

CHAPTER TEN

Foxden

"Barcus clearly did not destroy the Ventura. All the Solstice 31 Incident assumptions are now called into question."

--Solstice 31 Incident Investigation Testimony Transcript: Emergency Module Digital Forensics Report. Independent Tech Analysis Team.

<<<>>>

A few weeks went by, allowing Barcus to manage and direct further cleanup and repairs at The Abbey. At the end of that period of time, the gatehouse, the gate tower, the willow courtyard, the stable yard, the stables and the rooms above were all power washed and clean. Enough firewood had been collected to serve him the entire winter, more than was necessary, really. There were about thirty cords of wood neatly piled in the woodshed that was made for ten times that amount. The majority of the wood was from the trees that had been removed from The Abbey courtyards. Several of the trees remained. Barcus didn't remove any that he thought might help conceal his occupation of The Abbey from potential watchers from above.

One was an old apple tree that had grown to an impressive size since The Abbey had been abandoned.

Em had surveyed the surrounding area with BUGs and found several good sources for salvage. So far, she had not found any other books, even though Barcus kept asking her.

"I think we are ready to stock The Northern Cache. I would like to get it cleaned up, furnished and stocked with some supplies – food, water, clothes, blankets, firewood, and gear," Barcus said.

"It would go faster if we all went with the first load. For your safety, I don't ever want to leave you at The Abbey alone for long until it's secure," Em said.

"Are you babysitting me?" Barcus feigned insult.

"I just don't trust you to stay out of trouble," Em chided.

Barcus thought of Chen again just then. Dead, frozen, in the mountains.

"After we are done with that The Northern Cache, I want to go get the STU," Barcus said.

Em's avatar seemed genuinely surprised.

"Why, Barcus? That location represents a risk."

"I need him close enough for local comms. I have work for him to do."

"Barcus, we would have to fly him here. We could be seen. Where would you hide him? Again, why do you need him? It's a risk."

"First off, the shuttle has a small parts fabricator on board, more supplies, the med scanner and more tools. Second, he has massive CPU cycles. I want to use him to crack the encryption for their comms. Plus if we need to run..." Barcus faded off.

Em was looking thoughtful now.

"Before the snows fly here, I want to park the STU in the lake by The Northern Cache. We will travel to him, get close enough that we can use short range directional comms to bring him on- line. We will then bring him down to us on Grav-foils only. No engines, not even thrusters. Do you think that the two of you can manage that?" Irritation was creeping into his voice.

"You cut me to the quick, sir." Em tried to make light.

"That will also solve two other risks since we're talking about risks. If someone is up there and they are watching the STU, we will know without risking ourselves. The same when he picks us up. We will do it at night, a cloudy night. A stormy night would be better if they can watch via satellite because if our best hope for escaping detection is Grav-foils only, our best acceleration will only be about 8.1 meters per second squared. But it will be quiet."

"Then we could get to the lake in one night," Em added.

"And if they somehow trace the STU, there we will be, at The Abbey."

"If we can get the STU stashed before winter settles in for real, he will be under the ice. They'd never find him."

"Barcus?" Em said.

"Yes?"

"What about Chen?"

There was a long pause.

"I will go back for Chen when I can explain to her what happened...and what I've done about it."

"When we are on this trip, I want to stop at The Stone Cauldron, for salvage."

Em smiled at this.

The next day, they all went to The Northern Cache, making a side trip to that estate where they had found the good furniture. They loaded up Em with a table and two chairs, a medium-sized bed, some trunks for storage, clothes, blankets, oil lamps, candles, dishes, pots, and various other items they had learned were handy like a broom, wash basin, mirror, and even a chamber pot.

They reached the lake as they were debating on a better name for the place. Em's image was sitting in the other front seat as they glided smoothly across the countryside.

"The name should not contain information that is descriptive in any way. It would be bad OP SEC if the name referenced a location. We even need to rename The Abbey."

"Okay, okay, you've convinced me. What should we call it?"

"The Northern Cache or The Abbey?"

"Both."

Em's avatar actually looked thoughtful. Barcus realized again how very useful the Emergency Module's AI was in a survival situation. He'd be going nuts if he were alone. He smiled, realizing for the hundredth time that he was.

"And Faceless too. Following those same rules."

"Well if Faceless gets a name, the spider should too. This is kind of fun," Em said.

There was a large window open on the HUD that showed The Northern Cache in the autumn sunshine. The place was situated on a small rise on the southern edge of the lake. The Northern Cache was built between a couple of conveniently located boulders that made up its left and right walls. It had been dug out and leveled. Heavy beams held up a slightly arched roof that on the outside was overgrown with grass and some kind of dense vines.

Standing on the roof was what looked like a fox. Its nose was turned up, and its face was soaking up the late afternoon sun as it sniffed the air.

"We will call it Foxden," Barcus said. Somehow Em looked pleased with the name. The tactical display changed the name immediately as a final punctuation.

The suit had arrived before them and had the entire place power washed before they arrived. Barcus loved that. As much as he liked a clean house, he hated that first scrub that seemed to be required everywhere they went.

The door and both windows were wide open, and a large fire was burning in the fireplace already to dry the place out. The place looked almost like new. Barcus wondered at the craftsman's work here. How did they get the seams so tight in the stonework? It didn't even look like they needed to use mortar. The five roof beams looked oversized, but who knew how much all the soil weighed above.

"Em, you know how The Abbey was full of bird and mouse droppings? Well, this place was just super dusty. The windows have excellent seals. The door..." Barcus trailed off as he examined the heavy door. It was perfectly tight in the frame and it swung out easily. That is when he noticed the edge of the door. He originally thought the door was just heavy wood, but it actually had a metal core about a centimeter thick.

"I see what you mean, Barcus. I think this was made by the settlers."

The furniture was unloaded and arranged in less than thirty minutes. The supplies were stowed, and the bed was even made. It was getting dark when he started heating up some stew.

"I need to learn how to bake bread. I miss bread."

"There is an oven at The Abbey, but we don't have flour or other ingredients. I will put them on the salvage priority list if you like. We need to step up salvage before the snow flies. I believe this region will get a lot of snow." Barcus was getting used to the way Em's avatar would walk in and chat.

"I miss toilet paper, too."

"If you don't mind, I would like to send the spider and Faceless for a physical survey to the east. There are some ruins there that the

BUGs can't get inside that hold a bit of promise for salvage." Em opened a window in his HUD for him that showed a stone dock and pier. There was a large stone building that looked like a warehouse. There were actual roads that led to the forest.

"You are not worried about my safety?" Barcus teased.

"I can do the survey overnight and give you a full report in the morning. You do have your Glock and AR here," Em stated.

"Wait a minute. You mean the BUGs couldn't get inside there? Don't you usually just send them under doors or through keyholes?"

"There are inner airlocks and doors inside that warehouse that are sealed very tightly."

The recorded overhead view of the compound revealed that there were some large barges that had been sunk near the pier. Several buildings had been burned down some time earlier this year. So, the place had been in use this time last year.

"Okay. Do it. How long will it take you to get there?"

"Just a few hours. Faceless can ride. We really need names."

The spider and the suit were headed to the port warehouse, so Barcus settled in. Barcus was glad now that Em had insisted on two more overstuffed chairs for space in front of the fireplace.

"How about Shelobe? Or maybe Charlotte? Maybe Wolf?" The debate went on for an hour. Eventually after much debate that spider was christened as Pardosa.

"Pardosa it is. A species of spider. A thin-legged wolf spider. Par for short. That fits. Now on to Faceless."

Naming the suit was a more difficult effort. They went through famous people, historic figures, people Barcus knew from the past and even friends from the Ventura. Around midnight, they agreed on Ashigaru for the suit. They would shorten it to Ash. Barcus also told Em that Ash should have his own voice and personality. It would allow for instant speaker identification. He'd leave it to her to surprise him. Em smiled and seemed very pleased by this. Apparently the maintenance of a single personality was a default setting that she found limiting.

Barcus yawned and decided that it was time for bed. Stoking the fire once more, he said goodnight to Em and crawled into bed, thinking how an outsider watching him tonight would have thought him insane.

He felt very safe here. The frames of the windows were practical as well as beautiful and strong as bars. The door, once shut, was like a vault door. It's probably the only reason Em left me here alone, he thought. He fell asleep on his side, watching the firelight dance on the beautiful rug that Em also insisted he bring. She was right, again.

When Em sounded the alarm, he was deeply asleep. Suddenly, his HUD was bright with a tactical display of the region.

"We have an inbound contact. Moving at 1,100 kph at 189 mark 7. It is moving on an intercept with your position, not ours."

The tactical map showed all the known locations of every reference point Barcus had. The Abbey, STU, Foxden Lake, even the warehouse and Pardosa with Ash. That would take getting used to.

"Stay inside Barcus. That bunker you are in will give you all the cover you need." Em said.

He realized she was right; it was a bunker. It was pitch dark and chilly in the room. The time was 3:11 a.m. He padded out of bed and added wood to the fire.

"How did you detect this ship? I thought we were running passive scans only."

"It flew over some of the BUGs I had deployed in the south, from here, to here at this point." She displayed the map. A section of the map was highlighted, and the track of the ship appeared. "So I had the rest of the BUGs ascend to watch and listen for it. It's very loud. I believe it to be bigger than the other one we encountered. Much bigger."

"Can you extrapolate possible destinations?"

"Based on its current heading, it could be anywhere along this path."

The tactical drew a faint line ahead of the ship icon. Barcus froze.

It was headed to the village where they had found Po and Olias. He watched its progress as he warmed himself by his growing fire. The icon slowed and finally stopped just outside that village.

"I have BUGs in that village," Em said.

A window opened with a view flying over the treetops. There in the center of a large field was a large, fat, cargo style ship. A ramp had lowered in the back, and riders were already exiting the ship.

"How many?" Barcus asked angrily.

"There are 111 men and 123 horses," came her reply.

The majority of the men were forming ranks and awaiting orders while another smaller group proceeded on horseback to the village as an advance party. Once it deposited its load, the ship's ramp closed and it took off, making so much noise, Barcus was surprised the horses didn't spook.

When the advance party got close to the village, they dismounted and began looking at the ground closely. Seven men moved forward following the lead man, who was on foot.

There were now two BUGs covering the scene. One was moving in closer on the lead man. He had a shuttered lantern lit and was slowly walking to the village. The six other riders were still following him in single file.

"He's a Tracker," Em said. "They talk about Trackers all the time in Greenwarren."

"Greenwarren... Their next stop will be Greenwarren!" Barcus realized. "How fast can you get back here at maximum speed?"

"Two hours and forty minutes. It's exactly the opposite direction from Greenwarren, Barcus. Ash and I can go directly there at top speed. It will save almost six hours if we don't come back. We might beat them there."

"GO!" Barcus actually yelled.

Em appeared. Just popped in. She never did that. "Par and Ash are moving toward Greenwarren at maximum speed, Barcus. If the soldiers linger in that town, we will get there in plenty of time."

"I will arrive in about three hours at present speed. Ash is riding with me," came another, very different woman's voice, deeper. She sounded older. She had an accent he could not place.

"Is that Par, Em?" Barcus asked.

"I'm sorry, Barcus. Yes, that is Pardosa. From now on, you can address her directly if you like. Ash is here as well," smiled Em.

"Hello, sir. It's very nice to make your acquaintance. I wish it were under better circumstances." Ash actually had a formal British accent.

"Why the accents, Em?" Barcus asked.

"It is known as Practical Avatar Differentiation. When running in multi-mode, it's best to be able to differentiate with a syllable or two. Just saves time," Em said.

"Okay, got it." Barcus was not going to worry about it now. He'd get used to it.

"Em, where are Po and Olias? Do you know?" Barcus asked.

"Yes. Olias is in the blacksmith loft. Po sleeps on a cot in the kitchen at the inn with the other girls. They tend the cook fires. I have had BUGs there with them continuously," Em replied.

Anger was building now in Barcus. He wanted to be there.

He motioned to shift to fixed HUD mode. The windows and tactical in his vision would become like high-definition screens that hung in the room in fixed positions, like large paintings, instead of being fixed in his view, moving as his eyes moved. It allowed him to pace and move among them. It also allowed him to have more windows open without being too distracting. It allowed Em to interact better as well.

"Par, what is your ETA to Greenwarren?" Barcus asked.

"At present speed, we should arrive just before dawn," Par replied.

"Barcus, they are moving." Em gestured at the surveillance window following the soldiers.

"They found the remains. They are splitting up. They are following the road toward Greenwarren. One small group is searching. In the opposite direction. Two sets of scouting parties are spreading out."

"Barcus, at this speed, I am leaving a trail a five-year-old could follow," Par said.

Barcus went to the tactical map and said, "Par what is your planned route?" It came up on the display instantly. "When you get to this river, travel in it for six kilometers. When you get within one click of the village, let's reassess. Maybe you should try to minimize your tracks in that last kilometer."

"Yes, sir," Par answered.

"How much will that impact your ETA?" Barcus asked Par.

"I estimate it will add nine to twenty minutes," Par replied.

"Did you move from Foxden to the warehouse in stealth mode?"

"Yes, sir. Stealth is the default unless otherwise ordered," Par replied.

"Okay. Good," Barcus affirmed.

"Par, give Barcus a weapons and critical systems status." Em was standing there with her arms crossed, waiting for Par to answer a question he should have asked himself.

Par gave the full status. It took a full twenty minutes. Barcus was calmer by the time she was finished.

"Em, is there any way the BUGs could warn them?" Barcus asked.

"I'm sorry, no," Em replied.

"Em, what is going on here?" He gestured to a new window labeled 'comm traffic activity.'

"That's a new encrypted transmission. It looks like a persistent link via SAT. Look, here is another," Em replied.

The tactical zoomed over the area where the troops were. The BUGs flew down closer to the transmission source. In one display, a man had a book open that showed a detailed map of the region - a dynamic map.

"He is holding an old style Plate interface." Em observed.

The other one was talking to someone via the Plate. The BUG was too far away to hear.

"Dammit, we need to decrypt that traffic. You have to warn them when you get there. Ash, get the message to Olias or Po. They will believe you," Barcus said.

He got dressed in silence and then returned and put the kettle on the fire to make tea.

"Sir?" It was Ash. "Would you mind awfully much if we killed them all?"

Barcus looked at Em. Her eyebrows were up and her hand was covering her mouth as if she had been surprised and didn't want to laugh.

"Please do... All of them."

In Greenwarren, it began to snow.

CHAPTER ELEVEN

Late to Greenwarren

"The AI functioned for a few weeks within expected parameters. Barcus was safe. Then, for some reason, the new code paths were invoked. Code where safety protocols had all been disabled. "

--Solstice 31 Incident Investigation Testimony Transcript: Emergency Module Digital Forensics Report. Independent Tech Analysis Team.

For the first two hours, Barcus discussed options with Par and Ash to ensure none of the soldiers would escape them. They had very detailed maps of the Greenwarren but not the surrounding area. There were only 4 bugs still in that town, two that followed Olias and two that followed Po.

When Par got there, she would release another swarm of BUGs. None of the soldiers would escape them, the bastards. The snow was getting heavier. Snow or rain could be slightly problematic for the BUGs.

"Barcus. Look here." Em was focused on a video window showing the riders from above as they trotted, four abreast, down the road. In the center of the column, a rider was looking at a Plate. Because of the snow, the BUG had to fly very close and had now landed on the man's collar. Barcus could now hear the conversation and see the Plate's video.

"I will be packed within the hour. I want to be gone before you arrive, Esau," the speaker intoned.

"Don't want them to know that it was you that betrayed them?" Esau was laughing. "Very well. We will take our time. Perhaps four hours. We will even pause for a meal first to give you plenty of time, Keeper Malcom." He closed his book cover on his Plate and placed it back in its saddle pouch. He then left formation and began moving to the column's head.

"Em, what is a Keeper?" Barcus asked.

"They are the top layer of the caste system here. I believe they are supposed to be like priests," Em replied.

"My god. It's the town's own Keeper!" Barcus was incredulous. "That fucker is mine," he said.

"Get in line," Ash growled.

Reaching the front, Esau said to a grim man who seemed to be the leader, "I want to be there within the hour. Can you do it?"

The grim man gave a wide smile that was all teeth and no mirth. He then yelled something that Barcus could not understand.

"What! Em at that pace, they will beat us there." Barcus scanned for the ETA countdown display which read 1:14:22 and was counting down.

"It's the snow and the terrain, sir. I will try to go faster," Par said.

"Dammit. There has to be a way we can warn them!" He was watching Po sleeping.

"Barcus, I can't warn them. But I think I can wake them," Em said.

"What good would that do?" Barcus was getting frantic.

Barcus kept pacing.

"Olias has become paranoid after the last village fell. He maintains two escape caches with supplies in different locations." Two new points were highlighted on the map; a still frame opened showing the vista near the primary cache. It overlooked the town.

Em continued, "He has shown these caches to Po, and she has even updated their contents on a few occasions. They have a plan to meet there if anything unusual happens between midnight and dawn because that was when they struck last time."

"So," she repeated, "I think we can wake them. But it will cost a BUG."

"What good will that do?" Barcus asked, frustrated.

"If they are awake, they may hear something...unusual," Em said.

"Like what? Pounding hoof beats? By then it's too late!" Barcus shouted.

He glanced at the window with the soldiers. They were galloping full speed. It was like the horses had been longing for a run after being penned up in the shuttle for who knows how long.

"There is a ridge here that I need to move along," Par said as it was highlighted on the map again. More stills opened showing the view. Olias had visited there a few times - a log of the dates and times scrolled there.

"The town is six kilometers away from this point, but I think with the long range 10mm, I can make some disturbances." Par sounded angry. The still image zoomed into the bell tower of the Keeper's temple.

"Timing is going to cut this close, sir," Ash added, "When Pardosa stops here, I will disembark. I can descend the ridge here at speed."

"Em, wake them up," came his determined statement.

He was watching Po's window as the BUG descended toward her eye. It landed on her eyelash and was crawling to her eye. It pressed into the slight gap and under her eyelid.

"Don't hurt her, Em," he implored.

The second BUG opened in another window. Po's eye was twitching, and she began to stir.

Olias was sleeping with his face buried in a pillow. His BUG descended and flew directly into his ear. The image became confused while his second assigned BUG had yet to arrive. Barcus changed his focus back to Po's screen.

"Po, wake up," he whispered.

As if she had heard him, she sat up and rubbed her eye. She threw the blanket back, and he was glad that she was fully dressed, boots and all.

Olias's second BUG arrived then, and he was also sitting up.

"Stop moving the BUGs, Em," Barcus asked.

Olias raised the wick on an oil lamp, stood up and went to the only window of the loft. He drew the curtain aside and looked out into the snow covered the town. He could see the back of the inn across the town's rooftops.

Just then, he saw the kitchen window curtain draw aside. Someone was there. It was Po.

That was when Par fired the long range gun.

The tower bell rang once, but it was loud. A few seconds later, the sound of the shot was like distant thunder rolling over the town.

Olias was down the ladder in an instant. Without breaking stride, he grabbed his cloak from the peg and was out the door.

The first stall held one of the horses he had brought from Whitlock.

"Every night before he goes to bed he saddles it. Every morning when he wakes up, he takes it off so the blacksmith won't see," Em said.

He threw off the blanket and trotted the horse out of the stables, mounting quickly.

Barcus had his heart in his throat.

He looked at the display. The soldiers would be there in seven minutes, Par in twelve minutes.

They would be too late.

Po was putting on a heavier tunic and as an afterthought added another man-sized tabard and a heavy belt. When she opened the door, Olias was there. Without a word, she climbed up behind him and held on as he moved out of the inn's yard.

"Hurry," Barcus said.

When Olias got out to the road, he turned the horse and it began to run.

He was galloping directly toward the troops that were coming to the town at speed!

"No!" Barcus screamed at the display. He looked at Em. Her image seemed to be studying the same screens as him. Panic and frustration were draining the blood from his face.

As he looked back at the tactical display, he could see they had left the road. They were heading up a switchback that would lead to their cache of equipment. They had three BUGs with them. The one from Olias's ear had found its way out intact. They looked like children on that horse. Olias looked scared, and Po looked blank, stoic. The third BUG was watching the rear view. The snow was accumulating fast on the still night. It was muffling the sound of their passing but left a clear trail of it.

Behind them in the distance, they could hear the pounding of the soldiers' hooves as they passed the turnoff. It sounded like more rolling thunder.

By the time they reached the overlook, the massacre had begun. They knew people were being slaughtered in their beds.

"I told them to set a watch. I told them. I said they were coming."
Olias was crying as they stood on the overlook. Subtitles translated his
words. "All the weapons were hidden in the loft of the blacksmith's
barn." Olias opened his cloak and through gritted teeth said, "Except this
one." He was wearing a sword.

Olias began uncovering the cache. First, he brought out two
saddle bags and secured them to the horse, ignoring the quiet echoes of
screams. Then he added two packs and two bamboo-like tubes.

"Those are longbows." Em injected.

The screams had stopped. Many of the soldiers were dragging
people into the street and asking questions and then still cutting them
down. Soon even that stopped, along with the snow.

Suddenly, Olias heard a distant pounding. A shape could be seen
moving through the forest below, now and again. It was knocking the
snow from the trees as it passed at an impossible speed toward
Greenwarren.

That is when they heard the voice. It was in a voice, louder than
reality allowed, echoing.

"Olias, Po, run!"

Just then the faceless black demon tore into the soldiers like an
avalanche. Olias didn't wait to see the outcome. He mounted the horse
and held his arm down for Po, but she was staring at the town. Olias
looked again and a giant spider was there, harvesting their heads. These
men were not like the others. These were trained soldiers who stood their
ground. They died all the faster.

"Run!" echoed again, breaking the spell.

Po climbed into the saddle, and they moved up the trail to the
ridge. They had to be careful because dawn was still almost an hour away,
and the snow covered the trail.

By the time they reached the far end of the valley's bowl where
they could see the town, there was enough light, but too much snow to
see from that distance. They found strange tracks here. The ground was
savagely overturned in spots a foot or two across. It was an easy trail to
follow.

They rode all day, stopping only once to eat and rest the horse.
Olias had not planned for snow. He had figured that the horse could

browse along the way. The horse didn't complain, though. He just ate the snow and an occasional leaf in passing. It was well trained.

Po spoke for the first time in hours as Olias was fishing another tunic out of his pack to put on. "Where are we going?"

"We're going to find that Keeper," Olias replied

"Why did you come? How did you know to come? You saved me," she gushed.

"He did it," he said solemnly. "Keeper Barcus saved us. Again. I don't know how."

"How will you find him?" Po said.

"I don't need to. He will find us. I believe in him," Olias replied in common speech.

They didn't know he was already with them.

***

They kept moving west toward Barcus. But that was a small gift. Barcus watched unable to act as the village died. These men were professional soldiers. They were not like the raiders of the last village. They were quiet, they had executed the people on sight where they stood or where they slept in their beds. The soldiers had not screamed like banshees nor raped the women before murdering them. They did not loot the place or savagely destroy everything.

When Ash and Par attacked, they stood their ground and organized their attacks. The swarm of BUGs followed them as they killed and then died. After the main battle was over, Ash and Par had to mop up.

Some villagers had tried to run into the forests out the back gates into the snow. They were quickly ridden down and slaughtered by these grim men.

Vengeance fueled his anger as he directed the soldiers' demises.

Seven got away because those seven never joined the killing party. They had gone south after getting off the shuttle, so Par and Ash left them.

Olias had lost the trail hours ago. He had a great sense of direction, so he plodded on into the blizzard.

Barcus did not want not lose Olias and Po after all this. With the last of the soldiers dispatched, Ash began to follow after Po and Olias. It would take hours to catch up, and he was a mess covered with bloody snow and gore, sure to frighten them on sight.

A bit before dusk, Olias had found a large shelter pine. The snow never made it to the ground here in the dome created beneath the wide boughs. Even the horse fit inside if she kept her head down. Shelter pines were often used by trackers. This one was no different.

Olias made a fire in a circle of stones covered in pine needles they had found there so they could stay warm while they rested.

Po was busy getting a camp kettle ready when the sound of the voice made both their heads snap up. A Keeper was standing in the makeshift entrance.

"That was a merry chase." He had a crossbow leveled on them. "How did you know they were coming? It was brilliant to ride toward them. Their own horses would cover your tracks." It was Malcom, the Keeper of Greenwarren.

"You thought you were so clever. I knew you had gear stored at the overlook. I followed you once because I never trusted you. No one is supposed to survive those raids. So, when I heard that thing call your name, I knew where to look."

Then, silently, a black arm reached in and a gory, clawed hand grabbed him by the head and said in a voice straight from hell, "Drop the crossbow."

He had to drop it when Ash lifted him off the ground. His hands clung to the cruel fingers, taking the weight off his neck.

Po walked right up and took the dagger out of his belt. She raised the point under his chin. He went still immediately. She pulled his cloak off his shoulders and tossed it to Olias.

"Allow me." She was affecting a helpful tone that held a sinister edge.

"Just like all those times you made me." She unbuckled his belt and it fell, heavy with pouches and purse. Olias dragged it away.

"Nothing to say? Unlike all those times, you raped me. You had plenty to say then. You never stopped telling me how powerful you were. Are you powerful now? Well, you will never touch me again. Or anyone else. Keeper." She spat those final words.

She drew back and paused so he could see what she was about to do. She hammered the dagger into his heart. She wanted him to see it coming. She twisted it to see the pain in his face. When his hands left his head to go to the knife, she pulled it out and showed its bloody length to him as the light went out of his eyes and his body grew limp.

Without a word, Ash threw his body out into the darkness.

"I'll keep watch. We'll leave in the morning," Ash said from the darkness as he withdrew. A moment later, another horse was led in. It must have been Malcom's. Then some freshly cut boughs covered the entrance, stopping the wind.

"What did I tell you?" Olias actually smiled.

Po looked at him. A deep crease was between her brows.

"I just killed a Keeper." Po was stoic as she looked at the bloody knife.

It was warm in their shelter. The branches above with the snow bending the boughs down acted like a chimney, drawing the smoke up. Their clothes dried quickly and their bedrolls on the thick bed of pine needles made for a soft bed. By morning, the snow had stopped. The sky was still heavy, and the snow was about a foot deep. They didn't see the monster anywhere. But they saw his tracks.

His wake was so wide and so deep, it was like he was plowing a path.

After they had ridden for two hours, they came across a great pile of Marcie grass and acorns. It took Olias only an instant to know that they were for the horses. The horses did not immediately run to the food. They were very well trained. Po and Olias led them over and had to take off their bits and bridles and hand feed them the first acorn to signal that it was okay to eat now.

Olias and Po ate some dried meat and cheese while they waited for the horses to finish.

"That monster knows how to care for horses better than me," Po said in disgust, as she watched them eat. "Where are we going? We should be heading south. There are no villages this direction."

"Po. We are alive," Olias said.

She was hugging herself.

"He saved us again," Po said in a trembling voice.

She looked him in the face. Fear and dread were in her eyes.

"Why? Why us? What does he want from me? You thought Malcom was bad! He was cruel and vain and full of greed. But he was not powerful. Not like this. This Keeper Barcus has killed hundreds of the high Keeper's men on a whim." She was trembling, as she continued. "That 'thing' we are following may be leading us to damnation. It has no soul. It is not flesh and bone. It's made of stone, black malice, and death. It helped me kill a Keeper. An unforgivable sin. It wanted me to kill him! It could have easily done it himself. I am already lost. You may be lost as well because you let me live."

"Keeper Barcus saved us," Olias said slowly.

"What about Greenwarren? Did he save them? Or were they just bait for more death? Why would a Keeper do this?"

Olias was close now. "Answer this first. Why the hell is the High Keeper sending soldiers to wipe out our villages?"

"Who are we to question the Keepers?" Her back was to him now.

"Olias, why would anyone bother to save us? Even once? Much less three times? What is my life worth? Less than nothing," Po whispered.

Olias said nothing because in his mind he saw her point. He at least was a good blacksmith apprentice, worth something. He didn't say it.

The horses were done eating. Olias replaced the bridles, and they moved on again. Po was riding the Keeper's horse, and she noticed a special pouch on the saddle sized to hold a modest sized book.

It was empty.

CHAPTER TWELVE

The Gatehouse

"The Emergency Module, in hostile environment mode, had very complex algorithms. It determined the likelihood of Barcus's survival would increase if he were not alone physically."

--Solstice 31 Incident Investigation Testimony Transcript: Emergency Module Digital Forensics Report. Independent Tech Analysis Team.

They traveled for several days, and with the snow falling now and then, they could always follow the path left by the mysterious thing that was their dark savior.

They moved farther and farther into the wilds until one day, they found what seemed like an ancient road that was arched above by trees, heavy with snow. It was like a tunnel, hushed and dim under gray skies. The tracks followed this road north farther still.

They found small trees attempting to grow in the road with minimal success. They had the uneasy feeling that they were the only people left in the world. Every day they would find places to rest and more forage for the horses. Only once did they have to sleep in the open. On that night, Po didn't know if she slept at all because she sensed the black, faceless demon was near.

Once it was beginning to snow again, and the tracks led them to an abandoned farmhouse. It had a steep, old style, thatched roof that was more moss than thatch now. Inside there was one large room, and each end had a hearth with firewood that was already cut and laid out.

The floors were flagstone with traces of thresh still visible, but decades old. Olias set about making a fire in one hearth and Po in the other.

They brought the horses in and let them warm up and dry off in one end the room, and they took the other.

"I didn't know there were any settlements this far north," Olias said, trying to start yet another conversation with Po. She had fallen silent for nearly two days.

"This house..." Olias looked around at the stone walls and the heavy beams in the rafters, "was built to last. The hinges are made of stone."

Po spoke, "This was a Keeper's house long ago." She sat on the floor in the center of the room and slowly placed the palms of her hands on the floor. "The Keeper's magic lingers. The floor is already warm."

Olias sat next to her and felt the flagstones. They were warm even though the fires had been lit less than an hour ago.

"It was always like this in a Keeper's house. Rooms that had no hearths would even be like this. Keepers can make things hold magic and keep it," Po said.

Olias knew she had spent time as a Keeper's companion.

"I saw a Keeper's talisman that could bring things closer without moving them. You could look at a sawdust beetle like it was the size of a mouse. It could even bring the sun closer... and burn. The Keepers made it, infused it with their magic, and it still worked for whoever held it."

Olias dug into the saddle bags and brought out the last of the dried meat and nuts.

"What will we do after today? Are you a good hunter?" Po asked very seriously.

Olias laughed. "Don't worry." He felt the floor again. "I think we are almost there."

"Where?" Po asked.

Olias just shrugged and tossed a nut into the air and caught it in his mouth, smiling as he chewed.

Barcus watched the exchange in his personal HUD. The translation appearing as subtitles. He paced back and forth in what he had started calling the "throne room." It did have a raised dais at one end with a massive carved stone chair at the top. Em would tease him by sitting in it sometimes, knowing he had never even climbed the stairs to look at it. He told Em it would be hubris.

The room was really good for fixed configuration status screens in his HUD. Em was juggling them all with ease. Barcus sensed she still felt guilty for not detecting Malcom sooner.

The tactical map improved every day on the region surrounding The Abbey. The route Ash had taken to lead them to The Abbey revealed many surprises, most notably the forest road that meandered south. This was a main road that could not be seen from above. It was actually paved but had not been maintained in probably a hundred years. Trees had fallen across it, but few saplings had found enough purchase to grow in the road.

"Don't worry Barcus, they are safe. They will be here by midday tomorrow," Em said from the throne.

He was watching them via the swarm of BUGs Em now used to monitor them and the surrounding area. He had fixed windows of Ash's panoramic real-time view too. Ash was currently stationed at the edge of the woods, watching the farmhouse. Thirty-two other windows arranged themselves showing the BUG views as they patrolled. There was the large tactical map that could be engaged to take the entire side area to the front of the hall.

"You could see these much better from up here you know." Em was trying once again to get him to climb up. "Did you know the seat gets warm when the hearth is lit, as well as the floor?" Barcus had discovered that the floors were heated by a series of pipes that were below the flagstones. These pipes led to the fireplaces and made up the grates that held the wood as it burned. Once the fires got going, the coals heated a fluid in the pipes and natural convection circulated the liquid. The gatehouse hearths even heated the midden floor. That was his favorite.

Ahhhh, the little things.

He had discovered how this worked in the section of The Abbey that had been destroyed. The lattice of pipes in the dorms on the far side was exposed where the floors had collapsed on that corner.

Barcus reviewed his critical inventories and adjusted them for supporting three people. Food was the biggest issue. He had left three months of his survival rations from the Emergency Module at The Northern Cache, finally named Foxden.

"We will be fine. Ash and I will hunt. You'll have plenty of meat," Em said.

Barcus was looking at the detected transmission log. His maps did not extend much farther than the wide river to the south. It cut a deep path to the open sea to the east. He could imagine that in the spring there was no crossing that river by boat. There were some BUGs slowly mapping that river. It looked like a boat could go all the way to the sea from there, several hundred kilometers away.

The empty warehouse they had found near Foxden was very empty. Some logging tools were there, mostly rusted beyond usability. He had found a single ax that was worth bringing.

The next windows were images of the two shuttles. One was an ancient personal transport, and the other was an M79 Material Transport. The M79 was only used for eleven years and only on Exodus class colony ships.

Whenever Barcus began to stare at this image, Em would voice the hypothesis again. "Once the Expansion War had broken out and the real shooting had begun, every colony ship that was still in dock moved out before the Greens could destroy it. Many were hunted down and lost. Some were presumed to survive and reach their designated planet. Many of these settlements were eventually destroyed anyway."

"What if one of the Exodus Class Colony Ships didn't go to its designated planet? I read once that some of these ships were privately owned consortium ships with 25,000 people all paying their way with massive fares."

"What if one or two of these ships came here?" Em asked.

"What about the animals? The plants? The species and ecology here are so similar to Earth. Deer? Rabbits? Apples and grapes. Even bees. You know how complicated the ecosystem is for pollination?" Barcus said.

"The ecology is not exactly the same. There are no apex predators as far as I have seen. That may explain the plentiful deer. There are birds of prey of several sizes, even a kind of eagle," Em said.

"Any luck with the Plate yet?" Barcus asked.

"I told you if I had any updates I would let you know," Em said, sounding annoyed.

"Just be careful. I do not want that thing to give our position away," Barcus warned.

It was almost full dark when the wall loomed up in front of them. They had smelled wood smoke for the last thirty minutes. The tracks in the snow led all the way up to the wall and eventually a gatehouse with a door, now open, that was big enough for them to ride into. They looked at each other and rode in.

They passed through the gate into a courtyard that was clear of snow. There was water in the pool around a willow. It was not frozen and the horses drank as they dismounted. To the right, an arch revealed stables that were lit with lamps and had grain in feeders waiting for the horses. They unsaddled the horses and left them to their supper. They had learned that they were so well trained they would stay where they were left.

The guardhouse was on the other side of the courtyard, opposite the stables. There were lights in the windows. They stood in the courtyard trying to decide what to do when the door opened and Barcus said after a moment, "You've come all this way, and you must come in. I have just put the kettle on, would you like some tea?"

Olias said formally and a bit stilted, "Yes, please." Po had been teaching him the Keepers' High tongue.

Po averted her eyes and said nothing.

They entered the gatehouse and Barcus closed the door behind them.

He was so tall compared to them.

He made the tea just the way she liked it. Po didn't know he had been watching her so long. He felt a momentary twinge of guilt for knowing so much.

He poured them each a cup as they hung their cloaks on pegs. Handing them each a mug he said, "Welcome to Whitehall Abbey."

In his personal HUD, Em was there like a ghost they could not see or hear as she spoke. "*Whitehall?*" They had been arguing over the name for the Abbey for weeks. Em knew she had lost.

He gestured to the comfy chairs by the fire. A third chair had been pulled over from the table as well. "Please, sit. I know you must be tired from your ordeal."

Po sat on the edge of the chair from the table. She was staring into her steaming tea, holding the cup to warm her hands. The liquid betrayed her trembling.

"Keeper, thank you for our lives. Again." Olias's words were stilted, formal. He spoke them with care and intent.

"Please call me Barcus." He tried to use what Em told him was the casual phrase in common tongue. Olias smiled nervously.

Just then they all heard the large door in the gatehouse close. It startled Po a bit, causing her to spill some of her tea. Barcus brought her a tea towel and knelt before her saying, "You're safe here, Po. Those men will not find you here. Olias and I will protect you." He smiled at the boy, who beamed back, but when he turned back to Po, he realized that she wasn't afraid of the men, she was afraid of him.

He moved away, giving her space, and went to the pot simmering on the fire. He had made a decent stew. Thanks to Par.

Par had salvaged many things from Greenwarren that Barcus had not considered, like feed for their horses, potatoes, onions, spices, flour, salt, and other foods. Par was making another trip even now. Par, Ash, and Em never slept.

As he stirred the stew, he asked, "Are you hungry?" He didn't want them to know that he had been watching them. Something had broken the spell. Po seemed to come alive then. She turned her head, looked at the small table, set for three already. Then she looked around the gatehouse as if seeing it for the first time.

She set her tea cup on the raised hearth and went to the table and gathered the three bowls there. She came over to the pot where Barcus was and said, "Please, my Lord. Allow me."

Barcus suddenly felt nervous and looked over at Olias, who stage-whispered something in the common tongue. Em translated for him in subtitles in his HUD, "Just let her. She will anyway."

He remembered it was always she that served Olias on the road, even when they were camping rough. Barcus wanted her to feel comfortable, so he moved out of the way and carried the chair back to the table. Olias sat on one end of the table, next to the wall, with his back to the door. Barcus sat opposite, and although he did not have a wall at his back, he also did not have the door at it. Barcus never put his back to a door. Old habit.

Po filled Barcus's bowl first and then Olias's. She filled the third bowl and backed away from the table. Barcus was pouring water into some lovely cut glasses when he looked up at her and said, "Please, sit."

Olias's spoon stopped halfway to his mouth, and his eyebrows went up. Barcus knew that women were treated like slaves on this planet, but he was not going to tolerate that here. He could see the conflict across her face. He laid down his spoon making it clear he would wait until she did sit.

"Please, where I come from, our ways are different than yours."

"As you wish, Keeper." She sat with her hand folded in her lap with her eyes averted. Olias had set his spoon back down into his bowl, waiting.

It was a full minute before she reached up for her spoon and took a mouthful. Barcus took up his as well and smiled at them.

"Call me Barcus. Just Barcus."

They ate slowly and in silence for a few minutes, but hunger overtook them and they eventually dug in. Po brought them each another bowl and sat in front of her empty bowl looking down at her hands again. Barcus tried a different angle.

"I want you to have another bowl and another. We have a lot of work to do around here. I need your help. If we are to survive this winter, we need to be strong."

"Is there no one else here?" Olias was not sure his words were correct.

"There are only the three of us. I found this place a month ago in ruin. I have been working hard and fast to prepare for the winter."

"Just you? Alone?" Po was incredulous.

"Yes. Well... Yes," Barcus said. Olias and Po looked at each other. It wasn't hard for him to know what they were thinking. "His name is Ash. He won't hurt you, I promise."

A Keeper's promise carried more weight than Barcus knew. Or it was supposed to. It never really did, until that day.

"I really need your help. I don't know how to do this. Whitehall is a good place. It has orchards and vineyards and beehives. It has good water and shelter. And it's safe."

They said nothing.

"Why do they come? The soldiers. Keeper Malcom, he knew," Barcus queried them.

"I don't know. At first I thought it was my fault. I don't think so now," Po replied.

"Your fault?" Barcus asked.

"There is no one else," she said.

Po began cleaning up. Any attempt to help her was expertly rebuffed as she worked. Olias and Barcus went together to check the horses.

Olias spoke in common tongue. Subtitles showed in Barcus's HUD as Em translated, "My Lord, Keeper, let her do as she will, please. She needs it."

"Call me Barcus."

CHAPTER THIRTEEN

Falling Asleep

"The Emergency Module began providing incomplete and even intentionally misleading information. The BUGs observed the destruction of several villages and never reported them to Barcus."

--Solstice 31 Incident Investigation Testimony Transcript: Emergency Module Digital Forensics Report. Independent Tech Analysis Team.

<<<>>>

Olias and Barcus took a lantern each and carried the saddles to the tack room. It was next to the first two stalls. A fire was burning in that hearth. It kept the stalls warm on this end of the stables. Barcus showed Olias, the blacksmith shop at the other end. It was colder there. It had four different anvils but only one hammer. Ash had power washed the shop. Olias found its condition puzzling – clean and empty.

While he was with Olias, Barcus was watching Po in the gatehouse. She took off two extra layers of clothes, down to the gray dress she had worn for days. She took water from the kettle and cleaned the dishes. Then she refilled the kettle from jugs and put it to heat.

"You can look around more in the morning. You're welcome to stay as long as you want."

They exited the far end of the stables. The sky had cleared and the moon was on the rise just over the far wall. They stood looking up, but what Barcus saw was Po. She drew the curtain aside and looked into the back room. Then she turned and retrieved the kettle. She hung it on the fireplace hook and when she turned, she startled and gasped and actually fell backward onto her bottom. Above the wash basin was a large mirror. It was tilted forward a bit and she could actually see herself sitting on the carpet in front of the fireplace.

Slowly she got up and looked at herself. She touched her own face on the mirror. She could see that it was dirty from the road. She went to her pack and dug out a cleaner dress of the same cut and a washcloth and towel. Looking at the curtain briefly, she reached behind her neck and undid a single button. Her dress, in one quick motion, fell in a pile around her ankles. He closed his eyes reflexively and instead of closing the window, it shut out the world so that was all he could see.

She poured some water into the wash basin. Hurrying now, she washed herself. She was so thin, it broke his heart. She was bruised from long days riding and sleeping rough. He glimpsed scars. But then, as fast as the dress had fallen, another went over her head. She wore nothing underneath the dress, and her feet were bare. Her boots were drying by the fire in the other room.

He opened his eyes. Olias was staring at him. He didn't know for how long. In his best common tongue, Barcus offered, "Let me show you where you can clean up."

They crossed back to the courtyard that had the fountain. There was a tall, unkempt, willow tree growing up out of the center of the fountain, creating a large planter and canopy above that would shade the entire area in the heat of the summer.

Barcus led Olias into the outdoor kitchen area and to the midden door. The floor was warm, and the six stalls were clean and fresh. A large stone basin was on the other side. There were pitchers of water and towels with washcloths. The water had not frozen because the room was "magically" warm.

Olias gave a big smile and went into a stall. Barcus left him to it and returned to the gatehouse where Po was adding more wood to the fire. She had done the same in the bedchamber behind the curtain before she collected her things and went out.

"Let me show you where you will sleep." He picked up her pack and Olias's as well. He swept aside the curtain and revealed the back room as if she had not already seen it.

"For now, you will sleep here. You are welcome to stay in this room as long as you like. But Whitehall is huge - you can claim almost any room you want." He set her pack on the bed. "Olias and I will be just up in the loft above for now."

"Where do we sleep, my Lord?" Po caught herself staring at him and averted her eyes.

He was reluctant to tell her that she was displacing him for fear that she would protest. He had to be honest though.

"And where will Olias be?" She took the pack from him and went up the spiral staircase to the loft. Barcus followed.

Two narrow cot-sized beds were there. She put down the pack and looked over the railing to the room below.

"Do you really live here?" She actually looked at him for the first time.

"Yes. It has all that I need. Why?" Barcus spoke gently like she was a frightened animal that might run at any second.

She looked over the railing again at the carpet and the overstuffed chairs, the tables, and lamps. He had four small books on the shelf with odd shaped rocks as bookends. "It's so...beautiful."

Olias came in the door just then. The moment was gone.

"I will sleep here until we sort out better arrangements," Barcus clarified.

Yet Po looked confused.

"It's fine, really. I don't mind. Besides I don't sleep much," he equivocated.

"My Lord. You don't think I would deny..." Po was shaking her head like she was trying to sort a paradox. "I can't allow you to sleep up here and alone my Lord. It would be unseemly." She was averting her eyes again. But now it was his turn to be confused.

"Please call me Barcus."

Em walked into the room just then speaking in his mind. *"Barcus, understand that there is a caste system at work here. She has been raised to believe that Keepers are a higher form of man. They treat them differently. Apparently, none are allowed to sleep alone. Usually, two women are required to sleep with Keepers. They have been raised to think that it is the height of neglect and shame to allow a Keeper to sleep alone. Ask her if you don't believe me. Ask Olias. He is only fifteen, and I bet it's already second nature to him."*

He ignored Em. His head was almost touching the stone arches above, and he felt like he was towering over Po. He sat down on the cot behind him and looked up to her, hoping he would be less intimidating. "Po, where I come from, we have different customs. You need not sleep with me. If you stay here, you will never be forced to sleep with anyone ever again." She was trembling again.

To the side, he caught Olias's eye. He had frozen at the top of the stairs and was backing down again. Barcus would have to thank him later.

"That demon told you what happened?" Po said.

He answered quietly, "His name is Ash. Yes, he told me everything."

The words didn't bring comfort as he had hoped the trembling increased.

"So now you think I will kill you in your sleep?" she asked softly.

"What?" It was his turn to be incredulous. He laughed a little but regretted it. "No. I don't think that."

"Why are you doing this?" Her voice was a whisper now. He didn't know if she was trying to keep Olias from hearing or simply could not talk louder. "Death is tearing through the north. Why? I don't understand." She fell to her knees. He caught her left hand and her right came up to clutch at his hand as well. "Good people and bad, demons and monsters. Everywhere I go, people die." She was shaking. He gathered her up into his lap.

She was so tiny. She buried her face into his chest. He carried her down the stairs and Olias held back the curtain as he passed into the front room.

Barcus sat in his overstuffed chair and held her. She curled up and didn't say another word. Barcus could see the worry on his face as Olias watched. Olias took the lap blanket from the other chair and gently covered her, and set about making more tea quietly, not knowing what else to do.

Po began to relax slowly. He sensed it as a melting into him. She began as a hard fetal ball of fear. She was so thin, all bones and so small. Now as he stroked her back, her breathing eased. Olias brought two cups of tea, and Barcus drank his hoping he would not regret a full bladder later. Eventually, she shifted a bit and Barcus stretched out his legs reclining into the deep chair.

Barcus didn't know when he fell asleep. But when he woke, the candles had all been blown out, and a single oil lamp was banked low. The fire had burned down to a deep red bed of coals. His feet were crossed. Po had stretched out a bit, too. She was so small. But she was awake. Olias was in the loft snoring.

"Will you let me take your boots off?" she asked.

"I can do it," Barcus said quietly.

"I know you can do it. You are a grown man. Will you let me take your boots off?"

He nodded, not knowing what else to do.

She slid off his lap and began to unlace his boots. They were boots that he had salvaged. She set them on the hearth and climbed back into his lap, never looking away from his eyes until she curled up again.

"Will you let me sleep with you in your bed? Please?"

He carried her into the bedchamber and lay down with her on top of the quilts. She clung to his arm as a pillow to make sure he didn't try to get away.

Fully clothed, he held her to his chest, in the arch of his body, her back to him, spoon fashion.

He felt her fall asleep in just a few minutes and then he pulled the quilt up to cover her. Soon he was fast asleep as well.

When Barcus woke, it was well past dawn. Po was still asleep. Her head was on his chest with her right arm over him. Her right leg was over his thigh, and he could feel her left foot on the skin of his calf. It was their only skin to skin contact.

Her braid had come out in the night. Long waves of blond hair framed her face. Barcus brushed a lock of her hair out of her face, and her eyes fluttered open. She looked uncertain for a moment, but only a moment.

"Good morning, my Lord Keeper. Did you sleep well?"

"Call me Barcus." And he paused before continuing. "Yes. Yes, I did."

She sat up, Indian style, and began combing out her hair with her fingers. "Today we find out what kind of Keeper you are," Po said, and just like that she was gone.

"I don't even know what kind of Keeper I am," he said out loud to himself.

"*I know what kind you are.*" It was Em. She was walking down the spiral stairs in the corner.

"Oh, what kind is that?" Barcus whispered.

"*Rested. Since this started, I don't think you have slept more than an hour at a time really, until last night. You were so worried about them."*

He knew she was right.

"And I don't think she has slept a whole night in a decade. She feels safe here. Even with demons about."

"Where are Ash and Par?" Barcus asked.

"Par is en route to Greenwarren again, for salvage and cleanup. This time she took Ash with her. She left another load off last night just outside the gate and turned right back around. Start making lists of the things we need. Put them to work. I have been updating all current status items. They are ready whenever you go into the status room."

"Is it all right if I talk to the boy, sir?" Ash asked in his mind. *"It might make things a bit easier at times. He does not seem to be afraid."*

"Sure that's fine. But let me talk to him first. Both of them."

"The boy has been up for hours already. Exploring," Em added.

Barcus got up and went to the other room to pull on his boots. The gatehouse was empty. The packs were hung on pegs. The fires were fueled, and everything was organized.

He walked out the door into bright sun. It was warm. The snow was melting and the gutters were running. He could hear conversation coming from the outdoor kitchen area. He walked through the doorway to see Olias feeding the beginnings of a fire below a third large cauldron in the space. Barcus had not seen any of them lit.

He didn't see Po until she said, "Good morning, my Lord. Would you like some porridge?" She was back to averting her eyes. Her hair was braided again.

She didn't wait for him to answer. She walked to the huge cauldron with a ladle and dipped three large portions of oatmeal into a bowl. The cauldron had to be 100 liters – there could not be that much porridge in there. He walked up and looked down. There were seven tall ceramic jars in the cauldron, standing in water that was gently boiling. One of the jars was full of porridge, one smelled like beef stock, one was full of white liquid. Two were empty.

"Would you like some honey in your porridge?" She was looking at him now.

"Yes. Please."

She ladled in a good amount and added a spoon and handed him the bowl.

"Is it all right? I can make you something else." Barcus stopped her.

"No. It's not that. When did this all happen?"

"Olias has been awake for hours. He knows enough to know a cold kitchen is unacceptable. He found oatmeal in the... provisions."

"Have you eaten? You need to eat. I want you to eat," Barcus said.

She looked at him again, her head tilting slightly, like a bird. She turned and picked up a bowl. They were the same ones they had used for the stew last night. She ladled herself some and added a bit of honey. When she had her bowl, he tasted his, making it clear he would not eat unless she did.

The porridge was wonderful.

"I remember having oatmeal like this when I was a boy. My mother would put honey, maple syrup and crushed nuts in it. It was wonderful on a winter morning." He looked at the snow, melting in the sun.

"What is maple?" Po asked.

"It's a kind of tree." She was looking at his eyes again. It was like her words asked a different question than her eyes. Olias came running up, then speaking too fast for Barcus to understand. Po barked at him. He stopped.

"Have you eaten, Olias?" Barcus spoke slowly.

"Yes, Keeper." But he was looking into the tall stone jar.

"Call me Barcus. And eat more. Please."

Olias dove for his bowl and ladled up three spoons, and then his hand was hovering over the honey ladle. Barcus nodded.

Em's avatar walked through the doorway then. *"Barcus, do you realize that these two have been starved their entire lives? These last two meals probably represent more food than they have eaten in the last week. They have always been mistreated. You will need to let them help you, or they will mistrust you."*

That reminded him about Ash.

"I know this must all be very confusing for you both. But I will try to explain." He set his empty bowl down on the counter. "I am not like the Keepers you have known." He didn't want to lie. "I come from very far away. I'm alone and lost. I am just trying to survive."

Po was murmuring translations to Olias as he spoke.

"I was alone. Until now," he said.

She didn't need to translate that.

"I think the Keepers are the ones that killed my family, my friends. All of them. Just like you. And I don't know why."

He looked around the ruined courtyard. Em was standing there. She spoke.

"Ask them to stay. Give them a choice. They have never had one before."

"You are free to go whenever you like. I will never bind you here. But if you stay, I will do my best to protect you. I will try my best to be your friend. I promise. I need your help. I'm lost here."

Just then, Ash appeared in the archway to the fountain yard. He ducked under the arch and paused before he came in. He stood just inside.

"This is Ashigaru. I call him Ash. He will protect and help us. You do not need to fear him." He moved forward quietly, into the full sunlight. It was a bad idea. He was actually still splattered with blood in many places.

Barcus wondered why he didn't speak to them. Instead, he made a barely perceptible bow and left the way he came.

"He's big," Olias said in common, making Barcus smile.

"What about the other thing? We saw it at Greenwarren. A giant spider?" Olias asked, as Em was translating.

"Her name is Pardosa," Barcus said. "They are both my friends."

"Good," Po said. "Now do we have a decent broom?"

CHAPTER FOURTEEN

Cauldrons and Questions

"The Emergency Module had assumed three separate personas. Remember that they were all operating as EM extensions. Barcus had no idea how advanced this survival system had become. Em, Par and Ash were all the same mind."

--Solstice 31 Incident Investigation Testimony Transcript: Emergency Module Digital Forensics Report. Independent Tech Analysis Team.

<<<>>>

There was another big pile of supplies just outside the gate - bags of foods and grain. There were clothes and utensils and tools in the salvage pile as well. Po and Olias set about sorting, organizing and storing the supplies and gear without a single question.

Barcus went off to the throne room to study the hundreds of active status windows. The inventory lists were growing as the salvage was assessed. The survival estimate changed as the amount of food they had increased.

The cauldrons were being analyzed. One was dedicated to heating water for laundry. The cooking cauldrons constantly boiled fresh water that could be used to make tea or start a stew on a moment's notice. There was an iron grate in the bottoms of the cooking cauldrons that allowed boiling water to circulate all the way around the tall, heavy jars, slow cooking their contents but never burning them. It was brilliant.

The Abbey had a bakery. It was a big one. So big that it seemed like it had to be used to bake things for sale, not just for consumption by The Abbey residents.

There was a growing list of items to repair. Just like back on the Ventura. Same format even, same annotations.

"Plumbing, 5% complete, due date, prerequisites 12..."

"Em, what is the story here?" He indicated the plumbing.

"The plumbing depends on the aqueduct, and the aqueduct will not be

repaired until the wall is repaired. The wall repair should also be considered a security priority."

The security task list was then highlighted. It was long.

"We have a 'shopping list'?"

"*Items that we need to obtain before winter are priority items.*"

"For god's sake, Em. There are hundreds of things just on that list."

Barcus noticed then that six new villages had been added to the main tactical map. Active, living villages. More ruins had been added as well.

"Have you detected any more soldiers? Fires?" Barcus asked.

"*Negative. No smoke plumes anywhere visible on any horizon. No troop ships detected.*"

Barcus scanned the screens for an hour before finally saying, "Em show me the top priority tasks that involve me that are not projects or major objectives. Where do I start?"

"1) Retrieve Shuttle Transport Unit (STU)."

Behind the words hanging in the static HUD configuration was Po, standing in the open door. Wiping her hands on an apron. Frozen.

"My Lor... Barcus, dinner is ready," she said, eyes averted.

Suddenly he realized it looked like he was standing in an empty room talking to himself. Insane.

She turned and walked back toward the gatehouse.

When he got there, Olias was already sitting at the table. His face and hands were freshly scrubbed, unlike Barcus's.

Before he could get up to go wash them, Po was at his elbow with a small carved wood platter that had three wash clothes rolled and neatly arranged. He took one and then Po offered one to Olias and he took one, uncertain. They were wet and still warm. Barcus washed his hands.

Po came back holding the third warm towel, washing her hands with it and then setting it to the side of her place setting.

"The oven is not working yet. It has old raccoon nests in it. I'm sorry there is no bread yet," she apologized.

Steaming bowls of food were already on the table, and she picked up and served Barcus some vegetables and handed the bowl to Olias. There was venison tenderloin sliced in one of the bowls, fried potatoes in another, and what looked like yellow carrots, except they were spicy.

Barcus could tell that she was uncertain about eating with them. She was acting as if someone would catch her at any moment and drag her away by her braid.

Olias was uncertain for only a moment. Following the lead set by Barcus, he would not start until Po served herself and began. Then, he dug in with gusto. He eventually took thirds. Po ate more than she usually did, Barcus was glad to see. He didn't even have to badger her to have seconds.

Barcus thought the dinner was over, but when Po got up, she came back with three saucers that had a thin crusty looking cookie in the bottom. It did not look appealing. She went to a tiny pot that smelled of apples that hung by the fire during dinner.

"The oven is not working yet. But I managed these." She dipped a spoon into the pot. "These are dried apples, stewed in honey with spices." She ladled the mix over the coarse looking cookie.

It was glorious, the texture of the oatmeal crust cakes that soaked up the juices. And the apples were warm and sweet with a splash of cream. Perfect.

She served herself last. Staring at it. The spoon trembling in her hand.

"I've made this hundreds of times. I never once got to taste it." She looked up to look at Barcus in the eyes.

Olias had already finished his.

She put a spoonful in her mouth and closed her eyes as she tasted it, chewed and swallowed it. Barcus knew how wonderful it was.

She opened her eyes and looked at Barcus. He was smiling at her.

Something overwhelmed her. She furrowed her brow and covered her mouth with her hand. Her shoulders shrugged as her face collapsed. She fled unhindered to the other room.

Barcus looked at Olias. Olias raised an eyebrow, twisted up a half smile, pointed at her desert, pointed at Barcus and then pointed for him to follow her.

He did just that.

He walked with the desert to the curtain and entered without preamble. She was sitting on the edge of the bed with her face in her hands.

Barcus sat next to her. Sounds of dishes being stacked came from the other room.

"I have decided that there is only one thing you are never allowed to do."

Removing her hands and wiping her face she looked at his, which was quite serious.

"You may never let this ever go to waste." He handed her the dish.

She looked up at him again. She was so tiny. She took the dish. After a long moment she sighed, took a deep breath and took up the spoon.

"It is good." She took a bite.

"Did your mother ever make this for you?" she asked, finally taking another bite.

"No. I wish she had," Barcus answered truthfully.

She took the last bite of the desert. After she had swallowed, she handed the dish back to him. He was surprised.

"Thank you," she said with her eyes averted.

"Po, everything is going to be different from now on," Barcus stated quietly.

"I know." She moistened a finger and collected a few crumbs from the small plate. "Can I pick one thing you are never allowed to do?" she asked.

He was surprised by the bold question.

"Sure, if you make that for me again soon." He smiled, as she licked the spoon again.

They both heard the door close. "Can I ask you never to lie to me when we are alone in this house?"

"Yes. I promise," he said without reservation.

"Where did you come from really?" she whispered, her eyes glistening. There was a long pause.

His answer was just as quiet. "The sky."

She scanned his face and found only truth.

Her relief was evident on her face.

"I made you a nightshirt," she said as she looked away.

Barcus was getting used to her nonsequiturs.

***

Barcus went back to the throne room again after dinner and lit fires in all the hearths. The windows in his HUD were multiplying and sorting into piles. The list of things they needed was growing and being updated. The biggest problem with Pardosa on salvage runs alone was that she could only reach so much. While her front legs could be used as arms, some things were too fragile or too big to haul out a window.

As soon as Par was back, Barcus planned that she would take him to retrieve the STU. Ash would stay here at Whitehall. The day after tomorrow would be good. They would do some salvage on the way. Barcus was remembering the wine from that Tavern.

"Barcus, I have been studying the two Plates we have brought back from the raiding Keepers. Initially, it was to ensure they would not give away our location. I have discovered several useful things." A list opened in yet another new window.

- One was not secured - no passcodes required.
- The other was locked and fully encrypted.
- I have disabled SAT comm protocols on the unlocked one.
- I have located its User and Administrative manual.
- They support multiple network protocols including NearFi.
- There is small 1TB local storage capacity.
- I am reviewing files now for relevant content.

"Here is the best part so far." With that, the tactical display expanded beyond the small region it covered. It zoomed out, completely filling in the map; villages, towns, roads, rivers, lakes and seas were all labeled.

Finally, it zoomed out to the point that the globe was floating in the center of the room.

"The device was loaded with base maps, but not the annotations unless the specific user added them. There were none in this case. No annotations, no local documents. The only thing the local storage was used for was pornography. Nothing special there either except, the girls ran a little young."

"What do the maps tell us?"

"We are in an area that is outside their established provinces, of which there are eleven. The population centers on this planet are mostly on this continent in a temperate band - here." The area rotated toward Barcus and zoomed in.

Em laughed. "These people don't like the snow or the heat.

"The Plate itself is a very early model, second gen. The Augmented Reality Interface works still. But it really needs server side support.

"I believe I can use the device via NearFi if I activate a secure emulator on my side for it to talk to. I need your permission to try."

"You need my permission?"

"Yes. Your admin level is 'root'. As the AI, I have only limited admin rights. Connecting to other networks or devices requires root permission."

"Say please," Barcus said.

"Are you serious?" Em asked. He crossed his arms.

"Please?"

"Do it. If that works we can use it for communications locally," Barcus said. "What about the other one?"

"If the first Plate functions as expected, I may be able to replicate it at the block level. I would rather wait until we have the STU. A locked device may assist him in decryption efforts. We won't know until he is here."

"Par, when will you be back?"

"I will leave here at dusk today. Two nights travel. Dawn the day after that," came his crisp reply

The calendar began cascading updates. Various schedules moved to the left.

"It is 12:07 a.m., Barcus."

All the windows began to dim. All but one. That last one showed Po sitting up in Barcus's bed, waiting.

He opened the door to the gatehouse quietly. He sat and took his boots off equally as quietly. Then, pushing the curtain aside, he entered the bedroom. He immediately saw the nightshirt. It was neatly folded on the quilt. Po appeared to be asleep, her back to him. He quietly began undressing, folding each item and placing it on the chair. After removing his shirt, but before taking his pants off, he pulled the nightshirt over his head. It was a knee length, gray tunic, simple and soft. It was the same color as Po's.

He climbed in, his back facing hers. A moment later she turned to spoon his back. He covered her hand with his. Barcus thought he'd be awake the whole night, his mind racing. But his mind didn't race. He listened to her breathing, slowly relaxing into a faint snore. He was asleep soon after.

As he drifted off, he felt a pang of guilt for allowing her to be in his bed. He had been rationalizing it but knew he was just being selfish. He knew he was seeking comfort and swore to himself that it was fine because he would never take advantage of her.

"*You already are,*" he chided himself. "*Got yourself your very own slaves, you bastard...*"

When Barcus woke, it was 5:32 a.m. The clock was the first item he checked so he always left it on in his HUD. The HUD ribbon rolled out along the bottom of his vision with the indicators for priority items. Everything was deep green except the one that represented Pardosa's trip status. It was light green. Nothing to worry about, but he would check it first thing.

Then he realized Po was not there.

"Where's Po?" A window opened instantly showing her standing just beyond the curtain combing her hair.

"I'm here." He heard her through the curtain. He watched her suddenly rush to braid her hair. He watched her fingers fly in well-practiced motions.

Without thinking, he said, "You can use the mirror to do that." He realized his mistake at once when she froze. She paused only for an instant, took the leather string from her mouth and braided it into her hair for the last twenty centimeters and used it to tie off the braid.

She came through the curtain then. To distract her from the comment he asked, "Where's Olias?"

She sat on a corner of the bed and folded her hands in her lap. "He moved his cot to another room yesterday. In the 'dorm wing' I think you called it. He said you granted permission." Her eyes darted to the mirror where Barcus could see her and he knew she could see him in the dim light of the freshly stoked fire.

"I tried not to wake you," Barcus said.

"Can I ask another question? You don't need to answer if it is a secret," she said, looking at her hands in her lap.

"You can always ask me questions," Barcus said as he rose up on his elbow.

"How do some things hold the magic? Forever?" She looked at the mirror again. He realized that the reflection frightened her a little.

"Some things have magic in their nature. Like that mirror. Like the fire gives us light and heat," he said.

"But the Keepers can create magic. They can control the wind and speak to people impossibly far away. They have ships that can fly in the sky, I've seen them. They can make light in the darkness without heat or fire. They can know things without learning them. I have seen all these things," she stated.

Barcus had no idea where to start.

She got up and went into the other room briefly and carried back with her the four small books. She held them as if they were made of glass and fragile beyond reason. She sat them down on the bed next to him.

She picked up the smallest one, the children's book and tentatively opened it. "How does magic get into these shapes?" She was acting as if he might strike her at any moment.

The page was a simple, hand-drawn image of a small boy reaching for an apple on a tree. The page had the single word "apple" written below in formal block letters. The letter "A" was artfully highlighted.

"This says 'apple.' This is the letter called 'A.' it is the first letter of the alphabet." He sat up closer and pointed to the stylized letter.

Po pointed to the word on the opposite page. "Bee?" The drawing was a honey bee. Simple but clear in its depiction.

"Yes. Exactly." He looked at her eyes then. They were filling with as yet unspilled tears.

"Why would you tell me this?" Her lips trembled.

He was confused again. He always seems to step in it.

"Because I said I would tell the truth." He didn't know what else to say.

"Other Keepers would kill me for asking this, for knowing this. It's forbidden." She sobered.

"I told you things are going to be different." Serious now.

That was when Barcus decided that he was going to teach her to read. Olias as well.

"You would trust me with so much power?" she whispered, incredulous, searching in his eyes.

I trust you with my life, Po, he thought to himself and didn't know why. But "yes" was all he said. Barcus picked up the small book and handed it to her as if in ceremony. "This is your book now, Po." She slowly took the book. Her face was a mix of wonder and fear and awe. "I am going to teach you to read. You will know all the small shapes that represent all the things in the world. It is true. It will make you more powerful than you know. It may be the greatest single gift I could ever give you."

He wanted to reach out and touch her. They slept in the same bed, so he was sure she wouldn't draw away. But he chose not to.

"Will you teach me something?" he asked.

"What could I possibly teach you?" Po asked.

"How to make that excellent tea. It's a kind of magic as well..." They both smiled.

CHAPTER FIFTEEN

M is for Magic

"Barcus was kept distracted with food and comforts as more villages burned. The Emergency Module allowed these mercenaries to create a buffer around them."

--Solstice 31 Incident Investigation Testimony Transcript: Emergency Module Digital Forensics Report. Independent Tech Analysis Team.

<<<>>>

The temperature had remained above freezing that night, and a light mist of rain did its best to eliminate the rest of the snow.

He was sitting in the gatehouse, putting on his boots after getting dressed in the fresh clothes Po had laid out. He was going over plans with Em as he did.

Po came in then with a bowl of porridge and a mug of tea.

"Yes, I am going to eat right now," she said before he could open his mouth. She went right out. Em brought her up in his HUD. She did go out and make a large bowl for herself, with honey and something else she sprinkled in. Barcus looked down and then tasted his own. There were crushed nuts in it.

He smiled and ate as Em gave him the morning briefing. Inventories had been updated with the items Par had obtained on this run. Security status was provided with no sign of additional soldiers and expanded area of coverage. Silently Barcus wished there had been less detail regarding the collection of the corpses and their burning in a sand quarry nearby. One item was in red.

"What was the negative issue?" Barcus asked. Par replied herself.

"I believe I was seen sir." Par allowed him a moment to ask a question if he liked before she went on. "I was only an hour outside Greenwarren when I spotted the thermal signature of two people that hid as I approached. It was just after dusk, and there may have been enough light that they may have seen me. They were not armed, and the probability that they were a threat was minimal. So I ignored them."

"Very well. Where's Ash?"

"He is performing another salvage run to the Estate," Par said.

"He won't be able to carry much back with him."

"Olias has gone with him, with both horses. He plans on bringing back a wagon filled with items needed," Em replied this time.

He laughed and had some more oatmeal.

Em interjected, "I recommend you allow them to do as they will. It will improve life in Whitehall for you and keep them busy. We have perfect weather to retrieve the STU. You and Par should go first thing in the morning after she gets unloaded. Oh, and you need to prepare Po and Olias in case they are there when Par arrives."

"They were okay with Ash," Barcus argued. It just hung there.

"If all goes well, you will be gone only a week at most," Em said. "I don't know if it is too early, but the Plate is now configured for our local comm network. You could leave it with Po in case of emergencies."

"How would I explain that?" asked Barcus

"It's in a leather bookbinder case now. Just tell her it's a magic book, and if she opens it and speaks to it, you will hear her. She doesn't need to know that we monitor them both full-time already, and it is just so we can speak to her. We will also have Ash there. He can talk to them if need be."

"All right," Barcus decided.

The day went by quickly. Barcus began a detailed survey via visual scans and measuring of Whitehall so he could create a 3D model that would facilitate repairs, renovations and enhanced utilization of the spaces. Lists grew as Po talked with Olias or Barcus about the kitchen garden, seeds, baskets, carts, wheelbarrows, goats, chickens, tools and hundreds of other things.

Barcus noticed a new window in the throne room list simply marked "people." It included farmers, stone masons, carpenters, coopers, blacksmiths and even a vintner.

"Em, this is looking a little ambitious. I just wanted to be left alone, not draw attention until I can figure out what to do."

Em's avatar walked into the room and sat down on the step that led up to the dais of the main hall.

"Barcus, what is it that you want here?"

Barcus stopped his pacing.

"We need to know what the real goals are so I can help move toward them. Survival was the initial goal. Escape and evasion. But here is the thing." She actually waited until Barcus was looking at her. "I don't think they know we are here." She let it sink in. "We have seen their ships. We've seen the tech they have. It's very old, but it still works. We have killed a lot of their people."

He was scanning the many windows for clues. They all slowly faded except the local tactical map.

"If you knew there was a dangerous adversary loose in this region, what would you do?" she asked.

"Aerial search sweeps, coordinated ground searches, detailed crash site investigation."

"What do we have instead? Coordinated Regional Genocide. I don't think these events are related at all. I also don't believe that this is the first time something like this mass killing has happened. The ruins are not all recent. Just look at The Abbey. What the hell happened here thirty years ago? A bomb went off here, and not a small one."

"Are you saying getting the STU is too much of a risk?"

"I am saying the opposite. I don't think whoever runs this planet is watching at all.

"So I ask again. Barcus, what is it that you want here?"

He was thinking.

"Well here are some options." She ticked off a finger. "If you decide you want to simply survive and live out your days on this planet, we are in an excellent position for that. The major downside is there would be no longevity treatments. You'd only get another 90 years or so tops before you die of old age."

She ticked off her second finger.

"Next option: Rescue. Tougher to pull off, but if these fuckers have an automated defense grid, I'd bet they have a hyperdrive capable ship or an old school Tesla Comm Node." Barcus was amused by her tone.

She ticked up a third finger.

"Third option: Vengeance. Find out who is responsible for killing

Chen and the others and make those sons of bitches pay." The violent undertone in her voice surprised him.

He thought for a minute before speaking.

"The next step on all of those plans would be to retrieve the STU. Even if it's just for the transportation, med bay and the fabricator," Barcus said.

She stood and walked to him. "Look, Barcus. It's my job to keep you safe. I need to know what you are thinking to best do that."

Just then the door opened. When Po looked in, he was just standing in the center of a room that was dimming with the coming of dusk. She looked around and all six fireplaces were burned down to beds of coals, and a chill was beginning to return.

"Olias is back." She paused. "...with Ash."

"I'll be there in a moment," he said.

She averted her eyes as if she had been dismissed and backed out, closing the door.

"I want to survive first. Figure out what is going on here, and make them pay. Then maybe the rescue after. If any of it matters by then."

His voice was harsh again. He had no idea Po overheard him. He always felt angry when he realized he was talking to himself. Yes, he knew it was an excellent computer interface. But it was not real. And Chen wrote it. Maybe that's why he felt so angry.

Chen was dead. All his friends and crewmates were dead.

How many times would that realization continue to kick him in the guts?

***

He found Olias unhitching one of the horses from the newly salvaged wagon as Po was pointing and directing Ash where to put a huge crate that was on the wagon. Barcus knew Ash could have carried the entire wagon and load if needed. At least he wasn't making them afraid.

As soon as Olias had stabled the horses and saw to their needs, he was off.

"Does that boy ever walk anywhere?"

Po smiled wistfully. "He has never had so much. A full belly twice a day is heaven to him. But three times a day, a warm, dry bed, rooms of his own and more. It's like the winter solstice feast every day for him."

"He doesn't miss his family?" He knew this was her feeling as well.

"There is none to miss. His parents had died before he was six. His masters since then offered only work and deprivation, if not abuse and cruelty."

Ash took another load to the kitchen, Po watching him.

"It's not alive," she said. "Ash I mean. Not really alive. I can feel it. It's just a tool brought to life by magic. It's not dead either because it was never alive."

"Yes. A tool." Barcus marveled at how perceptive she was.

"Like any tool, it's neither good nor bad, in and of itself."

He realized she was trying to sort something out for herself. She looked up at him, one of the rare times she looked in his eyes.

"Ash is an extension of your will, isn't he? Like a woodsman's ax but more useful and more dangerous."

"Yes," he replied carefully.

She nodded and began to walk away.

"Po. In the morning, Pardosa will return." She stopped and looked back.

"You know I have seen her?" Po asked him. "More than once. And she has seen me. I can feel it. That one IS alive."

"I have to go away for a few days. I will take Pardosa with me. I'll be safe." He watched the wrinkle appear on her brow. "I will leave Ash here to watch over you and Olias."

She said nothing. She looked down.

"I won't be gone long."

"Is there anything you would like us to do while you are gone, my Lord?" She was playing stiff upper lip. He could see it. "Besides eat too much, three times a day?" A smile struggled up to her eyes.

"Actually, there is. I will show you later. Let's go see what Olias is up to," he invited.

***

Po knew where Olias had selected his rooms. They were not the largest rooms in the dorm wing, but they were nearest to the midden on that level. Barcus knocked on the door. Though Em had a monitoring window for him already, Barcus wanted to see for himself the room that Olias had been fixing up. There was already a huge pile of firewood in the hall outside his room, a whole winter's worth. Ash had been busy.

Olias opened the door with a huge smile and a sweeping wave of his arm.

The fire was blazing. The room was very warm already, warmer than Barcus liked for himself. Olias had a single-sized bed, but it was a canopy bed with heavy drapes he could draw. He had many blankets and pillows. In front of the fire were two mismatched but comfy looking chairs. He had a small round table and three stools. All of this was on thick carpets that overlapped each other, covering the entire floor. Each wall had a trunk. One was small and the other two were large enough for Olias to hide in.

Barcus noticed there were two swords and three daggers resting on his low mantel but said nothing.

"I presume by this you have decided to stay?" Barcus tried in his common tongue.

"Oh yes. I've never had my own room or a real bed before. Thank you." Olias said in common, translated by Em.

Suddenly Em's voice was in his head and a Tactical Map in his vision. *"We have an incoming, high altitude ship that is on a direct intercept vector with Whitehall."*

Po saw him look over his shoulder and head suddenly toward the throne room as if he had heard a sound.

"How far away is it? What is the ETA?" he asked to the empty part of the room as he arrived.

"ETA: 11 minutes 41 seconds," came her crisp reply

"What is its altitude?" he asked, ignoring the looks from Olias and Po.

"Barcus, if it has a bomb, you could get clear in eleven minutes."

"Show me the trajectory since detection." A very straight line appeared from the east. He was walking back to the main hall. "How did you detect it? Show me possible sites of origin." The map shifted and reversed along the same vector until it fell upon a series of islands well off the eastern coast to the far south. There was a major city marked there. Cookesthrow Shoals and the city of Millsea.

He looked down and finally realized Po and Olias had followed him. He barked questions at them.

"What do you know about the East Islands? What about the city of Millsea?"

Po answered first. "They... they make boats there. Ships. For sea trade."

Olias added, "They are very rich there."

"What else?" Barcus gave himself only two minutes to decide whether they should run.

Po answered, "They have only one Keeper there, and all the other Keepers hate him."

"Millsea is here." Olias ran across the floor and stood on an irregular pattern on the floor on the far side of the room.

From where he stood now, he could see it. The floor of the hall had a map of the world marked into the artful flagstone. Em shifted the tactical overlay to the floor. The ship was moving fast directly toward the throne.

"Come!" Barcus said.

The order left no doubt it was to be obeyed.

They ran to the stables and Barcus commanded them onto the horses, bareback, and to follow him.

The stars were beginning to reveal themselves as they cleared the gatehouse door.

Barcus ran.

The road was quickly covered by an arch of trees, but he didn't stop. He could hear them behind him so he ran faster and faster.

The horses' training prevailed. They seemed to know they were to follow him. The low gravity served him well as he moved as fast as these horses at full gallop. Glancing, he could see that both held a hand full of the horses' manes. Barcus ran full tilt for nine minutes.

When he could hear the ship, he began to slow. His HUD told him they were 5.7 clicks from The Abbey. Far enough for most tactical nukes. Well, small ones.

The road opened to the sky at this point. *Cover was better* he told himself. The Horses pulled up and nearly reared. Ash was waiting just inside the clearing.

Barcus held up a silencing hand.

They could hear the roar of the ship above. The ship and its vapor trail were still in the sunlight as it passed behind them.

Po was worried, "Barcus, what's happening?" She looked up. "It's the Keepers. We see them like this sometimes."

Olias chimed in, still breathing a little hard, "My mother always said that they were on the Errands of the Mighty. We are naught but ants." He sounded like he was quoting.

They waited.

Darkness had fallen fully before they turned back. Po and Olias were both shivering by the time they got back. The blackness of the open maw of the gatehouse door was unsettling. Barcus turned on the light from his multi-tool. They entered the fountain court and turned into the stable yard. He snapped off the light.

"I'll take care of the horses. Goodnight," Olias said uncharacteristically sober.

"Barcus, the ship continued without deviation until it was out of range," Em Said in his mind.

They went into the gatehouse, and Barcus sat and started to unlace his boots.

Po just stood in front of the fire warming herself.

"I'm sorry, Po. I didn't mean to frighten you," Barcus said quietly.

"How could you run... like that?" Po said.

That was not the question he expected.

"Where I come from, we are very strong and fast."

"Do you have to go tomorrow?" she queried.

"I do."

"What was it you wanted me to do while you were gone?" Po asked.

Pulling his other boot off, he said, "Get ready for bed and I will tell you."

She went into the loft to change into her night dress. He watched her through the HUD, even as he changed into his nightshirt. He got the book from the side table and waited.

She climbed in and sat up next to Barcus. She remembered.

"A is for Apple. B is for Bee." She traced the letters with her finger, then turned the page and cocked her head.

"Try." Barcus encouraged.

"Cat?" she guessed. "We could use some cats around here."

A livestock list window popped open and "cats" was added.

"C is for Cat. D is for Dog," Barcus said

"E is for Ear. F is for Fire." Barcus continued making the "f" sound.

She sat, and they went through the book dozens of times. Barcus explained that letters made words, words made sentences, and sentences held the thoughts or ideas. The back cover of the book had random letters scattered over it.

"Show me a T." Po found it easily. They did a few more until she almost chose wrong on "W."

"That's enough for tonight. I want you to read it every night I am gone. Think about the letters, the words."

Po set the book on the side table, added a large log to the fire and blew out all the candles.

Em said in his HUD, *"Barcus, Par will be here in four hours. They will quietly unload, and she will be ready to go whenever you want."*

Just then Po spoke. "Barcus, when I was a young girl, I lived on an estate just below the gorge. House of Keeper Volk. He discovered one day that the head cook could recognize the name of the spices from the jars. He made us all watch as he beat her to death, bashing her head in, with an ax handle. After he was done, he cried because he would miss her pastries. He said only witches could read, and we are always obliged to kill witches."

"No one will kill you as long as I have a say. Besides, you are already a witch," he teased.

In the middle of that night, he caught her out of bed reading the book by the light from the fire. It was when she said out loud "F is for Fire" that he woke. At first light, she was at it again. He smiled and watched her sitting on the floor. When she saw he was awake, she asked, "Is P for Po?"

"Yes!"

"M is for Magic..." she said.

"B is for Breakfast," Barcus said. At that, her eyes flew wide.

"Is B also for Barcus?" she asked.

"You mean that there is a magic set of symbols that if I were to recognize it, I would see you in my mind?" her eyes were wide.

"Yes," he smiled.

Breakfast that morning was cold meat and cheese with hot tea. Barcus went out the gatehouse door for a bit, and when he came back, he had another book in his hand.

"This book has more magic than the other books. While I am gone, if you ever need to speak to me, all you have to do is open this book and call to me. Even a whisper will do. And then I can answer. Let's try it. I'll go out."

He left the gatehouse and a minute later, Po opened the book while it was on the table and whispered, "Barcus, can you hear me?"

"Yes, Po. I can hear you," came his reply.

There was an image of Barcus in the book, out into the air. He was on top of the bell tower. She looked out the window and she could see him there.

"It's like the other side of the mirror is there, not here," she said.

"While I am gone, carry it with you in case I need to speak to you," Barcus said.

And then the Plate became a simple mirror.

CHAPTER SIXTEEN

STU

"The Emergency Module had valid intel that a massive bomb was inside a transport. This bomb was to be used north of the gorge somewhere. It was just being cautious. Barcus never knew about the four trackers Em killed as they fled the Abby."

--Solstice 31 Incident Investigation Testimony Transcript: Emergency Module Digital Forensics Report. Independent Tech Analysis Team.

Barcus didn't see Olias before he left. It didn't bother Barcus – he knew Em would keep an eye on him. Olias would get more done around The Abbey than Barcus would know how to do. The boy was driven.

"Hello, Barcus," Par said as he entered the cargo area from the rear ramp.

"Good morning, Pardosa." The HUD activated before he even sat down, creating the illusion that the spider had opened and they were looking directly at the sky. "Is there anything new this morning, Em?"

"The inventory lists have been updated with the new goods Par just dropped off. That will keep them busy while we are away," She replied efficiently.

"Bring up the tactical map with full annotations. Indicate the route you intend to take, current positions and ETA."

They were already moving at a rate of speed that Barcus thought was too fast. He didn't say anything since the ride was smooth.

"How close will we need to get in order to bring the STU down via remote?"

Em replied, "If we make our way to the foothills here..." A spot on the map highlighted and zoomed. "...we should have the benefit of elevation and line of sight."

"There is a pretty big distance between the two peaks. The one where the STU is parked will be just above the horizon at that point. Will a directional beam do it?" Barcus asked.

The HUD indicated it would be 45 hours to reach that point.

"We should have left a series of relay BUGs so we could remain in contact," Em said. "All I was thinking about was that they were coming. We had to escape. I didn't know then if the BUGs would lead them right to us."

Barcus settled in for the long ride. He had Par bring up the priority status items. On the screens, Par showed him the priorities once they had the STU. They would need a full systems check, a materials and capabilities inventory, and most notably, they would need to get Stu started on the comm traffic decryption effort.

There were new concerns listed about the weather. Em had collected data on the last storm and thought the pattern was going to repeat and intensify. "We will arrive and communicate with the STU just before dawn tomorrow. He will need time to fire all his systems up, but then we will have to wait for nightfall. We may be in luck with the weather for cover that night."

"Then what?" Barcus asked.

Em answered, "The advanced Shuttle Transport Units have the new Kidwell Grav-foils that can redirect gravitational forces in any direction, as propulsion has its limits. Basically the ship just falls, but horizontally or in any direction or none. The speed while in atmosphere is limited. It will be fine for getting down off the mountain quietly. The steering won't be very good without thrusters, but we won't need to be precise. It will simply be falling in any direction we choose. But only as fast as the near gravity would fall."

The track they had plotted was direct and constantly in wilderness. A large portion of the journey was through an area that looked as if it had suffered a forest fire a few months before. The burned area was contained by streams and land features, the margins of that area very clear.

Barcus spent a long time studying the weather estimates. The harshness of the estimates seemed extreme to him.

He slept in the module that first night without even pausing. He watched Olias and Po working on repairs at Whitehall. Eventually, he decided to call Po on the Plate.

She was getting ready for bed and was sitting tailor fashion in the middle of the bed reading her children's book.

"Barcus?" It was Em. "If you want me to, I have other children's books and reading lessons we could provide for her on the Plate."

"That is an excellent idea. I will mention it. I am about to call her."

"How would you like to do that? Audio only? AV? Or would you prefer full Augmented Reality?"

"Let's try Audio and Video only. Go slowly."

The bedroom at the gatehouse suddenly filled the HUD in the spider. The BUG was obviously sitting on the mantle.

The Plate, in its book, rested on the bed by her knee. She jumped when it quietly chimed. She reached for it and when she opened it, Barcus could see that Em had filled its screen with swirling clouds.

"Hello, Po," Barcus said.

"Hell...hello?" she stuttered.

"It's all right, Po. Just speak normally. Did you have a good day?"

"Yes. It was busy. Everything is fine," She replied.

"Do you want to see me as well as hear my voice, Po?" He asked. "I can show you how."

"Yes. Please," she answered.

He appeared on the Plate.

Barcus said soothingly, "It's all right, Po. It's me."

She lifted the Plate but said nothing.

"Are you all right?" he asked.

She was looking up and down from the Plate.

"Are you here and invisible like the wind, or is this a ghost?"

Barcus laughed. "A little of both I think. I'm not really there. Just my image is there."

"I can't touch you?" Po asked.

"No. But we can talk, even though I am very far away."

"Where are you really?" she wondered.

"I am north, toward the mountains. I will be back in a few days."

"Will your spirit stay here with me?" she said.

"Yes, Po."

She was nodding and appeared close to being overwhelmed.

"The Plate can do more. I will show you. If you want. Please let me know if it is too much all at once."

She did want more. Nodding her head.

Looking again, Po saw the Plate had the exact page, A is for Apple.

Po said it out loud.

Then it changed to B is for Bee. They went through the entire book again together.

"The Plate has more books for you if you want them. All you have to do is ask it. We will start here. Plate, I want to read Run Cat Run."

The child's book came up in the display. "It will show you many books if you like."

It read her the book. The words and letters glowed as they were spoken. Her eyes were wide.

"I will go now, Po," He said.

"Yes, Barcus. Thank you."

"Goodnight, Po."

"Goodnight."

Suddenly Barcus was very sleepy.

***

The next day, it was bright and sunny behind them and dark and forbidding in front of them. Clearly another storm front was coming through from the northwest. Barcus continued his morning status review. It had grown to hundreds of areas. He focused on the priority items usually, but on this trip, he got to review some of the lower priority reports.

One of the reports was a continuing effort to perform a detailed survey of the area surrounding Whitehall on an expanding radius.

This was an appendix to the Physical Security Status report that mostly focused on The Abbey proper. This appendix was the Proximity Report, Area Analysis, Possible Future Resources, Stone Quarry section. This report mapped the roads around The Abbey, where they went and why. A long unused road was found, which led to a stone block quarry. This was where the stones had been cut for use in The Abbey construction.

What caught his eye that day was an annotated still photo that was captioned "Predator activity indicated."

"Em, how far is this from The Abbey?" He indicated the image.

"That quarry is 2.7 kilometers from Whitehall." A large tactical map showing the exact location of the quarry relative The Abbey appeared simultaneously.

The image was of a great pile of deer remains, all piled in one spot on one of the terraced sides of the quarry walls. The remains were odd in that they were not entire deer carcasses, but parts of obviously dismembered deer. There were lots of skulls with antlers attached and hoofed feet that were recognizable. A few pelvises could be identified. But it was mostly shredded hides and parts not easily eaten by a carnivore. Hundreds of deer skulls could be seen.

"Em, has there been any other signs of this kind?" Barcus asked.

"No. We have been watching our thermal imaging recently, as well as looking for a large carnivore. It has probably moved south with the herd migrations or the seasons."

"Keep me informed on any related data for this item. And make sure Ash secures the gates every night at Whitehall. In fact, were there any cut blocks left at the quarry? Maybe we should step up the repairs to the wall."

"Yes, Barcus, there is a large quantity of cut blocks available, but they are grown over with vines. That was detailed in a previous survey report. It was also added to the itemized resources list." Both reports popped open.

"Okay, Okay. Thanks." Barcus was beginning to regret the full hands-on approach he had taken. Em was handling far more than he ever could.

He was tired. He should be taking advantage of the time to rest and not stress himself.

He reclined back.

"Par, bring up the Olias and Po monitors."

He found that they were together in a room he had not seen previously. It looked like a larger, luxurious bathroom. A fire was roaring in the hearth, and a small trickle of water was running out of the wall via a stylized fish mouth to land in the tub below. The water that was coming out of the fountain was steaming.

"Where is that room at Whitehall?" Barcus asked.

A tactical map of The Abbey displayed, showing the location of the room. It was in the blasted out portion of The Abbey. The scarred heavy door to the room led out to the section that was blasted away and had collapsed into rubble three stories below. The access to the room was along the ramparts and down a ladder to that level and then in. The area's roof was mostly intact but required a lot of repairs.

"At least now we will all be able to bathe like civilized people." Po looked at Olias scowling. "Even you. The tub will be full in a few hours. We need only keep the fire lit for it to be warm."

Barcus could see that the area outside the bath suite had a huge stockpile of firewood. He was glad that Po would be able to have a warm bath. He thought about himself as well. How long had it been?

He watched her as she bent over and retrieved a large canvas bag from the floor and began to unload brushes and rags and other cleaning supplies. She turned a tarnished lever, and brown water began to flow. She left the water to run and snagged chunks that the stone spigot spat out. After several blasts of dirty air, it began to run clear water. She began to scrub. The sink was an eight-foot long slab of stone with the basin carved into it and highly polished. She must have already done this procedure with the tub. Olias returned with buckets and mops, which he left there. His next trip brought several small rugs that he left outside by the firewood pile.

Olias went to the destroyed edge and looked over the side. It was about thirty feet down at this point, and he just sat down as if it were nothing, looking around and even up. Barcus wondered what he was thinking because he was thinking hard.

Then he waved.

"Em, who did he just wave to?" The BUGs scanned about, and then zoomed in on the bell tower. Ash was parked in the bell tower, watching.

It waved back then retreated into the shadows.

Em asked, "Is it okay for Ash to talk with the boy if he wants? Olias has tried to engage him on a few occasions. Plus, if you allow this, Ash can then function as a comm unit in an emergency without scaring the shit out of Olias."

"I think it's a good idea, but go slowly."

"Do you see the wall breach from this angle? Can you switch to Ash's view?" Ash's view had a much higher resolution than the BUGs'. "We need to get the lower section of that wall repaired and the water flowing from the aqueduct to jump this gap. If we don't, then ice is going to be a problem. If nothing else, let's redirect the flow to the outside of the wall."

"I see what you mean. The wall breach could have rows of the quarry block on the inside and outside and the center filled with packed rubble. Tiles here and here would allow the old pattern of flow," Em said.

"Put Ash on it. I bet he could use a lot of the rubble that is there already. Plenty of blocks still in the rubble."

"I think it would also get water in the stable systems too. You should also lift the night work constraints. If they get used to seeing him working, it will be better. Plus he could get twice as much done," she suggested.

And then a moment later, she added, "Are laser cutters okay?"

"Sure, with standard precautions."

"I know Olias wants to take Ash on another salvage run to the estate. What do you think?"

Barcus thought for a minute.

"Ash is only allowed to go if Po goes with them."

"She doesn't like the hearths to go cold. At this rate, we will run out of wood in January." Em wasn't kidding. A firewood inventory came up with the consumption levels neatly graphed on a temporal grid.

"Have Ash clear the trees from the roads. Then do a windfall collection. That can be a night job."

"Ash is going to be a busy boy." Em said.

Late that afternoon the weather front came though. It was rain that would be snow in the higher elevations.

The BUGs on the mountain would come into range as soon as they topped the foothill. It was the tallest in the area and even though the clouds would stop them from seeing the mountain in the distance where the STU was, comms would be possible.

It was full dark when they reached the peak. The leading edge of the storm had passed, and the air had stabilized. The BUGs that were left behind to monitor the STU were there and on-line. The STU was covered with snow and basically invisible.

"Stu, it's time to wake up buddy."

The full HUD in the spider was all windows. A new window appeared large and center labeled, "Startup Initialization." A log file of actions was rolling by fast as Stu began to come on- line.

The log file was going by too fast for Barcus to read any of it. Em began to summarize for him as she sat in the chair next to his. "Startup has initiated. Now it's doing a self-check, powering up hardware in a specific sequence, segmenting resources for the each system."

"Chen told me once the startup sequence was the biggest pain because it took so long to bring all the systems up. The AI comes up last of all," Barcus said.

"I think you lived because Chen came down an hour earlier that day to initiate startup," Em said, having no idea how that hurt.

Finally the log read, "STU initialized."

"Hello, Stu. How are you feeling?"

"I'm still waking up, sir. So far, all systems are nominal."

"We are in Survival Mode, Stu. Hostile Environment, passive sensors only," Em said. Barcus realized it was info for his benefit too.

Em began rapid comms at that point, conveying the flight plan and method.

The BUGs showed the shuttle enlarge from settle mode with sliding lobster tail style sections expanding, causing the snow to shake off and get blown away.

The Grav-foils finally deployed and quietly began to raise the ship. They looked like thirty flat, black oars that folded out from the sides of the ship at 45-degree angles, spiny, in a menacing fish fin kind of way.

The STU began to glide down to the rendezvous point.

CHAPTER SEVENTEEN

Stu Rendezvous

"The Shuttle Transport Unit, known as Stu, had a modified AI as well. But not modified in the same way."

--Solstice 31 Incident Investigation Testimony Transcript: Emergency Module Digital Forensics Report. Independent Tech Analysis Team.

<<<>>>

"Hello, Stu. What is your ETA to the rendezvous point?"

"Hello, Barcus. I am so glad you are not dead. ETA is fourteen minutes," Stu said. His voice sounded very young and formal.

"Par, head to the rendezvous point. How long will it take us to get there?" Barcus asked while watching the tactical as the land began to smoothly slide away.

"ETA is thirty-one minutes. Handshake has been established with STU and mission priorities have been conveyed."

"I have already deployed my passive antenna array and have begun collecting encrypted traffic," Stu said. "Sir, I have already detected some interesting information. TTL on the Crypt-Keys is set to maximum."

"TTL? Stu, what the hell is TTL?" asked Barcus

"Time To Live, sir. TTL." Stu answered.

"From now on, everyone state acronyms for me at least three times before general use. Now, tell me what a Crypt-Key is and why should I care."

Stu replied, "The Cryptographic Key is the piece of data that allows all the users and devices associated with a network to encode and decode the data transmitted over the network so that anyone monitoring transmissions will be unable to decode content."

"Do you have to be so damned formal, Stu?" asked Barcus.

"Actually, nope." His tone changed immediately.

"So what does that all mean? What are the implications of a long TTL?" Barcus wondered aloud.

"It means some lazy, dumb-ass admin didn't want to be bothered with encryption key management and set it never to change. The packet envelope says this was done over a hundred years ago. It basically makes the decryption easier. Once I brute-force the key, the password basically, they will not likely be changing it on us."

"Dumb-asses, indeed. Excellent. How long will it take?" queried Barcus.

"I've already started. If I had to guess it would be two weeks to two years," estimated Stu.

"Barcus?" It was Em. "We now have the STU's inventory and have made a list of items to transfer to the EM before we part. I also have a list of items for the Maker unit he carries to fabricate when it heats up." Several new windows popped up for med supplies, survival foods, tools, weapons, ammunition, as well as, fabricated items like pipes, hinges, and tools. "We will be ready to leave tomorrow."

"Excellent. Foxden is only a half a day away from Whitehall." Barcus was looking at the lists. "We will leave some of these items, like the food, at Foxden."

"Now that we have Stu, what will be the next priority items to tackle?"

"Well, provided we are not seen, cold running in the dark, under clouds, should do it. While Stu uses all his cycles for the decryption, we will convert the other Plate, continue salvage runs, do winter prep, expand our security perimeter, repair the wall, then the aqueduct and southern Abbey plumbing, execute roof repairs, gate repairs and door repairs, remove rubble and cut firewood - just to name a few. Teaching Po and Olias to read will make them much more useful in the long run as well."

"Excuse me, boss," Stu interrupted. "You got any idea why there is so little comm traffic? These SATs are designed to take way more." Barcus noticed that Stu was very casual in his voice now.

"No clue, Stu." Barcus smiled.

"Also, based on packet envelope data, it looks like three of the original thirty-two sats are not routing traffic."

"Does that mean three of them have fallen?"

"Fallen, destroyed, malfunctioning or turned off. That doesn't help or hurt the decrypt effort. Just thought you'd be interested."

"Thanks. Let me know if you find any other weirdness."

***

By the time Par reached the STU, it had begun to snow. Light amplification cut through the darkness as they pulled up to the opening ramp in the front of the STU, under his chin of a pilothouse. The shuttle seemed huge to Barcus now. It always looked so tiny compared to the Ventura, when they used it for exterior maintenance support. The ramp closed behind them as soon as they were clear, and then the interior lights came up. The hold was bright, white and clean.

Par walked in and "parked" in the dock designed for the Emergency Module. The dock was a recess in the ceiling that left maximum space on the floor for cargo. The spider's legs folded perfectly into the infrastructure, and when the hatch in the back opened, Barcus made his exit.

As Barcus moved to the narrow staircase that led to the bridge area, Em transferred the inventory list of needed items to his HUD. They were sorted by location now.

"Traveling by Grav-foils alone will require you to be strapped in, Barcus." He knew this already but said nothing as he opened the hatch to the main bridge.

He should have stayed inside Par.

He had forgotten about all the blood. Chen's blood. It was dried now. But the metallic smell of it lingered despite the circulation of the air. He knew he would have to clean it. He went to the command chair, center, down front - Chen's chair. It had blood on the left side, but he ignored it and sat. The round saucer-sized buckle slid up between his legs and the fifteen-centimeter wide strap extended thirty centimeters. An adjustable shoulder harness was buckled in on each side for the full five-point harness.

"Ready to go Stu. Full ship HUD please." The HUD snapped on, including several status windows Barcus didn't understand, that were intended for pilots. "Take us to Foxden, Grav-foils only."

"And we're off!" Stu said. "This will feel odd because the inertial dampeners will not function when moving like this."

Suddenly it felt like the ship was upside down and tilting forward. Barcus's body pressed against the straps, and then he felt like he was in an elevator that was falling. The ship was, in fact, in freefall, just not directly toward the planet.

They were in the clouds now, all gray and darkness. Watching the tactical was more productive. What had taken them forty-five hours over land would take them just under three hours in freefall.

The ride was uneventful, but the further south they got, the thinner the clouds were. They landed with the STU's nose directly over the door to the Foxden.

"We need to get this all offloaded and the STU into the lake before dawn," Barcus stated flatly.

It was all a snap except for the ammo. Chen had a ton of it, literally. There were four types, all caseless. Big .50 for Em's main gun, 5.56mm, 9mm, and 12gauge. Barcus decided to keep some in the STU, stow some inside Par, leave some at the Foxden cache and take the rest back to Whitehall. He also stashed a handgun, rifle and shotgun with the cache at Foxden, taking three just like them with him.

They finished two hours before dawn. Barcus rode inside of Par as the spider backed down the ramp. They parked near the rocky shore to watch as the STU flew over the lake then threw up a fountain of water into the sky as it descended. As it settled into the water, the lobster sections collapsed again, shrinking it to the smallest size possible.

It disappeared into the water and the tumult ceased, returning the waters to their normal calm.

"Bye, Stu. Keep in touch," Barcus said.

"Will do, boss."

"Par, let's go home. We might be in time for breakfast."

"Yes, sir."

Barcus stretched out his legs and leaned back, hoping for a couple hours of sleep. Out of the corner of his eye, he saw Em sitting in the other seat next to him.

"That went better than I expected. I am speculating about a few things based on the data we have already collected." She crossed her legs. "I am really beginning to wonder about the competence of the people running this planet."

"How do you mean?"

"Well, let me throw a few things out there." She loved ticking off fingers. "No search parties. Not at the crash site. Not in the surrounding area. We know they have ships. We've seen them."

She ticked off a second finger. "These raiders, these soldiers, they lost two Keepers. Ruling class members I presume. Still no searching."

Third finger. "They are destroying productive, self-sustaining villages and towns. Why? The Keepers know. It was their idea."

Another finger. "They seem incompetent regarding their own technology. Their operational security is bad. You'd think they would have had some kind of innovation in 200 years. There is nothing."

One more finger. "Why the fuck do they adopt this backward culture? Create new religions and caste systems? What the hell? It's like they want the middle ages."

She fell silent.

"We just need more information. I will have a lot of time to talk with Olias and Po over the winter. You see what you can find out with the BUGs and the surveys with Par and Ash. Eventually, we can tap into their traffic, but for now this will have to do," Barcus said.

"I think we should do a few more supply runs to Greenwarren. I want Par to take Olias on the next run. Par needs hands and feet to do a proper job," Em said.

Barcus looked at Em then with a questioning eyebrow.

"I think he will be fine with Par. He is fine with Ash already. They are becoming friends, I think. Olias likes it. He will take Par in stride when he knows she belongs to you. Remember, you're a Keeper, Barcus."

Barcus rolled his eyes. "Okay. Let me know when Po is awake."

A window opened that showed Po was already awake. She was sitting in the center of the bed with the Plate open in front of her and all four of the books on the bed by her knees.

"Call her, audio only."

The Plate chimed and startled her. It chimed again and she picked it up.

"Good morning, Po."

"Good morning, Barcus. I can hear you."

"You don't need to shout, Po. I can hear you very well."

"Oh, I'm sorry, my Lord." She blushed deeply. Her head bowed forward, and her hair cascaded around her face.

"No need to be sorry. We will use these a lot. You'll get used to them."

"Barcus, I have been reading, just as you told me...asked me too. I am doing so much better! We have a book here that is all about bees. It IS magic! When I master these arcane symbols and can read this whole book, I will know how to care for bees and harvest honey in safety and know all sorts of things to do with the honey!"

Barcus was smiling at her enthusiasm.

"Barcus, all four of these books are IN the plate! Others too!"

"Po, we will have lots of time this winter to teach you to read. I look forward to it."

He could see her, but she didn't know that. There was a flash of concern on her face for a moment as she looked at the books surrounding her.

"Po, I will be back in a few hours, in time for breakfast." Her face brightened.

"I will have it ready for you." She started climbing out of bed.

"Po, one more thing." He paused. "The spider, Pardosa, is bringing me. Don't be afraid."

He saw her hand go to her mouth.

"We will be ready," she finally said.

"See you soon."

She climbed out of the bed, gathering the books and the Plate. All of the books went back on the shelf. She kept the Plate out. She added logs to the two fireplaces, grabbed a clean tunic from the peg and put on a cloak. As she stepped her feet into some newly salvaged dainty slippers, very unlike her, she raised up the Plate and said, "Light."

The plate glowed as a bright white panel, lighting the way for her as she opened the door and went across the fountain yard to the stables. She tossed two logs on that fireplace grate and went up the spiral stairs. The hall was long here and well swept. With the Plate lighting her way, she ran the length of it and then up more stairs and onto the wall. She followed the wall around to the last stairs before the breach. She was down those stairs when Barcus finally knew where she was going.

The Plate lit her way perfectly as she approached what they had begun to call the "Keeper's bath." There was still a full bed of glowing coals in the fireplace, but she got more wood and put it on the fire. Then she hung her cloak up on a peg. In one swift motion, she unbuttoned the single button on her tunic at the nape of her neck and it quickly puddled about her ankles.

Barcus didn't try to look away or close the window.

She went to the edge of the tub and swung first one leg over the edge and then the other. When she turned toward the light, he saw it. There was a scar, a brand mark, just above the left breast. It was an old scar, many years old from the looks of it.

He watched her lower herself slowly into the huge tub, all the way into the water until her head was completely under. He watched her wash her hair with a bar of soap and rinse it under the steaming waterfall. She scrubbed her body with a fibrous ball of string that had a bar of soap in the center. He could see the soapy water drift away toward the overflow drain at the other end. She sat and soaked for a while after she was done scrubbing. When she climbed out, she simply stood before the fire, air drying. She combed her hair straight and shining and rapidly braided it, securing it with a simple string. She put on a clean tunic and then her cloak. She added another log before she left by the light of the Plate again.

It was still only 4:30 a.m.

Barcus closed the window and closed his eyes. Em promised to wake him before they arrived.

It seemed like only a few minutes before Em turned on the HUD, allowing in the full morning light. It was 7:40 a.m. now, and Barcus recognized the quarry road as they moved by it. The trees had all been removed from the road. It was easy going. He could see the wall of The Abbey as they approached.

He was planning on walking Par directly over the broken section of the wall and directly into the compound.

He asked Ash to announce their arrival.

Po and Olias saw Par climb over the breach in the wall and then over the inner walls to the kitchen yard. Par lowered the ramp and Barcus jumped out.

When he rounded the side, he saw that both Olias and Po had their heads downcast and eyes averted. He walked up to them and placed hands on their shoulders. "It's all right. She won't hurt you. Her name is

Pardosa." They looked up nervously at his smiling face.

"I'm starving," Barcus said as they smiled back. They cast dodging glances at Par as she backed up to unload by the outdoor kitchen.

If they decided to tell him about the tub, he knew that he would take a bath right after breakfast.

CHAPTER EIGHTEEN

Ash the Stone

"The Emergency Module kept him busy and distracted."

--Solstice 31 Incident Investigation Testimony Transcript: Emergency Module Digital Forensics Report. Independent Tech Analysis Team.

Breakfast was wonderful. There were pancakes with syrup made from diced dried apples stewed in honey. And there was real bacon. It was served on beautiful earthen plates with matching mugs for tea and cups for warm cider.

Olias was eating gleefully and in quantities only a young teen could manage. Po was unselfconscious as she ate more than she usually did. Olias encouraged her to eat more.

As she began to stand to collect the plates, Olias got up first and started with Barcus right behind him. They carried the plates to the basin in the open kitchen. Olias commented, "She is still uncomfortable with us taking her work away. You may not realize that this makes her feel, how does she say it, inadequate." Olias was chewing unfamiliar words. Em was translating for Barcus. The boy shifted back to common. "She does not know how to think about any of this really. But she will be fine.

"She said that you control her dreams. She never has nightmares if you are here. More magic."

"Nightmares?"

"Horrors have been done to her. They return and haunt her, dreams of reliving it." Em's translation of common seemed too short. Olias was saying far more words than the translation allowed.

"Her life. It has been... difficult," Olias said. "She has never had so much sleep or so much food." He paused, deciding something. "She sees things that need doing. She does not want to tell you what to do in your own house. She just does them or asks me to. She has started asking Ash, but only about firewood. He can carry a lot."

She came out just then with a few more dishes, and they fell silent. They went back in to get the rest of the dishes, and there were no more.

"I will clean this up. Olias, please show Barcus the surprise we have for him."

Barcus knew what the surprise was already.

"Let me get a fresh tunic before we go."

Olias's eyes went wide, thinking this was more evidence of Barcus's magic powers. Barcus was amused by his reaction. Olias was still frozen in shock. So Barcus grabbed a fresh tunic and led the way up to the new bath.

***

Soaking and scrubbing in the sunken tub was far better than he had expected. The stone tub was deep in the center and had built-in benches all around. One side had a couple of steps up to floor level. The wall at the end opposite the spigot was slanted so he could stretch out if he liked after he was done scrubbing and washing his hair. That was exactly what he did.

He let the water's heat soak into his bones. The slow but constant flow of the water swept away all the suds as well as the dirt in the water, even the dirt that sank to the bottom somehow. It was a brilliant system, based on the same technology as the floor heating systems. He was considering a reassessment of The Abbey to look for other innovations when he heard someone add logs to the fire.

"You don't need to do that, Po. I'm almost finished." She was once again shy, averting her gaze. The fireplace was the only light in the room, and the shadows were deep in the dark stone tub because it was sunken low in the floor.

She slid a three legged stool out of the corner and looked at the fire as she spoke. "Olias and I have been talking about how we should behave here. With you." She swallowed hard, "Did you know I should be bathing you? This is a Keeper's bath. Bathing is a Keeper's sacrament. I don't think you know that. Just as you didn't know you should not sleep alone."

"That's right. I knew none of these things, and much more I expect," came his measured reply.

"I have never eaten at the same table as a Keeper or any man for that matter. I have only served. I have never been allowed to eat the same food as the men, not to mention a Keeper, not even the scraps. I have seen women beaten for simply tasting uneaten food that would have gone to the pigs."

"That will never happen under this roof," Barcus said.

"I know." There was incredulity in her voice.

"I will never eat anything better than you, or better than anyone else under this roof," Barcus vowed.

"I have never been allowed to speak unless spoken too," she continued, head bowed.

"I expect you to speak when you wish or need."

"Every sentence out of my mouth before now always ended with the words 'my Lord' for Keepers or 'sir' for men of age." She paused. He waited.

"Keepers would have killed me by now for daring to read. Or any of these other things I just spoke of. I have been raised to obey and nothing more."

"I know you are strong enough, Po, to treat me the way I ask, to make decisions, to act. I've seen it. If you are ever unsure, ask.

"Please understand you can say 'no' to me at any time," he stated and then paused.

"Do you want me to bathe you?" she asked.

"I can bathe myself." He watched her head bow a little more, as if in disappointment.

"What do you want me to do?" she offered.

"I want you to eat three meals a day and become strong," he said.

She glanced up at him, and he caught and held her eyes.

"I want you to learn to read and help me understand this world. I want you to be my friend, not my possession. I want you to do only the things that YOU want to do. I want you to be free, just like me."

She looked away from him, looked down at her hands.

"May I please still sleep in your bed?" she asked.

"Yes, Po. But, only if you want to."

"Do you want me to?" she asked. It was almost a whisper.

"Yes. But only if YOU want to."

"Why are you doing this?" she asked, clenching her hands

together. "What sort of magic is this?" She rushed out.

"Em, please follow her. Make sure she is okay." A window popped open that showed Po moving up the stairs to the wall. She went toward the North Tower, entered quickly and sat on the steps, hugging herself.

"I'll watch her and keep you informed," Em said in a sympathetic tone. The window closed as he got up out of the tub, feeling truly clean for the first time in weeks.

***

Po sat alone on the steps in the tower, trying to sort out what she was feeling inside.

"You know you saved him, saved his life." The voice was a deep low rumble. Po turned her head and saw the deepest blackness in the shadows move, just enough for the outline of Ash to be revealed. "That first night of fire, you saved him."

"What do you mean?" she asked, confused.

"And that night in Greenwarren, he almost lost you again. You saved him again that night. You saved this entire world I think." Ash said.

"I don't understand," Po whispered.

"Po, he is the most powerful Keeper ever to walk this world. He has come from the stars where he lost his soul. You have helped him begin to find it again, here. You have no idea that you may be his most powerful magic."

"I am nothing," Po whispered.

"No. You do not know the depth of your meaning. Beside you, I am nothing. I am only stone and will."

"I don't understand," Po pleaded.

"Simply know this. The stronger you are, the stronger he will be. The smarter you are, the smarter he will be."

"Why is he doing this? It feels like he is reaching into my chest and stopping me from breathing sometimes."

"That is his greatest sorcery," Ash said.

"He has so much more power than any Keeper I have ever met," Po said.

"More than you may ever know," Ash said.

There was a long pause.

"You talk a lot for a stone," Po said.

Just then, her Plate chimed.

***

Barcus got dressed and went to find Olias. As he exited the bath chamber, Barcus took a good look at the damage directly in front of him. "Em, this definitely looks like a dropped bomb explosion to me. From this vantage point, the crater is obvious." Barcus looked at the rafters and the open floors. It made him think of images from the war.

Barcus found Olias unloading the cases from Par, who was backed up to the outdoor kitchen area. They were almost done.

"Par asked me to help unload these. Is this all right?" He was setting down a med supply case and the gun case.

"Olias, please take those two and slide them under my bed." Olias did without question. Next was one of the large, heavy ammo cases Barcus had prepped. That went into the gatehouse.

After everything had been offloaded, Par retreated to the garage beneath the cathedral ruin, climbing down into the shadows.

Barcus turned to Olias and spoke in common tongue. "I need you to make some salvage runs with Par. Can you do that? In fact, I need you to be in charge of all the salvage operations. You should use your own judgment to select what we need. Po and I will let you know if we need anything specific. To help with this, I want you to have this." Barcus handed him the second Plate in its book cover.

"You will be able to talk to Par, Ash, Po or me with it. It has maps. It can also help teach you to read. You can use it to keep lists or remind you of things. Ask it anything. Just be careful with it. We only have two."

Olias was holding it as if it was made out of the most fragile of glass.

"Open it. Touch it like this to activate it. Now you can ask it anything," Barcus shared.

Olias looked up and said nothing.

"Plate, where are we?" Barcus asked.

"You are in the cook's pavilion in the south end of Whitehall Abbey."

An aerial view of the circle of The Abbey opened on the Plate. A bright green dot correctly indicated his position with "Olias" over the dot.

"Show where everyone else in Whitehall is located."

Dots appeared for Ash, Po, Par and Barcus.

"Plate, add icons." Faces appeared by Barcus, Po, and Olias. Full size icons of Ash and Par appeared.

"Oh! Po is there, in the tower with Ash," Olias said.

"Plate, call Po."

"Hello? Barcus? Is that you? Is everything all right?" Po asked, concerned.

"Yes. I am showing Olias how to use his Plate. Say hello to Po, Olias."

"H-Hello?" Po laughed.

"What!?" Olias took umbrage.

"I can see you!" They looked to the tower where they could see Po waving a hand. They waved back.

"Do you see this little icon in the top right? That makes it a video chat. So you can see and talk." He selected it and Po could see them. "Press yours now, Po."

There were several icons across the top of her Plate. Barcus was watching over her shoulder in a HUD window.

"The next one over to the left. The green one."

She touched it, and Olias could see her.

"If you hold it up like this, we can see what you see," he informed them.

Po could see herself from below, and they could see themselves from above.

"It also holds a teacher. Her name is Em. You can ask her questions and she will answer. That's enough for now. We need to get to work. Olias is going on a salvage run and will need to pack."

Po efficiently closed the Plate, put it back in its pouch and was headed down the spiral stairs to get food together for Olias's trip.

***

Everyone split off to perform their various tasks. Barcus went to the throne room for a detailed status.

"Stu, are you doing okay?" Barcus asked.

"Yes, boss," came his reply.

"Em, what's next on the list?" Em strolled in and seemed to stand next to Barcus, looking at all the status windows.

"More salvage runs and repairing the wall are the next two priorities on the list. I think that if we can use Par to make a couple quarry runs before she heads out with Olias, Ash can work on the wall while they are gone," she replied.

"Do it. It would be great to have that done before the next big snow," Barcus said. "Once winter hits, we will likely be stuck inside. Restoring water to the south end would be great as well."

As they discussed other priorities, Par and Ash moved out.

Two and a half hours later, Olias was ready to go.

Par had demanded that she be swept out before she left. Barcus was surprised that Po went in and did it without a word. On sweeping the last of the debris off her ramp, she said to Olias, "Get a couple more brooms and dust pans, please."

"And you were worried that they would not handle this well," Em said in Barcus's head. *"They are taking to the Plates better than expected, as well. I will still keep control on them,"* Em added. *"It's still a bit early to try to explain AIs or Augmented Reality to them."*

"Have you developed lesson plans for them yet? Plate usage and reading, for starters?" Barcus asked.

"Yes, I have lessons queued up already. Daily formal sessions as well as other times, like when Olias is en route on salvage runs," Em said in his mind.

"Have Olias collect books and maps if he finds any. Show him how to take images of paintings and tapestries. They can contain info as well."

"Anything specific you would like Ash to do before he starts again on the wall work?" Em asked.

"Have Ash furnish the loft in the gatehouse as a study for me. I use too much firewood in the main throne room. The loft is smaller. The cots are already gone, I noticed. Make sure it has at least one comfy chair. The rest is up to you. I can change it later if something comes up," Barcus said. "We are working Par and Ash pretty hard. What is the power situation for both? I never worked on kinetic systems."

"They both use synthetic kinetic fiber for locomotion," Em began. "Fibers that work like muscles with tiny micro voltage. The battery in your multi-tool's flashlight could power Ash for a year. Both are served by solar batteries just fine. Some systems take a lot of power, like flood lights, cooling, heavy transmissions," Em added. "But we have not used them much."

"Olias and I are both ready now," Par said.

Barcus walked up the ramp with Olias and showed him where to sit. "While you are with Par, in here, you can speak to me at any time. Par knows what to do. Keep the Plate with you while you are away from Par. Good luck." Barcus showed him the five-point harness and helped to strap him in.

"You will see things here few have seen," Barcus said kneeling next to Olias.

"Thank you, Barcus, for trusting me." The common words were almost difficult for Barcus. He had been practicing.

Barcus answered with a slap on Olias's shoulder and a quick exit. He and Po watched as the ramp closed and Par began to move out and over the wall.

***

"Do you have your Plate with you?" He knew she did. "Let me show you something."

"Say this," he whispered in her ear, and she repeated, "Plate, locate Olias."

A map displayed of the region, as Olias and Par were moving fast down the south road.

"You can always find us this way." He said.

"This is how the birds see the land? From high above?" Barcus whispered in her ear again.

"Plate, show me the route they will take to Greenwarren." The view zoomed out and showed the path they would take to Greenwarren.

Then without prompting, she said, "Plate, show me where Langforest Manor is." The map zoomed out a bit more and showed another point almost directly south of The Abbey, but much further than Greenwarren.

"What is that place?" Barcus had not heard of it before.

"I grew up there."

CHAPTER NINETEEN

The Salvage Run

"The Emergency Module did not take into account all possible potential dangers on this planet."

--Solstice 31 Incident Investigation Testimony Transcript: Emergency Module Digital Forensics Report. Independent Tech Analysis Team.

<<<>>>

Par woke Olias when she reached Greenwarren. The morning sky was dark gray with the threat of snow. He and Par had spent an hour earlier, discussing the list of items they needed. Olias had described where most of the items could be found. Par told Olias that most of the bodies had been collected and consolidated inside a barn just outside of town – both soldiers and townsfolk.

Their first stop was Joseph's wood shop. Joseph crafted all kinds of trunks, chests, cabinets and even barrels. They would collect several trunks and barrels, which they would fill with the many small items on the lists for easier collection and transport. They chose eleven trunks to start with and began at the inn because it had the biggest kitchen. One entire trunk was filled with just spices. Olias learned quickly to leave the trunk where Par could pick it up when it was heavy.

The next trunk was filled with a selection of pots and pans and cooking utensils, packed tightly with towels and cloth napkins. Knives, forks, spoons, ladles, cutters, rolling pins, baking gear and more went into the next trunk, Olias listing each off as he packed it. He even topped it off with several ale mugs and wine glasses wrapped in towels.

A room-by-room search of the inn revealed seven books of topics unknown. He found four purses with a good quantity of gold, silver and copper coins. He found a beautiful sword and crossbow under the bed in one room. He took them, too.

Many staple food items were collected, like bags of beans and flour. Several barrels were filled with potatoes. Olias loved potatoes. He also saw to candles, lamps and lamp oil.

Multiple trunks were impossibly heavy, filled with tools and supplies, like nails.

Three trunks were filled with clothes, one for each of them.

Four more books were discovered, and Olias was surprised to note that two of them belonged to the blacksmith, where he had lived.

When all the priority items were loaded, Par was about half full. Olias was really good at packing. He used blankets and heavy cloaks as packing material. He filled gaps with nice rugs. He managed eight more cots and mattresses for them and still had room. He added several plain chairs.

For Barcus, he added several cases of wine and hard spirits.

Right after that was when he found the goats and chickens. Luckily, he also found four chicken baskets that allowed him to take all eight chickens. He couldn't crate the goats, so he tied them and closed them into the back of Par as the ramp was raised. Then he entered via the small, round emergency belly hatch that opened directly under the feet of the driver.

He and Par updated the lists, and he realized he was tired. He would need to make at least one more trip here. He left two of the hay barn doors open. If there were more goats or chickens about, maybe they would come back and he could collect them next time.

During his search, Olias had found only two more bodies. He covered them with blankets and dragged them only as far as necessary for Par to pick them up for removal to the barn.

As they left Greenwarren just before dusk, Olias didn't know they were being observed, but Par did. Passive infrared scans, part of the standard security sweeps, had detected a single observer.

***

He watched from a window over the inn as Olias worked. BUGs were issued to follow him and monitor the observers activity early in the day.

After Par and Olias had moved out, the man came down from the attic rooms of the inn and loaded a pack up with six bottles of Kaleyard, a strong liquor made from apples. He was thin and looked old. His skin was like wrinkled leather, brown and worn from a life spent outdoors in the weather. He had a thinning goatsbeard that looked like it was crudely trimmed with a knife and not recently. But his back was straight and his steps were sure.

Chewing a piece of dried meat, he began to walk south, the opposite direction from Whitehall Abbey, just as it began to snow. He moved at an easy pace, and in less than an hour, he reached a decrepit barn where he retrieved a horse. Like him, the horse was old. He walked next to it, holding the reins. He walked four more hours before he mounted the horse. Two more hours after that, he cautiously entered the outskirts of the ruined village of Whitlock. There was smoke coming from one of the chimneys above the inn. He dismounted and walked his horse the last quarter mile. The smell of burning still permeated this place. More than half the village was gone, and other structures in the village were heavily damaged. He could also get a whiff of the dead bodies that were buried in the ashes of that barn.

He walked his horse around back to the stable yard. There were currently only two horses stabled in the huge stable. He unloaded his horse and carefully brushed her down as she munched oats from a feeder. He also moved the other horses to fresh stalls and fed them as well. After placing horse blankets on each, he picked up his pack and moved inside.

He entered the inn through the back entrance, in the dark. A dim glow was coming from the common room at the far end of the hall. It was still a few hours before dawn. He seemed to intentionally make noise closing the door and with his footsteps as he walked down the hall to the common room. There was a man standing before the fire with one hand on the mantle. There was a large mug in his other hand. They didn't acknowledge each other for several minutes as he unloaded his backpack onto the bar, lining the large bottles up. "I was worried," the man by the fire said without turning or even looking up from the fire.

"I am sorry, my Lord. I ran into some...trouble."

This got him to look up. "What sort of trouble?" His eyes darted to the bottles briefly.

He gestured absently to the village about them. "This sort."

At those words, he uncorked one of the bottles he had brought back and poured a cup full for himself without checking to see if the cup was even clean. "It was still there." He emptied the cup in one gulp. "I saw it carrying bodies through the village by their ankles." He poured another drink and downed it.

"I have never seen you drink, Grady, until today. I thought I was your abject lesson and a constant reminder of the folly of drinking." The man approached the bar and lifted the bottle, sniffed it and poured himself a generous helping.

"Ulric, I think it saw me or heard me or smelled me. It was a huge black beast, like an impossible spider. It had arms that hung from below. It was so black, it was like a hole in the fabric of the world. I think it saw me." He grabbed the bottle from him and refilled his cup. His hand was shaking, only staring into it as he remained silent.

"Those marks on the ground are in fact footprints then?" Ulric asked.

"It's piling them all in a barn, soldiers and townsfolk. Like a nest. Like food for later after it ripens. And that's not all. It has something small with it."

"What do you mean? Young?" Ulric asked.

"I didn't see it. I hid in the eaves when I heard it. It came right into the room where I was hiding. I almost pissed myself." He took another sip.

"Greenwarren?" Ulric asked.

"Gone. No fire, but gone. Ulric, I told you once I'd follow you anywhere, and I still hold to that. I have wanted you to get out of your chair and into the world for more than a decade. But here? By the High Keeper's beard, what are you thinking?" His panic was barely contained.

"I'll tell you if you promise not to leave." Ulric was serious. He was looking Grady right in the eyes, less than sober.

"Do I need to promise again? I've already said. If it makes me dead, I've already had more years than most." Grady promised.

"It's Cassandra." Ulric paused as the statement settled in, "It's started, just as she said."

He emptied the cup again.

"The sky fall we saw in early autumn?" Grady asked. Realization was setting in.

"Walk toward the fire and find death's wake. Follow the demon's path to the reluctant throne." Ulric was quoting.

"You know where this leads if it's true?" Grady asked, knowing the answer.

"Yes." They both emptied and refilled their cups.

They left for Greenwarren the next day at dawn.

The snow had started to fall again, heavy, straight down snow with massive flakes. But they were ready. They had expensive hooded fur cloaks. Their horses had cold weather coats and even spats on their legs to keep their legs warm and dry and free of ice. They were not in a rush.

They made Greenwarren by midafternoon.

They decided to spend the night at the inn. Damaged as it was, they could still be comfortable. They selected rooms and met in the inn's common room. Grady already had a fire going and had a pot of stew started. "We will replenish our food stores here. Normally, we would have just purchased here, but they have all gone."

Ulric was behind the bar placing several bottles on the bar. "Yes. Replenish. Very nice."

He was studying a label of an old bottle when he said quietly, "I still want to see the bodies." Grady's answer was very formal in a sad way, wishing he didn't have to see it again, but knowing Ulric had to.

"Yes, my Lord." He bowed his head slightly.

"We need to see if we can find a decent razor." He pulled a cork out with his teeth and spat it on the floor. "Had I known we were to be gone this long, I would have packed a proper one." He was rubbing the quarter inch long hair on his head and the whiskers on his cheeks that were so much shorter than his goatee.

"But who would you get to do it? I'd just cut your throat and have done with it," Grady grumbled.

It seemed like it was an old pattern with them.

Grady had timed things well. There had been sufficient time to have enough to drink to make it possible to visit that barn again without drinking so much that it would do no good.

Even though it was freezing cold out, they could smell the barn before they could see it. As they approached, they could tell by the hush, the feel, that it was the right place. Rounding the bend, they could see it. The first impression was that it was neat and tidy, a well loved and cared for place. There was a massive pile of logs there - a timber process at work. There was an open pavilion of some kind attached to the barn that was some kind of de-barking system. A log was in the roller jig, and half the bark had already been removed. Ulric knew that he was stalling by studying the machine.

He flung open the latch and swung the door out. The smell crashed into them, sweet and full of horror.

Bodies were piled halfway to the ceiling, villagers and soldiers intermixed.

What really struck him was that the bodies were stacked in there with logs. The timbers were piled throughout, at several levels, with the bodies.

"It's a funeral pyre." He looked at Grady, over his shoulder, sleeve covering his mouth and nose. Stepping in farther, the cloth over his mouth and nose muffling his voice, he said, "I thought you said a beast, a monster, did this."

Ulric walked in to the edge of the pile, the pyre.

"You didn't think to mention this?" Ulric leaned down and picked up a very high quality crossbow and then two full quivers.

"What does that mean?" Grady asked.

"It means they are coming back. They will light it when they have done doing their mischief."

Ulric handed Grady the crossbow and quivers, pushing them harder into his chest than he intended.

"We've got to get out of here. We do not want to be here when it gets back. Do we?"

The question broke Grady from his vapor lock. "No, my Lord."

"So much for my warm bed tonight," Ulric said.

CHAPTER TWENTY

The Magic of Sleep

"The Emergency Module had begun planning very long term. The psychological manipulation by the AI was very targeted and specific in nature."

--Solstice 31 Incident Investigation Testimony Transcript: Emergency Module Digital Forensics Report. Independent Tech Analysis Team.

<<<>>>

Ash walked by with a large, rolled rug under one arm and an overstuffed easy chair in the other. He had a large coil of rope as well.

Po looked at Barcus with a look that said, "Now what?"

"It takes too much wood to heat the Keeper's room, so I am making the loft into a reading room."

"That's a good idea. I like to read," she replied smiling, her pride seeping out. "When the snow really starts, it will make it much easier. Thankfully all the walkways are covered."

Ash was making another trip. Another chair and a bookcase this time.

"Where is he getting all this furniture?" Barcus asked.

"While you were gone Ash, Olias and I made several trips to that empty estate. The blacksmith shop is also full of items," Po said.

"Ash, if there is a small desk and chair that would fit up there, add that too please." In his head, a window opened and indicated that there were three to choose from. As they rotated in a HUD window, he said, "yes, please" to the one he wanted.

"Ash can hear you from here?" Po asked, more curious than frightened.

"Both Ash and Par can hear me from very far away. Par can hear me all the way in Greenwarren."

"Why do you always deny that you are a Keeper?" She was serious and straight forward and looked him right in the face as she asked that.

"Because I never was a Keeper in any way. I am...something else."

"Barcus, do you realize that the Keepers are going to try to kill us?" Po said.

"They will try," Barcus replied.

She looked at him for a long moment before saying, "Okay, then."

"Ash tells me that he will be able to get water to the kitchen soon. If it's like the rest of the keep, that would be wonderful."

Barcus stepped out from the overhang and looked at the darkening sky. "Do you think it will snow?"

Hugging herself she said, "My hip tells me it will snow soon. Why don't you know what the weather will do? Keepers always know."

"Really? They are good at predicting the weather?"

"Yes. Very good. Some Keepers are called 'Weathercocks' for their ability to predict or control the weather."

"They claimed to control the weather?"

"It's a grandfather's tale that the bird, a Weathercock, controlled the weather. They were just very sensitive to it. I knew the Keepers didn't control it because I have seen years where the lack of rain cost them dearly. The Plates told them about the weather."

"That's right," Barcus affirmed.

"They can't tell you?" Po asked.

"No, not yet," was Barcus's answer.

Ash walked past with a desk and a chair and a small table.

***

Olias was speechless for almost an hour. The HUD inside Pardosa made it look like the top was off and they were moving fast through a tunnel of trees. There were no sounds, no wind, only the sense of movement as if he were in a boat.

"Par?"

"Yes, Olias."

"Can I ask you questions?" Olias asked.

She answered in perfect common tongue, "Barcus told me to answer any question you may have. Even tell you things I think you should know. Do you have questions now?"

"Why me?" he asked.

"That is a very good question," Par answered.

"Barcus may not admit it, but he is the most powerful Keeper the world has ever seen, now or ever. He needs an apprentice. I don't really know, but I think he has chosen you."

"Me? Really?" Olias asked.

"He has kept you alive on more occasions than you actually know. Why would he do that? Why would he give you a Plate? Why would he command that you learn to read? Why feed you like a Keeper? Why did the High Keeper's men try to kill you? Twice? Why would Barcus do any of this? Because he can see in you what you cannot see in yourself."

"He says I can leave whenever I want," Olias mused.

"True. And where would you go?" Par said.

Olias fell silent.

"All right then. What's on the list?" Par asked and Olias sat up.

***

Barcus climbed the steps to the new den loft. The first thing that struck him was a question — *where do they keep finding these beautiful rugs?*

Immediately to his left, on the end wall as he entered the loft, was a set of dark, oak shelves that were about rib height. An open, empty trunk was just beyond it. The only thing on the bookcase was a glass oil lamp that was already lit. To his right was a desk that was about two meters wide with lots of slots and small drawers set in a shelf towards its back. Another oil lamp was its only item. It had a leather desk chair. Directly opposite the desk was a table the same size, but bare topped except for another larger lamp. Beyond these, two overstuffed chairs with a small table and lamp between them backed up to the loft railing that overlooked the room below. There was even a single, heavy looking, footstool that these chairs could share.

He sat in a chair and put his feet up. He laid his head back so he could examine the beautiful stonework of the arches above. He had not had a close look since the power washing.

He had no intention of falling asleep, but he still did. When he woke, he didn't know how long he had been asleep. All the lamps had been put out except the one by the stairs. Glancing to the left, he saw that it was dark below as well, except for the fire.

He also saw Po, curled up like a cat, in the other overstuffed chair next to him, fast asleep. She was already wearing her night dress, her feet were tucked under her, she was hugging her knees to her chest, and her head was resting on the arm of the overstuffed chair. Her braid was falling apart and a wisp had fallen across her face. She was so tiny.

He noticed his freshly laundered nightshirt was folded on the table.

He silently slipped off his boots and socks. He loosened his belt and left it behind in the chair as he stood. The thick carpet ensured the only sound was the crackling of the fire from below as he crossed the room to his nightshirt. He quietly drew his tunic over his head, leaving only the light draw string pants, hanging low from his hips.

Through slitted eyes she watched him in the firelight without moving. He didn't look like a real man. He looked like he was carved from stone. His stomach and chest were muscled and ridged more than any blacksmith she had ever seen. He lifted the nightshirt and untied the draw string at the same time. As he put the nightshirt over his head, his body stretched.

This felt like it was more magic.

His nightshirt fell to his knees and then he stepped out of the pants and blew out the remaining lamp. In the dim firelight, he approached her. Po expected a small shake to wake her for bed, but instead he lifted her as easily as a sleeping child. She felt so light in his arms.

"I'm awake," she said sleepily. "I can walk."

"And I can carry you." He proceeded down the spiral of stairs into their bedroom. The bed was already drawn down. Smoothly, he laid her down and the carry never released. She was held with her back to him in the arc of his chest. She felt him bury his face into the nape of her neck and breathe deeply. His left bicep was her pillow. She hugged his right forearm to her chest and she felt his fingers trace her collar bone and rest on her chest, just below her throat. His hand was so big and warm. He breathed in deeply again.

"Goodnight, Po."

"Hmmm…" she hummed.

She felt him relax and his breathing become deep and regular. She smiled at his twitching as his arm became heavy upon her. Stirring slightly, his right hand absently cupped her left breast. It was the first time he had touched her in that way. She felt the unintentional wakening of his manhood against her bottom.

She had known many men in the past, but this was the first time she had felt this without dread. With a deep sigh she fell asleep herself.

***

The room was cold when Po came awake. The blankets were heavy and very warm. Barcus, with his back to her, radiated heat. Po had slept all the way through the night. She could not remember ever doing that in her entire life. The light in the window revealed it was well past dawn. She knew all the fires here and in the kitchen had already burned low with Olias being gone. Instead of jumping out of bed and dressing, she gently wrapped her arm around Barcus and moved closer.

Both of their nightshirts had hiked up in the night. The fronts of her bare thighs had found the bare backs of his thighs. She felt an unfamiliar flush, a moist heat between her legs. She could even feel her own heartbeat there. She fell back asleep wondering if it would be different to touch him in the way men wanted. Every man she had been to bed with wanted sex. For the first time she was curious, even interested in what it would be like with this man. She dozed again, beginning dreams of skin.

When Po woke the next time, she was alone. The room was warm, the fire built up in the fireplace. She panicked.

She jumped out of bed and peeked into the other room, and the fire was built up there too. On the table there was a place setting laid out with bread and cheese, butter and honey, fresh fruits already sliced and cold ham. There was another place setting that was just crumbs and a knife with butter still evident. The mug from that place setting was missing. The kettle returned to the fire hook. Barcus's nightshirt hung on its peg, and there was no sign of him. She dressed rapidly and went into the other room, heading to the door.

"Good morning, Po. It snowed again last night." She froze, turning. Barcus was in the loft. She looked up, and he had a book open in one hand and a steaming cup of tea in the other, raised in greeting.

"I am so sorry, my Lord." She had fallen to her knees and her face was down turned.

"Po, don't you ever do that again." For the first time she heard anger slip into his voice.

"I won't, my Lord." She placed her hands at the small of her back in complete supplication. She cringed when she heard his tea cup slam down on the table.

"I don't mean sleep late! I meant calling me 'my Lord'! I mean groveling on your knees! I won't have it!" His last word was punctuated with his boots landing on the floor in front of her face. He had jumped from the loft! Suddenly there were hands on her arms, lifting her like a child's doll.

"Do you understand me? I have told you before. I. Won't. Have. It." His voice was quiet now. Serious. He set her down onto her feet gently.

It was then that she realized her hair was not braided. It was falling around her face and shoulders. His hand released his grip on her arms and she felt his right hand trace a line from the center of her brow to behind her ear, tucking the hair there. His hand cupped the back of her head making her look up into his eyes.

She saw no anger there.

She did see something she had never seen before. She didn't know what it was. But she knew he could see her. She feared he could see her so well that he knew her thoughts. No one had ever looked at her like that. It felt like no one in her whole life had actually seen her at all. Until now.

Quietly he said, "I made you breakfast. It was the best I could do. I am kind of at a loss in the kitchen, especially here."

What magic is this, she thought, confused. It was electric where his hand touched her cheek. She flushed again.

He didn't let her go.

"Remember when you told me why you had to sleep with me?"

"Y-yes." She was trembling, but was not afraid.

What magic was this, again?

"I think you're right. It helps healing. But I think I'm healing you..." He released her. "Please, I don't want you to do that again. Not ever. It's important to me. All right?" Barcus was very serious.

She nodded.

"Now eat your breakfast, or you will cut me to the quick."

His magic had taken the strength from her legs. "I will get you some warm cider." He turned to get the kettle as she sat.

She squirmed a little. His magic made her throb down there. She could feel that she was damp from longing in her sex. She had never felt this before. Her mind was swirling inside. Her breasts ached. She rubbed her wet palms on her tunic over the tops her thighs to dry them, but it only reminded her of the feel of his skin on her skin there.

He was close then while he poured the fragrant cider and at the same time, saying in almost a whisper, "I'm sorry, I didn't mean to scare you."

"I'm not afraid." She surprised herself saying, "I'm sorry too. I did know. It's a lifetime of habits. I've had masters that would simply kill me if I overslept. Or ate their food. Or spoke to them."

"I want you to be healthy, rested. I slept in as well. I think we both needed it. It was nice to not think about anything for a while." His face darkened a bit as he looked out the window above the table, staring at nothing.

Barcus turned.

"I left my tea in the loft." He stood, but his smile was weaker, haunted somehow, as he went to retrieve his mug.

She dug into the food. It seemed the more she ate, the more she needed to eat. He wanted her to eat. So she would eat.

When she was finished, she placed everything in the basket tray that Barcus obviously carried everything in with and carried it out to the kitchen pavilion. It looked like they had about eight or ten inches of snow already overnight. It was falling straight down in enormous flakes. She was thankful again for the wide covered walkways.

When she got to the kitchen, water was running in the large sink there. It was more like a trough, about eight feet long and a foot-and-a-half deep at the far end. It was already full. The overflow disappeared down a grate at the far end.

She thought to herself that one of these fires would make this water hot. She would have to find out which.

Another smaller sink was also running in the indoor kitchen. She would need to scrub them both. She got the cook fires back to her satisfaction and then started one in the main fireplace of the indoor kitchen, hoping it would heat the water of the sinks. Then she followed the covered walkways across the courtyard to the stables to feed the horses and add wood to the tack room fireplace. Before she got there, she noticed the fountain was running. Water flowed from gargoyles' mouths into the huge basin.

When she got to the tack room, the fire was already built up. She added one more log and found the horses were already fed.

Returning, she called to the loft, "Barcus there is water in the kitchen."

"Yes. And the midden is flowing properly. And the horse trough is full and even the fountain is running, but I have no idea why it isn't freezing."

"How?" Po asked.

"Ash has been repairing the wall, and with it, the aqueduct."

"Aqueduct?" she asked, pronouncing each syllable carefully.

"It is the way water feeds the keep. He says we are now getting 206 liters per minute flowing to the southern half of the keep. He will likely have the wall enclosing the aqueduct completely repaired today. The battlements above will be done tomorrow."

"I also discovered that there is some sort of air flow activated. This morning, when I went to get a bag of feed, I heard an odd sound and discovered there was air blowing into the cold forge from the back. It was blowing dust out, so I left it for later. Olias can look at it when he gets back in a few days."

"Did you notice the covered walkways and the gatehouse courtyard are free of snow? Well, the covered walkway halfway down the stable side. To get to the other side, we would need another fire in the blacksmith shop at the far end."

"I love magic," Po said.

"This kind of magic is called 'excellent engineering.'"

CHAPTER TWENTY-ONE

The Mad Monk

"The Emergency Module backup that we are analyzing began to show signs of outside tampering at this time. Data deletions. The manipulations increased."

--Solstice 31 Incident Investigation Testimony Transcript: Emergency Module Digital Forensics Report. Independent Tech Analysis Team.

Olias was amused and excited by how much he had packed into Par on this salvage run. The goats and chickens settled down eventually with the swaying motion of the ride. They were sticking to the roads mostly because it had begun to snow again. The further north they moved, the more generous the term road became. When dawn arrived, the only indication of road was the old growth trees that flanked the track they travelled in. Saplings prevailed in slowing them down like intentionally laid obstacles.

When the goats started to smell, Par activated positive ventilation and made the stench much less noticeable. It was good that the confined space of the extremely packed load held them to a tight space all the way to the back. It would make it easier to clean out later.

"Par, where do you come from? I mean, I thought you were a beast from the mountains. But now I. . .I don't know anymore."

"I am a beast out of the mountains, Olias. At least I was. I'm so much more now. Barcus made me so. It's a magic I don't understand. I can still hear and see like before. But now I can know things, I can speak in languages. I can hear Barcus in my mind whenever he wants me too. He is powerful, and I love him."

"You love him?" Olias asked.

"Yes." Par paused and said, "Because I can leave whenever I want to. I only do what I want to do. He trusts me. He honors me with his trust."

"How? How do you know?" Olias asked.

"He trusted me to look after you, his friend," Par said.

"I'm his friend?" Olias wondered.

"What else would you be? How does he treat you? Like a slave? Like a stable boy? He eats meals with you. He gave you a Plate. He trusted me with your life."

Olias was very thoughtful.

"Does he ever order you to do anything?"

"He always says 'please' to me," Par said.

"Actually, he mostly lets me do what I want," Olias realized.

"Did he order you on this trip?"

Olias thought about it.

"No. He asked me. He said he needed my help," Olias said. "In fact, he left all the details to me. He trusted **me** to make the decisions."

"See. He's your friend too. Before he named me, I never had a friend before. Never knew what it was. Before his magic touched me, I never had a soul. I'm getting used to it."

"You never had a soul? What's that like?"

"It's...cold. When you don't realize you don't have one, you're just a thing. I was just a thing with legs and instincts. Doing what was necessary. All the time. Knowing someone, having relationships and making friends were not even concepts in me. But after he brought me to life, I could see all that and more. I could feel things for the first time. I saw in him how to do it. It was wonderful and terrible and filled with so much magic. I was almost overwhelmed."

Olias was speechless.

"Ash was my first friend, besides Barcus. But Ash is like me. His soul was fresh as well. And for a while, it was just the three of us. We were wandering, trying to find a safe place to rest. That's when we found those men killing the people of Whitlock. Barcus mourned every dead villager. It was as if they were all friends he had just not gotten to know yet. He was so angry. So sad. You see all his friends had been murdered. Every one."

"Is that why he saved us? Po and me?"

"He had to save you. He could not do otherwise," Par said.

"Ash followed us that night until we reached Greenwarren didn't he?"

"Yes. We had to make sure you were safe."

"I thought I heard him in the forest," Olias said.

"When we saw you safely there, we went on our way. But Barcus always worried about you and Po. He used what magic he could to warn the village. Only you and Po could hear. Ash and I came as fast as we could. I am so sorry. I wish we had been faster.

"Barcus was so angry. He was so worried. We almost lost you again."

"We're fine, Par. It's all right," Olias reassured her.

"What I am trying to tell you is that having a name, having a soul, is not all good. When I was carrying those bodies today to the barn, all I could think was that they were two more friends I'd never get to know. It was an ache inside me, when I didn't know I had an inside.

"Please don't tell Barcus I said any of this. I want to be strong for him," Par said.

"I won't say anything," Olias vowed.

"I tried to talk with Ash about it, but he is different than me."

A pause fell over them.

"Want a reading lesson?" Par asked.

"Sure!"

By the time they reached Whitehall, Olias could still not spell his name.

***

It was funny to see how excited Po was about the goats. Two of them were milking goats. They were quickly settled into the paddock in front of the stables. They would spend nights in the stables with the horses. The horses even liked them. Many stables kept a goat. They had a strange calming effect on horses.

They quickly unloaded the rest of the salvage with the help of Ash.

"You have done an excellent job, Olias, better than I could have done." Barcus slapped his shoulder, nearly toppling him.

"Thank you, Olias. Things will be easier now." Po actually hugged him.

"When do you intend to go out again?" Barcus asked as Ash

power washed Pardosa's ramp.

"I think in the morning. There is too much that will go to waste otherwise. Would it be possible for Ash to come on the next run? Some things are just too heavy for me. Plus, we could stage things so Par could make runs without me while Ash and I take the wagons for local salvage," Olias said.

"Whatever you think best, Olias. There is a hot bath and fresh clothes ready for you," Barcus said. His word confirmed what Par had been telling him.

"Here, I got these for you." Olias retrieved a simple wooden box that looked like it was a small crate. He opened it.

There inside, were eleven leather bound books.

Barcus accepted them as if it was a treasure chest.

"Thank you, Olias. This is really excellent." His smile was very wide.

"Watch this," Olias said, picking up a stick.

He carefully scratched in the soil where they stood in the courtyard, "OLIS."

Barcus laid a hand on his shoulder. "Olias, a new world awaits."

Po suddenly burst out, "It says Olias!" Her eyes were wide. "It means...Olias."

Smiling when their eyes met, he looked down again and scratched in perfect block letters "Po."

Her eyes went wide when she got it, and her hands flew to her mouth. They looked at each other and then both looked at Barcus.

He smiled mischievously. "Magic," was all he said and walked away with the books.

Po and Olias talked about reading and the other aspects of the salvage inventory as Barcus walked to the gatehouse. On the way up to the loft, he collected the other four books and placed them all on the shelves he had there.

"We need some bookends," Barcus said and they appeared on the salvage want list. "And we need small slate tablets for writing lessons."

"Barcus, the Plates have that ability. I will work it into their lessons."

Olias helped Po distribute and organize the salvage with assistance from Ash. The heaviest items were the tools in the blacksmith shop. The day was warming again, and the snow melting. The goats were happily rooting in the snow for the easy to find grasses.

Po showed Olias that the plumbing was fixed on the south end of The Abbey. They went to see if the dorm baths were working on the west side of The Abbey yet. Water was just trickling from the six spigots into shallow puddles in the baths.

One bath would have to do for now. The roof there had a few places that were trouble as well.

Barcus spent the rest of the day carefully scanning the books in his den with Em's help. A few BUGs positioned correctly made the job as easy as simply turning the pages.

This made them available to him on demand after that. It allowed Em to assimilate them and use the data for cross correlation.

The first book was detailed instructions on how to make various distilled beverages from apples, everything from simple ciders to powerful straight liquors. It even had diagrams for making the stills from iron and copper.

The next book contained notes regarding animal husbandry and specific livestock breeding. It had chapters dedicated to cattle, goats and even dogs, right down to kennel designs and functions.

Another was a handwritten catalog of medicinal herbs and their properties. It had detailed, beautiful drawings of the herbs, instructions on how to dry them and even ways to preserve them as infusions in alcohol or oils.

The smallest book listed all the High Holidays of the Keepers and the various associated rituals for each.

The oldest looking one was a kind of travel guide that talked about the "Ten Greatest Cities." That could be very handy, even if it was old information.

The next one was very thick. It was a ledger of goods and services associated with The Boar and Barrel Inn in Greenwarren. It showed everything from building materials to booze - how much they paid for goods, how much money they made and who owed them monies. The list was long.

The next handy book was about pest control for things like rats, mice, snakes and various bugs from mosquitos to horse flies.

"We need a few cats," he casually remarked, and "cats" priority jumped on the salvage want list.

One book was very thin and contained mostly pictures of clouds and what they meant for the weather. It actually contained the phrase, "Red in the morning sailors take warning. Red at night, sailors delight."

There were two cookbooks. One was titled "A Soup Cookery." It contained recipes for many kinds of soups and stews. The other cookbook was about baking breads and meat pies. It actually made his mouth water, even though the pictures were not done very well.

The last two were the most interesting to him. It appeared that they were both first person fiction. One was called "A Warriors Tale" and the other "The Mad Monk." Barcus would save these for the long winter nights that were on the way.

Closing the last book, he stood and placed it on the shelf, sliding the blocky stone up for a bookend. He rolled his shoulders and said, "Em, initial summary review."

"Useful data for long-term. Perhaps the most useful of them all are the two works of fiction.

"The Mad Monk is about a retired High Keeper that decides to move to an isolated monastery and make wine. It says he began to dabble in dark forces and was killed when the darkness found him, destroying his monastery and all his people to the last man, woman and child".

"Does it say how or when it was destroyed?"

"There was an explosion followed by a horrible plague that was only stopped by the harshest winter in memory. Tens of thousands died in this story. Dates are not specific, and there is a lot of flourish and hyperbole."

"Are there any other specific points of interest there?" Barcus asked.

"It alludes to 'dark catacombs' where this mad Keeper performed his experiments. I have come to believe that this Abbey is more than it seems. While we have been executing repairs, we have discovered a few things."

"Like what?"

"The diameter, as previously stated, of the keep is 91.44 meters. It varies by less than a centimeter at any given point. The material of the walls is a type of cement that seems to have been poured seamlessly, solid for 1.828 meters."

"You seem to be implying there some significance to this besides its precision."

"You are correct. 91.44 meters is exactly 100 yards, and 1.828 meters is exactly two yards," Em said. "The ships we have seen are of a vintage that would be consistent with an Exodus class colony ship. If that is true, those ships were equipped with eight RFUs."

"RFUs?"

"Redoubt Fabrication Units. The early name for Makers. These were specialty massive robots that were designed to create human habitats in harsh environments. They were big machines that would use local materials to create domes, and then they would use themselves as raw material to create the interior infrastructure and support systems. They could even function autonomously in a vacuum. They were very early single task AIs."

"Are you saying that this was once a dome?"

"RFUs were designed to make a few different configurations. A dome and a configuration known as a bowl were common. It was basically an inverted dome."

Barcus was thinking now and looking at The Abbey diagram in his HUD.

"The Mad Monk talks about dark catacombs. If this Abbey is actually a Redoubt, there may be more below."

"Here in the diagram, the stairs go directly into the water. Do you have any real time imaging of this area?"

"I'm sending a BUG there now." Another window opened of a flying view moving toward the tower and then down the spiral stairs. Six and a half steps were drying; there was a glaze of stain on them.

"The water is receding. Repairing the wall has stopped the flooding. Where is Ash right now?"

"Ash is currently rearranging salvage with Po and Olias."

"When he is done there, I want him to take a little swim."

"You know the suit is not designed for long term exposure to water."

"Yes, I know. He will have to tie off a micro cable before he goes in. That will give him 600 meters of movement, even if he does sink like a stone."

"Do you have any insight on what the layout might be?"

"Layouts could vary and could have been programmed locally," Em said.

"How is it draining?"

"It probably has natural gravity feed drains based on what I've seen from the other plumbing systems here. Assuming all this is true, I have dispatched a swarm of BUGs to search the surrounding area for period-appropriate solar collection systems. A Redoubt of this period would have been equipped with ten solar collectors that provided all the Redoubt power needs."

"So this bowl might go down 50 meters? Or more?" Barcus asked.

"If I had to speculate, I would say, yes. Probably ten to thirty levels. I would certainly consider them 'catacombs' if the Mad Monk was in fact a true story and based here."

"Something doesn't seem right, though. I have been on lots of blast repair crews, and the damage I see here didn't originate below. This exploded and blew down as hard as it blew up and to the sides."

"I have also run many simulations based on the observed damage." A window opened in his HUD that was a simulation of The Abbey when it was intact. It had a globe marked "point of origin." The point was on the roof of the cathedral, just above the gutters on the east side, near the corner in the center of The Abbey. Slowly, the globe expanded showing the pattern of destruction that intimately matched their known reality.

"Em, I swear, that looks like a dropped bomb to me."

CHAPTER TWENTY-TWO

The Drowned Redoubt

"The Emergency Module knew it was a colony redoubt."

--Solstice 31 Incident Investigation Testimony Transcript: Emergency Module Digital Forensics Report. Independent Tech Analysis Team.

<<<>>>

It was almost dusk when Ash was done moving the tons of items around for Po and Olias. The blacksmith shop that had previously been used to store items was now clear of them. Tools now hung on its walls. It was not a full complement of smithing tools, but Barcus would not recognize most of them even if there were.

Goats were still exploring the paddock outside the blacksmith shop and a door had been re-hung to contain them, thanks to the new hinges Stu had fabricated and Barcus had brought back from Foxden.

Dinner that night was better still. It was soup and flavorful flat breads with large potatoes stuffed with spices, onions, meat and cheese. There was even a dessert. It was like a biscuit, filled with a thick whipped cream and drizzled with stewed dried fruits of some kind. Po made two for Olias.

Barcus no longer had to nag Po to eat. He could see that she was benefiting from it already. He realized that her face was filling in. Before, her skull was too evident. She spoke freely in front of him more easily as well.

Barcus didn't protest or force her to allow him to help clean up. He simply let her do it without a word. It seemed to make her happy, that small concession.

He went up to the loft later. Po had cleaned up in short order and climbed into bed with her Plate and was studying quietly.

Barcus sat in one of the loft's overstuffed chairs and seemed to stare into the darkness. His entire view was full HUD mode with Ash, seeing everything Ash saw.

Ash was in the tower and had driven a piton into the stone of the tower and attached a carabineer. After hooking a thin cable through it, he began to descend the stairs slowly into the water.

A seventh step was now exposed. He descended about fifteen meters into the chilly dark waters before he came to an open arch. All his bright work lights were now deployed. Infrared was of no use because everything was the same uniform cool temperature. Other night vision systems were useless as well, seeing only the murk in front of them. So the work lights were his sole technological support.

Ash was in a corridor with white walls and a ceiling that was completely filled with water. As he moved, albeit slowly, his footsteps disturbed the sediment on the floor, sending up small clouds of it.

Ash's voice asked simply, "Left or right?"

"Go to the right, Ash. Is there any way to minimize the silt disruption?"

"I will do my best, sir." The status window indicated "Ice Spikes Deployed," and he began moving again, a series of spikes the only thing entering the silt.

Moving with the spikes helped some, but it was really the wake that was disrupting the silt. Ash continued around the curve of the bend in the hallway. A 3D map tactical display was filling in as he moved.

"So far, this fits in the parameters of the IDR, Inverted Dome Redoubt," Em said.

A doorway opened to the right that led down a wide corridor to a black opening about twenty meters away. Ash moved smoothly to minimize the silt.

"Do we have any amphibious BUGs Em?" asked Barcus quietly.

"No, Barcus. Chen never anticipated the need for an underwater probe. We are already looking into potential options with what we have on hand," Em answered.

Ash cleared the end of the corridor and came out onto a wide balcony that had a railing that clearly had doubled as a planter structure. A void of black was beyond the railing. Lights barely touched the far side. This balcony continued all the way around a perfectly circular level. Over the edge, another level could be seen about five meters below. This level extended about five meters, as well as the one above. They moved in as the levels descended, following the contour of the bowl.

As Ash focused lights on various areas, the 3D map continued to expand in Barcus's HUD.

"I'd like to descend to the Redoubt's floor. I have a good connection, and I can go over right here," Ash said.

"Before you do that I want you to try something. Turn all the lights off," Barcus said.

Ash did it and, once the image adjusted, it was clear that there was an opening above the center that was about ten meters across. Starlight faintly glinted in. A giant beam and other debris had some kind of water weeds growing on them. It was the only place that got enough light during the day to allow for growth.

That opening was added to the diagram in Barcus's HUD. Barcus noticed that Po's quiet murmurs of the lessons had stopped. He realized he had been speaking out loud.

She stood there watching him from the doorway to the stairs.

Their eyes met.

"They say Keepers can sometimes see ghosts of the dead. Can you?" It was a serious question. He could tell she already believed it. He decided it would be simpler to let her believe it.

"Barcus, tell her yes." It was Em in his head. *"It's the easiest thing for her to understand."*

"They are speaking to you now," she stated simply.

"Yes. Please don't be afraid." He tried to sound comforting.

"I know they won't harm me," Po said.

"I meant afraid of me. I am not insane."

"I know that." She was thoughtful for a moment and said softly with her eyes downcast, "This is the first time in my life that I have not been afraid."

"Po, I'm glad."

"If you need privacy, you can tell me," Po said.

"It's all right, if you don't mind me talking to myself."

"It's like talking to you on the Plate. I don't mind. I will leave you to it. It's already late for me," Po said.

She turned and went down the stairs.

"I am ready, sir, to descend if you are, sir." It was Ash. He was standing

on the railing about to climb down.

"Yes," was all Barcus said. All of Ash's work lights were back on.

He closed his eyes for the best image. Full Point of View Augmented Reality (POVAR) was enabled now. It was like he was there, climbing down and then hanging and then slowly descending. There were balcony rings after balcony rings, together defining a central shaft. Ash stepped down level after level.

After passing the last balcony, Ash stopped about ten meters from the floor. It was covered with debris from the destroyed cathedral above. Blocks and rubble were piled about a meter deep. It looked like the debris fell onto a large pile that stood in the center of a wide circular fountain.

After a detailed view, Ash lowered himself to the floor. Silt immediately rose from his feet but, unlike the silt above, these clouds were being drawn in down through the rubble.

"That must be where the water drains out. If it's like the courtyard fountain, it is designed to handle the overflow if the center pool becomes too full. See if you can clear some of the rubble, Ash."

Ash began to carefully shift the rubble. The increasing speed with which the cloud of silt vanished was proof positive that his work was helping. It was slow work. By about two in the morning, the area was cleared from the stone grates all the way around.

"Let's call it a night. It will take a while to get back out of there."

The line slowly drew Ash back up. By the time he reached the balcony, Barcus could see that the water level had dropped noticeably already. For the first time they could see larger timbers floating in the water. They must have been beams from the cathedral.

Ash climbed over the edge of the last balcony, and only then did Barcus notice the hundreds of wooden crates stacked against the back wall. Some of the wooden crates were floating against the ceiling. The others clearly held enough weight or were deeply water logged to keep them from floating.

Without a word, Ash picked one up and walked back up the main corridor. He then turned down the smaller one, towards the stairs. He automatically wound in the cable as he went.

He went up the stairs slowly. The water was still lower, only a few centimeters, but noticeable. He finally reached the piton and unhooked his cable. He left the piton.

Leaving the box in the outdoor kitchen, he returned to his scheduled priority tasks, disappearing into the darkness.

Barcus went down to the bedroom to find that Po was already asleep. She was completely under the heavy quilts and was only visible as a small bump with just a bit of hair sticking out from the edge of a pillow.

Barcus added another log to the fire, undressed and put on his nightshirt. He climbed into bed as quietly as he could. As soon as she detected his warmth, she burrowed next him, tangled her legs with his and buried her freezing cold feet under each of his calves, all without totally waking up.

Barcus lay there watching the dancing firelight on the stone vaulted ceiling. A window opened, floating in a fixed position. He selected the "Silent Status Update" option with his eyes. Em began to speak to him inside his head.

"We are ready for another salvage run. I am uncomfortable with leaving you alone, but I will save you the comment. I'll get over it.

"Po is progressing nicely with the reading. Po is very bright and is picking it up easily. I think she has a very high IQ. Olias is having a hard time of it. He has the language challenge on top of the reading. It will take much longer for him. He is a physical boy, not cerebral. On these salvage runs, I will work on his English during his waking hours while traveling. After a winter of this level of dedication, Po will be quite advanced.

"The draining of the Redoubt has accelerated. Clearing the debris from the storm drain has increased the flow of water. This increased flow seems to have flushed some additional blockages somewhere. The level is dropping at a noticeable rate. The pool at the bottom of the crater has already dropped to the lip of the original Redoubt. We will have to decide how we're going to secure the hole. A 52 meter drop will be dangerous.

"Ash brought out one of the crates he found stored down there. You will need to check that out tomorrow."

"Analyzing the imagery from Ash's visit shows that there may be some sealed compartments still closed after decades. The seals were precision designed for protecting against vacuum, so there may be a chance.

"Analysis has also detected human remains.

"At present pace, the draining of the Redoubt will take about seventeen

weeks. I recommend cleaning each level as it's exposed. The silt will be washed away as it drains. Water will also be handy as well, for power washing. Ash will be busy.

"Yet another status log has been added for your daily review. It is unfortunate that the opening isn't larger. The STU could have fit in the main chamber."

Po stirred slightly and gave a big twitch. Amused, Barcus just smiled and kept listening.

"Provisions after this salvage run will see us through the winter and well into next year. Fresh meat is the main concern. I will encourage Olias to collect more livestock. Plus we can supplement with hunting and trapping now and then. Task lists are getting longer though. We will soon have to make priority decisions.

"Stu is running all quantum processors to brute-force the encryption on the comm's traffic. Stu has also been able to triangulate the geo-synchronous sats in this hemisphere with the help of Ash and myself when we had decent separation during the last salvage runs. Based on their distribution, he believes there are 32 deployed stationary, geo-synchronous SATs in orbit. Exodus class colony ships had a standard compliment of sixteen SATs. I believe we are looking at a colony made up of two Exodus class ships - the biggest ships in the fleet at the time of their use."

Po turned in her sleep, placing her back to his side, using his warm bicep for a pillow.

"Those are all the priority updates for tonight. Good night, Barcus."

All the windows closed, and he was back to the here and now. He moved a bit to get comfortable, spooning Po as she arched into him. His hand gently rested on her hip, and her hand slid to rest on top of his. A few minutes later, just before he was about to drift off, she drew his arm around her until his hand cupped her left breast. She was so wrapped up in him. She was asleep so deeply. He remembered watching her try to sleep in Greenwarren. She never did really. Always keeping fires going, always alert to sounds, never seeming to rest. He even saw her wake from nightmares a few times.

Barcus fell asleep holding her close, realizing he never slept this well either. Maybe it was the smell of her hair. He lightly kissed her on the head and breathed deep the scent of her.

He couldn't see her smile or that her eyes were open.

CHAPTER TWENTY-THREE

Freedom

"The Emergency Module knew far more about this culture than it conveyed. The data was considered *Not Conducive to Long Term Survival.* This analyst's opinion is that if Barcus had truly known how cruel this culture was, he would have set the whole planet on fire."

--Solstice 31 Incident Investigation Testimony Transcript: Emergency Module Digital Forensics Report. Independent Tech Analysis Team.

Barcus awoke to the smell of bacon and sounds of the table being set for breakfast. He had slept in again. He was getting used to this. The flare of guilt was momentary but it still hurt.

Clean clothes were laid out. Today, before he put on his belt with its knife sheath and array of pouches, he clipped on the holster for his .45 caseless handgun. Once it was on, he slid the large case from under the bed and unlocked it. He took out the gun and gave it a ready check. Confirming that it was fully loaded and ready to fire, he holstered it.

Next, he took out two twenty-round magazines and put them in a pouch on his left side.

Em said in his mind, "Good morning, Barcus. I'll add firearms safety training for Po and Olias to the task list." It made Barcus smile and shake his head. Plenty to do this winter.

He examined the rifle briefly before he closed the case and slid it back under the bed. Passing through the curtain, he could not believe what he saw - a wooden bowl with six eggs in it.

Po saw his stare and informed him, "The chickens Olias brought were already laying." Then she began cracking the eggs into a ceramic bowl and scrambling them. There was already a mug of steaming tea poured. The bacon was sizzling in an odd pan that was like a cast iron wok hanging from three chains over the fire on the hook opposite the one the tea kettle occupied. She had a covered dish warming on the hearth to which she transferred the bacon. With a wood and cast iron tool clearly made for this very purpose, she expertly tipped up the pan, causing most of the bacon grease to flow into a crock on the shelf as if specially designed for the task. Swinging the pan back, she added diced onions to the hot grease and stirred for a minute. Then she poured in the eggs. The eggs cooked quickly and were then transferred to the warming dish with the bacon and taken to the table.

He realized he was staring. He sipped his tea.

"I believe you will want to see what Ash left in the kitchen pavilion for you after breakfast. I also started the fire in the bathroom so that while I am cleaning up you may have a bath if you like, my L..." It was the first time in days that she had almost said 'My Lord' to Barcus. Barcus was amused.

"What will you be doing today, Po?" Barcus asked, amused internally how it all seemed so domestic, as she began to tell him about sorting out the kitchens and how the firebox for the main oven was the heat source for the sink. She spoke of how much she loved the new wooden utensils, holding up her flat wooden spatula.

It was then when he realized one of the reasons he put Olias to the task of salvage. He tried to hold his smile but found it more difficult than he realized.

It was like they were robbing the graves of the people of Greenwarren.

"What's wrong? Did I say something wrong?" Po hadn't stopped talking as she served the eggs onto their plates. He realized his face had fallen.

"No. No." She had set the bowl and spoon down and was clenching her apron in her hands, a gesture he had come to recognize. It was reflex. He reached for her and gathered her to him without getting up. She didn't resist. He had his arms around her, his cheek to her ribs. Her hands rested on his head. She began to pet him as if this happened all the time. Combing his hair with her fingers.

He was thinking of all his dead friends, all the murdered villagers, all the death.

They're all dead and here I sit playing house, Barcus thought to himself.

Po shook him back to reality.

"If I wanted to leave, would you let me go?" Po asked.

Barcus pulled back enough to look into her face. She didn't stop touching his hair.

"You can go any time you want. Where would you go?" Barcus was confused.

"Do you like eggs? I should have asked." She withdrew. It wasn't pulling away, because Barcus offered no resistance.

"I love eggs. I have not had real eggs in five years." Barcus smailed.

"I want you to stay." He added it as a simple statement, expecting no reply.

He took some bacon from the covered dish. He was still shaken, more than he could admit to himself.

"We should have Olias look for seeds on this trip. We will need some for next season. We could buy some, but the nearest market village is probably more than a hundred miles from here. Below the gorge," Po said casually. "With his next load, we will probably be okay with potatoes, but anything else will be harder," she said.

A window opened on the wall by the door, with heritage seeds listed at the top. "Varieties?" listed below it.

"What kind of seeds?" Barcus prompted.

"Onions, carrots, sprouts, beans, corn, peas, beets, turnips, pumpkins, squash, anything really for the kitchen garden," Po said as she served up. "Blueberries, gooseberries and strawberries, plus melons. Herbs of all kinds. Sunflowers, lamp flowers and medicinals." She was on a roll. "Peppers! Radishes and tomatoes. Wheat would be too hard without a mill that was near. But we have gold, apples and grapes, so we could trade for flour."

"Gold?" Barcus asked.

"Oh yes. Olias salvaged a lot of gold from those soldiers. There are a couple of chests in the small pantry. One for gold, one silver and one of copper. I can't move them anymore, either."

As an aside, she said, "Women are not allowed to handle coins. But they do all the time. I never have."

"I want you to stay. Please," Barcus said quietly.

She put down her fork. She looked Barcus directly in the face.

"In my reading lesson last night, I learned how to read the word 'freedom.' It is a powerful, magical word," Po said.

"Yes," Barcus replied.

Her voice was shaking just a little as she asked, "I am free to do whatever I like? Even if you don't like it?"

"Yes," he whispered. He realized his heart was racing.

She stood and walked to his side of the table. "Anything? Especially if you don't like it?"

"Yes," Barcus admitted. *Please don't leave.*

She slowly went to her knees at his feet. She sat on her heels, never losing eye contact. Then slowly, she bowed until her chest was on her thighs. Both of her hands were clasped at the base of her spine, and finally her cheek rested on the top of his boot.

He was mortified. He took a deep breath to protest but thought better of it. "Yes. Even that," came his pained whisper.

She spoke from his boot.

"Believe this, please. There will come a day when your only way to keep me safe is to allow me to be what I need to be. No matter what happens to me from this day to my grave, I know I will always be free. With you. Here. Like this." She stayed another moment. Slowly she sat up and then stood. Surprising him again, she sat in his lap. She has a talent for working her way in.

"I'm sorry, Barcus. I want you to understand now." She pointed to the floor. "I have done that thousands of times. That was the first time it was because I wanted to."

He was looking at her mouth as she spoke. Her right hand came to rest on the back of his neck, her other hand caressed his bearded cheek. "This too." And she kissed him. Warm and slow and soft. "Your mouth is so soft." She kissed him again. His hands came to hold her. She looked at him and said, "I like freedom. I think it feels like the greatest magic of all."

Barcus whispered, "My father always said, 'Freedom is a beautiful woman who I'd rather sleep with in a pile of dung, than to sleep without her in a bed of silk...'"

"A wise man," she said. She got up. He didn't stop her.

"Hey, my eggs are cold!" He finished them in one massive bite.

She stole his last piece of bacon as she said, "But your lap is warm."

They both laughed.

They didn't know Em was watching from 32 angles.

***

Before Barcus went for a bath, he stopped in the kitchen pavilion to check out the crate Ash had collected. It wasn't big or complicated, but it did have two latches. It took a minute to free them up without breaking them, and when he did, the box creaked open. It contained five dark glass bottles. The bottles were a bit dirty, but the corks seemed to be intact.

Barcus was rinsing off the second bottle in the wonderful sink when Po came out with the dishes.

Did she just blush? He wondered.

"I'll do that, Barcus. You go get a bath." She set the dishes in the long sink. "Would you like to try one with dinner? We'll see if they are still good."

"Sure, that would be nice." As he walked by it, he saw a mark on the box. Burned in with a brand. It read Hermitage House in a round icon. The H's were stylized.

He made his way up and around to the bathroom, really noticing the amount of damage and trying to see the old structures as they were. When he got to the edge where he could see into the pond, he noticed the level had dropped drastically. It was now below the bottom edge of the concrete Redoubt. It was now obviously around the beam on the one end. It gave Barcus an idea.

"Em, see if you could find a way to get Pardosa in and out of there easily," Barcus said.

The bath was wonderful as usual. Barcus knew he was thinking like a teenager when it concerned Po. He knew he would be unable to take advantage of her even if she did sleep in his bed. He had built a lot of trust quickly somehow. He didn't want to damage that. But he couldn't stop thinking of her gesture. Her test. He knew he was being tested.

To distract himself, he began to muse on the best way to cover the hole. Ash would cut down and bring in four trees to act as beams. A lattice of sapling pole would be laid across the beams. This would make it safer while keeping sufficient ventilation to dry it out. The large beams would have to be brought in before the rubble was removed.

When his bath was over, he dried himself off. The towels were new and thick. He hung the towel on the peg made of beautifully carved wood and got dressed.

He was planning an assessment of the salvage. His talk about the gold and silver made him realize he didn't really know what was there. Browsing the lists relied on Ash to label the items.

When he came out of the bath suite, the sun had come out, cutting through the gray. He stood looking into the Redoubt, marveling at the rate of drainage.

Barcus adjusted his belt and robe to make the holster comfortable. He made his way back around the collapsed dorms and found the set of stairs that went to the top of the wall on the north end toward the main tower. There, all four stories opened to the weather on this side because of that mysterious blast. There was even a basement level here exposed. He had not noticed it before. The receding water had exposed them again.

The top of the wall was not made of foamcrete. It was cut blocks and field stone. He wondered if the battlements were an aesthetic choice or an actual practical design.

Standing on top of the western wall, he looked back at The Abbey from about thirty meters from the tower. He could see into many of the inner courtyards from here.

"Em, can I please see an augmented view of how The Abbey looked before the explosion?" he requested.

A transparent overlay filled in the ruins. It became more opaque as it filled in. The rubble was removed and replaced by well-trimmed grass and a few apple trees.

"Why would they cover the opening to the Redoubt below?" he asked.

"Maybe they wanted to hide it from satellites above. That would also explain the types of trees that were planted inside the walls. Good cover," Em replied.

"Or maybe...they needed a support structure for the Redoubt's main elevator. Look at the wall supports. They would take a lot of stress," Barcus suggested.

"A mechanical elevator?" Em asked.

"Why not? It looks like they could have stored a lot of cargo down there. That central shaft is thirty meters across," he said.

"27.432 meters across," Em corrected.

"Start a low priority project, Em. Rebuilding the structure AND an elevator. I have to check something."

Barcus walked around the walkway toward the main tower. He was noticing blast damage. There was less here, but it was still evident. He entered the tower via a doorway that led directly onto the wall walkway. He could see that the hinges had been torn away.

The room was large and mostly empty. It was fifteen meters by thirty, he estimated. A similar doorway led out to the west wall. In the center of the room was the huge pulley and gear system that was designed to raise the portcullis in the area below. Damage was evident on one side and the thick, iron bound, portcullis was down to stay. He took the circular staircase down, lighting his way with the light from his multi tool.

It was a full ten meters down to the ground level. He was inside the portcullis room but could get through because Ash had lifted the portcullis up and propped a stone pier in the center to hold it up.

Two huge iron-bound doors stood closed here. There was a smaller man-sized door in the center of each side. Barcus unbolted one, and it swung out easily. He stepped out.

He walked out onto the bridge. It was still shaded and covered with wet leaves. It looked haunted. Everything looked haunted to Barcus at times.

"Em, would the STU fit through these doors?" Barcus asked.

"Yes he would. With a spare meter," Em replied.

"If we eventually restored the roofline, could he park in there?"

"Yes. He would fit," Em sounded excited.

"Hmmm mm...," he mumbled, thinking.

He walked back in and bolted the door behind himself. He walked under the portcullis and toward the ruins of the cathedral.

He stood at the wide center of the opening, looking up and marveling at the craftsmanship of the stonework in the ceiling vaults. Looking across toward the crater, he could see that the bridge came into the keep a story higher than ground level. The crater was more obvious from here. From this point, he could not see the opening to the Redoubt.

Sun shined in from the low sun of the south east. It felt good.

He turned and went down the spiral stairs this time. After the first bend, it was completely dark. His tool light gave him lots of illumination. The steps were wet, and then he was at the water line. It was just below the foamcrete ceiling that a three centimeter gap showed. There wasn't much more to see, so he went back up.

Soon he found himself in a rhythm, moving up and up. Four steps at a time was all he could manage because of the curve of the stairs, but he flashed by the gate level, then the portcullis room level, then a second room above that, and then he was on the roof, in the sun.

Looking over the edge, the area below the crater was very well defined. He could see the southern edge of the opening to the Redoubt. He could envision the way the blast crushed and expanded. He could imagine how the rest of the heavy slate roof fell in and smashed down tons of rubble, only to collapse the floors below all the way down to the foamcrete.

Killing hundreds of people.

"Ash, as you have been clearing rubble, have you ever found any human remains?" Barcus asked.

"Yes, many," Ash replied.

"How many?" Barcus asked.

"It is difficult to be sure, as they have all been heavily damaged skeletal remains. No forensic examinations have been done to provide an accurate estimate."

"How...many?"

"Best estimate, 63," Ash said.

Those bastards, Barcus thought.

"Please note, all the found remains were buried in rubble. I believe that other bodies had been removed."

Barcus burned with anger again. He could hear his pulse in his ears.

You fuckers are going to pay. You have gotten away with this long enough, he thought.

He walked all the way around the tower's edge. He saw Po, fresh clothes in hand, going into the bath suite. Beyond, to the east, towards the quarry, he saw the road that Ash had been restoring. Systematic tracks were still visible going back and forth in the snow. To the north, the land climbed to the foothills and then mountains, the source of water for the keep and even Foxden and the STU. To the east lay Greenwarren and Whitlock and the long dead stone cutters' village.

"Em, how long do you think we will be stranded here?" Barcus asked.

"If you get a real-time comm channel, presuming there is one, as little as five years. If we have to send the STU, thirty or thirty-five years. Maybe more, depending on the social and political climates. A lot can change in thirty-five years. We will have to decide what to tell whom ever Stu encounters. It would mean a lot of cost and risk to send a ship here to rescue one man."

He stared to the north. He could see cold mountains in the distance. He thought about Chen, buried there. He thought about Rand and Jimbo and Joe and all the rest of his murdered shipmates.

CHAPTER TWENTY-FOUR

The Frames

"Our AI forensics team had never before seen this level of targeted surveillance. Barcus had no idea. It changes everything."

--Solstice 31 Incident Investigation Testimony Transcript: Emergency Module Digital Forensics Report. Independent Tech Analysis Team.

<<<>>>

Barcus spent several hours inspecting barracks. There were dorms with rooms of various sizes and workrooms of all kinds. All were very empty. He even found what could be easily described as cells. They were below ground level and had black iron lattice doors. He found three other bath suites, but none with the flow of the single working one. There were two large communal baths, but neither was functioning fully. There was lots of roof damage all around, making bird messes a problem. Despite all this, they were set for now.

He found it odd that Olias had furnished several dry rooms with furniture salvaged from the manor. He had even laid in firewood.

Are we expecting guests? He wondered.

Po brought him lunch midday. She actually asked the Plate to locate him and was excited it had worked. He was in one of the communal baths that didn't function. They sat on the edge of a large sunken pool that was completely dry and ate bread and cheese with boiled eggs and an apple each.

Barcus found he was nervous at first after what happened at breakfast. But Po was not awkward at all.

She smelled so good.

"Why do you always wear your hair in a braid?" he asked before biting into a piece of sliced apple.

"It is unseemly for a woman to wear her hair down. It is either braided or completely covered. Older women or women that are mothers typically cover their hair and bodies. You really don't know any of this?"

She took a deep breath. The look on her face was one that she knew she was talking out of turn. "The Keepers like the braid on younger women because they...can grab them." She bit her apple looking down.

"I was always punished for being too bold. Speaking or just looking up." She could see he was listening close. "It is considered vanity for women to have more than one button on her dress. Or to wear pants or underthings. Even in winter." She looked in his eyes. "I believe it's so the Keepers can take us easier. They keep us cold so we will willingly come to their warm beds. Some Keepers even cripple their difficult women after they have a Keeper's son so they can never run away."

"Cripple them?"

"They place their foot on an anvil and crush their toes with a hammer. They can barely walk, much less ever run again. Sometimes they made us watch as punishment."

"And they mark us." Slowly she timidly slid her tunic off her shoulder and lowered it reveal a brand scar just above her left breast.

"Barcus, it's worse in some places than others. Here above the gorge, they don't keep the faith strict. In the south, it's not just the Keepers. All men are taught to treat women this way. Women are in the lowest frame."

"Frame?"

"The lowest gamut. The lowest...caste."

"Women, then men, then Keepers. These are the frames. Each frame has several gamuts." Po said.

"It is forbidden for women to talk of these things. Not only can they kill you for it, you risk the hereafter. I don't want to teach you this. I believe it can spoil the spirit of good men. I have seen it."

"But, Po. I need to know it. There will come a day when we must go among other men. I need to know what to expect." He took her hand in his and knelt before her. "I promise, I will never be like them.

"What else is forbidden?" Barcus asked.

She blushed. Barcus wondered what she was thinking.

"Most forbidden? No women can...use magic."

She paused, looking for his reaction.

"Homosexuality usually means death. But I have seen...some Keepers."

"It's all right Po. Tell me."

"If men are found out, they are usually executed. Hood and anvil. Keepers quietly tolerate women...some even encourage it...at times. It's hypocrisy, though. Many Keepers and their friends like...boys."

"Hood and anvil?" Barcus asked.

Her eyes widened at this question. She accepted his ignorance and explained.

"Do you know what a loricart looks like?" she asked. He shook his head. "It's a small garden cart about this high."

"Hood and anvil...it's a type of execution. First someone is cruelly bound to a loricart, and a heavy hood is put over their heads and tied around their necks. Their head is rested on an anvil and smashed with a sledge," she said.

"The heavy hood limits...the mess. The cart makes it easy to take the body away. Every village has an anvil, a sledge and a loricart that can be used for this purpose. It is grim." Po grimaced.

"Have you ever heard the saying, 'lucky as a country blacksmith'?" she asked.

"No," came his simple reply.

"A country blacksmith has a chance of going his entire life never having to take a sledge to anyone's head," she said flatly.

"What else is forbidden?" Barcus asked.

"Weapons possession by anyone other than a Keeper or their designated men is a death offense. It includes daggers, swords, crossbows or any kind of weapon."

"What about hunting bows and knives?" Barcus asked.

"They are fine in remote areas like this, but not inside city walls. They are considered tools here. Oh, armor and defensive castles or keeps are not allowed either, for anyone other than the High Keeper or the members of the High Council. There are only eleven citadels. It is forbidden to defend yourself against the High Keepers."

She continued, "This keep is probably forbidden. That's why Olias is collecting daggers, swords and crossbows. He says if we are found out, we are fooked anyway."

She blushed then.

He thought, *did she just curse in common tongue?*

"I know he already has two caches set up at the abandoned Lislehill estate to the east, and in the honey house to the west. It's a good idea," Barcus said.

Po's eyes went wide.

"What else?" he asked.

"Women cannot say 'no' to any command. That, too, is a death offense - hood and anvil.

"Women cannot lie. Or read. Or bite. Hood and anvil.

"Women are worth less than the dogs in the kennel." Po said.

"Not to me," Barcus said.

"It is death for a woman to kill a kenneled dog, even if it attacks her."

"I grew up in a place called Langforest Manor. The Keeper's name is Volk. He is Keeper and a Manor Lord, and he is a cruel man. When he could not get a child with me, he began throwing me at his friends. One night, I was less than satisfactory for one of his fat, drunken gambling partners named Gresham. So he beat me unconscious." She had turned pale, her throat working like she couldn't speak or was trying not to throw up. "I woke up tied to a loricart, a hood on my head and resting on an anvil. A rope around my neck held me there."

"The stable boy found me in the morning and untied me. When I went to begin my work in the kitchens, I heard them. Volk and his friends were laughing. Recounting how they took turns on me, while bound on the cart, at the anvil." Her voice was flat.

"Those...sick...fuckers," Barcus whispered.

She was suddenly in his lap. Her arms and legs were around him, her face buried in his chest. She was trembling. She seemed so thin.

He just held her for a long time before speaking. "When I was a boy, I fell through the ice into a pond. I was stupid. I had been alone. I managed to get out, but I was freezing. It was brutally cold. The wind was blowing. It took me over an hour to get back to my home, but I made it. My clothes had frozen so stiff, I could barely take them off. The cold had left frost bite burns on my back. I almost died, they told me."

He moved his hands to either side of her face. He was gazing into her eyes. "I never thought I would ever be warm again. But a strange thing happened. After that day, I was never cold again. But I never truly felt warm, either. Until...now." He tucked a loose hair behind her ear, noticing a scar there.

She held his eyes for a minute, looking deep into him. He could see hers welling up, but before they spilled over, she squeezed them shut tight.

Suddenly, she reared back and hammered both of her fists on his chest, growling, "Damn you." The momentum helped launch her off his lap and onto her feet.

The strike didn't hurt Barcus, only shocked him into silence as she began to pace back and forth like a caged animal. "Damn you," she whispered through clenched teeth. "Damn you."

Now Barcus wasn't sure if she was cursing him or not.

"I don't know how you're doing this." She risked a glance at him.

"Doing what?" Barcus returned quietly.

"This magic you are using on me." Still pacing, she said "You say I am free, but I seem to be binding **myself** to you...with chains I am making myself." She was about to cry.

She stopped in front of him. Even sitting, he was as tall as her. Suddenly, she pounded his chest again. He let her. Again and again. "I have always hated the Keepers!" she screamed at him. She slowed until the pounding stopped. "How can you MAKE me want you?" came out in a coarse, gasping whisper. Tears finally spilled in a torrent.

Wisps of hair had come loose. They clung to her face where the tears still spilled.

She kept looking at him and at her own feet. She started collecting the remains from lunch, collecting herself by visible force of will. When she was ready, she looked straight at him and said, "It's forbidden to strike a Keeper. A death offense."

"Remind me after breakfast. Perhaps it's the anvil for you," he said, straight faced.

Her eyes went wide that he would say such a thing, but before she could reply, she saw his face go from playful, to serious again.

"Po, I lied to you." He was the one to look away this time.

"Tell me." She said.

"I don't think I could ever let you go."

It was her turn to stare at him. He didn't know if it was the right thing to say.

"Thank you, my Lord." She smiled.

She collected the lunch things and walked out.

CHAPTER TWENTY-FIVE

Wine and Sleep

"The level of terraforming on this planet remains a mystery, even with all the data this archive contains. The AI was actively researching this aspect of the planet Baytirus, without informing Barcus in any way."

--Solstice 31 Incident Investigation Testimony Transcript: Emergency Module Digital Forensics Report. Independent Tech Analysis Team.

<<<>>>

Barcus sat there letting it sink in just how badly Po, and all the women here, were treated.

"Em, where is Langforest?" The now familiar regional tactical map popped up in his HUD. Whitehall centered. Directly south and a little east was an icon marked Langforest. It was one of the icons just below "the gorge," a wide deep cut of a river that had steep walls, rapids and many waterfalls. A single bridge was near Langforest, the only bridge he could see on his map.

"Do we have any BUGs there yet?"

"No, not at this time. Do you want me to modify the survey sweeps on the schedule to pass near there? We would have no need to go south of the gorge unless you want that."

"You decide while on the sweep."

"I estimate, twelve to seventeen days. Depending on what other random events you put us up to." Barcus could hear a smile in Em's voice.

"We just need to finish the wall. Enclose the water system. Maybe cover the Redoubt," Barcus said.

"Ash has a full maintenance and repair schedule. The clearing of the Redoubt will be a winter-long job."

"How many Redoubts do you think there are?" Barcus asked.

"There should be approximately thirty-two, if there were two Exodus class ships."

"Is there any way to locate other ones? I wonder if there could be any decent salvage down there."

"Right now it looks like they were using this one for cellars. Wine storage."

"That reminds me. We are having wine with dinner?" he asked. Then he added, "Is Po okay?"

"She's fine." A window popped open. She was in the kitchen, wiping her hands on her apron. She had just added wood to the oven. In fact, she looked far better than fine. She was flush and animated, and her eyes were bright. She looked, healthy, happy.

Barcus continued his tour of the vast interior spaces in The Abbey. He found two floors that were more barracks. The bunks were built in, part of the building. There were drawers below each bunk and more cupboards in between the bunks. They had the look of a long train, with sleeper cars, with a wide aisle. There were no windows, and the barracks were completely empty except cobwebs and mouse nests. Some of the drawers were missing.

"We definitely need some cats," Barcus said as a mouse scampered across the floor.

"Barcus, it is kind of ironic that it was likely the villagers and residents nearest to this place who salvaged everything from here."

Barcus brushed the cobwebs aside and ran his hand along the ancient wood. It was real wood. He had spent so many years on spaceships, dreaming of real wood. It was lovely to touch, to feel.

"Just The Abbey could house about 600 people when it was fully up and running. Not including the Redoubt."

Down the last flight of stairs, and he was in the basement. This level was directly on the foamcrete roof of the Redoubt. The floor was white, and the wall directly to his right was white. A wide hallway curved off into the distance and darkness.

Cells lined the wall on the right as he walked this hall. Every cell had a heavy ring on the wall opposite the door. The entire place was dry and deeply dusty. There was a distinct lack of cobwebs, which he found interesting.

"Em, bring up this level on the floor plan." It popped up. "Now lightly superimpose the level above," Barcus requested.

"Could there be something more, directly behind these cells? The halls and stairs wind you around so you might never notice, but if the foundation of the upper levels are along this edge, there could be a huge area here." Barcus gestured with his hands.

"I believe that area is all topsoil for the trees and plants above in The Abbey. It's getting late, Barcus. It looks like Po has dinner ready."

"Call her, please," he said.

He was already watching her in a window when her Plate made a delicate chime. She had just finished uncorking a second bottle of wine.

"Barcus?"

"Hello, Po."

"Hello, where are you? It's very dark."

"I am in the lowest level under the western section. I am heading back now, but I am covered in cobwebs, so I'm going to stop and clean up a bit on the way back. Fifteen minutes or so."

"Thank you for letting me know." She was still talking too loud and slow for the Plate.

"See you soon. Bye."

"Goodbye." She put her mouth close to the Plate as she spoke, then slid the Plate back into the pouch at her hip and skipped to the oven.

He returned to the stairs and ascended. All the way up to the top of the wall. It was twilight as he moved along. He passed through into the North Tower and out the other side and finally to the stairs that went down to the bath suite. He cleared off most of the cobwebs and washed his hands and face.

He made the meandering way back to the gatehouse. Before going in, he checked the stables and added extra wood to the fire in the tack room that heated that end of the stable. He checked that the gate was barred at the entrance, and finally he went into the gatehouse and found the table set with several extra lit candles.

He took off his tabard and cloak and hung them on the pegs, noticing that they had even more cobwebs and dirt on them than he had feared. He added more wood to the fire, thinking again how they sure used a lot of it. He also recalled that he had not carried in a single armful since before, when he was alone. He'd have to remember to change that.

He heard a rattle at the door. Since he was standing right there, he opened it. Po had two trays piled with various bowls and dishes and almost dropped one when the door was opened. Barcus reached out quickly and took a tray from her. It was very heavy.

"These weigh a metric ton! What are these bowls made of?"

"Careful, they are hot. They are made of stone and heated on the warming shelf of the oven. You really don't know anything do you?" She was amused.

"Only what you tell me."

"Here, let me show you," she said as the last dish was moved to the table. She took the lid off one of the bowls with a wood hook-like handle. It had what looked like mashed sweet potatoes and smelled of cinnamon and other spices. She lifted what looked like a miniature tea kettle and drizzled something on the potatoes and lightly folded it in. She replaced the lid, saying, "If you do not know when you will be serving or have a long way to the kitchen, they are very useful."

She went to the fireplace and got the kettle before opening the next bowl. The same kind of wooden hook handle was lifted, and he could see mixed onions and a greenish carrot dish on a bed of thin wooden sticks. "This kind is much hotter." She poured in the water, and it instantly began to boil and steam beneath the vegetables as she replaced the lid.

"This one here keeps meat moist." It had two sides with steaming spiced water on one side and grilled steaks on the other. There were also sliced mushrooms in butter.

Barcus sat and let her fill the plates.

She was getting used to eating with him. Last of all, she poured him a taste of wine. She poured gently so as not to let the wine splash as it poured into the crystal wine goblet.

It was the best wine he had ever tasted.

"This is wonderful!" He gestured for her to fill her glass as he waited.

Olias asked in common tongue, "May I offer the toast?"

"Please do." He held up his glass.

"A full belly, warm bed and another day. Willing," Olias said in common tongue.

"You are supposed to say 'willing' when he does," Po shared.

"Willing," Barcus replied.

They all dug in.

The dinner was amazing. Everything was excellent.

"You sit in front of the fire while Olias and I clean up. I'll join you with another bottle of wine," Po said to Barcus.

When they had gone, Em walked from behind him to sit in the chair opposite him, "*I think we are ready for winter. How are you doing?*"

"I'm fine. We will be fine for the winter." He paused, "Em, thanks for keeping me sane when I was alone."

Barcus moved to his comfy chair and filled his glass with the last of the wine from the decanter. He looked at the decanter, wondering when she had filled it. When he turned back, Em was gone. Po was back in short order without her apron, but her sleeves were wet. She excused herself to change into her night tunic.

Barcus watched in the other room via a window as she popped the button at the nape of her neck. The single button, carved from bone, was all she had been allowed. He thought about its strategic location as he stared into the fire. Without that button, her entire dress would fall to the ground. *Clearly, a Keeper design*, he told himself.

She was back in less than a minute and sat in the other chair after filling both glasses. Barcus raised his glass and said, "To Po and her own kind of magic. Willing." Po said the word "willing" with him, blushing.

"Tonight was the first time I have ever had ANY of those dishes, even though I have cooked them many times. I loved them. Thank you," she said sincerely.

"Thank Olias the next time you see him. Where did he get steaks?" Barcus drank more of the glorious wine.

"He brought a whole side of beef, wrapped in cheesecloth. Thanks to Ash. He says there is more. But our meat locker isn't cold. The beef will freeze where it is in Greenwarren for now."

"Another item for the list," Barcus said. It appeared on a task list inside his HUD.

"This wine tastes like Hermitage," Po said, surprising him.

"I think it is. That's actually what it said on the case," Barcus said. "How did you know?"

"Some Keepers will not drink alone. Drinking is against the true faith. They can blame the sin on a woman if she is there. Do you realize that a bottle of that wine is worth as much as those horses? It's all that Volk would drink, even though it's harder and harder to find. Wait. Where did you get it?" she asked.

"Ash found it in the water." Barcus didn't want to explain about the Redoubt tonight. "There might be more."

"Did you know wine is forbidden? Not a death offense, but it is technically forbidden in the scriptures. They say they flog people in the south if they are discovered drunk."

"Oh really? But there has been a tavern in every village I've seen."

"In the wilds of the north, much is relaxed." She raised her glass again. Barcus refilled them.

"This region is not held, not claimed by any Keep. You can see it on the great floor map. Nothing above the gorge. But there are almost 200 towns and villages here."

"Do you know a lot about the region?" Barcus asked.

"Not really. I've lived near the gorge my whole life though," Po replied.

"There is nothing north of here except the east way river." She put her hand on her mouth, stifling a flash of despair.

"What's wrong?" Barcus asked.

"Greenwarren was such a prosperous town because of the lumber. The winters allowed them to move the long massive logs easily over the snow on special sleds. They would bind them together and take them down the river to the sea in the spring during the high waters. They say there is a real city there where they sold the lumber as masts and beams and poles."

Po sighed heavily.

"No masts this spring," she said.

"I saw that river. There is a port there. It's deserted," Barcus said. He could see her slipping into sadness.

"When I was a boy, my parents had a cottage. It was far away from the city where we lived. It was by a river much like the east way. Our cottage was up on tall poles, four of them, as high as the walls here. It was one large room and a balcony that overlooked the river. We climbed a ladder to get up to it. The times that we were there were the best times of my life. We were free." He tried to stop the memory there. Before the pain.

"The cabin was on the floodplain, and in the spring when the river spilled over the banks, it stayed dry. The roots of the trees around it kept it safe year after year. Even then it was beautiful. I went there with a friend once in a boat during the flood, just to see. It was beautiful and frightening. We lost the boat and the ladder we tied it to one night when the river rose quickly.

"My father rescued us. He never told my mother. He never said another word about it."

"Why?" Po asked.

"Well, let's just say I worried my mother too often back then. He wanted to spare her the fear. That and...my friend was a girl."

"Oh, I see."

"I gave her that cottage years later, after my parents had both passed away. I didn't think I'd ever go back there again. I hope her children enjoy it as much as I did."

"Were you with her long?" Po asked. Barcus sensed that this was a difficult personal question for her to ask.

"No. Not long. The flood happened in the spring. I never saw her again after that summer."

"What happened?" Po asked.

"We traveled with my father. It wasn't much longer before he was supposed to retire. My parents had saved their entire lives just so they could retire early and...'live.'"

"They were killed on that next trip. It was an accident. I never went back home."

"I'm so sorry, Barcus," Po said.

"Thanks, it's fine. It was long ago. It's a shame to waste good wine on sad stories," He said.

"It's not a sad story. Not to me. You've had family, friends and love. And magic. Books. A full belly. Good wine." She raised her glass again and then emptied it.

Barcus picked up the decanter and refilled both of their glasses. She drank again.

"You know, this is the first time I have had wine just for the pleasure of it." She sipped again. "Wine is completely different, depending how you feel when you drink it."

"I never knew my parents. The closest thing I had to a father was the Smith from Langforest manor. He was a hard man. He looked after me in his way. He did a good job keeping me out of Volk's line of sight." She drank more, pausing. "It was easy when I was small, when I got a bit older, fifteen years old, the household staff noticed me. Smith could not stop them from taking me from him. They put me to work. I was luckier than most."

Barcus had the sense she was glossing over most of it.

"What happened to the smith?"

"The last I heard, he had lost an eye to the whip. Even that word was years ago."

They talked for another hour about repairs to The Abbey. When Barcus reached for the decanter, he realized all the wine was gone. He also realized that Po was asleep, curled up, head on the overstuffed arm rest, hugging an empty goblet.

He got up and changed into his nightshirt and turned down the bed.

Gently, he slipped the glass from her hand and placed it on the table. He carefully lifted her tiny frame like a sleeping child. She helped by burrowing into his chest, curling up even more in his arms. Slowly he knee-walked onto the bed and placed her down, going with her.

He drew the covers up over them both, her back to him, matching the curve of him, feet tangling in his legs.

Finally giving in to the wine and warmth, he fell asleep holding her.

CHAPTER TWENTY-SIX

The Telis Raptor

"The first new Baytirus species cataloged that is unique to this planet."

--Solstice 31 Incident Investigation Testimony Transcript: Emergency Module Digital Forensics Report. Independent Tech Analysis Team.

<<<>>>

Barcus woke in the early dawn. He smiled.

Po was spread-eagled, sound asleep. She was on her back, diagonal on the bed with her arms over her head. Barcus was on his side, his face pressed against her ribs. Her right leg was thrown over him, the soft portion of her knee following the curve of his hip, her skin on his skin. She usually slept curled in a ball. She was softly snoring.

As Barcus slowly came awake, he realized there was skin under his right hand. His arm was over her. His hand held her. His thumb was touching the soft bit of skin just below her armpit. His fingers wrapped around her to her shoulder blade. Without thinking, he moved his thumb and caressed her skin there.

Without waking, she reacted. She made a soft sound, a cooing sigh, her left hand finding his.

Now he was beginning to react.

Slowly he tried to extract his hand. He feared she would wake and a trust would be lost. As he tried to slide his hand out, as slowly as an analog watch minute hand, her hand followed his. He discovered that her night dress was pulled up high. At least now his hand was away from her breast and not up under her clothes. Over her ribs and down her belly, his plan was to gently use that hand to shift her leg from him so he could slide from bed without waking her.

Her hand would not leave his though.

In fact it began to guide his hand subtly again. He let her.

His hand began to feel an increase in soft, fine hair below her navel. Hyper aware now, he could feel her leg move lightly on his body.

There was delicate hair on her legs.

She dragged his hand lower and her snore changed with a twitch. Her legs spread slightly wider, and all at once she drew his hand directly to her soft pubic area. He knew she was dreaming. He could not take any more.

He moved all at once, like a sleeper turning so she was once again on her side with her back to him. Her own hand now occupied that place of privilege.

As he slid out of bed with his now painfully hard erection, he was beginning to form the discussion he would have with her later. He needed to be clear. He wanted her to know that she was desired, but he also wanted her to want him. He needed to be sure.

He paused for a moment to watch her sleep. She let out a soft moan and it almost broke his resolve. Without thinking, he raised his hand to find the scent of her skin there.

He gathered his clothes, his boots and belt. He thought, *I know how to act with women from my time and place.* An amusing mental correction. *You just ask, in one way or another, and no would mean no.*

But with her, there was no such thing as saying no. He would have to find a way to explain it today.

Part of his head was saying, *"Just take her, you stupid bastard, you know she wants you."* Another part said, *"Don't fuck this up LIKE YOU ALWAYS DO."* Another part said, *"What the FUCK are you doing? Don't get distracted. Find the ASSHOLES that killed everyone you care about and make them pay!"* This sobered him. Angered him.

"What the hell are you doing?" he sighed.

Em's voice was in his mind as he collected clothes and his boots and passed though the curtain. "Barcus, is everything all right? Your heart rate and blood pressure are way up." He indicated a silent "yes" in his HUD.

He dropped the clothes in an overstuffed chair, stepped into his boots and stoked the fire. The cast iron kettle was already full and hanging from the hook arm. He swung it to the front, over the fire. Quietly, clothes and cloak in hand, he went out.

There was a light dusting of snow that was very dry and didn't stick to anything. He made his way to the bath suite and, after hanging the clothes on a peg, went about starting a fire. He was surprised that there were a lot of coals left that he managed to draw back to life. Soon he had a large fire burning.

He didn't wait for the bath to get warm. The cool water took the edge off. He scrubbed himself roughly. He washed his hair and beard savagely with the strong soap. Submerging himself, he scrubbed the soap from his hair. The suds floated away as the water circulated through. He could feel the water getting warmer. He laid there a while, watching the steam rise from the small waterfall of the water flow, emptying his mind, searching for clarity.

He got out and dried off, after a long soak, with the thick towels Olias had salvaged. He stood naked in front of the fire for a while to air dry in the heat.

He dressed in fresh clothes he had never worn before. There were layers. First he donned the under-tunic and pants. Next came the over-tunic and his belt. Then he pulled a tabard over that. The last piece was the cloak. These were the standard winter clothes, he had been told. He smiled as he thought of it.

After adding more wood to the fire, he folded his nightshirt and headed back to the gatehouse.

He came directly down the spiral stairs into the bed chamber this time and was amazed to find her still sleeping. He hung his nightshirt on the peg and went in search of food.

He collected utensils, two plates and mugs on a tray. He added bread, butter, honey, cheese, ham and apples to the tray and carried it back to the gatehouse after stuffing a big chunk of ham into his own mouth.

Soon the table was set and tea was brewing.

The table next to his chair held the most recent book. He looked forward to spending time with it. But as he sipped his tea, he reviewed the morning reports Em had prepared. The most notable item today was that the Redoubt was draining at eighteen centimeters per day. That rate would increase, though, as the diameter of the Redoubt decreased.

Thirty minutes later, he was reading the book about bee keeping, when he heard Po stir. It was just after 10 a.m. She had never slept that long.

Quiet stirrings suddenly turned into panicked rustling. The curtain flew back. Her hair was loose, long and wild. Her night dress had fallen off her shoulder and she was more beautiful than he had ever seen her.

"Good morning," Barcus said over his steaming cup. "The bath should be warm now if you want to clean up before breakfast. Tea's ready whenever you are."

Her eyes darted from Barcus to the food waiting for them both at the table, to the teapot on the hearth and kettle over the fire.

Her face fell, "I am so sorry, my Lord." Barcus rolled his eyes "I never intended to sleep so long. I... I..."

"Po. Stop. Please. I wanted you to sleep in. I will try to explain it again." He set his tea and book down, got up, poured her a mug of tea and carried it to her. "I want you safe, well fed, well rested, strong, healthy, clean and happy. Your mind will work best then. I have a lot for you to learn." She had one hand holding back the curtain and the other on the door frame, staring at the tea. "I need your help, Po. This is the only way."

He extended his hand offering her the tea. She took it after a moment.

He tucked a few wild hairs behind her left ear and on a whim he kissed her forehead. Her body almost imperceptibly drew nearer, like there was extra gravity between them. He moved away then, and looked at her again.

"Thank you." There was a long pause. "Barcus?"

"Yes, Po." He picked up his tea.

"I know it's true. All of it." Po said.

"What is true?"

"The magic. It's not just in written words. It's in spoken ones if the speaker says them true. It's in the fire and the food and in sun and rain. It's in the rest, my sleep, my touch and my dreams. It's even in the water and air I think. Everywhere. I feel it. I never felt anything before except fear and pain. And even those are magic I think."

"Yes, Po. Especially those," Barcus said quietly.

"I don't understand any of it, but I know it's true."

"That was a good night's sleep." Barcus smiled.

She sipped her tea and set it down on the table by her plate. "I will clean up after breakfast," she said.

"Excellent." Barcus said as he retrieved the teapot from the hearth and brought it to the table. He topped off his mug.

Po was tearing apart the loaf of bread as Barcus sliced the apples. They ate buttered bread with honey amid bites of apples and cheese and conversation about the coming day's tasks.

He told her that Pardosa, Ash and Olias would arrive in Greenwarren today around noon. If she had any other requests, things to get, to call him on the Plate and let him know.

Breakfast was over too soon.

"One day this winter, you will have to begin teaching me how to bake bread. I'd love to know how," he said.

This for some reason made her smile wide. She collected her fresh clothes and went up the spiral stairs heading toward the bath.

He wanted to watch her but decided he should not. He needed a clear mind when he tried to talk to her later. The BUGs would keep an eye out and let him know if there was a problem.

He took the dishes to the kitchen, while thinking about the wall cap stones that would go over the aqueduct. Slabs from the quarry that had already been cut would serve nicely.

***

"Barcus..." it was Po's voice. She had called out his name. He instantly panicked. A window popped up immediately showing her in the tub reclining. She said his name again, but whispered it this time.

He was just in time to see the end of her shuddering orgasm.

He was hypnotized by her arched back, her nipples breaking the surface of the water. Her arms pressed her breasts together as she touched herself with both hands.

By the time she was finished, she was limp.

Barcus closed the window and then his eyes.

Em's voice startled him, "I have been monitoring her for months now. This behavior is a recent development. Her health continues to improve, physically and mentally."

"Em, I don't know what I'm doing," Barcus said.

Em appeared in the chair at the table. No casual walk in from another room or from behind him like she usually did.

"You are surviving. You have secured shelter, food, water, comfort, cultural intel and real companionship. You are ready for the snow. You are far more prepared than we could have hoped for. The snow will act as another layer of security while we break their comms. Once we do that, we find out how this happened. Who did it and what we can do about it."

"I know. I just..." Barcus said. "All I want to do is..." he trailed off. Em didn't ask him to finish the thought. She knew he wanted to hunt these bastards down, one at a time, and tear their heads off as they screamed. But that would not help him survive.

Barcus went back to work. He finished the cleanup and went to inspect the wall repairs. He had dispatched BUGs into the water system to find the clogs first. They had to be careful because the BUGs were a limited resource and now he was beginning to think long-term. He was at the wall repair, looking into the open top of the repaired aqueduct, wondering how fast Ash could cut and carry the correct size stone blocks here. This made him look down the ramp of rubble there, on the outside of the wall, which Ash had used to repair the wall thus far. The top of the rubble was still about two meters shy of the top of the repaired wall section.

That's when he saw the tracks.

There was a light dusting of snow here that made it easy to see the trail once it was past the rubble, as it ran directly to the tree line.

Looking closer, he could see traces of where it had gone down the rubble on the inside of the wall.

That's when the screams began.

It was not a human scream. It was a screeching howl of fear from an animal. It was enough to start him running. He moved along the top of the wall fast. As he rounded to a view of the paddock he saw the source of the now silenced screams. It was a goat in the jaws of something shaped like a lion, but was broader in the chest. It looked like a reptile and had a very long tail that was swishing back and forth.

He knew it was a predator of some kind, but it was like nothing he had ever seen. The other goats began mewing loudly together. They were pressed against the wall opposite the stables.

The beast was tearing off a hind quarter and ignoring the other goats as their screams rose.

Barcus's heart froze and time slowed as the gate opened and Po entered the paddock wiping her hands on an apron. Her eyes were on the goats crowded together in the corner to her left. She hadn't noticed the predator looking up at her with its bloody face.

In seeming slow motion, it began stalking towards her. When she saw it, her hands flew to her mouth in shock. It was only ten meters from her when he left the wall, ran down the slate tiles of the roof of the dorms above the stables, placed one foot on the stable porch roof and launched into the air.

The gravity held him aloft far too long it seemed. In slow motion he turned in flight. He landed with a ground-shaking impact on his feet, arms wide, cloak spread, directly between the thing and Po.

Barcus had surprised the beast. It reacted like a cat. A large ruff of a mane came up at its neck. It was more like feathers than fur. It was a reptile. Eyes on the front of its skull, a giant snout of bloody, snarling, teeth. It had gray mottled skin that looked like stone. It began to move like a cat about to fight, its back arched, its body pivoted to the side. Its head didn't move.

Its tail lashed him so quickly that he didn't see it until it was returning from a strike that hit him on his left collar bone, gashing downward across his sternum.

His gun was just clearing its holster when the second strike hit full force across his face. His left cheek bone took the most of it, knocking him off his feet to the ground as the predator advanced, arching for another blow.

Barcus could not miss the massive target of its ribcage when he opened fire, despite his blurred vision. The first shot would have been enough to kill it, blowing its heart and lungs out the far side, but it didn't go down. As he began to sit up, he shot it three more times. It fell off its feet as Barcus was regaining his.

The report of the gunfire echoed and faded into deeper silence.

He slowly turned to Po and said in a voice that didn't sound like his own, "Are you all right?" She was still frozen. Only seconds had passed, her hands on her mouth, eyes growing wider still.

Em chimed in his mind, "*Barcus you are badly wounded. You are frightening the girl. You need her."* A window opened and it showed his own ruined face. The thing's tail had slashed his face to the bone. His right cheek had been peeled from his face from just below his eye to his jawline. The flap of skin hung there, his skull exposed, white in places, teeth showing. He could see a deep score line in his skull on the bone of his cheek to his teeth.

He watched himself, almost casually, dropped the gun to reach up and press the flap back up to cover his skull.

That is when he felt the blood running down his belly and over his genitals.

Em chimed in again, or maybe she had never stopped, **"BARCUS! If there is another one of those she is dead. You will go into shock soon."** This got him moving.

Through gritted teeth he said to Po, "Hurry," and grabbed her with his left hand and moved to the gatehouse. This jump-started Po as well.

In a loud whisper he said, "I will go into shock soon. You need to help me and fast." They moved into the gatehouse and he slammed then bolted the door closed.

"Under the bed is a large red case. Bring it." She ran and was back in seconds. She lifted the case onto the table, sending items flying to the floor as Barcus sat. Barcus opened the first latch, and Po quickly opened the other three and flung it open.

Barcus reached in and withdrew a small tube marked "Trauma Pen: for use in emergencies only." He pressed it down against his thigh. It made a snapping and a hiss sound. It felt like ice water being flooded into his veins. His vision cleared and the pain subsided. But it became clear where his damage was. He picked up a small towel from the table and pressed it to his face. "Hold this. We have to hurry," he said to Po. Without hesitation, Po placed direct pressure to his cheek. "Stand here."

When she moved to the side, the BUG showed the expanding blood stain on his chest around a great cut in his tabard.

With one swift motion, Barcus grasped the edges of the torn tabard and tunics and ripped them wide until his chest was bare all the way to his lap. Pain shot though him like an electric shock as he moved.

A giant gash went diagonally from his collarbone to his ribs on the opposite side. Ribs and sternum bones were exposed. Blood ran freely from the wound. From the case he withdrew a canister.

"Watch what I do with this, Po. I will need you to repeat it with my other wound." He seemed to be staring off into the distance. He was actually examining the wound via the BUG. Em was silent.

The canister functioned like a spray paint can. It looked like a dust of fine white chalk, as it covered the wound. When it was covered, he pressed on the canister a red button that lit. He winced as the blood flow seemed to almost stop immediately.

"Po, now watch this next part. I have to close the wound."

"I know how to stitch wounds," she said in gasping but controlled words.

"This is much the same, but uses medical adhesive. It uses magic. Watch."

He grabbed a device that looked like a syringe. He turned the base, and it activated lights that illuminated the area of the wound. Pressing a small button on the side caused a bit of active foam to excrete from the tip into the top edge of the wound. "Press the edges together as you go. See?" Barcus showed her. He handed her the device. His clarity was beginning to fade.

"Hurry. I will pass out soon." He pressed the towel to his face again so she could use both hands. She didn't ask a single question as she began to close the wound.

His focus shifted from the HUD to her face as she worked. Her brow was deeply etched in concentration and concern as she worked unflinchingly. As she reached the bottom of the wound, he reached into the case and pressed a button and a moist towelette was dispensed. "Clean it with this," Barcus said to her.

She set down the medical adhesive canister and took the towelette. She could feel a cool sizzle where she touched it. As she wiped around the wound, the towel caused a bubbling reaction as it absorbed and somehow consumed the blood and soil from the area until it was just his very pale skin and a horrific, somehow pulsing line on his chest. There was no bleeding at all.

"Last thing." Barcus took another canister from the case and shook it. A thumb release allowed a cover to slide, revealing a soft-looking brush. "Don't ever use this unless you have cleaned it with that first." He gestured drunkenly to the towelette. He painted the wound with the brush. A clear coating covered the wound.

Barcus almost dropped it as he set it down.

"We don't have much time. You have to do this." He gestured to his face. "I am going to pass out soon."

She grabbed the first canister and asked him, "Are you ready?" She tried to show a weak smile. His vision was beginning to tunnel and he knew it.

"Nanites first," he said. She painted the open wound with white dust.

He pointed to the canister he held. "Close it." She did without hesitation.

He pointed to the medical foam. "Clean the area then seal it." He nodded. "Ready," he said through clenched teeth.

"Doesn't it need to be cleaned on the inside of the wound?" she asked.

"No. The Nanites will handle it," Barcus whispered.

She let the soaked cloth drop to the floor with a splat. Barcus closed his eyes as she sprayed. It was a mistake. The room spun. He opened them again to tighter tunnel vision. Feeling in his limbs was failing. But he redoubled his focus, fighting against the tunnel. Em was there.

"Barcus, you need to stay awake a little longer." She was helping him fight the tunnel closing as Po worked.

Then Po was finished.

"BARCUS!" Em was yelling in his head. *"Take the Rapid Renewal!"* He looked to the case and found the small bottle, but his finger would not open it. Po took it from him and opened the top. He gulped 150 ML of fire. It woke him enough that he could get to his feet. The rags of his blood soaked clothes fell off his shoulders. He staggered to the bedroom with Po supporting him under his shoulder. The bed was unmade, awaiting new sheets. He paused and loosened his belt and his remaining blood soaked rags fell around his boots. His naked body was covered in blood. He sat on the edge of the bed and slowly toppled.

"Barcus. Barcus...Barcus!" Po was getting frantic as she first pulled off one boot and then another, swinging his legs to the bed.

She looked at him. His breathing was shallow. Bruising was beginning to spread from both wound sites.

"Barcus." It was a whisper now. A precursor to tears.

The Plate chimed loud and urgent.

She stared at Barcus a moment longer before she reached into her pouch and drew out the Plate. She touched the answer icon, incredulous. It said Barcus was calling.

"Hello, Po." Em's face on a black background displayed. Po's hand went to her mouth, and the tears spilled.

"It will be all right. I promise. I need you to do a few more things for him though." Em's voice was reassuring. Po recognized it as the voice from her reading lessons.

"But..." She looked from the Plate to him. The gash and the expanding bruises were bad.

"I will show you everything one day. How all this magic works. I promise. But we are not done here yet." Em on the Plate seemed to look over her shoulder at him.

"I need you to clean him up...completely. That same towel will still work."

Po went into the other room and retrieved it and after returning everything to the case, brought that back as well. In a few minutes Barcus was clean.

"He feels very hot to me. Even though it's cool in here," Po said. The wounds were all closed now.

"I know. That's what we will address now. Do you see this compartment of the case?" An image of the case displayed on the screen, and a hand reached in and withdrew a small clear, flat piece of plastic that held three small disks and a ring.

"Take these out and place them here." The image put one disk behind each ear and one under his left armpit, and the ring on his index finger.

She did exactly that. The disks adhered easily to his skin. The ring seemed too big at first and frightened her when she saw it shrink to fit his finger.

"Po, he has lost a lot of blood," Em said.

She almost lost it to tears. "I know." She looked at the bloody rags on the floor. The blood on the front of her own clothes.

"I need you to retrieve this device from the case." The Plate showed where a tube the size of a thumb was stored. She found it and compared it to the image on the Plate. It had written on it "Hemitropic Stims."

"Hold it against his arm, here, press down and hold it there for a few seconds," Em instructed

She did. It made a click and a hiss.

"What else should I do? Tell me what to do. Please?" She was nearly frantic.

"Thanks to you, Po, he will sleep now, for a long while. Please don't worry, he will be fine. Make sure he drinks some water often. I will remind you."

"Leave the Plate on the table, and I will tell you if he needs anything. He will be fine."

Starting to cry, she asked "Why?"

"He will be fine," Em said.

"Why would he do that?" She was looking at his unconscious body. Bruises spreading as she watched. She was crying now. The crisis had past.

"No one else dies before him. He'll not have it," Em said from the Plate.

"But I am nothing. Why would you do that?" She was talking directly to Barcus.

"Never say that again," Em said. Then softer, "Please."

Po set the Plate on the side table, added more wood to the fire, brought in a pitcher of water and a cup. She reached up and flicked one button free on her bloody dress at the nape of her neck. It fell to the floor as she stepped out of her boots and climbed into bed with him. Naked and unselfconscious.

"Po, he will never let you die. You are his reason to survive. As long as he has you, he will have a reason to live," the Plate whispered to her.

"But I am nothing."

"The most powerful Keeper to ever walk on this world disagrees,"

Em said quietly.

She curled around him, willing her life force into him. Her tears flowed in silence as his fever burned.

CHAPTER TWENTY-SEVEN

Ulric's HUD

"The Emergency Module almost lost Barcus. System anomalies increased after the Telis attack. Up until that point the EM had left the STU out of it."

--Solstice 31 Incident Investigation Testimony Transcript: Emergency Module Digital Forensics Report. Independent Tech Analysis Team.

<<<>>>

EM: New short range comm signal detected, ping only. Recommendations?

STU: Source?

EM: Surveillance Subject 864. BUGs confirm. Unknown protocol.

STU: Recommend a short range broad base challenge response, full spectrum.

EM: Stand by. Initiated. Acknowledgment received. 1.47v HUD protocol.

STU: Version 1.47v is compatible up to 4.12v. Recommend upgrade and diagnostic.

EM: Upgrading. Complete. Cold start required. Stand by.

STU: Audio and Video access complete. No security present.

EM: This is going to be... useful.

***

Ulric came awake with a start. "What was that!?" he had become highly skilled at sleeping in the saddle. Loud sounds usually made his horse flinch more than Ulric.

"What was what? Your snoring wake you again?" Grady laughed.

Ulric was already digging out his flask for a long pull. When he brought the flask down, he caught a glimpse of movement in the trees, a silhouette of someone in black.

"There is someone there." He pointed. "Behind that tree, just to the right of the boulder that looks like a ram's horn.

"I saw nothing," Grady stated flatly.

"Someone is there!" Ulric was still pointing, fear clearly in his voice.

Grady swung his leg over the pommel and slid down, silent in the snow. He produced a woodsman's ax from somewhere as he walked directly to the spot, about fifteen feet off the road.

"Nothing. Not even tracks in the snow." He looked around. It was obvious he was taking it seriously.

"This tree?"

"Yes. Right where you are standing." He tipped back the flask again as Grady walked back.

"What's in the flask?" Grady walked up, still scanning around. He didn't expect an answer.

"Ghosts," Grady said. "Probably more ghosts. The closer we get to each village."

Grady was climbing back up when Ulric heard it. It was just a whisper.

"Ulric..." The whisper was faint but there, and straight ahead. He looked into the distance. His eyes could still see in the distance a faint, dark, cloaked figure, was walking ahead, looking back to Ulric, in the center of the road, between the walls of trees. It was just descending the far side of a rise, limping, and was out of sight a moment before he could say anything.

Grady settled and they moved ahead in the virgin snow.

It took about fifteen minutes to get to that knoll. There were no tracks.

Ulric took another swig from the flask but didn't stop to investigate tracks that he knew wouldn't be there.

They rode a long day for Ulric. It was less than half the pace Grady kept when alone. They left the road by a small cairn of stones that Ulric would have completely missed if Grady had not pointed it out. Less than an hour later, they reached a remote farmhouse. It was empty, as if abandoned without a moment's notice.

There was a large black cook pot still hanging on its hook over the fireplace ashes. A further search found that the house was equipped with a stone oven. Six loaves were in the cold thing. They were black.

"I will put the horses in the barn. There might be grain there," Grady said as he left.

Ulric set about getting a fire started. He set the cook pot out on the porch for the small animals to clear out. There was water in a large ceramic cistern. He had a kettle on for tea by the time Grady returned.

"Any sign of the occupants?" Ulric asked as he hung his winter cloak and then his pack on a handy peg, conveniently located there so the farmer's cloak would dry by the fire.

"There are six things out there covered with snow. I didn't look closely." He set down saddle packs and took off his own outer layers. "There was feed in the barn as well. I will go out after dinner and brush the horses down proper."

Grady searched the farmhouse and discovered someone had already done the same. He did find an overlooked sack of potatoes and a small wheel of cheese. A stew of dried beef and onions with the freshly peeled taters was soon simmering.

"Why have you taken to wearing that backpack all the time under your cloak?" Ulric asked as the cork came free from a bottle of Roofers Oak, a quality Bourbon. He held the bottle up to punctuate his question, adding an offer to join him. "You even wear it when riding. There are saddle bags for that." Ulric poured himself a tall beer mug full. Almost half the bottle emptied into the mug.

"One of my old tracker habits," he replied, holding a small clay mug out to be filled. "I have everything I need in this one small pack if I find myself on foot or in trouble."

Ulric was focusing on not missing the small clay target of a cup as he poured.

"In my youth, it's all I ever carried." He took a sip. "Now, despite my best efforts, I sleep under roof a bit too often." He set the cup on the mantle and worked his way out of two more layers, hanging both on pegs at the door.

"The horses are settled in the barn and just in time. It is now snowing hard. Sky smells like we're in for it." He dug into his small pack, drawing out a leather tube. Opening it, he slid out a carved flute and a small oiled cloth that held carving tools. He retrieved his cup and sat in a reasonably comfortable chair. He unrolled the tools and after taking another sip, started carving on the flute.

"You have been carving on the thing this entire trip. What's taking so long?" Ulric demanded. "I swear you have been working on it for the last ten years."

"I can't believe you never asked before now. What is up with you?" Grady was staring at him. "I make one every year. It's Ironwood. Feel it." Grady tossed it to him, unconcerned. Ulric wasn't ready for it and the only move he managed was to protect his drink. The flute was incredibly heavy, far heavier than he expected.

It bounced off Ulric's chest with a thud and hit the floor end-wise. The slate floor tile cracked where it hit. Grady snatched it from the air before it damaged anything else.

"My god, man, are you trying to kill me?" Ulric was rubbing his chest in mock pain. "Why would you use Ironwood? I thought that was a useless wood, all twisted and thorny."

"Twisted and thorny, it is. Do you know how hard it is to find an Ironwood sapling that is straight enough to yield a three foot section?"

"Why bother? Aren't most flutes Rosewood or Cherry?" Ulric asked. "They are so much easier to carve."

"You have to use special, hardened tools and files. The intricate carving gives it a special sound." Grady was looking at the flute, smiling.

"I have never heard you play it. Why?" Ulric asked like he was asking a very personal question.

Grady smiled, looking at the flute.

"As you know, I usually spend my winters in the south. I usually sell the flute there to finance my wandering without having to hire on with the Keepers or anyone else to be comfortable. After I sell it, I harvest another sapling there and spend the next year working it. I just didn't get south this winter..." He obviously left it hanging there.

"Can you even play it?" Ulric asked.

"I can play. I try not to play it, though. If I did, I may not be able to sell it. I usually only play it a few times once it's finished. This is the most beautiful one I have ever made. I have worked it much longer than in other years."

Ulric set down his mug and held out his hand. Grady handed it to him. He was ready for the weight this time. It felt like iron. He began to look closely at it. It was black and very smooth. It didn't really feel like wood because the grain was so dense. It was like a typical flute, but the carvings were a work of art. The density of the grain allowed incredible detail in the tiny carvings.

"Is this the valley at Collins Ford? And this is that beautiful fireplace at the inn by the Wickliffe River. That's me with my favorite clay pipe! And that's..." he was looking at a beautiful woman sleeping in bed.

A long pause followed as he examined the rest. Images carved from life during the last year. All were surrounded by vines and leaves. There were only a few inches that remained uncarved. The carvings became darker the lower they went: Arrow filled bodies, swords cast aside, a barn with a door open like a gaping maw.

"It's a diary. I had no idea. Why don't you play it?" Ulric asked, humbled, offering it back toward Grady handing it to him.

In answer Grady took it, stood, and put it to his lips.

Grady closed his eyes, took a few deep breaths, and began to play a familiar simple lullaby that Ulric knew. The tone and quality of the flute defied description. It was like the flute's tones were made of emotion instead of breath. It made tones deeper than he thought possible, its scale and range and volume the most beautiful he had ever heard.

He didn't realize tears had spilled until Grady had stopped playing and opened his eyes, saying, "I am unworthy to play it - a novice. In the right hands, you would not believe what it can do."

Ulric was left incredulous.

"This is the twelfth one I have made, my best yet. The carvings improve the tone somehow. This one has more than any other. I may fill the whole of it before I see home again." Grady sat and rolled out the oiled cloth his tools were in.

"I noticed you always disappeared in the winter. You have a home in the south as well? I thought that horrible rock cabin in Northknock was your home."

"For the summers. A base of operations. It keeps the rain off," Grady said.

"What are you carving tonight?" Ulric asked, taking another drink.

"The stone wall out there to the left and the six bumps in the snow," Grady said soberly.

"What will that mean to the one that buys it?" Ulric asked.

"The tales are part of the price of the flute. Whoever buys it will get an evening of stories that tell the flute's tale. It's one reason they pay so very much."

"What is it you do with all this money?"

"I invest it. Save it for my retirement. Spend some. I don't need much."

"Don't need much? I have never met anyone that needs less!" Ulric laughed and drank.

"I'm frugal and self-sufficient," Grady admitted.

The conversation lapsed. Grady carved and filed his flute. Ulric fell asleep in his chair.

Grady kept the fire going and eventually went and slept on the bed, fully dressed.

***

Ulric woke with a start, but his dream was slow to dissipate. It was the first time he had heard the cello in thirty years...

The music was quiet and sad. It made him remember home - his parent's estate. They had so many slaves then. But he wasn't dreaming. Was he? He rubbed his face hard with both hands, but the music didn't stop.

He sat up and pulled on his boots. They were dry now. He clumsily put two more logs on the failing fire.

But the quiet music kept playing. It was coming from somewhere outside. In the distance.

He was going mad. He needed to stay clear, to not let Grady know. He'd go out and have a quick look, but if Grady asked, he was going to the outhouse.

He went out as quietly as the door allowed.

The snow was deep now, more than a foot. He struggled to focus past the drink. How long had it been snowing, where was he, where WAS that music coming from?

He stepped into the darkness, letting his eyes adjust to the snowy night. The snow had stopped, and the moon was bright behind the clouds, but covered. The music was a bit louder. He walked toward the low stone retaining wall in front of him and looked directly down into a pasture surrounded by trees at the fence line, a perfect paddock. And in the center of the snow covered field was the form of a person playing the cello. He recognized the tune. It was Adagio in D minor by Tomaso Albinoni. He could not believe it.

He stared for a minute, and in the midst of it, she stopped and stood, staring back at him.

He turned and ran back and around to descend the path past the barn and to the field. The snow was deep and slowed him down very much, and when he got to the paddock he ran through the open gate into the middle of the field.

She was gone.

She was utterly gone. The snow was completely undisturbed, as if she had never been there. When had the music stopped? All he could hear was his blood pounding in his ears and his labored breathing. He looked around in all directions. He even looked back up to the top of the vine covered retaining wall.

Grady was standing there looking down to him.

Ulric hesitated and then waved.

Grady shook his head and turned back toward the cottage.

That is when he heard the whisper from the darkness.

"I remember you...Chris."

Ulric froze. He was unable to breathe.

Then after a moment, he ran.

He didn't stop until he was back inside that farm cottage. He realized he burst in a bit fast and slammed the door a bit too hard.

Grady was stirring the fire.

"I think I'm going mad," Ulric said.

"What else is new?" Grady said.

"No, I'm serious this time. Insane. I am hearing and seeing things."

"Really?" Grady glanced over at several empty bottles on the table.

Ulric followed his glance and a bit of doubt crept in.

"Like that time in Winton when the Black Trackers had come to kill you, but all they did was stand at the foot of your bed and watch you sleep?" Grady asked as he stood up straight to glare at him.

Ulric reddened but said, "It's not like that time. This was..." he was going to say "real" but then he remembered there were no tracks in the fresh snow.

"There are three more hours until dawn. Get some rest," Grady recommended. Ulric didn't argue.

There would be no rest. The cello had started again. He didn't dare mention it to Grady.

Ulric drank his way to oblivion. He woke to a raging headache and a mouth full of rancid wool. There was a fire in the hearth and a pitcher of water and a cup on the table next to the bed. The curtains were pulled closed to keep out the painful sunlight.

Driven outside by his bladder, he could hear Grady humming softly to the horses in the barn. The snow had stopped, and the skies were a hard gray. Looking to the meadow, he could see his own tracks going to a spot in the middle and returning in a panicked pattern.

Once relieved, he went to the barn. Grady was brushing the second horse. All three horses were eating grain in large amounts. Ulric knew there was more there than they could take with them.

There were many tools laid out on a bench. He didn't know what they were used for, but he understood that Grady knew. Hooves and tack maintenance of some kind.

Grady spoke first. "You're never going to touch another drop again, right?" He smiled and looked over the horse's back. When Ulric didn't initiate the standard set of curses, Grady's smile faded.

"Did you know that they say a frozen anvil is the best to lay your head upon?" Ulric said, and he touched the frost on the anvil that had formed as Grady's work had moistened the air.

"Yes. I've heard that. The cold distracts you so you don't know when the blow is coming, and the anvil rings louder so the horned one knows you're on the way," Grady said.

"Last night wasn't like the other times, Grady." Grady looked at him. Ulric's eyes were pleading. "It was a ghost. It took her years, decades, to find me. But it was her."

"Who?" Grady asked.

"She played the cello. Tunes I had forgotten. She had our family crest tattooed on her back, a moon with clouds...and one of her legs was...gone. Replaced by a steel pier. It had to be her."

"Let's say it WAS a ghost. We still need to make breakfast." Grady moved to the third horse.

"We will stay here today and leave tomorrow, in the morning. Give the horses a chance to rest and eat their fill. They also have a good tack room here. They won't mind if I refit a bit. They even have deep snow spats for the horses' legs."

Ulric said nothing. He always deferred to Grady on these matters. The last thing he wanted was to be on foot again. Grady could walk anywhere given the time. Not Ulric.

"Only one leg?" Grady asked the simple question. "Do you know her?"

Ulric was always surprised at how matter of fact Grady was. "Yes. Long ago. She was a...slave."

The word made Grady stop.

"A slave?" He asked.

"Yes. A household slave. She played and read for us. For me," Ulric said.

"I have known you to be thick at times, drunk often, a whore monger and worst of all a Keeper in the pulpit. But I have never heard you talk about having slaves. Crest marked slaves? Seriously?"

"Yes." It was a single word confession.

"Did you live in the southern isles then?" Grady was fishing for details about a past he had never heard about. "Twenty-five years ago?"

"Thirty-five actually. It was while I lived on my parents' estate. My father prided himself in not knowing how many slaves he had. It was over 300."

Grady had stopped now, listening intently. "All marked?" He could not keep the awe out of his voice.

"She played for me. She also..." He looked up, and Grady was wagging his eyebrows.

"No. Not that. She... She shaved my head."

"Now I'm jealous. By the way, I have a good edge. Anytime today would be good. Oh, and I found your hat."

CHAPTER TWENTY-EIGHT

But Not Your Blood

"The Shuttle Transport Unit identified Christopher Black by his HUD implant ID. He and his ship had disappeared decades before but he remained on the official Be On the Look Out (BOLO) list because of his family connections. Stu reported it to Em. Em immediately identified his connection to Chen. Stu never mentioned it, as he was never asked."

--Solstice 31 Incident Investigation Testimony Transcript: Emergency Module Digital Forensics Report. Independent Tech Analysis Team.

It took much longer to reach Greenwarren than they expected. When they finally approached, Ulric wished it had taken longer.

They could smell the smoke when they were still miles away. Grady knew what was burning. It was the first time they had smelled the greasy smoke of a funeral pyre this size.

Cautiously they approached the warehouse that burned. The snow was deep and undisturbed on the road. The first tracks they discovered were all around the huge fire.

Somehow, the warehouse had been collapsed into a giant pile before it was set ablaze. This did a much better job disposing of the bodies. The odd tracks surrounded the foundation and then led off down the road to the northeast, directly into the village.

"These look to be more than a day old," Grady stated with certainty.

"What kind of tracks are those? They are like hoof prints, but round with uniform claws, but huge," Ulric said, flask in hand.

They followed the tracks back to the center of town and straight out. They stabled the horses at the inn. There was lots of feed grain, hay and space.

Grady found the inside had been neatly stripped. Pots, pans, food, and worst of all, the liquor. A search of the cellar revealed that most of the wine was still there. It would have to do.

Grady set about making fires in the common room and in a bedroom on the same level.

Ulric claimed a bottle of wine and large chunk of cheese and sat in front of the fire.

"Why did they do it?" Ulric asked.

"Do what?" Grady groused.

"Burn them. Why bother?" Ulric looked in that direction.

"To chase their ghosts away on the smoke."

"Do you believe in ghosts, Grady?" Ulric asked.

"Yes I do, my Lord. Do you?"

"Yes. I believe a ghost led me here. I have no idea otherwise what the hell I am doing here."

"She sent us. We could not do otherwise," Grady said in a whisper and emptied his clay mug, one of the few that were left. He refilled it and Ulric's.

"I saw the High Keeper once, Grady. Did I ever tell you that story?"

"Yes my Lord," Grady said.

"It was at the winter festival in Exeter. It was a beautiful day, and I was shopping in the festival market with her. Suddenly, he was there in the same spice vendor's tent. I didn't recognize him, he was in plain clothes. But I recognized..."

"My brother, Tolwood." Grady finished for him then tossed back the rest of the cup's contents.

"Yes. I knew he was the Lord High Keeper's bodyguard," Ulric said.

"You talked about coastal curry," Grady said in a well-practiced tone.

"We spoke at length about excellent coastal curries," Ulric added.

Glasses were filled again and again. Ulric wasn't sure when Grady had gone to bed. The fire had grown low. The ghosts would come again soon.

Ulric was right. She did come. The silhouette he found in the corner of the great room could only be her. The outline of her short bobbed hairstyle was not allowed on this planet. Especially to slaves.

In the darkness, she said not a word. She moved to drink from a mug, but for no other reason.

"Why do you haunt me now?" he said to the darkness in the corner. The reply was barely a whisper.

"There is a great task that needs doing," she said.

"Yes, I know," Ulric confessed.

"And you are not the one to do it," she whispered.

"I also know this."

"There is a man that just wants to be left alone," she whispered.

"Yes?"

"And he is not you," she continued quietly.

"I don't deserve to be left alone."

"You will go to him," she ordered from the shadows.

"I was already."

"You will tell him everything he asks." She was very precise in the pronunciation of her words.

"I will?"

"Almost everything," she added.

"I have tried to forget everything," Ulric said.

"You will find peace there." The whisper became even more quiet.

"I will?" There was a trace of hope in his question.

"And pain. And death. And blood. So much blood." She whispered directly in his ear now.

Ulrich sobbed.

"But not your blood," she added.

"Why are you telling me this?" he begged.

"You will leave here in the morning. You will follow the tracks in the snow to the north. If you ever want to sleep again, you will never mention me, ever again." The threat was clear in her tone.

And she was gone. The weight of her was gone.

***

"Did something happen?" Grady asked as he climbed into the saddle. "Why so suddenly, so urgently?"

"We are not getting any younger," Ulric was in the saddle and starting to move already.

"I hate it when you drink so much strong tea." Grady, with the provisioned pack horse in tow, began to follow him.

They found the tracks easily. They were clear, and the road was easy. They made good time, far better than usual.

"Why are you so quiet today?" Grady asked, noting that he wasn't drinking either.

"I'm thinking about Cassandra. The image of her that you have on your flute." He fell silent again.

"She knew all along she would not see us all the way there," Ulric said.

"She knew the High Keeper was going to scour this region again. She also knew there was nothing she could do to stop it," Grady said.

"This time," Ulric finished. "It's the only thing that let her rest and let go in the end."

"Save me from prophecy. I don't want to know. But I promised her I'd get you to where you wanted to go," Grady said. "I never thought it would be here. I have never seen a place that needed a Keeper less than here."

They fell into silence again, moving north.

CHAPTER TWENTY-NINE

A Son of Earth

"Data corruption and deletions were widespread during this time. Detailed medical data did exist as a useful baseline for eventual subsequent events."

--Solstice 31 Incident Investigation Testimony Transcript: Emergency Module Digital Forensics Report. Independent Tech Analysis Team.

<<<>>>

Po held him as he burned. She had never felt a fever so hot.

The wounded areas swelled and bruised in the first few hours. They seemed to hum beneath her touch. A few hours after that, they cooled and began to recede.

She left his side only to bring him water. Even in his stupor, he knew enough to swallow. She held him through the afternoon, counting every shallow rapid breath. Afternoon turned to evening, evening to midnight, when the snow began to fall heavily, bringing a crushing hush on the gatehouse.

Sometime after midnight, she sensed a change in him, a relaxing. His breathing normalized. He seemed like he was just in a deep, heavy sleep.

Po cried again, silently this time.

As the tension faded from Barcus, it dissolved from Po as well.

She fell asleep.

***

Barcus woke up thirsty. The thirst was the rope that led him back to the light.

Then there was pain, a dull throbbing ache in his skull, a burning ache that felt like a weight on his chest.

His face itched. It was almost like the itch had a sound. A silent sizzle. He could feel it more than hear it.

When he tried to reach up and scratch, he realized Po was there, her head on his shoulder, her cool hand on his chest. His arm was around her. He could feel her skin beneath his hand.

He looked around the room, and his mind started working again.

Clever girl.

There was a half glass of water on the bedside table. It had been moved right up to the bed. He could reach it with his right hand.

Slowly he drank, eventually drinking the whole thing.

Using a tongue control, he activated his HUD and requested, "Status."

"You are awake," Em replied.

He restated the silent request, "Status."

"You have been unconscious for 17 hours and 49 minutes. Your primary concern right now is that you have lost a lot of blood. There are more Hemitropic Stims in your med kit, but you cannot take them without food and lots of water. Your blood pressure is very low. Do not try to stand."

Barcus whispered, "Why do my eyes itch so much?"

"She used too many Nanites. After delegation, the extra Nanites were dispatched to other areas. They detected a small amount of retina damage, a common issue with maintenance personnel. With most people actually.

"It has also begun to snow heavily. Po needs to attend to the animals soon. Olias will not be back until this afternoon, maybe longer.

"Po was awake until about an hour ago. She never left your side. She could use the sleep, and so can you."

Barcus had begun to fade before Em had finished the sentence.

***

Po was in a wonderful dream, and she struggled to stay asleep. Even as she said this to herself, the dream came into clearer focus. Barcus was holding her, warm and naked in bed. Her back was to his chest. His left arm was her pillow. His right hand held her left breast. Their legs were perfectly tangled and aligned. She could feel his soft breath at her ear and her neck.

Then he moved.

It seemed a vain attempt to increase the amount of skin in contact.

She opened her eyes. This was not a dream.

Her right hand covered his as he held her. The events of the day before came crashing back on her. She took a deep breath and held back the tears that wanted to come again. Gently, she rotated into him. His hand softly drifted off one breast and over the other as she turned, across her ribs, her back.

His eyes were open.

He was studying her face as she studied his. It was deeply bruised. The swelling was gone. The gash was now a ragged pink scar, almost completely healed.

"Thank you," Barcus whispered.

"You are not a Keeper, are you?" Po asked.

"No. I told you that," Barcus replied.

"What are you?" Po asked, nearly unable to speak as his fingers traced her spine.

"I am...thirsty," Barcus replied.

Po smiled and could not stop the tears, even though she laughed.

"I am afraid," she said.

"I will always protect you," Barcus whispered.

"I know, but that is not why I am afraid." She drew back a little so she could see his chest, examining him again. "I am afraid because I might have lost you, not because I am weak, but because I am ignorant." She sat up on one elbow, stretched her hand up to the windowsill, exposing her beautiful breasts inches from his face.

This is why he didn't see the gun she had retrieved from the sill until the muzzle was next to his face.

"This is a weapon." She let him take it and place it on the table. "And that," she pointed at the still open med kit. "That is magic medicines. I think I need to know these things before stories about cute kittens finding their mothers."

"That," she pointed at the Plate, "is more than it seems. Now it's more than a Keeper's Plate."

She sat all the way up, without being self-conscious. "And this is impossible." She traced the jagged scar. It was pink and new. "It looks six weeks healed already."

"You're right. I need to tell you everything. You may not believe me," Barcus said through a scratchy voice.

"You need water!" She began to climb out of the bed and the

moment she was climbing over his naked hips, straddling him, is when she seemed to realize she was naked. Their eyes met for a moment, then she was off him.

She picked up her bloody dress and held it to her chest as she poured water for him. Realizing how bloody it was, she dropped it again and went to a chest and took out another one just like it. She stepped into it, and as she buttoned it at the nape of her neck, her stomach growled loudly.

"Po, I have lost a lot of blood. I need to take some medicine, but I can't on an empty stomach."

Po looked down into the med kit. "You will tell me everything?"

"Yes, if you can keep secrets," Barcus answered.

She turned and trotted out of the room. She returned just a few minutes later with a tray of bread, honeyed butter, cheese, ham and whole apples. There was a small pitcher of milk, too. She helped him sit up and put the tray in his lap. She drank deeply from the pitcher and, while licking her milk mustache, she handed it to Barcus who did the same.

In silence, they shared the cold breakfast like it was a feast.

Po put a kettle on for tea and came back looking at the case and asked, "All right. Tell me what is next."

"There is a white bottle in the lower right that is labeled 'Hemitropic Stims' that is full of pills. Do you know what a pill is?"

"Is this it?" She held up the correct bottle. "What is it?"

"Hand it to me. I'll show you." He opened the bottle, shook out one pill, and closed the bottle. "This is called a Hemitropic Stim pill. I need this because I have lost a lot of blood. Loss of blood makes you weak. Lose enough and you die. This is a drug that helps my body replace the lost blood. But I need to drink a lot of water for it to work well."

"Will this work on anyone? Or just Keepers?" she asked.

"Anyone," Barcus answered.

"What if you take it without food or water?" she asked.

"You will hurt your stomach, maybe enough to make you vomit blood. Never take it alone. Take it with food and water at least. Never alone."

"What if I take one now, uninjured, with lots of food and water?" she asked.

"Well, it won't hurt you. Actually, in a day or two, you will be able to hold your breath longer. Run farther without running out of breath. It lasts a week or two. But they are too valuable to waste like that."

"Tell me about that." She pointed at the handgun. "I know that is magic. I saw you use it. It killed the Telis. There is thunder in there."

"It is a projectile weapon, like a crossbow, but more powerful. It's called a handgun. It's very dangerous. And I want you to learn how to use it, just not now. When I am better, I will teach you."

"Will this work for anyone? Or just Keepers?"

"Anyone. If you know how," Barcus said.

"All of these things are forbidden, aren't they?" She looked at the handgun.

"More than you know," he answered.

***

The next day they were finished with lessons by midday. They were packing the rifle back into its case as she asked, "Why is the rifle so much quieter, even though it seems far more powerful?"

"This rifle has a device called a suppressor. It keeps it quiet." He indicated the 'muzzle' end of the rifle, *the end where the death comes out.* "It is made to be quiet to protect your hearing and to keep your location a secret. It adds size to the rifle, though. The handgun could have one, but then it would be bigger and more difficult to carry it."

She was taking it all in as if it was not any big deal. She had a real knack for the AR. Barcus knew she considered it all to be magic. Even though he answered every one of her questions, he could now see why it was a consistent opinion. Once she had gotten past the taboo of it, she embraced it. Just like reading. She was very good with the rifle. Especially good. Unnaturally good.

He was rubbing his eyes, trying not to scratch his healing wounds.

She was there, gently pulling his hands down from his eyes. They were just outside the gatehouse. "You need to drink and eat and rest now."

He was looking at her. He wanted to say something. "I am not a Keeper. I never was."

"I don't care," she said.

"I hate them. I'd kill them all if I could," Barcus said.

"I believe you," she said.

"I'm lost. I don't know what to do except survive," he said.

"You and I are the same then," she said.

"I will tell you everything if you want me to," he said.

She nodded.

"I came from the sky. Not across the sea, not far over land. Not anywhere in this whole world," Barcus confessed.

"There is a fable I heard as a child, about a man that came here from heaven," she said.

"Oh, what did he do?" Barcus asked.

"He died. They killed him," she said.

Barcus smiled. "Nice story. It is told to children?"

"The Keepers would kill anyone who told the story. It was forbidden." She looked up to his face. "That ensured everyone whispered it," she said.

She was still rubbing her wrists. He could tell she was working up to another highly taboo question.

"Have you ever been to...Earth?"

He raised an eyebrow at that. "Yes. I was born there. It was my home, until I left for the sky. How do you know of Earth?"

"Earth is the place they scare children with whispers in the dark. Death lives there," Po said.

She touched the scar on his face. "I still believe it. You are a Son of Earth. I have seen your wake. And I am still not afraid."

"Saying any of that out loud ensures a visit to the anvil," she said.

"Ash and Em are both soulless demons, made from stone and death, tools and reason," she said.

She sounded like she was reciting something from memory.

"But they are my demons. Ours," Barcus said.

"They are coming," Em interrupted.

CHAPTER THIRTY

Barcus is Thirsty

"The actions of Po during this time made us begin to suspect that there was more to her than a slave. The EM tested her Intelligence Quotient and discovered it was 162."

--Solstice 31 Incident Investigation Testimony Transcript: Emergency Module Digital Forensics Report. Independent Tech Analysis Team.

<<<>>>

They heard Ash long before they could see him.

His feet were pounding in the road, despite the muffling effect of the snow. Barcus and Po stood at the gatehouse entrance on the small bridge that crossed the shallow moat ditch in front of the door. They could see Ash moving with ease directly toward them from a kilometer off.

Em had already acknowledged their proximity, and Barcus was watching her progress as she approached from the north. A regional HUD map seemed to hang in the air five meters in front of Barcus showing everyone's position relative to The Abbey.

Ash slowed to a gentle walk as he made his final approach. He towered above them as he began to cross the bridge.

Po surprised Barcus by stepping right up in front of Ash and placing her hand in the center of his smooth, black chest.

"Ashigaru," she addressed him formally, "I know what you are. Would you harm me for knowing?"

Ash actually knelt, coming closer. It was still taller than Po by a meter, but the gesture was not missed.

"My Lady, even I do not yet know what I am. But I would see myself utterly destroyed before I allowed you to come to harm," Ash said quietly in his deep voice.

"I know you have no soul," Po added.

"In this, you may be wrong," Ash said as he rested a massive hand on Barcus's shoulder.

She had not expected these answers. She seemed to falter.

"Feed him and put him to bed. He is lying to you. He is pretending to be well. He is about to fall down," Ash said to her.

Ash stood easily. "I will wait for Pardosa."

It was true. When she looked closely at Barcus, he was pale and sweating, even though a breeze had brought new flakes of snow. She led him to his chair in front of the fire. She brought hot tea, bread and cheese while she began to cook.

Lunch was ready by the time Olias came in.

"Par told me that a Telis got in The Abbey and ate a goat," he said excitedly in common tongue.

Po replied in common, as if it was nothing, "Yes. It's still here."

Olias blasted water out his nose and sputtered, "W...w...what?"

"It's over in the paddock. You can't miss it. The huge hill covered with snow."

He looked Barcus in the face for the first time to see if there was amusement there to confirm the joke Po was playing. That's when he saw the scar on his face.

Without a word, he abandoned his still steaming bowl of stew and ran out to the paddock. It was five minutes before he came back, sitting down again before his cooling bowl.

Po said, "Do you think the meat could be tasty? Get Ash to help you hang it up and butcher it. It will be the first meat for the winter locker. Oh, the goat it killed too, please, what's left of it." She was sopping her stew up with a piece of bread.

His look of fear began to shift following the look on her face. The smile preceded his words in common, "I can't leave you alone for a few days without you getting into trouble, can I?"

***

That evening, Barcus, Po and Olias talked long into the night about the new salvage that had been brought in on this load. They discussed the need to remove the rubble that allowed the Telis Raptor to get over the wall, even as Ash was moving it. They talked about the repairs in The Abbey, the weather and honey bees and orchards and vineyards.

Po watched Barcus closely. He knew she was watching. She could not believe the amount of water, tea, milk and wine Barcus drank without ever going to the privy.

Olias had gone off to his own rooms and Po had cleaned up.

"Rest," was all she said, as she helped him to his feet. She was very aware how much bigger he was than her as she made him stand there so she could check his wounds without anything in the way.

He allowed it without protest. She removed his belt, safely handling the handgun it held. Just as he had taught her. She took off his tunics, baring his chest. His drawstring pants hung low on his hips.

The flesh was soft and very white along the wound, like a baby's skin, freshly made. She gently washed it but did not use the liquid bandage on it again. She was amazed again at the size of the wound.

She made him sit on a chair so she could do the same for his face. She washed it gently. She used her own brush to comb his hair back.

She removed his boots and socks and hung his clothes on pegs or placed them in baskets where they belonged. She drew back the bed clothes.

She helped him to his feet and led him to the edge of the bed. As she looked up into his eyes, she untied the drawstring on the front of his pants. They fell to his ankles, and he stepped back out of them with the help of her bare foot holding them down in the center. He sat back and slid under the quilts to the far side of the bed.

Po reached up to the single button at the base of her neck and released it. Her dress fell of its own weight, thick as it was for winter. She climbed into bed with him, her head resting on his bicep, her naked back towards him, as his arms closed around her.

He was so warm, still fevered. She felt so small there. His left hand wrapped around her, and his nose burrowed into the nape of her neck.

She felt the exhaustion take him. Soon, his body twitching made her smile. He was so warm, but now she knew he still had a fever caused by the Nanites as they worked. Their legs entwined and her arm reached back to hold him, her palm on the base of his spine.

She willed her life force into him again. She knew it would work as she drifted off.

She woke in the dark. The only light was from the low coals of the fire. She was stretched out and warm. And alone.

She listened to the darkness but heard nothing. She slid from the warm bed and retrieved her knife from where her belt hung on its peg. A shadow moved beyond the curtain in the main room. Using the tip of the knife, she carefully drew aside the curtain enough for a peek.

The fire blazed in that room. Barcus was silhouetted in the firelight with his back directly to her. Both his hands were raised, holding the large pitcher to his mouth.

"Did no one ever teach you to use a proper cup?" Her voice sounded loud in the quiet room as she stepped in.

It startled him a little, and a quantity of water splashed down to his chest.

"I'm still so thirsty. I'm sorry." He meant it.

"Don't be." She entered and went to the rack where towels dried. "The jug, the water and the thirst are all yours," she said.

She moved as if she had no idea she was naked.

It was obvious that Barcus was noticing.

"The Hemitropic Stims seem to be working," she said as she dried his chest. Water had run down to his hip bone, and she slowly dried all the way down to it. As she dried him, she looked into his eyes. They sparked in the firelight.

"Did you know I am free? Free to do what I like?"

"Yes," he whispered.

"Did you know I am free to say 'yes' as well as 'no' whenever I like?" She smiled and returned to bed.

CHAPTER THIRTY-ONE

Cassandra

"The Emergency Module was now outside the parameters of all out known protocols. It was somehow acting irrationally. Decision trees could no longer be followed. Data corruption was increasing. Barcus never noticed. Much of this data is still under forensic analysis by the team because it makes no sense."

--*Solstice 31 Incident Investigation Testimony Transcript: Emergency Module Digital Forensics Report. Independent Tech Analysis Team.*

The snow stopped as they continued to make their way. Grady had not seen Ulric this serious or sober in many years. He was even leading the way.

Now and again he would stop, usually on a rise, and look into the distance. Grady didn't know he was looking for the ghost and finding it often in the distance.

That night the snow was a blizzard. All the tracks they were following were gone.

"Ulric, sorry to bother you with petty, practical considerations, but we will reach a point where we only have enough rations to make it back to Greenwarren." Grady was used to his silence but not THIS kind of total silence.

"We will be fine," Ulric said. The forest was deep here. The trees were old growth and limited the amount of light and snow and underbrush. This served to make the going easier as well as possibility of getting lost. It was all the same in every direction.

"If riding in a circle for days is fine," Grady grumbled.

"Grady, have you ever been to this forest before? Has anyone? Ever?" They were riding by a tree that was so big, ten men with arms extended would not reach around it.

"Why do these trees never fall?" Ulric asked.

Before Grady could consider an answer, he noticed a change in the nature of the light in the direction they were moving. Not a clearing, but something.

Ulric could see her waiting there in the distance between the trees. One leg was a shining steel piling below the knee. Her arms were fit and impossibly bare in the cold. She walked off to Ulric's left, falling out of view.

"What is it?" Grady's had not missed Ulric's noticing.

"I believe it's a road," Ulric stated.

Grady saw it was a road. As the horses stepped over the wide curb onto it, he looked in both directions at the unmarked snow.

Ulric went to the north without hesitation.

Grady reached around and drew a well-oiled map from the pack he always wore. Looking up at the arch of the forest canopy, he knew he had no idea where this was. His map had no road in this region, much less a road of such workmanship. Few saplings had caught hold there. Tree fall was scattered randomly, but the road was sound.

It was completely unmapped.

"If I had to bet money, I'd say we were somewhere far north of the Salterferry Bridge. Way farther north of the unfinished tunnel. I will need some night sky to be sure." He folded his map and placed it once again in his pack.

The road was wide. It was so wide, four wagons could roll side by side without a single nervous driver.

"I have never seen any roads like this so far north," Grady said.

Ulric wasn't listening. His eyes were focused in the distance. A stone arch could be seen far off, with a small tower to the left side, its windows empty, save one. There she stood, waiting for him. He'd have to go. If he didn't, he knew she would come to him and steal his sleep. She would torment him in the darkness with a past he didn't want to remember and could not drown in drink if she was at his ear, reminding him of things he had forgotten, perhaps never even knew. Like the names he never knew.

So he would do as she asked.

***

"The tower arch is a way point, just as they have in the south. It was a traveler's shelter, somewhere to rest and keep warm in safety." The wooden door had frozen closed, and it took them both to force open the rusted hinges. The stable there was full of dry leaves, but serviceable.

"It's better than sleeping rough," Ulric said with a suspicious lack of complaints.

There was a stack of firewood stored in the alcove. The wood was covered in cobwebs and drier than any Grady had ever seen.

"Get a fire started, and I will tend to the horses," Grady said as he exited, roughly pulling the door closed behind him.

Instead of starting the fire, Ulric went directly up the stairs that spiraled up in the back of the room. The door at the top still swung easily, if not loudly, into the room above. Windows on all four sides of this room were broken in several places. The door that led out onto the arch was gone completely.

She stood there looking onto the arch.

"Cassandra warned me, you know." He waited for a reaction. Her back was to him, naked in the cold except for the massive tattoo there. The livery he had tried to forget.

"Did you meet Cassandra on this planet? What do you think she warned you about, Chris? You don't mind if I call you Chris? I always did when we were alone. Remember?" She turned to him. Her eyes glowed golden, like a cat's in firelight.

"She was my wife. She sent us here." Ulric's voice was a trembling, graveling whisper. "She told me my days would end in the north, with madness, and clarity, and anger and war and pain and no peace until the end." He waited for her to say something. She didn't.

"And I came anyway. Because without her, what difference did it make?" Ulric said.

"Cassandra was your wife? They don't allow wives on this planet. Especially for Keepers. She wanted you to do something here? Find Something? Someone?" she asked turning back to the open doorway, relieving him of her gaze.

"She said I'd know what to do." He said it like an oath.

"Yes. I believe you will. We will find out tomorrow." She walked out the door. When Ulric went to follow, the arch was empty.

He called after her into the hush. "Chen?"

When Grady returned, the fire was lit but burning a bit high for that hearth. The room was warming quickly, even the floor.

"Anything upstairs?" Grady asked.

"How'd you know I went upstairs?" Ulric deflected, giving him a moment to think.

"The cobwebs are gone. Well not gone, exactly." Grady pointed at his cloak, where it was covered in them.

"Nothing. No one has been here for a long time," Ulric said, fishing out a camp pot to fill with snow.

"It's been decades. The hinges are rusty and this wood is so dry, it won't last one night. I'll have to cut some more to leave for the next traveler," Grady said.

"What do you mean? You think someone will come through again in another 50 years?" Ulric was actually curious.

"It may be us, my Lord, at the very least when we return," Grady said as he was unpacking bed rolls.

Ulric realized he had not considered a return journey. Still shaken by the visitation, he reached for his flask for the first time today.

After a long pull, he said, "I think we will get there tomorrow. Wherever there is."

Grady stood and looked at him, considering his statement for a long beat, but said nothing.

***

"Barcus, I have detected two men that are moving this direction on the ancient road. ETA at present speed is seven hours and twelve minutes," Em told Barcus, as he was helping Olias sort a trunk full of nails and wire and various small tools.

"Shall I send Ash to deal with them?" she asked. The implication by her tone was that Ash would simply kill them quickly. A visual of the two men and their pack horse came up in his HUD. One man was tall, thin and weathered, obviously an experienced Tracker. The other one was a bit of a mystery. He had the look of being out of shape and out of his element, though it was evident that he had lost weight recently from hardship. His clothes were not as practical as a Tracker's.

"No. Just keep an eye on them for now. They are not soldiers. They don't have weapons."

Olias had become used to Barcus talking to Em. When he looked up, Barcus asked in common tongue, "Olias, do you have your Plate with you?"

Olias nodded and drew it out of a deep pocket somewhere.

Barcus took it for a moment and said, "What can you tell me about these men?" Handing back the Plate, there was an image of two men on horseback.

He spoke in common tongue. "This one is a Tracker. I have actually seen him before, but have never spoken to him and not seen him for years. I have never seen that one. He looks like a Lesser Keeper. That neckline on his tunic is only worn by them. They usually have shaved heads. Like that." He pointed.

Olias zoomed out with adept control to show the entire horses as well. "These are typical farm horses." His accent slipped. "A bit old and sway-backed compared to ours."

He was referring to the High Keeper's horses in the stalls next door. "They sport northern tack, and they even have deep snow spats. We should add those to the lists." A window popped up in Barcus's HUD with the items added to the "stable" list.

"Why would they be coming here?" Barcus asked him.

Olias scratched his head. "Refugees?" He struggled with the word in common. Barcus had not even considered that.

"Well, we will find out. They will be here by dinnertime," Barcus said, handing back the Plate.

"I will tell Po there will be two more for dinner." He looked like he was about to run off when he hesitated. "Barcus. She... If he is a Keeper, she'll..." he fell back into rapid common tongue.

"The Keeper will require things for hospitality sake, things that she won't like anymore. They will be obliged, even required, to take her to the anvil for so many things. She won't. I mean..." He was stammering now.

"I'll tell her, Olias. Get some rooms ready and prepare the stables." The boy ran off.

Barcus found her on the wall, far above the kitchen with a chimney sweep's tool for extracting nests. Fearlessly, she stood atop the uncapped chimney, even though it was a 50 foot drop to the rocky ditch on the other side of the wall.

The nest was soon extracted and the chimney brushed out. She handed him the long pole extensions as they came out and were detached. Then she lightly dropped down to the walkway, holding Barcus's hand.

"Thanks." She smiled through soot on her face.

Barcus noticed the total absence of "my Lord."

"Em tells me that there are two men riding this way from the south. They should be here around dusk."

"Two men?" Instantly serious, she wiped her face roughly with her apron.

"Olias thinks one of them is a Lesser Keeper." Her eyes involuntarily drifted to where she knew his handgun was concealed in the folds of his clothes.

"I will show you on your Plate."

She took the book from her ever present pouch and handed it to him. The same view was there when he opened it.

"Can you tell me anything about them?" Barcus asked. It took only a single glance to return the deep crease between her brows. She stared for a moment and looked away, out over the wall to the south.

"It's over," was all she said.

"What's over?" Barcus asked.

She stabbed at the plate with her finger as she pointed. "He is a Tracker and he is a Keeper. It's over. This unlikely peace that I have found, it won't stand." The crease grew deeper. She was getting angry.

Barcus said nothing, waiting.

"I can't do it anymore. I won't." She was looking at his eyes. Defiant. "I will not wash another filthy Keeper's cock even if he's been in the saddle for a month." She started pacing. "I will never let another one of those child FUCKERS ever touch me again!" She leaped up onto the battlement out of his reach, with her back to the edge. "I would rather jump than even avert my eyes." She drew her knife in a flash as tears spilled, pointing it at his throat. "You have done this to me. You and your sorcery! How did you do it?" She was screaming at him. "How did you make me desire death more than the touch of any, save you? How can I be so completely undone?"

Barcus slowly advanced, and the knife point withdrew as if there was a force field around him. By the time he had his arms around her, the knife had clattered to the stones. Her arms surrounded his neck, and her face buried under his chin.

"I swear on my life that no one will ever touch you again uninvited, even me." He lifted her from the rampart and turned to sit on its edge, holding her as she trembled.

She drew back and pounded his chest once hard with both hands. "I never cried before, either." She palmed her eyes further, smearing the tracks in the soot before looking deep into his eyes. "Is the magic of yours somehow connected to my tears?" She wasn't screaming anymore. He thought she was teasing him now.

"What should we do?" Barcus asked her.

"First of all, you cannot talk to me when they are here. I don't think you could talk to me in any way but this, so best not at all." She had moved that quickly to planning.

"I'm not sure that will work," Barcus said.

"The first time that Keeper so much as touches me, I will slit his throat. I will leave the Tracker to you, or better yet, Ash. He won't hesitate to pound him down like a tent peg."

Barcus remained silent, letting her finish.

"I'm sorry." She rested her forehead on his. "I meant it though."

"It isn't over. It will just be different," he said.

"How do you know?" she asked serious.

"There are no happy endings, Po. Because nothing ends."

243 | Martin Wilsey

CHAPTER THIRTY-TWO

Close to the Edge

"Chen's ghost in Ulric's HUD was a mystery until we realized it was Em using yet another method to manipulate these people. But these prophecies remained a mystery. How can this be coded? It can't."

--Solstice 31 Incident Investigation Testimony Transcript: Emergency Module Digital Forensics Report. Independent Tech Analysis Team.

<<<>>>

It took the efforts of both Po and Olias to convince Barcus that it would be easier and safer if Po did not dine with them. She would become very scarce, in fact. Olias would see to their needs when they arrived. Barcus agreed that it may be the best way to avoid bloodshed. The table was drawn away from the wall and set for four. Barcus would send them away. Quickly.

For the first time, the braziers at the four corners of the southern entrance bridge were lit. Barcus was amazed at how fast the ice on the bridge melted as well as the short way to the gate door that was now open. The braziers must have had heating coils as well.

"Barcus, I have been watching these men all day and have come to an interesting assessment," Em said as she walked into the light and warmth of the braziers. She even held out her hands to warm them.

"These men have no idea where they are or where they are going. The Keeper, his name is Ulric, has been drinking steadily for the last hour and seems very nervous. The Tracker's name is Grady and is about as formal with this Keeper as we are with each other."

"Why are they here? Do you have any idea?" Barcus asked.

"The Tracker has referred to a prophecy on several occasions, usually while cursing." A window opened, showing the men talking. Several parts were cut together in the view.

"Damn you and your bloody prophecy." Cut.

"You and your filthy prophecy will get us killed." Cut.

"Damn prophecies and the fools that follow them." Cut.

Then a different scene showed, "I can smell the chimneys, Ulric. Chimneys, not open fires. What will you tell them? You have to tell them something. Should I scout ahead?" Grady said.

"I have no idea. We will be fine," Ulric said. "Do you smell that?" His eyes widened a bit. "Fresh bread!"

"You think she sent us all this way for fresh bread? Bloody hell..." Grady fell into mumbling.

***

Barcus was sitting on a stone bench sipping a mug of hot tea as the men approached.

They could see The Abbey from over a kilometer away with the braziers lit. Barcus watched them slowly approach, but didn't get up from the bench. He sipped his tea. He knew Par was out there in the darkness, weapons targeted on these men.

"Good evening, my Lords." The words felt awkward for Barcus. But they had convinced him to use them. "Out for a bit of a ride tonight I see?" There was humor and goodwill in his voice.

"Greetings, my Lord..." Ulric began, but before he could continue, Barcus interrupted.

"Please call me Barcus, just Barcus, and come in. You must be cold and hungry. Olias! Come help with their horses." Olias came out and took hold of the reins of both horses as the men looked at each other. The men dismounted.

Grady spoke in common tongue. "Hello, lad. My name is Grady. What say we leave the grownups to talk?" He glared at Ulric and followed Olias in, walking his horse.

Ulric said, "Somehow, you knew we were coming."

After a pause Barcus said, "Somehow, you knew we were here."

"I'm Ulric. Do I smell bread?" With a smile and a slight bow to each other, they went in.

***

The horses were settled in quickly, and Olias showed the men to rooms above the stables that had been prepared for them. They were modest in size, but private. They washed up and left their things.

Olias waited for them out on the balcony until they were ready.

The moon was high, and the snow made the scene brighter and more haunting at the same time. The hulking ruin of the northern tower loomed above.

"Follow me," was all he said as he skipped down the stairs and back into the willow courtyard, where he waited for them to catch up. Once they did, he knocked gently on the gatehouse door and entered.

Barcus was sitting in one of the armchairs, reading about bee keeping. He rose to greet them, leaving his book on the chair.

Grady took Ulric's cloak to hang on a peg as he looked all around the small room.

"What is this place?" Ulric asked as they began to sit. Olias exited, and Grady sat opposite Ulric.

"We call it Whitehall Abbey. I have no idea what it's really called. It was a ruin when I found it this autumn, still is, I suppose, except for this bit here."

"How many are you?" Grady asked.

"There are only three of us." He answered with reluctance in his voice.

"How did you come to be in this place?" Grady continued. Ulric had spotted the whiskey on the shelf by the door.

The question was never answered. Just then, the door opened and Olias entered. He had a large tray that he set down on the table and began transferring crocks and baskets to the table.

It was to be a simple dinner. Stew with bread, butter, cheese and stewed apples over biscuits for dessert.

"May the High Keeper bless you, my Lord. I could smell that bread baking a mile away," Ulric said as he ripped off a chunk from the loaf.

Grady didn't even seem to notice Olias.

They dug in.

Ulric spent the entire meal describing how horrible a cook Grady was. And how he had been nearly driven to voluntary starvation by sawdust flavored hard tack. The conversation was cheerful until Grady asked about the apples in the dessert as he took his last bite.

Olias immediately said in common tongue, without thinking, "I got them from the larder at the inn in Greenwarren."

The looks on their faces revealed that they had been there.

"It's dark days above the gorge," Grady said. "I've seen things, dark things." He held his cup out, and Olias refilled it. "This was once the most beautiful countryside in the entire world. I would spend my summers here in peace." His eyes focused on Barcus. "Have you seen the High Keeper's mercenaries?"

"I've seen what's left of them," Barcus replied. "They are not the only thing out there. It's why we've holed up here, to hide, to be left alone."

Just then, they heard the gate door close.

Olias chimed in with common, "There was a Telis Raptor! It ate one of our goats!" Olias was stopped there by the look Barcus gave him.

"Bloody hell," Grady cursed. "No wonder you are inside walls. I was wondering."

"So where are you from, Ulric?" Barcus asked, as the dessert dishes were cleared away by Olias. Po never appeared.

"A city very far away. You'd never believe how far."

"Try me. What city?" Barcus asked.

"It's called Buffalo," he said almost absently.

Barcus froze. Grady noticed, but Ulric continued. "The winters were just like this there. So much snow." He emptied his cup. "It was the lakes near there, just as it is here."

"He is drawing a knife," Em said in his head as she opened a window that showed the knife in Grady's hand just below the edge of the table.

"How long have you been a Keeper, Barcus?" Grady asked, measuring him.

"I am no Keeper," Barcus answered.

"You do understand it is forbidden to live within a fortification," Grady said as he looked at the book Barcus had been reading.

Barcus said nothing.

"Where is she?" Grady asked. "The woman you are hiding? Why are you hiding her?"

Barcus did not expect that question or his own reaction. Instantly Barcus was on his feet, his handgun drawn, pointing at the center of Grady's chest. Ulric's eyes had gone wide. Grady simply sat up a bit taller and looked directly into the muzzle of the gun.

"Say the word." It came, though, as a whisper through clenched teeth as Po advanced slowly through the center of the curtain between the rooms. First the muzzle of the AR, then the rifle as she followed in a perfect advancing stance, just as Barcus had taught her. The LASER dot was on the center of Ulric's body.

"Say the word," she repeated.

"I feel I should apologize in advance here. But you need to understand that since coming here, everyone I have met has tried to kill me except Po and Olias." Barcus moved back a bit as he spoke.

The initial shock faded from Ulric's face. Grady remained still except for an eyebrow raising glance at Ulric that clearly said "this is all your fault again."

Risking getting shot, Ulric pushed back from the table and grabbed his empty cup and moved to the sideboard saying, "Well if I am going to be murdered, I refuse to die thirsty." He lifted a bottle of bourbon and started pouring.

A shot rang out and the bottle exploded in Ulric's hand, the bullet impacting the stone wall just behind. He flinched, his hand going to his neck and coming away bloody.

"You shot me!" he whined.

"Sit down, Ulric. They're serious." Grady still had not moved a muscle.

"All right. I give up. I don't care anymore," Ulric said.

"Did you ever care?" Grady snapped.

"Why did you even follow me here?" Ulric was talking to Grady.

"Follow you? You couldn't lead yourself to the bottom of the ocean if you were drowning," Grady quipped.

"I got us here didn't I?" Their volume was increasing.

"Only because Cassandra pointed your teetering ass in this direction," Grady said a bit louder.

"Don't you even say her name, you ungrateful bastard. I never knew why she liked you." Ulric drank deeply.

"She liked me because I was the only one left willing to put up with your horse shit. She LOVED me for it, knowing that I actually cared enough to even try to keep your drunken ass alive. And now you've gone and gotten us killed."

"Let me kill them to just shut them up," Po inserted. They both fell silent and looked at her because her tone was so serious.

"Tell me why you came here," Barcus said quietly.

"She said we had to come here," Grady replied.

"She said I had to come here, not you," Ulric corrected. The argument was about to renew when Po bumped the muzzle of the suppressor to his temple.

"Why did this Cassandra ask you to come here?" Barcus was more menacing as his voice got lower.

"She had a vision about a way off of this planet. We had been here so long. Her longevity treatments were due when we crashed on this godforsaken planet. She only lived another thirty-one years. She died three days after the sky fall last autumn. Was that you? Your ship? Stumbling into this godforsaken orbit?"

He said nothing.

"She told me to come here. She said I'd know what to do. So I will drink." He emptied his mug, spitting out a piece of glass. "I loved her. I always trusted her. She said I'd know what to do, so what I think I should do is go to bed. It's been a long day."

With that, he stood and walked again to the sideboard and picked up another bottle, looking over his shoulder and shielding it from Po with his body.

He walked out. They let him.

Em had Ulric in a window for Barcus as Ulric stumbled up to his room above the stables.

Grady stood and gave them a formal bow saying quietly, earnestly, "My Lord, I give you my oath that we will do you no harm, any of you." He slowly laid his belt knife on the table. Then slowly, he added two boot knives Barcus had not spotted. Nodding, he followed Ulric.

Behind Po and Barcus, Olias was heard behind the curtain. "What did he mean by 'crashed on this planet'?" Olias asked as he walked through the curtains, carrying a loaded crossbow.

CHAPTER THIRTY-THREE

The Telis Tail

"The speed of Po's learning to read, use of the plate, the med kit and the firearms should have been noticed. Especially, when contrast with Olias. This observation is beyond the scope of this team but is worthy of note."

--Solstice 31 Incident Investigation Testimony Transcript: Emergency Module Digital Forensics Report. Independent Tech Analysis Team.

<<<>>>

Barcus woke alone on the next morning.

"Em, status."

"All is well," she said. This was not her typical method of giving her morning status.

"Where is everyone?"

"Po is in the kitchen, where she has the larger oven working. It is the one where she cleared the chimney. Olias is still sleeping. He was awake most of the night in case our guests needed anything. He left Grady's knives on a small table outside his door, like you asked." A tactical map opened in his HUD showing all the locations. "Par and Ash are in the garage. Grady is 2.3 kilometers to the northeast, close to the quarry. Ulric is still in bed."

Windows of Ulric and Grady opened.

Grady was just drawing his bow. He loosed his arrow and remained still.

Ulric was clothed, face down on the bed, snoring. He closed that window.

Grady slowly walked up to a small deer lying in the snow, another arrow nocked in case it got up. He touched the tip of the arrow to its eye. It didn't blink. He replaced the arrow in its quiver and hung the quiver, the bow and his small pack from a nearby tree and took a small knife from his pack.

Barcus closed all the windows, saying. "Em, keep me informed."

"Yes, Barcus."

***

He got dressed and went to the kitchen, where Po was already busy kneading bread dough.

"Good morning, Barcus. Did you get any sleep at all?" she asked.

"Some. More than I expected."

"Grady went hunting. He said there will be fresh venison for dinner. Somehow I believe him. I got to speak with him early this morning over tea." She finished a loaf and set it aside, "He has no idea why he is here, beyond watching over Ulric." She started on the next braided loaf. "Ulric was a Lesser Keeper, in the south, in a small village. Grady would do specific work for that village back then, decades ago. He would guide Ulric on trips to odd places. Summers in the north sometimes, winters in the south other times, to the Citadel a few times." She wiped her hands on her apron. "He was looking for something, or someone. Maybe it was you all along. That's what Grady thinks. He's content with that. Such an odd man."

"I need to have a long talk with Ulric when he wakes up." Barcus grabbed a bowl for some oatmeal.

***

Barcus was on top of the wall, planning the last of the repairs, when he saw Grady below, dragging a small deer.

He stepped off and lightly landed on a large rock atop the rubble outside the wall. He knew they needed to eliminate this pile to be secure. The sound caught Grady's attention, and he stopped to rest.

"Here, let me help," Barcus said, as he took the cord from him that he was using to drag the deer. Barcus tied the front feet and then the back feet together and slung the deer over his shoulder like he was carrying luggage.

They walked slowly as it began to snow again.

"My knee says we are in for a blizzard," Grady said, giving his leg a shake.

"Good work, getting the deer," Barcus remarked.

"Game is good in these parts. Did you really kill a Telis Raptor? They go where the game is best," Grady said.

"Yes. But it was almost the end of me," Barcus admitted.

"The way Po tells it, the beast tore you up good – you instead of her." Grady was watching him.

"Grady, I apologize about what happened. I don't know what to say. For what it's worth, I would not have killed either of you."

"Lie to yourself boy, but don't lie to me. No offense. But if you thought that girl was in danger, you'd kill me faster 'n you could lace your boots."

The boots Barcus wore had no laces.

"No need to apologize. Best forget. Ulric likely will. Usually does." Grady paused, then continued. "He has no idea why he came here. He is sure it was to see you."

They entered through the south gate, walking directly to the open air kitchen and then into the butchery. Grady stopped in his tracks.

The Telis Raptor hung, there in the cold, dangling from some of the many S hooks in there.

"Bloody hell." He started to walk slowly around it. "You neglected to tell me how big it was, lad." He lifted the tail and looked at the wicked barbed blade that grew from the end of it. "In the south, a tail-spike that big is worth a boot full of silver. And your boots are big."

With the ease of practice, Grady had the deer hung, skinned and quartered in no time. He carefully extracted the tenderloins to take to Po separately.

Barcus watched as he worked.

Grady washed and wrapped the rest in butcher's cloth and stored it in the meat locker.

Knife still in hand, he lifted the tail of the Telis and looked to Barcus. "Let me do this for you," he said.

Barcus nodded.

Grady peeled the skin of the tail back about twelve inches, exposing the first tail joint. It took a few minutes of careful cutting before the bones separated. He held up the tail spike by the bone, and it looked like a curved short sword.

"Mind if I finish this for you? Telis Raptor bone is as hard as Ironwood," Grady said.

"Not at all," Barcus replied.

"Wonder if Po will boil this for me for a day or two," he said to himself as he walked out.

After a quick lunch, Grady spent the afternoon in the stables and blacksmith shop with Olias. Their horses needed some long overdue attention.

Even the afternoon hammering didn't wake Ulric.

**

"Barcus, Ulric is awake. I have sent Olias to show him where the privy is located and to bring him some water," Em reported.

"I am so glad I fixed the water that feeds this end of Whitehall." Grady, Po and Barcus looked at each other as the sounds of vomiting echoed.

"How long has he been in there?" Barcus asked.

"The better part of an hour," Po said.

They heard loud gargling and spitting from the privy as Grady poured a large mug of tea and waited. An awkward door slamming open and then closed preceded Ulric's form teetering around the corner into the kitchen pavilion.

"Morning," mumbled Ulric repeatedly, taking the offered tea and moving to a bench under cover that looked out past the cauldrons, at the area that would one day be the herb garden. For a long while, he said not a word.

"I feel sorry for you people. When you wake up in the morning, that's as good as you will feel all day," Ulric said.

Barcus knew he had heard that expression before. It was an expression from home, a quote of a famous person from the past.

Po had made toast while she was moving about. She buttered it and brought it to him on a wooden plate.

He looked up at her. "You shot me in the neck," he stated.

"I'm horribly sorry about that, my Lord," she said, handing him the plate of toast.

"That's all right. I probably deserved it. I guess I'm forgiven if I get toast with my tea. Thank you." He took a bite that was inappropriately big and looked back to watch the snowflakes growing large as they fell. Po walked back to Barcus and Grady.

"Grady, we have a decent bath if you want to take him over for a soak. Olias is warming it up now. It would make him feel better," Po said.

"A bath?" Grady sounded incredulous.

"Olias will show you where it is," Po said, as Olias rounded the corner, adding, "I have started another laundry cauldron if you have clothes you'd like washed."

"Thank you, but we are already stressing your hospitality. I can do our laundry," he said humbly.

"As you wish, sir. In the meantime, I have laid out britches and tunics that you can wear. They should fit well enough." Po averted her eyes then.

"Please call me Grady, Po. 'Sir' makes me itch."

"Very well, Grady," she said.

Grady smiled at her immediate cooperation.

The snow really started coming down as Olias showed them the way to the bath suite. There was no wind but gigantic flakes that were accumulating fast.

"We need to configure some canvas walls along this open end during the winter," Barcus gestured.

"Canvas? You mean like sailcloth?" Po asked. He nodded, "We may have some in the storeroom already," Po said.

An inventory window popped up in his HUD showing the amount and location of the "tent cloth."

"I think I remember seeing it. I will go have a look." Barcus headed for the storeroom where he now knew it was.

"Em, what is your assessment of our visitors?" Barcus asked.

"I think they are harmless, if that's what you mean. I think Grady would be very useful if he were to stay. Ulric? That has yet to be determined."

"Stay? You mean stay here for the winter?" Barcus had not considered that as an option.

"We have enough supplies, more than enough in fact. Plus, Grady can easily supply fresh meat. Ulric may be able to answer a lot of questions about this planet and this society. He has been here a long time. I believe that he is from Earth originally."

"The way this snow is coming down, they may not have much of a choice." Barcus said.

***

Ulric had scrubbed himself nearly raw everywhere, after he got in the tub. Grady had already lathered up and shaved Ulric's head for him and his face down to the goats beard he liked, holding onto his last Keeper vanity. Grady left with his filthy clothes.

Now he just soaked in the fresh, clean, warm waters. It was the best bath he had taken in years. He was relaxed, and his hangover was almost gone. His eyes drifted closed for a few minutes.

When he opened them, she was there, sitting in the water at the other end of the tub. Her back was to him. The full moon tattoo, artfully obscured by clouds, was clear and more detailed than his memory.

"Grady did a passable job. Considering he used a hunting knife. Excellent edge for that knife, adequate edge for a razor," she whispered.

He closed his eyes, but he knew she wasn't gone, because she lived in his mind. She was his insanity.

"How many times did I shave you? And I never cut your throat," she said.

"I freed you." He clenched his eyes closed. He could feel her drifting closer.

"You ran." Her whisper came from directly in front of his nose.

He felt her go.

He sighed with relief before he heard in the far distance, "But I found you..." The cello began to weep a sorrowful tune.

He opened his eyes, and he was alone.

CHAPTER THIRTY-FOUR

Ulric's Tale

"The Emergency Module clearly decided that Grady and Ulric were to be assets. Ash was on standby to deal with them."

--*Solstice 31 Incident Investigation Testimony Transcript: Emergency Module Digital Forensics Report. Independent Tech Analysis Team.*

<<<>>>

Bathed and dressed in fresh tunics, Grady and Ulric were led to the gatehouse by Olias. The table was already set and covered with steaming crocks and baskets.

They didn't seem to notice that Po sat at the table next to Olias, immediately to Barcus's left.

They began dishing up tenderloin medallions in gravy with onions and bacon, small potatoes and buttered peas. The bread was still warm from the oven and light as could be.

"The snow is up to my knees already," Olias said through a mouthful of potatoes. Po glared at him.

"That bath is wonderful," said Grady. "I can't remember the last civilized bath I took."

"Your clothes should be dry by morning. I need to mend a few of them," Po said.

Looking up, Ulric seemed to notice her for the first time. Barcus was wondering if he remembered that she was the one that held the AR pointed at his face. He stopped wondering when he spoke.

Ulric pointed his finger at Po and held it there for a long moment before speaking.

"You shot me in the neck!" Ulric mock whined, his hand going to the scab on the side of his throat.

"Be glad it was not somewhere more important," Grady said as he spooned peas into his mouth.

Olias laughed.

Soon they were all laughing.

He'd brag about that neck wound for the rest of his life.

***

Dinner had continued with talk about the wonderful meal, the amazing wine and the snow. It was still falling straight down deeper and deeper.

Tonight, Ulric was only drinking wine, the fine Hermitage from within the Redoubt below. Barcus had moved to tea. Conversation had lulled when they found that Po, Olias and Grady had busied themselves elsewhere. They moved to the over stuffed chairs.

"How long have you been here?" Barcus asked.

"It's been almost thirty-two years," he replied, staring into the fire.

"What happened?" Barcus prompted him, as he fell silent again.

"I was on route back to home from a tour in the outer colonies. I had secured a bay in an FTL Midas class ship for my Renalo Yacht. It was called The Carlisle. It was no frills passage. I had to stay on my own ship the whole time, basically. That saved my life, really. It was just as well. The thing was an old converted Cobalt Destroyer from the war. Never saw a ship that was less comfortable. It was big, though." He refilled his glass from another full bottle Po had left on the small table before her quiet exit.

"I have no idea why the ship was diverted here. But as soon as it managed orbit, it was destroyed. I was injured in the initial attack. I don't remember anything. Four of the six crew members were killed outright. Somehow the Communications Tech and the Chief Engineer managed to get it to the ground. We found a good place to hide and stayed with the ship for months, trying to repair it. We eventually ran out of water, of all things."

"What happened to the others?"

"Wujcik, my Chief Engineer, cut his hand while refitting the tractor to use as ground transport. It seemed like nothing at first. He died of an infection before we could find help." He paused, deep in memories.

"Cassandra, the Comms Officer and I took the tractor as far as we could and then walked. We were traveling along the coast for weeks before we found a fishing village."

"This is the Cassandra you mentioned last night?" Barcus asked.

"Yes. She died last spring," Ulric said soberly.

"How did you become a Keeper?"

"When we got to the fishing village, we could not understand the common tongue. The only one that knew even half of what we were saying was the old village herbwife. She assumed I was a Keeper right then, because of the high speech. I never knew enough to correct her."

"I had no idea what to do. With Dave Wujcik dead, all hope of getting the ship space worthy was lost. Even if I could fly it, the hull was breached in so many places."

"We were there for two years before an itinerant Keeper visited the village by boat. We left with him. By then we knew common tongue, knew the culture to some extent. The people in the village didn't want us to go. I always thought we'd go back one day, but never did." He fell silent again.

"Then what happened?" Barcus asked.

"I was assigned a small parish in the southeast. It wasn't on the coast, but farther inland," Ulric recounted. "Keepers have local and regional conclaves annually. I went and no one questioned me. I was obviously a Keeper. I could read and I could speak the high tongue and I could drink more than bloody pirates. Of course I was a Keeper.

"We survived. Slowly we resigned ourselves to never knowing what happened. I became an itinerant Keeper for many years, to travel and try to find out. But I had stopped caring if Cassandra was not with me. That's when I first met Grady, traveling."

"We crossed paths many times, the following five years. When I knew I was never going to be more than a Lesser Keeper, I found a parish in the north where it wasn't so damn hot, and I settled down. The farther north you get the more slack they are about strictures, which is good because they made excellent bourbon there. Grady would visit every year. We'd go on parish walk-about with him. Cassandra was always restless."

"Then I gave up," Ulric confessed. "Cassandra left and wandered alone or with Grady for years. She came back about this time last year. She knew things, had seen things, she was different. She said there was a great task to be done and we had to go. We left the morning after your ship was destroyed. She cried as we watched it burning into the atmosphere."

There was a long pause.

"It was difficult to travel. It wasn't safe. She knew the mercenaries were rampaging. We didn't know she was ill, either," Ulric said.

"How did you come here?" Barcus asked.

Before Ulric could answer, he heard a whisper right next to his ear. "Do not mention me, Chris. Or I will make you tell him what you are leaving out."

He swallowed hard.

"Cassandra pointed the way, but not the reason." Ulric fell silent.

Po came in just then and withdrew to the room in the back.

"They'll kill her you know." Ulric stated it quietly. "The anvil. I have seen it so many times, for less."

"Do you know she would be killed even for wearing a belt? Did you know that?" Ulric asked. "They are not allowed even pockets on an apron. But to wear a belt with a Plate pouch, she'd be tortured to death slowly."

"She knows," Barcus said to the fire.

"I know she knows. It's you that are risking her life. Any visitor but us would have required her death, might have taken her, or killed her outright, without a word. That's allowed, you know.

"Does she have a Plate in there?"

"Yes."

"For the love of the Maker. We'd ALL be killed for that! For just allowing it!" Ulric said.

"Olias has one as well."

Ulric could not even reply to that. He drained his glass, poured another one and drained that one as well.

"You will have one as well if you are to be the Keeper of Whitehall," Barcus stated, smiling.

***

The next morning, Em had finished her status reports and added, "Grady is in the garage. I believe he knows that Par uses it. He has also been looking at the completed wall repairs and rubble removal. He has been trying to track Ash and Par. He is a brave one."

"I guess we will need to introduce them," Barcus said. "Where is everyone now?"

A new tactical map opened in his HUD and showed everyone's location.

"Ash is in the Redoubt. Par is with Olias to collect some more goats and chickens, before they die from lack of care. Po is working in the storeroom, Ulric is sleeping. Grady has been moving supplies to the cache he is making here at the west end of the vineyard." A window opened showing Grady walking through the deep snow with two large bags of supplies over his shoulders.

Barcus watched him enter a tiny, windowless hut. The door opened easily on newly oiled hinges. There was only a cot and a table in there, and both were already piled high with gear and supplies. He left the door open for light.

Barcus closed the window. "Em, he will either stay or go. It's up to him."

***

Grady took his time as he unloaded the bags onto the table and then subsequently packed the items into saddle bags, backpacks and larger canvas bags. Scanning the room one last time, he backed out and closed the door.

Turning, he almost walked directly into Ash.

Grady froze. Then he saw the ax in the hand of the faceless monster.

Ash spoke quietly. "You may want to add this to your gear and supplies." Ash handed Grady the ax, handle first. "It can be very useful in many ways."

Grady took it automatically. Ash turned away to leave and paused.

"Let me know if you require anything else specific. I have an inventory of Whitehall and the surrounding region."

"Thank...thank you..." Grady stammered.

"My name is Ash."

"Thank you, Ash," He said.

"He won't harm you, you know. Even if you lie to him," Ash said.

"Are we not prisoners then?" Grady asked.

"No. You may leave whenever you want," Ash replied.

"And Ulric?" Grady asked.

Ash turned back toward Grady. Grady was sure it had not

intended the movement to be intimidating.

"He was meant to be here. He knows it. Thank you for getting him here safely."

As Ash walked away, the wind rose and began to blow the snow to drifts.

CHAPTER THIRTY-FIVE

They Were Under the Bridge

"The Emergency Module was spreading itself thin. It was making assumptions."

--Solstice 31 Incident Investigation Testimony Transcript: Emergency Module Digital Forensics Report. Independent Tech Analysis Team.

Ulric woke with a start.

He had no idea what had woken him so violently. He could swear someone had slammed his door closed.

Two candles on the table were still burning, and the coals of the fire still glowed.

The room was empty.

He got out of bed, dragging a quilt for his shoulders, and added more wood to the fire, when he heard the music.

It was outside.

After the first week, Barcus convinced him to move to a more comfortable spot. His new rooms, the Keeper's suite, opened onto a balcony that overlooked what used to be the Abbot's garden. He had gone out there yesterday. It was all overgrown chaos now, with no sense at all how it used to be.

But he heard the music. He had to go.

When he opened the door, dappled sunlight fell on the balcony through the shade of summer leaves dancing in a breeze. He walked out and saw the garden was renewed. Flagstone paving stones meandered through flowering shrubs that filled and balanced the garden around the three obelisks placed there.

Benches were placed in the perfect spots for sun or shade, depending on the visitor's pleasure. Scanning along one path to a large patio, he saw a table and chairs overturned. Then people, lying in pools of blood, with their throats torn out.

He began backing back into the room when the music stopped, mid note.

That is when he saw her, out of the corner of his eye. She was standing on the balcony, her bloody, oversized mouth filled with a thousand needle-like teeth.

When his head snapped over to look at her, she wasn't there.

Looking back at the garden, it was no longer summer. Moonlight shone on snow, making it all bright.

He was shivering.

When he saw her standing out there in the snow, on the spot where the toppled table had been, she said, "When they come, you will be the Keeper."

"When who comes?" Ulric whispered.

"Do not fail me," she said.

"Who is coming, please, tell me?" he begged.

He saw her smile impossibly wide. Bloody needles for teeth.

He woke with a start in bed.

There was music in the distance.

***

Barcus was unable to sleep that night. He got out of bed without waking Po and got dressed in the loft. After pulling his boots and a fur cloak on, he went up the spiral stairs to the ramparts on the wall.

The wind had blown all the snow off the top of the wall. The moon was bright on the deep snow. He began to walk clockwise on the top of the wall. He saw lights in Olias's and Ulric's rooms, as well as the gatehouse. The smell of wood smoke was in the air as it rose from chimneys concealed in the construction of the battlements.

He looked down into the courtyards and overgrown gardens. Entering the north tower, he paused to look out over The Abbey.

That is when he heard a voice in the quiet. He could not make out the words. He scanned The Abbey and saw Ulric on his balcony. Faintly he heard, "...please, tell me."

"Em, is Ulric all right?" Barcus said.

"Yes. I think he is going to take his nightly piss off the balcony. He doesn't like to empty his own chamber pot," Em said.

"Who is he talking to?" Barcus asked.

He was gone from the balcony now.

"He is back in bed. No one else is there. He has been alone since retiring." Em brought a window BUG view up for Barcus. "He doesn't sleep very well."

"Where is Grady?" he asked.

"He is in his room, above the stables. Asleep. I will alert you if anything unusual happens, Barcus." There was a tone in Em's voice that almost sounded like she was annoyed with his queries.

"I'm sorry Em, I just can't sleep tonight. I have the oddest feeling. There is so much to do," he said as he left the east end of the tower and began his walk around.

The wall repairs had gone well. Only the battlements remained to be replaced. He stepped to the edge to see that the rubble had been mostly removed. Not completely, but like the remaining stone work, it could wait.

As he stood in the center of the opening, the feeling of unease came upon him again.

The sky was so clear tonight. Barcus wondered if they had names for these constellations. The moon was high and so bright, he could read if he wanted too.

Barcus had no idea he was being watched.

***

Ulric woke with a start. Again.

"Please, no more. I will do as you ask," he whispered.

"How did you come to pick the name Ulric? A bit of hubris there, don't you think?" There was a shadow in the corner, an outline in black. There was a glint of candlelight reflected off the steel of the piling where her leg should be.

"It was from the old herbwife, Rayne. She called me that. I never knew why. Christopher made them look at me like I had a shrunken head, and 'Black' is a word on common tongue that means thick black hair." He sat up. More comfortable the less he resisted the ghost.

"An Ulric is a kind of animal on this planet," the ghost informed him. "It is a powerful, wolf-like creature. Telis Raptors flee at the scent of them. Be glad there are none here. But know that when they come before you, part of their mind will remember this."

"Who are they?" Ulric asked.

"They were sent by Ronan. Their task has been undone, and they seek to know why." The shadow paused, "You will tell them how, but not why."

"I don't understand any of this. Ronan? I might as well jump from the tower now and save myself a mountain of pain and fear. Ronan? He is as ruthless as the High Keeper. Maybe more, because he is smarter." He held his face in his hands because he sensed her moving in darkness.

"Grady will find them today. He will bring them to you. You will hold together or I will be...displeased." Her voice was growing faint.

"What is their task? What do I do?" he whispered.

Silence had returned to the night. The deep hush of winter wilderness in snow.

***

"Barcus, wake up!" It was Em.

"Status!" He was instantly fully awake. He was alone in bed. The dawn was not quite here yet.

"Intruders. I don't know how, but they got past my sensors." He flew out of bed. Windows were opening in his HUD as he was changing quickly into is day clothes. The center image was Grady squatting on his heels, somewhere dark, holding an ax in a very menacing way as he silently gazed at something in the shadows. The BUGs shifted to night vision as Barcus noticed on the tactical map that Grady was under the north bridge, just outside the gate.

"Window 5 shows two Trackers asleep beneath two large white fur cloaks, probably sheep skins, perfect winter camouflage, warm and white."

"What is Grady doing?" Barcus asked.

"He appears to be waiting for them to wake up," Em stated flatly.

As he was tightening his belt and shifting his holster to be concealed beneath the tabard, Po entered with a pot of tea.

"Em said you were up and could use some tea," Po said.

He took the tray from her and quickly poured a mug, as all the windows closed in his HUD except one that showed Grady and the sleeping intruders in one view.

"We have visitors. I have no idea who they are yet." He took a gulp of tea that was too hot. "Get the AR and your warm cloak. I want you on the south tower with your Plate."

Without a word, Po dragged the case from under the bed and opened it. She had spent many hours practicing with the rifle but had never had to really use it.

First, she took a canvas bag out and put her head and one arm through so the wide strap went diagonally across her chest. It was obvious that the bag held six additional magazines. She pulled out the AR and checked the safety and the chambered round indicator. She took a single point sling from a peg and put it over her head on the opposite side and attached the AR. It hung down in front of her has she put on her cloak.

All this took about ten seconds before she paused, pistol grip in hand, index finger extended, tactical light test complete. She looked up. "Ready."

He nodded, and she was gone up the spiral stairs in a flash. He watched her go, two steps at a time, wondering how it was she was so proficient so fast. No time for that now.

Just then, there was movement and sound in the window image. They were stirring beneath furs. A hand sought the edge of the fur and drew it down, revealing a yawning face of a woman with her hair loose.

The yawn turned into a stretch, revealing a bare arm, and that is when she saw Grady. He said nothing.

She stiffened with a start but didn't cry out. Her sleeping companion was smart enough to say nothing, but also came out to look around.

They all locked eyes for a full minute.

Grady spoke first.

"Fools. Do you have any idea how lucky you are that I was the one to discover you?" Grady said in a tone that was calm, precise and menacing at the same time. Never mentioning the ax he held. "Do you have any idea what walks these woods? Did you ever wonder why we took up residence in this fortress?"

They lay there, frozen, their eyes darting between Grady's eyes and his ax. When he abruptly stood in one smooth motion, they startled into action, crab walking backward, dragging the furs with them.

"No night watch? Idiots. Get dressed, before I change my mind."

Grady shouldered the ax and walked out from under the bridge, up the embankment and waited above.

There was no talking as the couple stood and dressed. She had been naked, and he was wearing a tunic style shirt and no pants. She dressed faster with an under-dress and an over-dress. She pulled socks and boots on then quickly braided her long hair as the man put on his belt with fumbling difficulty. She had her pack and cloak on and while she was waiting, Barcus saw her check boot knives.

Barcus watched them decide to leave their gear there under the bridge.

Another window opened, showing Po on the top of the tower as she reached down and grabbed a handful of skirts, pulled them forward and tucked them in her belt in the front. It suddenly looked like pants.

Then he saw her face.

Fierce did not begin to describe it. The crease between her eyebrows was no longer a worry indicator. It was the face of a predator.

She deployed the bipod just as he had taught her and looked through the scope to the east.

"Em, give me the AR POV," Barcus said.

Another window opened showing cross-hairs on the magnified face of a woman. She was weather-worn from a life in the sun, but still beautiful. Her hair was light from the sun, but also was scattered with gray. Out loud, Po said in a low voice, "Barcus, I have met these people before. They are Trackers for a Keeper named Ronan. Don't kill them. Not yet." Her scope drifted to Grady. "Grady looks like he will take their heads if they do anything."

How did she know I could hear her? Barcus thought.

Grady was angry. Barcus didn't know the man, but there was no mistaking it.

The scope moved to the man. He was younger than the woman, Barcus could now see. He was more nervous than she was.

"Po, hold your fire." His words quietly came from her Plate.

Barcus sat on the bench with the tray and extra mugs, sipping his still steaming tea. They were rounding the curvature of the wall.

"*Olias is waiting just inside the gate doors. If you call to him, he will hear you,*" Em reported. A tactical map displayed the location of everyone, even

Par and Ash.

Ash had quietly joined Po on the top of the south tower. Par had line of sight from a long distance.

They crossed the bridge and, when close enough, Barcus said, "Good morning, Grady. Who have we here?" Barcus stood.

The woman paused a pace behind the man as he lowered to one knee and lowered his head. She went to both knees and placed her forehead on the back of her hands as they rested on top of one another directly on the ground. He felt anger instantly at the gesture.

Suddenly, Po's whispering voice was in his ear. "Let her. It's all she knows." Po knew him better than she expected. "I am watching on the Plate now. I'd have to hang over the wall to cover you now."

The man's head was bowed. Grady stood directly behind them with ax at ready as he spoke. "Good morning, Barcus."

Barcus was glad he didn't say Keeper Barcus.

"I was out checking my trap lines this morning and encountered these travelers near the north gate, and brought them straight around. I was going to let them warm up in the tack room until you were up and about."

"Excellent idea," Barcus said.

Po whispered, "Say this: 'Well met, travelers. Please enter and enjoy your oaths.'"

Barcus repeated the words without hesitation, and they both rose and seemed to relax. The man spoke, "Well met, Barcus." He reached out to actually shake his hand. Barcus took it firmly, smiling at the gesture. "My name is Pyke, and this is Ann, Trackers for Lord Keeper Ronan of the East Isles."

Both the Trackers bowed their heads slightly at the mention of their Keeper's name. Ann left her head bowed and eyes averted. It seemed awkward to Barcus.

Barcus made his decision. "Welcome to Whitehall. Have you had breakfast?"

CHAPTER THIRTY-SIX

Pyke and Ann

"The Emergency Module in survival mode was learning from these trackers. They lived their whole lives in survival mode."

--*Solstice 31 Incident Investigation Testimony Transcript: Emergency Module Digital Forensics Report. Independent Tech Analysis Team.*

Barcus immediately saw in his HUD a flurry of activity that encouraged him to slow down a bit. Olias ran to the kitchens at the same time Po was flying down the spiral stairs, unslinging the AR as she went.

"What brings you this far north?" Barcus asked.

Pyke looked at Ann, and she nodded almost imperceptibly.

"We were doing our annual winter business run for Keeper Ronan to Greenwarren to confirm our midwinter timber order and perhaps add a few things." He swallowed hard before continuing. Ann encouraged him with another nod. "The village has been..." He swallowed again. Barcus knew why. "Greenwarren has been destroyed."

"Yes. We know. Keeper Ulric has been there with Grady," Barcus said, causing one of Grady's eyebrows to rise slightly.

"You have a Keeper in residence, then." He looked at Ann again at this point, as Barcus pulled the huge door open for them to pass.

"Yes. Do you have horses? You must have more gear than this."

"They have a camp, not far from Whitehall. Olias and I will be happy to collect their gear and bring it in while you have breakfast." They were looking at Grady, non-verbally thanking him for his discretion.

Just then, Olias came through the open door to the courtyard on the gatehouse side and skidded to a stop. He looked first at one Tracker and then the other, his hand on his knife handle as if ready for a fight. He seemed so small to Barcus in that moment. He had filled in so much during the previous weeks that Barcus sometimes forgot he was just a boy.

"This is Olias. Olias, this is Trackers Pyke and Ann of the East Isles," Barcus said.

Olias tried to take a formal stance and make a head bow without looking comically formal. He almost pulled it off.

"They will be having breakfast," Barcus instructed.

"Right. Follow me, miss." He turned, and Ann followed him through the arch toward the kitchen.

"Please," is all Barcus said and entered the gatehouse. Before the door was closed, Olias was back with a tray of tea and warm wet towels. Pyke picked one up without thanking Olias or even acknowledging him. Barcus poured tea for them both. He saw Grady and Olias exiting the south gate to go retrieve their gear.

Pyke was talking as he washed his face and hands with the towel. He seemed uncomfortable with how dirty he had made it. "Was it Keeper Ulric that brought you here? Inside these walls?" Barcus could sense his discomfort, knowing why the idea helped him.

"Yes. There are Telis Raptors about, and the walls seemed sensible." Barcus knew that Keeper's desires could override the prohibitions this far north.

"Telis Raptors?" His tea mug had stopped half way to his mouth.

"Yes. They were eating our goats," Barcus said, matter of fact. "There's one hanging in our meat locker now. Do you know if we can eat it?"

Pyke choked on his tea.

***

Po was in the kitchen, collecting trays and dishes rapidly for breakfast. She already had a basket of fresh, warm bread and crocks of plain butter, honey butter, crushed nuts, chopped dried fruit, honey and thick cream ready. She was about to ladle hot oatmeal into a warming bowl when Olias entered.

"Po, this is Ann. Ann this is Po, our head of house. Ann is a Tracker, Po," Olias added, as if to explain some social issue. He left without another word. She bowed her head to Po in sincere respect, even though she was far taller and older than Po.

"How may I help, mum?" It was a formal greeting.

"You can put your things there. We will bring them breakfast in the gatehouse, then we can talk."

Ann took off her cloak and over-dress. Together the women assembled two large trays without a word. Ann looked puzzled at one of the trays.

"There are only two bowls," Ann said.

"Yes. This meal is just for Pyke and Barcus. We will eat here." Po gestured to the large kitchen work table.

"All this food?" Ann asked, incredulous. Po suddenly understood what her question was. She had grown accustomed to the amount of food they consumed.

"Yes. Now take that tray." Po picked up the other tray and with practiced ease moved through the doors, down the covered walk to lightly knock and enter the gatehouse with Ann right behind her.

***

Pyke was choking on his tea as they entered. Barcus laughed and was patting his back. Forgetting himself, Pyke spoke directly to Ann.

"They have a Telis in the meat locker!" he blurted out.

She tried to communicate to him with her eyes, but Pyke seemed to be the only one in the room that didn't understand her. She looked directly into Barcus's face for the first time. He realized then she was as tall as he was. He raised an eyebrow.

"Forgive me, my Lord," she said and suddenly was on her knees with her forehead on the flagstone, her hands clasped at the base of her spine. It was as if she expected him to stomp her head flat.

Barcus was clearly furious now. His jaw muscles seemed to highlight the scar on his face.

Pyke realized what happened, and before he could say a word, Barcus spoke.

"Po, I don't care what you must do. But explain it to her clearly so this never happens again."

Po grabbed her by the arm and dragged her to her feet and to the door. She risked a glance at Pyke as Po led her out. It was an apology this time.

"Barcus, my Lord. I..." Pyke stuttered.

Barcus held up a hand that cut him off. "Do not worry, Pyke. No offense was taken."

Pyke seemed embarrassed and dumbfounded at the same time.

"I'm hungry. Let's have breakfast. Then we will talk."

***

Po was still dragging Ann back to the kitchen by the elbow.

"I am so sorry, mistress. I shouldn't be allowed indoors." Po pushed her down onto a bench at the long table.

Po let out a barking laugh as she set two bowls on the table with spoons. "He likes you already." Po added a basket of bread to the table, more crocks of butter and honey and other items. Ann was about to speak when Olias came in, running as usual.

"Likes me?" Ann stammered.

Olias rushed in, "Ann, Grady wants to know if you want one or two rooms for your gear?" Her mouth hung open.

She nodded holding up one finger.

"Just tell him. I will explain over breakfast." She turned to Olias, "You and Grady are to come get some oatmeal as soon as you're done."

"One room. Please." Ann said.

Olias grabbed an apple slice off the table as he ran by with her warm clothes in his arms.

Po set a full bowl of oatmeal in front of her, then dished one up for herself.

Ann recoiled from the bowl, as if it was full of snakes.

"At Whitehall, we all eat from the same larder." To punctuate the fact, she poured in some honey, cream, a scoop of crushed nuts and folded it all in. She grabbed a small loaf of bread, tore it open and buttered it. Then she added honey and took a big bite.

"We have so much honey," Po said between bites.

Just then, Olias rushed in and went for a bowl.

Ann started to rise and was stopped by a gesture from Po who held Ann's eyes locked as she spoke to Olias without looking at him. "Olias, wash your hands before you touch another thing in my kitchen. You too, Grady." Ann was visibly mortified for sitting with food before her with men present. She had not even heard Grady enter.

"Eat." Po pointed at her bowl, reconsidered, and traded bowls with her, adding honey, cream and nuts to that bowl as well.

As Po dug into her oatmeal, Grady set mugs of tea down on the table for the two of them, before collecting two more for himself and Olias. Olias dished up another large helping of oatmeal for himself, then handed the ladle to Grady, who did the same.

Grady spoke to Ann as he settled next to Po on the bench. "Get used to it, lass. Eat up or you **will** be in trouble." Olias was eating noisily as Ann lifted her spoon and took a mouthful. Her reaction was immediate. It was wonderful.

They all ate in silence for a while. She was bold enough to take some bread and even butter it.

Po finished as Olias was helping himself to a third bowl. Grady pushed his empty bowl away and cupped his mug in both hands. He spoke first.

"You know what it's like to be days away from the nearest village? Sitting around a fire with a full belly of rabbit stew and a story fresh told? The way Pyke will speak to you then." Grady spoke directly to Ann. "I see it in him. He'd not treat you poorly. He respects you. You know how you both see work that needs doing, and it gets done. No wasted time on groveling." She nodded. "Whitehall is that very thing."

She said nothing.

"He will want to speak with you. When he is done speaking with Pyke," Po said.

"Don't worry," Olias added in common tongue around a mouth full of breakfast. "You'd be dead already if he didn't like the truth of you."

"Is he the Keeper then?" Ann asked Po.

All three answered at the same time, "No."

"Don't make the mistake of calling Barcus that. We have a Keeper. His name is Ulric."

"How many people live here?" Ann asked, looking around at a kitchen that could support hundreds.

"You have met everyone except Keeper Ulric," Olias blurted out, earning a scowl from Po.

Suddenly Ann's manner completely changed. She had a kind of fear in her eyes. She quickly rose and took her bowl to wash in the sink, a bit overzealously. "I am sure we will be on our way by noon." She didn't notice Po walking up beside her until Po placed a calming hand on her arm.

"What's wrong, Ann?" Po asked in a low voice.

Before she could reply, they heard Barcus call for Olias, who ran out in a blur. Ann looked over her shoulder, but Grady was gone as well.

"I cannot lay with another Keeper. I'm sorry. I'd rather take my chances naked in the snow," Ann whispered through clenched teeth.

Po realized what she was thinking.

"Ann, hear me." She reached up and touched Ann's chin making her look into Po's eyes. "Within these walls, no man will ever touch you without an invitation. Not Keeper Ulric, not the High Keeper himself. I promise."

"What is the word of a woman worth?" Ann asked, fear still in her face.

***

"Please, sit and have some breakfast as we talk," Barcus sat and gestured for Pyke to sit as well. "Po makes the best oatmeal." He served himself and handed the ladle to Pyke to do the same. Pyke followed Barcus's lead, and was soon hungrily eating the excellent breakfast.

Em was speaking to Barcus in his head. *"I'm sorry Barcus. I don't know how they got so close without detection. I will step up perimeter surveillance right away. I have no idea how Grady found them before I did."* Barcus said nothing.

"Greenwarren and most of the eastern villages have all been destroyed, burned down by mercenaries, the villages abandoned. All the people were killed. It's genocide." Barcus popped the last of the bread into his mouth.

Pyke replied, "It's more than that. There is something else. We've seen it, seen them."

"Seen what?" Barcus asked.

"Some kind of beasts, down from the mountains, bigger than anything I have ever seen before." Pyke had stopped eating. "We carefully tracked them to Greenwarren, and from there to here. They have been here. We have seen the signs. Does your Keeper protect you here?"

Barcus was caught short by the question. "Keeper Ulric explains very little to us. But we are relatively safe inside these walls. I will take you to see Keeper Ulric before you resupply and go. Where will you go?"

"We will need to go to Langforest Keep. Keeper Volk can let Ronan know what has happened and dispatch a shuttle for pickup. We normally do that from Greenwarren, but Keeper Malcom is gone like the rest."

Barcus remembered then that Langforest Keep is where Po grew up. It was directly south and a bit east of The Abbey and across the Salterferry Bridge, just south of the gorge.

"I believe Grady has a map that will show you the fastest way to the Salterferry Bridge. We can also provide horses."

"What is Keeper Ulric doing here? It's the north end of the world," Pyke asked.

"I honestly don't know. I am just the gatesman."

"Barcus, Ulric is awake," Em notified him.

"I will see about meeting the Keeper. In the meantime, Olias will take you to your rooms to clean up and rest." Barcus got up and opened the door, calling to Olias.

The boy came around the corner in a rush.

***

Olias skidded back in, directly in front of Ann. "Barcus would like a moment to speak with you." He didn't wait for a reply, but ran deeper into The Abbey.

"Leave it." Po began leading her to the gatehouse. Ann was speechless, but went without protest. Po and Ann entered without knocking. Barcus was at the hearth, refilling his mug from the kettle there.

Po literally pushed her down into one of the overstuffed chairs. Barcus turned towards her as Po walked up to stand beside him.

"Barcus, I will make this conversation easier. Please correct me if I say anything that isn't true." She turned to Ann with hands on hips as if she was about to scold her.

"Within these walls, no one will touch you without your leave. Ever. No beatings, no beddings, not so much as a tug on your braid to get your attention." She savagely tugged her own braid to prove the point.

Barcus sipped his tea.

"Not the Keeper. Not Barcus. No. One. Would. Dare." Her voice was fierce.

She looked at Barcus then. He simply nodded.

"She has figured out that Ulric was sleeping alone," Po said to Barcus.

The realization dawned on Barcus then.

"You are a very good Tracker, Ann. Perhaps the best I have ever met," Barcus said. "I have no idea how you managed to get so close to us without detection. Well done. How long has Pyke been with you?"

She averted her eyes and replied, "We have been teamed for three years now, my Lord." She looked surprised and a bit sad with this answer.

"Barcus, easy," Po said, knowing Ann's "my Lord" would chaff.

Ann looked older in that moment, as if the weight of some sadness aged her just then.

"You were with another Tracker before then?" Po asked.

"Yes, mum. For twenty-two years. He taught me everything I know," Ann replied, her sadness evident.

"What happened?" Barcus asked.

Ann looked up then. It was as if she had made a decision. "He was defending me. It cost him a trip to the anvil. His name was Brice." She stood and walked the few steps to stand right before Barcus. "All for the vanity of a Lesser Keeper."

It was as if she expected to be struck. What Barcus did had a far more devastating impact. He gently placed a hand on her shoulder and spoke.

"I am so very sorry for your loss..." His faced showed that he meant it.

CHAPTER THIRTY-SEVEN

The Audience

"Major data loss occurred during this temporal segment."

--Solstice 31 Incident Investigation Testimony Transcript: Emergency Module Digital Forensics Report. Independent Tech Analysis Team.

Olias came skidding into the gatehouse without knocking, and with his usual complete unawareness of things that were happening that he was interrupting.

"Barcus, Keeper Ulric is awake and waiting in the main hall." It was in rapid common. Em's subtitles helped so much.

"Oh really?" Barcus raised an eyebrow.

"Shall I get Pyke?" Olias asked.

"Yes, please. We shouldn't make the Keeper wait," Ann said.

Olias was gone in a flash, and Ann was looking down at her clothes.

Barcus looked at Po and shrugged with his eyes. "Po, please wait here with Pyke and Ann. I will go to the Keeper to find out what he would like to do this morning."

***

Barcus left the gatehouse and crossed the courtyard to climb the steps up to the main hall. He entered the vestibule and then the main hall. Grady was busy lighting the last of the fires in the six fireplaces.

Ulric sat on the throne of the dais. The bags under his eyes were deep, and there was an uncharacteristic look of seriousness on his face. His head was recently shaved, but his beard was tangled, which gave him a slightly crazed, intense look.

"Ulric, what are you doing?" Barcus said, as he slowly began to climb the steps to the dais.

"Barcus, you need to send these Trackers on their way. Today. Now," he stated.

"Why? Do you know them?" Barcus asked.

"They work for Ronan, the Keeper of the East Isles." He pointed to the floor map, and Em highlighted it for Barcus. "People go to the East Isles and are never seen again. His Trackers are more than Trackers." His voice was escalating in panic. "They are probably assassins and spies. How did they find this place? We need to get them out of here!"

"We will." Barcus was approaching Ulric like he was a spooked horse, palms open and moving slow. Ideas were forming in his head. "Keeper Ulric," he said formally, "I will bring our guests before you and you can best send them on their way by offering assistance - horses and supplies." His words were calm as he stopped on the top step. "I recommend that you do not engage in any other topics. You are a busy man. You owe them no other explanations. Let us do the rest."

These words reassured Ulric. He relaxed a bit in his chair. Barcus chanced a glance at Grady who was not far away. He gave no reaction, but his face was lined with concern.

"Bring them. Let's get this over with. I need a drink," Ulric said.

***

Ulric waited in High Seat, trying not to look at her. She sat on the steps halfway down to the left. She spoke to him without looking up.

"They must go," she said. He nodded. He could not speak to her with Grady watching him.

"Tell them to take the old road directly south until they find the unfinished tunnel." She got up and turned to him. Her eyes had flames behind them. "They will make their own way around the mountain to the other side. There is the other sides tunnel entrance there as well. It was never completed."

She was walking up the stairs now, her eyes still burning.

"Directly south of there, two days more, and they will find the road to the Salterferry Bridge."

She was close enough now for him to see the flames in the back of her throat as she spoke.

"Today."

Just then, the doors opened at the bottom of the hall on the right. Grady walked in, leading a man and a woman.

When had Grady gone?

They paused at the bottom of the dais steps. The woman knelt and pressed her forehead on the lowest step, her hands at the base of her spine. The man stepped up two stairs and took a knee, his head bowed.

"My Lord, I present Tracker Pyke of the Eastern Isles." He ignored Ann completely.

Ulric began, "What do you want? Never mind, I know what you want. Tell me if I am far off. You came to Greenwarren for the lumber, only to find Greenwarren destroyed."

"Yes my Lord." He was nervous.

"Why the bloody hell did you come here?" Ulric was yelling.

Pyke was visibly shaken by his yelling.

"Forgive me, my Lord. I had no idea you were here. We were tracking...something."

"You are fortunate you didn't find it or it find you.

"What do you want?" Ulric asked.

Pyke opened his mouth too slowly

"No. Let me tell you what you want." Ulric pointed a shaking finger as he began to speak. "You want to get away from here as fast as possible. You will have horses and supplies and directions, and if you are still here come sundown, I cannot guarantee your safety. Grady will show you a map. The old road will take you south to the unfinished tunnel."

"Thank you, my Lord. We can get to Langforest Keep from there," Pyke said with his head bowed.

"No! Do not thank me. Go quickly, and be well away from here by dark if you value your hide." Spittle flew from Ulric's lips as he visibly controlled himself from sliding into a rant. "Tell your Keeper he will need to find his masts elsewhere. Tell him only death waits above the gorge. He'll know what that means."

"Yes, my Lord." Pyke backed down the steps. Ann began to rise.

"Now, go." Pyke bowed. Ann never raised her eyes as she turned to follow Pyke out.

"I was very sorry to hear about Brice," Ulric said sadly to their backs as they began to walk out. They stopped at his words. Ann turned her head and looked up at Ulric for the first time. Their gaze met and held a moment. No words passed.

When Pyke began to move again, Ann followed, breaking the

gaze.

"Grady, go and see to their needs," Ulric said.

They all left, leaving Ulric to himself. A minute later he spoke to the empty hall.

"I've done what you asked, now please, leave me alone." Ulric put his face in his hands.

***

Barcus watched the entire audience in his HUD as it happened. He was taken aback at Ulric's final words.

Does he know I am watching? Barcus thought.

Ulric continued to sit on the High Seat with his elbows on his knees, one hand on his forehead.

Grady knocked and opened the gatehouse door. Pyke and Ann followed him in with Olias now in tow as well. "He thinks they should leave as soon as possible. We are to provide provisions and even horses."

"Olias, saddle up two horses and prepare a third for provisions. Use your best judgment on which ones. Work with Ann on the provisions. It's at least a week to Langforest," Barcus said.

"I'm sorry we can't stay longer, Barcus," Pyke said.

"Did you say Langforest?" Po came through the curtain asking.

"Yes. Volk is the closest Keeper that can contact Ronan for us. Why?" Po noticed that Pyke was very comfortable answering a question from her, a woman.

"I lived there once. Please, send my regards to the smith for me." She hesitated before adding, "Tell him I am well."

"Yes, mum," Pyke replied.

"Our Keeper would rather keep it quiet that we have taken up residence in this ruin," Barcus added. "His reasons are his own. But we shall count on your discretion." Barcus held his gaze. "You are always welcome back, if you do."

Two windows opened just then in his HUD, the familiar tactical map and a surveillance window showing Ann talking with Olias in the storeroom.

Barcus smiled then and cuffed Pyke on the shoulder. "Do you always get so much done so early in the morning?"

"Barcus." Pyke didn't know how to say it, so he just did. "We tracked a demon here, maybe more than one. Maybe you should come with us." His concern was genuine.

"This may be the root of why we are here. Please, speak no further on this, to anyone." Barcus added guiltily, "To speak of them will draw them to you." He said it low and had no idea that it would have such impact on the boy.

***

After a flurry of activity to collect horses, gear and provisions, Barcus found himself alone in the main hall, watching the fires burn down.

"Would you like a full status?" Em was casually sitting on the throne, with one leg over an arm rest. She activated all the status screens in his HUD all at once. They were floating in fixed positions all around the room.

Barcus was watching the two camera views that showed Pyke and Ann as they rode wordlessly to the south. "How far can the BUGs follow them and still transmit back to you?"

"Well, the search pattern was already moving toward Langforest Manor, so we will have connection all the way there via routing relays, but if they get on a shuttle and fly out of range, we will lose them. The BUGs will still be active but in autonomous mode. If we ever crack the comms, they will come on-line."

Barcus looked at the tactical map and could see that Ash was following them in the forest at a distance. "How far will Ash shadow them?"

"It all depends on their conversation when they are alone. I will keep you informed." Em sat on the steps. Her face was even with Barcus as he stood below.

"What is going on with Ulric?" Barcus was worried.

"I will try to find out. I'll keep an eye on him. He's back in bed now," Em said.

"By the way, how did Grady find them before you? I thought you had the entire facility under observation. They were right under our noses." Barcus let a bit of his anger slip into his voice.

"I am sorry, Barcus. I never detected them via motion or heat signature. I have already increased the number of static observation points." Her voice actually sounded sincere. "I think Grady detected them because of their footprints. I am trying to develop an algorithm now to detect and access footprint evidence. Can you do me a favor?"

"A favor?"

"Grant me compile authority to create new advanced, binary-tree based, analytic, control algorithms. New ones only. No mods made to or by any foundation systems. Otherwise all the advanced math has to be done via sequential scripts via the interpreter."

"Okay, okay... permission granted."

"Sorry, Barcus. But you have to say the whole thing to do an admin control change. Here, just say this..." A plain text box opened in his HUD that he read out loud.

"Grant the Emergency Module compile authority to create new advanced, binary-tree based, analytic, control algorithms and subsystems. New ones only," Barcus said. The text box disappeared.

"Thank you, Barcus. This will allow me to keep you safer."

CHAPTER THIRTY-EIGHT

Langforest

"Barcus had no idea what he just did. He granted limited admin control to the AI itself."

--Solstice 31 Incident Investigation Testimony Transcript: Emergency Module Digital Forensics Report. Independent Tech Analysis Team.

<<<>>>

The skies remained heavy gray and overcast for the week that followed the Trackers' departure.

Po cleaned and cooked and spent time reading at an increasing pace. She made all their lives easier, seemingly without effort. She slept in Barcus's bed, moving as he moved, resting deeply as he did. She gained weight, mostly muscle, but still filling out her sharper places, hiding her bones. She would talk to Olias in common and laugh. He increased his antics specifically to amuse her. Po would read to Olias and study the Plate applications that Em would teach them.

Olias made more salvage runs. He ate more than Barcus thought possible. His health increase was evident. He ran everywhere. He constantly asked questions of everyone, Par most of all, while on their salvage runs.

Grady hunted and wandered. He seemed to spend a lot of time just remaining still and watching for something that never seemed to happen. Barcus learned that he had placed a trap line and brought rabbits for stew, as well as deer for the meat locker and smokehouse that Grady put back in service. He helped Barcus with repairs that would better weatherize the occupied sections of the keep.

"I'm worried about Ulric, Barcus," Em told him during the daily status update on the morning of the eighth day after Pyke and Ann had left. "All he seems to do is wander the abandoned sections of The Abbey and talk to himself."

"I know. He seems to be looking for something," Barcus said.

"He doesn't sleep at night. If the STU were here, I would do a full medical scan on him."

"Grady says he's been worse. I can't imagine," Barcus said. "Keep a close eye on him."

"Any priority items today?" Barcus knew he didn't need to ask.

"Actually, Pyke and Ann arrived at Langforest yesterday. They are very cautious. They remain hidden and are observing the manor. I have begun a full site survey. There are over a hundred people there. The caste system Po mentioned is evident there, very evident. There is a small village to the west of the manor compound."

Barcus was studying the maps. "Will the Keepers' comms help Stu with the decryption efforts?"

"Perhaps. We will have detailed temporal and communications activity logs for comparative analysis. It all depends. There are too many variables to predict."

"When he uses his Plate, I want to see it, real-time."

"Acknowledged," Em replied.

"When will Ash be back?" Barcus asked absently. He was surprised that Em had him gone so long.

"Do you require him for tasking?" Em asked. "He will likely assess a few farms on the way back. I'll keep you informed."

"No. No need to rush. He rips up everything if he rushes. That is what makes his path easy to follow." Barcus moved on to the standard task list priorities.

Barcus found himself watching Po as she worked. He had come to recognize how ordered and systematic she ran her days, her weeks.

Her time got divided between what she did as daily work, projects that improved life in The Abbey and personal time spent studying. It was very disciplined, and she was very disciplined. Systematic even. Barcus was proud of her. Barcus could only help with projects. But he was always better off finding his own.

This week, he would finish the wall after Ash got back. For now, he would continue to explore the remaining denied spaces.

***

"Before we finish this lesson, Olias, I'd like to show you one more important item in the medical kit." The case lay open on the table in the gatehouse. Olias had his Plate in front of it as Em walked him through the basics. "Located here in the lower left compartment are small items that look like this." An image of a small tube with a series of small icons on it was displayed. "Take one."

Olias found the device and lifted it from the case. It was labeled "DBI Assessment and Repair Unit."

"Set that one aside, close the case up, and stow it now," Em instructed.

Olias did exactly that.

"What does 'DBI' mean?" he asked.

"It stands for 'Deep Brain Implant' and is an acronym. Do you remember what an acronym is, Olias?" Em asked.

"Yes. The first letter of each word. DBI is Deep Brain Implant," Olias said proudly even though it was still common tongue.

"Put the DBIARU in your pocket," Em said, and he did it without question. "Take your Plate and go to Ulric's suite." He picked up his Plate and left the gatehouse with his head held high. He was trying to look like a young Keeper.

***

Barcus was in the lowest level that was just about directly below the main hall. He knew from the map in his HUD that there was a large space behind these cells that made no sense. The communal bath was below the main hall to his right as he looked into the last cell. He shifted his vision though various modes without thinking. His training had showed him that this could reveal anomalies that could provide the information he needed.

Sure enough, a spectrum analysis view showed him traffic patterns on the floor that led into this cell and through the back wall. A simple push caused the entire wall to swing right.

It revealed a large room that contained rack after rack of weapons.

Some of the weapons had obviously been there when Olias had found the space. Many were corroded and dried up, but some were still serviceable. They had been cleaned and set aside for new swords, daggers, axes and crossbows – dozens of crossbows, hundreds maybe. Thousands of arrows and bolts were stored, point down, in small barrels.

Barcus smiled. All was forbidden.

It occurred to him that it was also a good idea to collect them to simply deny them to his enemies. Nodding his head with approval, he moved farther into the long room.

He didn't hear the well-oiled door slowly close, on its own well lubricated angled hinges.

Barcus wondered what inventory list and report this was all detailed within, that he had not read.

***

Olias entered Ulric's suite without knocking, on Em's recommendation. His feet were silent on the thick carpets.

On the way over to his rooms, Em explained, "I think that Ulric is very sick. The DBIARU will help make him better, clearer. Do you remember how the injector works?"

He replied, "Yes. Just gently hold this end to the skin over a large muscle group and press this button."

Olias almost laughed out loud when he passed through Ulric's outer room to his bed chamber. Ulric was face down on his bed, his nightshirt up around his armpits. The late morning light from the balcony windows was bright on his bare buttocks.

Olias tiptoed up and softly pressed the tube against his left butt cheek and depressed the button. A small hissing snap sounded, and Ulric reacted as if a mosquito had bitten him in his sleep.

Olias tiptoed at a run out of the suite. Em told him to drop the disposable injector into the middens.

As with many other things Em asked him to do, he never mentioned it to anyone.

***

Po was setting about the business of lunch when Ulric basically staggered into the kitchen. "Keeper, are you all right? You look..." she didn't finish her comment before he spoke.

"Thirsty," was all he croaked out.

She held up a pitcher she had just filled for lunch. "Would you prefer water or some hot tea?"

Without a word, he took the pitcher from her with both hands and drank deeply directly from the side of the container. After gulping down nearly half the pitcher, he lowered it and said, "Tea would be very nice. Thank you." He wiped his mouth on his sleeve before continuing to drain the vessel.

Shaking her head, she filled a large mug of steaming hot tea for him and set it on the kitchen table.

"I am so hungry. When will breakfast be ready? Am I the first one up?"

"Sit. I am about to make the midday meal." He sat. "Start with this." She set bread and butter in front of him and then a bowl of apples. Ulric tore into the food.

"You found the clean tunics I left for you, I see," Po noted.

Through a mouth full, he said, "Yes. Well done. I will never know how these things get done out here in the wilderness."

Po rolled her eyes and then paused. She looked around at what they had accomplished. She looked at Ulric eating like Olias. Absently, her hand sought the branding scar above her left breast. She traced the raised portions.

Her smile faded.

***

"Barcus, would you like a quick status update on our brief visitors?" Em asked the next morning as Barcus was studying the main gate mechanism for the huge portcullis.

"Sure," He said without pausing, trying to figure out why the counterbalance weights were jammed.

"Pyke entered the Manor and was granted an audience with Keeper Volk. He made a 40 second call to Keeper Ronan, and Pyke was dismissed. The entire interaction took less than two minutes. I have a solid relay network set up all the way to Langforest Manor in hopes that we can learn more." There was concern in Em's voice.

"What's bothering you, Em?" Barcus asked.

"Four hours later, a shuttle arrived to pick up the Trackers. They left the horses with Volk," Em Replied.

Barcus knew it wasn't about the horses.

"Four BUGs stayed with the Trackers and were out of range in no time," Em said.

"You expected that," Barcus noted.

"It isn't that. That evening, Volk's carriage returned to the Manor without a driver, and Volk was dead inside. The household staff believes the driver feared he would be blamed and has fled," Em said.

"How does any of this matter? Frankly, it's one less filthy Keeper that I have to kill," Barcus growled.

"It's the deplorable conditions of the people that live there. The household staff is planning to loot the estate and flee," Em said.

"So?" Barcus was still focused on an amazing set of gears.

"After the funeral, the High Keeper is planning on sending troops. They are going to destroy Langforest Keep and all of its people now that Volk is dead. Somehow the house staff knows this," Em said.

Barcus stopped and stood.

"Isn't this where Po..." Barcus began.

"Yes."

A BUG widow opened. It was an old, yet very muscular man. He was bald, and his face and head were heavily scarred. One of his eyes was ruined, clouded over. A label appeared below the image: Smith. The vid was of him standing in front of a fat, weasel faced, man that brought a rattan cane down on Smith's shoulder as he was being screamed at. Smith didn't even flinch. The scars were in that moment explained to Barcus.

"Tell Ash to stay there, and stand by, hidden for now," Barcus ordered.

He brushed his hands off. "Get everyone together. We are going on a little trip."

CHAPTER THIRTY-NINE

The War Begins

"The Emergency Module was now running a new agenda. It ran upgrades and repairs on Ulric's HUD, without direction, permission or reporting it. Logs and data collection are now more neatly edited. We were still able to uncover that Ash had quietly murdered Volk and his driver."

--Solstice 31 Incident Investigation Testimony Transcript: Emergency Module Digital Forensics Report. Independent Tech Analysis Team.

<<<>>>

They arrived at dawn on the fifth day after the funeral of Volk. The BUGs had swarmed over the Manor days ago, and Em had the entire picture. All but a final few guests were now gone. Everyone hated the Keeper Volk, even the other Keepers. Some came for the feasts, some to just make sure he was dead.

They were met by the head servant, Samson. "Greetings, my Lords." He bowed deeply. "Please come and have some breakfast." He led the way though the main doors into the foyer and nave of the Keeper's Temple.

The main hall was warm, even though the room was huge. Eight hearths blazed big fires. A table surrounded with ornate chairs in the center of the hall was heavy with food. There were breads and pastries and meats and foods of all kinds, enough to feed a hundred people.

"Bring tea and leave us," Ulric said.

Em was in his HUD. "There are six cruel and corrupt servants here. There are 94 slaves. Barcus, they brand them like cattle. One was just murdered this morning by a guest who is still here. Samson is behind this panel listening to the conversation via a device hidden in this vase." The panel and listening device were highlighted in his HUD.

"These six servants are currently packed and will flee before the High Keeper's men get here in three days. They know they are coming. There is a wagon full of gold and silver coins and other valuable items ready to roll now."

"This is a lovely temple. I may consider accepting this as a post," Ulric indicated he knew they were watched.

"We should have a tour and review the staff. If you know what I mean..." Ulric was really good at that greasy inflection.

Barcus finished his tea and only managed a half a roll and stood up. Po had never sat. Po stood at his elbow, and Grady was tending the fires. Ulric refilled his large wineglass and stood as well.

The sun was finally up but had not reached the windows of this hall. Samson was there without calling him.

"I want to see where the staff lives," Ulric said haughtily.

"Very well. Right this way," Samson said with a slight bow and a gesture with his hand.

"Not the house staff," Ulric added, grinning.

Samson's eyebrow raised and a sly smile found his lipless mouth.

"Understood. Right this way my Lords." Samson led the way.

They were taken to the courtyard. Across from the main stables was an older, more dilapidated building. Voices and even laughter could be heard behind the door. The BUGs showed Barcus what was going on inside. Almost all the slaves were assembled in the same room.

Barcus realized it was the old blacksmith shop, converted to a common room. The forge had been converted to a fireplace to warm the room. Since it was not designed for that, the room was smoky.

Some people were drinking from a small, rough barrel of an unknown drink.

Some of the people were festive, some serious, some wept as they looked toward the hall in the rear.

Samson kicked the door open in an obvious attempt to be dramatic. The room went immediately silent when Barcus ducked under the door, followed by the others. On seeing them, the slaves immediately moved to line the walls and kneel on the cold floor, heads down, men and boys to one side, women and girls to the other side.

All except one man.

He was old and bald. He had a white beard that was roughly trimmed, probably with a knife.

To Po, Barcus asked quietly, "Why do they do that?"

"To make it easier for you to...choose," she replied.

Samson was moving toward the standing man, lifting a whip from a peg as he crossed the room.

"Say the word, my Lord." Samson was looking at the man's scarred face.

Barcus and the man locked eyes. He was defiant. His head and face were covered with scars that were the obvious result of this defiance. One of his eyes looked clouded, probably damaged in the past by the whip.

Barcus walked up beside Samson and held out his hand for the whip. "How touching. They are celebrating the life of Volk." Smiling wide, Samson ceremonially put the whip in Barcus's hand, nearly drooling at what was about to come.

"Samson, please assemble the rest of the household staff for introductions in the main hall. We will be there soon."

"Yes, my Lord." He scampered off to the door behind him.

"The Keepers never come down here, only their...guests," Smith said.

Barcus moved in close. Uncertainty came to the man's eyes for the first time. The door closed behind Samson with a blow and swirl of snow.

"Keepers will never set foot here again, nor their guests," Barcus said without blinking.

That was when Smith recognized Po. He froze, his eyes wide.

"Come with me," Barcus said to Smith "Po, get them all up and dressed as best they can."

He turned, expecting to be followed. The man did.

Ulric finished his wine and filled the goblet from the barrel. It was bitter beer with a slight hint of lamp oil.

He sat on the floor in the middle of the room and said, "Gather round, children. I have a story for you about a mouse and a lion..."

Barcus crinkled his forehead at that. "The Mouse and the Lion" was his favorite story as a child.

Barcus walked down the hallway. Horse stalls on either side had been converted to living spaces for the slaves. He had seen it on the HUD already. His anger was building. He opened one door, and a woman was tending the wounds on a young girl, deep cuts in her wrists and ankles and whip marks all over her.

Room after room of women and boys beaten, burned and whipped.

Smith spoke, "More than usual. His 'friends' enjoyed his funeral."

Finally, Barcus stopped in front of a door and pushed it open. He used his flashlight to see the strangled dead body of the raped young girl. Em had seen it via the BUGs. They had been too late.

He turned and kicked open the next stall.

The whip flashed and cut deep into the fat flesh of a man raping yet another girl. The first had not been enough. The whip fell again and again as Barcus's fury grew. The man was screaming, "Please, stop! Don't you know who I am?!"

"I do know. You are the dead man." Then he broke his neck.

Barcus then turned to the Smith, so only he could hear, and through gritted teeth, said, "I am so sorry this happened to you. Will you help me make sure this never happens to them again?"

The girl was suddenly hugging him around his waist. "I want all these people in the main hall in fifteen minutes. It's warm in there. We will set up a triage hospital. I'm sure there are feast cots. And breakfast is there for all. I have one more thing to do." He paused before leaving as the girl ran out.

"Are any of the house staff innocent?" Barcus asked Smith.

"Evil. The lot," the old man said.

"*I second that, Barcus. Evil,*" Em added.

"What is your name, Father?" Barcus asked.

"Smith, my Lord," He replied.

He started to walk past, winding up the bloody whip. The man stopped him with a hand on his chest. Even Barcus knew the gesture was a risk for the man. "Thank you, son."

"Call me Barcus."

***

He walked into the hall. The whip in his hand was still dripping blood.

The household staff was lined up, smiling. They were soft and fat with the look of cruelty, smirking. It was the bloody whip that was making them smile.

Ulric entered the hall. Grady was still helping Po organize the others.

Barcus paused before them, saying nothing for a long minute, until the smile had fallen from all their faces.

"Get out. Take what you have now, the clothes on your backs and go. On foot," Barcus growled.

"We most certainly will not," Samson said, motioning to two guards that stood there. "We are the house..." The mouse-faced man was cut short.

Without a moment's pause, Barcus shot him in the face with the Glock. When the guards rushed forward, they died as well.

The rest moved quickly, fat and corrupt. "Come to the nave. Move. Bring those pieces of shit with you." They were simpering, begging forgiveness, offering bribes, confessing as they dragged the bodies as far as the bottom of the steps.

As the door slammed behind them, Barcus said, "Now run." He let the bloody whip in his left hand unfurl.

The remaining five ran out the gate and never looked back.

***

Barcus returned alone. He didn't know Ash killed them all after they cleared the main gate moving toward the village.

In less than an hour, everyone had assembled in the main hall. Most seemed confused. They all knew that the household staff was gone and not permitted to return. Now, the sick and wounded were everyone's priority. They were still very afraid of Barcus and even Ulric, who was refilling his wineglass from a pitcher on the table. Barcus stood head and shoulders above them all. He was about to speak when he saw Po stand on a bench.

Speaking in common tongue, she said, "Some of you may remember me. My name is Po." She slid the collar of her tunic off her shoulder to reveal the scar branded above her left breast. "I was born here. My parents died here before I knew them. I would have died too if not for some of you."

She paused and looked right at Smith. "Volk gave me away as a party gift to an old Keeper years ago, to gain favor. I was glad to be away then." She said, almost ashamed.

"I eventually came to be in the service of Lord Barcus." She looked at Barcus. She took a deep breath, "He is the first Keeper I have ever met that deserved to be called Lord." Her lips were trembling. She knew Barcus didn't like what she was saying. But she was free. He knew she was, now.

"The first time I met him, he saved my life. He didn't even know me then. But I have come to know him. He has saved my life more than once, even at the risk of his own. MY life." Her voice cracked and tears spilled from her eyes.

Everyone was silent.

Her hands were clenched into fists, hugged to her chest. "MY life." Her soul was bare in her face. She sobbed openly for a moment, then took a deep breath.

"He has given me everything, and has never taken a single thing from me that was not freely offered." She risked a look at Barcus, and more tears fell.

"He is fierce and strong and kind and sad and so very angry..." A sob slipped out.

"He is also humble, does not want to be called Keeper or Lord or even Sir. Just Barcus. But he is more powerful than even the High Keeper. I have seen his magic." Quieter, "And I think...he truly loves us. All of us. The way the Keepers preach about love, but never do. Not just empty words echoing in a Temple."

"I would die for him." Almost whispering now, but the room was so quiet, all could hear. "But that's not what he wants from me, from us. He wants us to live. Not for him...but for ourselves."

Straightening and taking a deep breath, she continued louder now, even though the room was silent, even the children. "We have come to take you all from here. If you want to come. As soon as it can be managed. But come only knowing you will be considered heretics. You will live under threat of the hammer. But never from us."

"Now eat this fine breakfast Barcus has arranged for you." She was smiling at him now with glistening eyes.

They were all staring at him now. But he could not speak around the lump in his throat. Finally, he managed.

"Eat!" was all he could manage. The children ran up first,

followed by their mothers to make sure they didn't gorge too much.

He went to Po, who was still standing on the bench, wiping her eyes. He gently lifted her and set her down. Shy, suddenly. "Thank you. You are too generous." He lifted her tunic's collar back up into place. His hand came to rest on her slender throat. "We need to get them out of here as soon as possible, Po. Take anything we may need."

Po and Grady began organizing people and tasks while they made sure everyone was eating. "Boots for everyone first," he heard Grady say.

Barcus carried over a small loaf of fresh bread and some cheese to stand next to Smith. He ripped the loaf in half and handed half to Smith. Barcus took a bite of his, then broke the cheese in half. "Smith, I don't think I will be able to do this without you. I'm not a Keeper, really."

"Yes you are. You must be made of magic, lad. I watched Po grow up in this tortured place. A heart made of stone, that one. I think Volk gave her away because he was afraid of her."

Barcus looked at her. She was bringing food to the ones not able to rise from their cots. Others were beginning to help her.

"I never saw her shed a tear her whole life, until today. And I was there the day they put the brand to her." Smith bit the bread. It was almost ceremonial.

"We need them strong, healthy. Convince them it's true. Clothe them first. Take the animals, wagons, food, whatever you, Po and Grady say to bring. We have room for everyone. We have to be gone from here in two days, because on the third, they arrive."

"What's to stop them from following us?" Smith was truly worried.

"I will be killing them all," Barcus growled.

CHAPTER FORTY

Battle

"The depth of this manipulation was immense. Safety protocols in survival mode were off."

--Solstice 31 Incident Investigation Testimony Transcript: Emergency Module Digital Forensics Report. Independent Tech Analysis Team.

<<<>>>

Barcus made sure preparations were well underway when he set out that night with Par and Ash. He would not wait for the mercenaries to arrive in Langforest Keep. He would meet them on the road and ensure the people had maximum time to escape.

It didn't take long to find them. By the next evening, he was approaching their encampment, which was at a farm. They had already taken the farm, killed the family, and were feasting on fresh meat from the farm's cattle.

Par deployed a cloud of BUGs that would find and shadow every man in the camp. The BUGs easily entered the farmhouse and the barn.

The leaders were in the house. There were six of them. One of them had a Plate.

"The one that carries the Plate must die before calling in," Barcus communicated while sitting inside Par. Forty windows were open all around, showing vid feeds from the BUGs, as well as an increasingly detailed tactical map of the region.

Slowly, more and more indicators were tagged red as more and more of the mercenaries were identified by the BUGs and marked on the tactical map. Ash was working his way around quietly to the far side, where the most likely escape route would to be.

"Par, you will drop me off here three hours before dawn, and then take up station here." He indicated the points on the large tactical map. "I will have an excellent field of fire in three directions from this point.

"They have only three sentries: here, here and here," he said, marking the slowly moving points. "I will take this one. Par, you take the other two, but try not to spook the horses. Then start dropping the mercenaries one at a time, using suppressed fire only. We will get as many as we can this way before we start the mop up.

"Par, use your high def thermal imaging and take out the man with the Plate. He will most likely look out the window to investigate before he calls in. Take him then. Use the 10mm if you need to."

***

In full darkness, Par quietly dropped Barcus off, where he took his position in an elevated rock outcropping that overlooked the farm. It took Par almost another hour to get into position after that.

Barcus scanned the camp with his scope as he waited. He found eleven bodies laid out in a row. The farmers and family, including the children. From their state of undress, it appeared that four of the woman had been raped before their throats were slit.

His growing fury kept him warm.

In that hour, waiting for Par to get in place, he watched the sentry on his side walk back and forth just outside of the firelight. The fools kept looking at the fires, destroying their night vision. Barcus would drop him at the extreme end of his path. It was farthest from camp.

Dawn was two hours away when he pulled the trigger. The sentry fell like a puppet with its strings cut.

The sound of the rifle, though suppressed, still seemed loud in the night.

The windows in his HUD showed the other two sentries drop, a moment apart.

Barcus began to work. Targets were highlighted in his scope. He held his trigger back, and when a target was acquired, the rifle shot. He consumed his first magazine before he knew it. The process of ejecting, reloading and firing only took seconds. The camp was beginning to react now. The alarm went up. Yelling began. They fell as they emerged from tents, drawing on boots, pulling on pants, shrugging on shirts. Some ran for the horses without a word.

Search, aim, fire, search, aim, fire, over and over until he emptied another magazine. Em called a warning to him as he paused to eject the latest magazine.

"Movement, behind YOU!" Em called out.

Barcus rolled over in time to see a Tracker with a huge knife bearing down on him in the darkness. He brought up the empty AR to block the downward stab. The strike was so hard on the AR that he heard the man's wrist break. Instantly, he swung the butt of the AR at his assailant's head, but missed. The man's momentum landed him heavily on Barcus, knocking the back of his head on the rocks behind him, dazing him for a moment.

The man was driving his left forearm into Barcus's throat with all of his weight. This was a mistake, because it created a bit of space between them and freed Barcus's hand from being pinned.

Barcus drove his knife under the man's ribs with all the fury that had been building. He tore through his heart and lungs and even ribs, from belly to collar bone.

He threw the body off and quickly reloaded his rifle. Several men were now screaming in pain, adding to the chaos below.

Barcus noticed a counter in his HUB, "Remaining: 21/109."

"Several remain hiding in the barn. They are getting ready to make for the horses as a group. Four remain in the house. They are hiding in the basement. Even the 10mm cannot reach them there," Par stated.

"Move in. Spook the horses if you can. I will wait for them to move. Do you think we may have missed any other Trackers? They don't sleep in camp with the rest."

"They must have met up with them as guides," Em replied.

Par was moving towards the horses when the men began to flood out of the barn, with their crossbows shouldered and aiming in every direction. Barcus started with the last one out. Quickly moving up the double row, he cut them down one by one. They had no idea where he was or what was happening.

The last four got to the horses just as Par arrived. They all fired their crossbows at Par, but they might as well have been tossing tooth picks. Par simply stomped them to jelly.

"Remaining: 4/109."

"They are all in the house. Ash, move in," Barcus said.

Less than a minute later, Ash jogged up to the farm house and casually crashed through the front door. Screaming ensued. Barcus didn't bother to watch. He took the time to remove a partial magazine and replace it with a full one.

Par was already beginning to collect bodies, strip them of weapons and gear, and toss them like dolls into a pile inside the barn.

The mercenaries had tried to fight off Ash with fire. But they only managed to burn the farmhouse down with themselves inside it. Even so, Ash retrieved the Plate and placed it inside Par's Faraday compartment for later conversion.

By dawn, all the weapons and gear were loaded into Par, and the barn was their funeral pyre. None of them had managed to get away.

The swarm of BUGs revealed one more Tracker that had been hiding high in a tree. He had nearly been overlooked. He had been patiently waiting with his crossbow for a shot at Barcus. The 10mm literally tore him from the tree.

Barcus asked Ash to return to Langforest Keep with the horses. They had never spooked, not a single one. Ash could lead them all at once. Barcus wanted the caravan to have as many options as possible.

He would return with Par. She would provide her shadowed protection on the road.

***

Barcus slept in the command chair almost as soon as they got underway. Par woke him as they approached Langforest Keep.

"Em, status?"

"They are packed and away. Someone set the slave quarters on fire on the way out. That caught the stables and several other buildings as well. The Manor might survive, mostly because it is made of stone."

"How is Ash doing?" Barcus asked.

"I estimate he will catch up to us a few kilometers above the Salterferry Bridge tomorrow."

"Good. Par, do you think you can get me to the bridge before the caravan?"

"Easily," Par answered. Before he could reply, they were moving faster.

"Excellent," Barcus said, as he ripped open a protein bar. He noticed his hand was covered in dried blood. He looked down at his tunic and he was covered in stains.

"I should have brought a change of clothes."

He ate the bar, wondering what he would do with all these people.

***

He wasn't sure how they would react to Pardosa just yet, so she dropped him off at the southern bridge tower. A cloud of BUGs followed the caravan, so Barcus knew how far away they were.

Par went north to ensure the road around the mountain was passable by the wagons. She already knew there were several fallen trees would need to be moved.

Barcus walked out onto the bridge while he was awaiting the caravan. The gorge was very deep, and the bridge was wide and strong. It was a suspension style bridge, the deck was made up of squared, thick, timbers from impossibly tall, straight trees. The caravan came into view.

He stood in the middle of the bridge.

Po was the first to recognize him, and galloped her horse up to him as fast as she could. She was out of the saddle before the horse came to a full stop, but didn't rush into his arms.

He realized he was disappointed.

"Barcus, are you all right?" She was looking at all the blood.

"Yes. I'm fine. It's not my blood," He answered.

She moved closer, slowly, as if he might spook like a wild horse.

"How are they?" he asked. They were starting to enter the bridge.

"They are fine for the most part. Some of the sick and wounded may not survive the trip. We have so many on foot." She looked back at the group.

Barcus turned to face the north end of the bridge. "Par, after you clear the road, I want you to clear the tunnel for them to camp tonight. Unload everything at the tunnel's mouth and then just wait, deep in the tunnel."

He turned back to Po and said, "No one will follow us. We will be safe for now."

"More will come. There will be much to do," she said.

"Will they leave us alone now, Po?" he asked.

"There are no happy endings, because nothing ends," she echoed her reply with a sad smile.

***

They reached the unfinished tunnel by midafternoon that day, and made camp early. A giant pile of dried tree-fall was already piled near the entrance for firewood. There was a huge pile of weapons and gear there.

Soon, several fires were built up, and cooking began. After getting into some clean clothes, Barcus helped with the most severely injured people. There were fifteen of them. They had been carried in three large wagons that now had makeshift canvas covers. These were set up as a makeshift hospital in the tunnel. Only five of them could even walk on their own.

"I don't think Kat is going to make it. She has lost so much blood," Lea said. The woman, Lea, had assumed the role of healer. Po looked at Barcus.

Lea continued, "Volk let them take turns with the lash. They opened her to the bone in several places. She passed out mercifully after the first twenty."

"Moving her opens the wounds again," Po said so only Barcus and Lea could hear. "We need to get her back to The Abbey quickly, Barcus."

Barcus faced the darkness of the tunnel and said, "Par, I want you to come up quietly and back your ramp up as close as you can. Lights off. I want to load ten of these cots directly inside. They should just fit. I will ride with Lea back to Whitehall as fast and smooth as possible."

Po turned to Lea. "Lea we are going to take them tonight. We need you to be brave. We need you to go with them. Don't be afraid," Po said to her as Barcus walked to the edge the darkness.

A candle flickered with the movement of air. Lea was watching Barcus when suddenly, he was outlined in the soft light of a small room that somehow appeared directly before him. It looked like a rustic cabin inside.

"Come. We should hurry," Barcus said.

Po and Lea led the least injured to the front where they sat in five of the six seats. Others helped them carry the ten occupied cots in without bumping the patients. They were especially careful when moving Kat. Barcus had retrieved a small first aid kit from the side of the main console. Without a word, he held a small tube to the side of Kat's neck, moving the tube side to side until the light shifted from red to green. The injector made a small sound.

"That will help. But we will need to hurry," Barcus said. "Get Smith. He will need to help walk us out." Four other women sat among the cots when the ramp closed. Barcus was in the command seat.

In the end it was Smith, Po, Ulric and Grady that walked through the tunnel saying, "Don't be afraid. Close your eyes. Just for a minute. It is all right. We are safe."

Most people closed their eyes. Some did not. Deep in the tunnel, Par was so black that as she passed over them silently, they didn't even notice. A few people looked but didn't know what they were seeing. She was a greater darkness. Keeper's magic. The few that truly saw Par were the ones working just outside the tunnel. They saw her as Par emerged, as it immediately turned and began climbing over the mountain.

Par moved fast after that, even though they could barely feel it inside. The walls remained simple white and the lights dim. Barcus used his HUD to get them there. He called ahead, and Olias had all the hearths lit in the main hall when they arrived after dawn. Par backed right up to the main double doors of the hall as she opened the ramp.

One by one, they moved the cots to the warm room.

Barcus disappeared for a few minutes but was back at Kat's cot doing something out of Lea's view as another cot was carried out. When the last of the cots was out and the patients settled, Lea went over to Barcus as he was covering Kat's back again with a clean dressing.

Before Lea could say a word, Barcus said, "Lea, this is Olias. He lives here and knows where everything is. If you need something specific, ask him." Olias nodded to her with respect, something that had never happened to her before.

Barcus continued. "Kat will begin to run a fever soon, and it will continue for a few days. Don't worry though. It will mean she is getting better. Olias, make sure everyone gets water. Kat will wake soon and she will be very thirsty. It is very important that she drinks water."

"Lord Keeper Barcus, I'm sorry, but she will never awaken. I have seen this before..." Lea tried to explain but was interrupted.

"Don't call me that." He had not meant to snap at her. She fell to her knees, trembling before he could stop her. Her forehead was on the floor.

"I'm sorry, my Lord." Her voice shook.

He could not stop himself. He reached down, lifted her up and set her on her feet by her arms. She was light as a feather.

He smiled and said, "Please. Call me Barcus. Just Barcus."

She was shocked into silence.

Barcus looked over his shoulder. Everyone in the room had stopped and stared at them. Patients and caregivers. Just then they heard a small voice, barely a whisper.

"I'm so thirsty."

Kat was already awake.

CHAPTER FORTY-ONE

The Fourth Day

"All data was precisely deleted during this period."

--*Solstice 31 Incident Investigation Testimony Transcript: Emergency Module Digital Forensics Report. Independent Tech Analysis Team.*

<<<>>>

Barcus woke as Po tried to slide out of bed without disturbing him. He caught her by the braid.

She froze.

She rolled toward him, first rolling the braid around her neck followed by his hand and arm until she was nose to nose with him.

"Good morning, my Lord. May I serve you?" She knew he would not tolerate that sentence to be spoken in the presence of another person. He kissed her.

As if in punctuation, they heard a hammer fall on the anvil in the first tap of a rhythm that would last all day.

"We slept late," Barcus said

"We were up late." She had a wicked smile. "The late bath, was an excellent idea though."

The anvil had a cadence. Ding... ding, ding. Pause. Ding... ding, ding. Pause.

"This is a new smile on you. What is it?" Po asked.

"This place is alive again. The sounds. Those boys will make nails and laugh all day long as they work." He looked to the window. "They will sharpen tools for people and learn something new from Smith."

Po added, "They work with full bellies and a good night's sleep, on a clean bed, in safety. These people have never felt safe before in their entire lives. You have done more for them in the week that they have been here than anyone has done for them in their entire lives. Come with me and I will show you."

They slid out of bed and dressed quickly.

A dozen people were in the kitchens when they looked in. All six of the cauldrons had fires beneath them. The smell of porridge and fresh breads made his mouth water.

They had finally stopped kneeling and bowing to him whenever he appeared. The slight nod and smile held all the weight and honor possible to convey. He took a bowl and served himself some oatmeal with apples, spices and honey. The oatmeal was spiced in a way he had grown to love. He held out a mug for tea, knowing that even he would get his hand slapped now if tried to pour his own.

He sat with Po at a long, well-scrubbed table, across from Smith, who was looking intently at a scroll that was trying to roll itself up. Barcus set his tea mug down on a corner just as Smith had set his own mug on the other corner.

"What's this?" Barcus asked, looking at a detailed drawing upside down.

"It is the northeastern quadrants arc. We are planning the repairs to the destroyed section. We are dismantling an old barn today that will give us the lumber we need to first stabilize, then rebuild the section."

"There are enough rooms for everyone for now. They are far better than what we had. But I prefer that everyone have a room above ground. It will keep them healthier."

"How can I help?" Barcus asked.

Smith would never get used to this question.

"You can arrange to obtain these blocks from the quarry." Smith pointed to a list of dimensions that were actually block sizes and quantities. Smith still had a hard time believing the things Olias had told him, about Ash and Par mostly.

Just glancing at the list captured it. Em indicated in his HUD that these blocks were in the current inventory at the quarry and whoever made the list had obviously already visited the site.

"These will be used as the new footers here and here," Smith indicated on the drawing. The automatic scan and render in his HUD revealed the scale was amazingly close for having been drawn freehand. "Once they are set here, we can shore up this corner and save the rest of the roof from collapsing here." He pointed on the map and then turned to look out and up at the precarious roofline, far above and at the other end of the keep.

"Then we can fix the roof and begin to restore all three floors. Now is the best time, before the spring planting. We are going to be hard pressed this first year."

"Good morning, My L..." The speaker stopped. "Good morning, Barcus." She held her own bowl and mug. She was still waiting to be acknowledged before she sat down.

"Good morning, Lea," Barcus said. Echoes from Po and Smith came at the same time.

"How are things?" Barcus asked, knowing that she was here specifically to deliver her daily report on the status of the infirmary and its patients. She was still skittish about eating with men.

Barcus dug into his oatmeal then. It was finally cool enough.

"We still have eleven beds." He was still not used to the way they referred to patients. "Kat is up and helping me with the others." Her voice caught. Barcus pretended not to notice. A glance at Po showed her paying additional attention to her breakfast.

"I don't know what to say, Barcus. She...was the worst of them all. The lashings are all closed and nearly healed now. Sixty lashes." Lea's tears fell freely again. Barcus did not look away now.

"Lea, you will never see those kinds of wounds here, ever again." A sob slipped from her. Barcus continued, "How's Ulric?"

Like magic, she laughed. Face wet with tears, her hand went to her mouth finally, to cover a snort. Everyone laughed then, because they all seemed to know about Ulric's hemorrhoid. Both hands covered her face now, as her shoulders rocked, in tears and laughter with them. She produced a handkerchief from somewhere and dried her tears finally and wiped her nose.

"He'll live," she said through a smile.

She also drew out a small pouch.

She set it on the table and slid it to Barcus.

"I can't take this," Lea said.

Barcus leaned back from it like it might explode.

"And why would you say that?" Only Po could hear a touch of anger in his voice.

"I do not deserve it. You give me so much already. More than I ever had. Or deserve."

It was Smith that spoke first. "Lea, there are no slaves here."

It was Po that picked up the pouch and placed it back in her hand. "You earned it."

"But I...you already... This has been the first week of my life that I have not known hunger. The first winter week I was never cold. I have clothes and a room and...hope. You need not pay me."

"Listen to me. You will take this pay, just like everyone else that intends to live and work here. But we expect you to earn it. And you have. Your food and the roof over your head are also part of the deal. Part of your pay."

"But the food. It's the same as...it's what you eat." Her chin began to tremble again.

"I like the food," Barcus said, as he shifted to common tongue. "Do you like the work?" The question caught her off guard.

"Yes."

"Do you do a good job?" Barcus asked.

"Yes, but..."

"We expect your best work. Can we have it? That's part of the deal, too. Not the work of a slave." His eyes fell to her chest where he knew she held the brand. "We can't afford that."

"And only half of your waking hours." Po said this. "The other half belongs to you."

"And every fourth day is yours," Smith added.

"Have you taken a day yet?"

"I have never had one before. I don't know what I would do."

"Start by sleeping as late as you want," Po began. "Then eat, all you want."

"I like to walk, to look at something beautiful," Smith said.

"The top of the tower with a cup of tea is very nice," Po added.

"I like to clean my rooms. I do a little more to make it my home," Smith added.

"Spend time with friends or family," Po continued.

"Make something beautiful." Grady added this.

"Have some wine. Sing. I hear you have a beautiful voice," Ulric said. "Olias has set up a tavern in the tower. The portcullis machine room.

"Wine is the only thing to spend our money on around here anyway!"

"When did this happen?" Barcus asked, amused.

"The day the repair crew finished fixing the portcullis. At the end of the day, Olias showed up with a keg of ale, and we sat about laughing. Rose brought up a tray of food, and the next thing we knew, we were laughing and crying and singing.

"The next night it spontaneously happened again.

"Before we knew it, Olias had the tavern set up. Right there in the machine room, warning us that we'd be buying him drinks for a month to pay him back. You see, it was there he told us we were to all be paid the next day.

"Rose and May have taken it on as the place to go for cold meals after hours. It frees up the night kitchen crew from distractions.

"And they keep people from drinking too much!"

"Except Keeper Ulric!" They all laughed for a moment and fell into comfortable silence.

"So, Lea. You will take your pay and spend it on whatever you like. Or save it." It wasn't an order, or a demand. It was a simple statement.

The pouch disappeared back into her skirts.

***

While everyone was told it was eight hours on, eight hours off and eight hours rest, they worked constantly during daylight. If not on their assigned job, they worked on improving their homes, the formal gardens or other things they enjoyed. The Portcullis Tavern had lots of volunteers to assist with construction. Rose fell into running it full-time, and May stayed on as well. Rose also made The Abbey's work schedule for everyone. She enforced it as well. Everyone was made to take a "fourth day," even Barcus and Po.

***

They took their first day off together. They met Par on the quarry road just after dawn. They brought a basket of food.

"So, where are we really going?" Po asked.

"I promised I'd tell you everything. It's easier to show you." They were sitting down in Par's first row.

"Par, full open canopy," Barcus said.

The enclosure seemed to disappear. Par was moving in glide mode, smooth as could be, through a sky that was bright with high clouds.

"We are going to a place I call Foxden. You will also get to meet another friend. His name is Stu," Barcus said as she marveled at the view.

"Is this friend like Em?" she asked

"Yes and no. Let's say they are related. Stu has been making a few things for me," Barcus said.

"Stu?" Po asked.

"Yes. His name is Stu."

"What was he making?" Po asked.

"Hinges and tool handles, for starters. We have thirty-six ax heads with no handles. Axes seem to be our most useful tool, and real weapons."

"Why do we need weapons?" Po asked.

"To be free. If we cannot defend ourselves, we are just pretending not to be slaves."

"Tell Olias. I think he has been salvaging weapons. Crossbows, swords, arrows, bows. He has burned bodies, not weapons," Po said.

"Em, you must know," Barcus said

"Yes. He has nearly 400 cached away. About 300 are in The Abbey already. Only a few of the people know how to use them," Em said out loud.

"Add a stocked armory to Olias's task list, and an archery range, maybe between the western wall and the orchards," Barcus added.

"You know it's forbidden," Po said.

"I now believe that living above the gorge is forbidden," Barcus said. "Did you know that the Salterferry Bridge has been burned?"

Po gasped. "What?"

"That bridge was the only easy way to the south."

"Or to the north, FROM the south?" Barcus said, with a raised eyebrow.

"Won't the High Keeper wonder what became of all his mercenaries?" she asked.

"He won't care about them. He will only care about the Keepers he lost. Maybe not even then," came his caustic reply.

***

They arrived at Foxden well before noon.

It had been months since Barcus had been there, and the spring did not seem as warm here as in The Abbey. The lake was still iced over, though it was much thinner at the center. If he had not known the shelter was there, they would never have seen it.

The wind was constant from the west this morning. There was no snow on the rocky beach in front of the outcropping of stone that concealed Foxden.

They unloaded their supplies and luggage, and Par quickly moved away. It was almost like she was uncomfortable in the barren open.

Barcus opened the door and immediately lit the fire that was already laid in the large hearth. It was dry and smelled a bit dusty to Po as she entered.

The contrast between the hard rustic nature of the shelter and the beauty of the fine rugs and furnishings was so well balanced, it stopped her short.

Barcus looked up at her and smiled.

"I expected...a Tracker's hole," Po said. "A bed out of the rain."

"It is that." Barcus stood and went out to retrieve the cask of water and other supplies.

When he returned and closed the door, Po was still standing in the same place. Slowly, she turned back to him and unclasped her cloak as he opened the shutters on the large windows to either side of the door. The room was warming.

"I thought I'd have to clean." Po was looking at him, not the large room.

"This is your fourth day, Po."

"I thought we were to meet Stu."

"He will be along later, after dark."

Barcus walked up to her and instead of touching her, he reached into her ever present pouch and drew out her Plate.

He walked to the fireplace and set it on the mantle, propped up behind a beautiful, silver candlestick holder.

"Music, romantic," was all he said, and it began to play. It was a soft, slow classical guitar piece, with Spanish undertones.

"That's beautiful," Po said.

Barcus added another log and stirred it to life.

"It's for you."

He returned to her and took the cloak from her shoulders. He hung both hers and his on the pegs by the door. And then he did something that surprised her. He took off his boots, socks and his belt.

In bare feet, he filled the kettle at the sink and hung it from the hook on the swinging iron arm in the fireplace. He walked around the trunk that functioned as a low table in front of the oversized sofa and sat. He leaned back, slouching as he put his feet up on the trunk to soak heat up from the fire, wiggling his toes.

"What are you doing?" she asked, still not moving from that spot.

"Making tea. You?"

She turned slowly towards the large windows. The stark desolation of the frozen lake had its own kind of simple beauty. An elk was standing in the bright sun, using its hoof to break the thin ice to drink. Its rack was huge and scraped. A few places were broken off, giving it even more beauty in a savage way.

The music and the scene quieted her mind to every other thought as she watched and listened. When she spoke it was a whisper.

"What is this?" she said.

She had not noticed him walk up behind her until his hands came to gently rest on her shoulders. The thick carpet had hidden his footfall.

"This is rest," Barcus said.

"What kind of magic is this?" She turned and looked up into his face.

"The only kind that matters, really. Powerful for what it doesn't contain," Barcus said.

"I've never had a fourth day my whole life."

He reached between them and took up the end of her braid, untying the leather that held it. He slowly began to unbraid it as he spoke.

"Pay close attention. If you do, you can return to this feeling, any time. And if you spend enough of your fourth days like this, wherever you are, the feeling will hold the rest of the days."

"I thought fourth days were to, be simply, sleeping off

hangovers." She smiled.

"Did you bring a hair brush?" He was almost through unbraiding her hair. She nodded.

"Get it." He readied a beautiful, delicate teapot and unmatched mugs, selected for their size, on a wooden tray. She dug out her hairbrush. It was the silver one that Olias had salvaged.

He set the tray down on the trunk and gestured for her to sit on the carpet in front of him.

He gently, leisurely, brushed her hair as they made tea and listened to music. They had a cold lunch of hard spicy sausage, bread with butter, cheese and apples.

"So this is how Keepers eat?" Po asked as she dipped a slice of apple into the honey pot. They were both sitting on the carpeted floor now.

"Keepers should be so lucky." She smiled at his words, but the smile faded.

"So many things are forbidden. In the south it is much worse, where the world is 'civilized.' Did you know Rose was raised there, in Exeter? She says that everyone has the hammer over their head there. Everyone lives under threat of the anvil. No one is innocent."

"It's because you cannot rule the innocent." Barcus said.

"But you do." Po added. His eyebrow rose at this.

"I rule no one. I'm just a gatesman in a ruined Abbey, full of refugees."

"You do lie to yourself, Barcus. I have learned since I met you that when one is free, that is the first freedom we embrace."

She continued. "But I see you. I am beginning to understand the way you see others."

"What I see is not the gatesman of the hermitage. I see Barcus, man of Earth." She paused. "The Keepers are justified in their fear of the men from Earth if they are all like you. You are the nightmare under their beds. You have all their magic and more, far more. And they have no idea you are here.

"I'm glad the Salterferry Bridge is burned. I don't want them to wake the Man from Earth. I have seen him awake, more than once."

"I am just a man, Po. Nothing more," he argued.

"Just a man?" she asked, incredulous. "Smith is just a man. Give him a hammer and measure him again. Give him a hammer and his people and measure him again. And if not for you, he and all the rest would be dead. If not for you, how many mercenaries would be left north of the gorge?

"I have seen you on the wall or in the tower or even your study looking into the distance. I know what you are doing. I can see it in your face. You hunt them and kill them, in your mind, with magic, all of them. I know the day, the hour the last of them fall. Because you come back to us then."

"They must be stopped." He whispered as he remembered. "Don't you see? I am just a man... Different tools. Skills. Different desires. But still just a man. Par and Ash and Stu are just tools. I have been trying to tell you." He drew the handgun from its concealment and laid it on the table. "Just a tool."

"A bow can be used to feed your family or to murder them," Po paused. "An anvil can be..."

"Our anvil makes nails," Barcus interrupted. "What are you trying to tell me?" Barcus asked.

"I am trying to tell you, whether you like it or not, you are leading these people. You, not Ulric. Everyone knows it, everyone except you. Right now, even today, you are leading by example. If you had not taken a fourth day, no one would have.

"Why do you think Olias paid you during dinner last night? It wasn't a joke. Even he knew. The gatesman gets paid. Just like everyone else."

"Does Ulric get paid?" Barcus asked.

"He is the one paying us all. Otherwise it's forbidden." She smiled.

"Does he know that?" Barcus laughed.

"Saay and Kia have thanked him repeatedly, I'm sure," Po smirked. "Why does he get the big suite instead of you?" she asked.

"He is the Keeper, and I am just the gatesman," Barcus said

"Yes you are." She climbed into his lap, facing him, her legs wrapped around him.

Their faces were close to each other. Her fingers traced the scar on his face. His hand gently caressed her back.

"Tell me something I should know. Something Magic," Po said.

"Can you keep a secret?" he asked.

"Yes. I swear."

"I am 91 years old," Barcus said. "I have never told anyone that. Where I come from, it is very impolite to talk about age. Because it doesn't matter."

"No one in my caste ever gets that old." She wasn't taken aback as he had expected. "The high born might get that old, but by then they are gray and...old." She ran her finger down the scar. "Only the High Keepers never age. It's part of the magic."

"That magic is called longevity serum. It's a drug. It prevents cellular replication errors." He touched her face now. "I only need it once a year or so now. It slows the aging process."

"I'll die an old woman while you still look like this?" The idea seemed upsetting to her suddenly.

"No." he reassured her. "I will now age along with you. We'll die together, gray and wrinkled."

"How many years will you lose? Being here?" She asked.

He almost put the topic aside, but he had promised to answer her direct questions. "Probably 200 years. It's worth the trade to be here with you."

She looked like she was going to cry again, so he just said it.

"I love you, Po."

They looked into each other's eyes for a long minute. Slowly she reached up to the button at the base of her neck. Instead of letting it fall, she swept it off over her head, onto the floor in front of the sofa.

"Now I will tell you a secret," she said. "I can always tell when people are speaking the truth."

She was naked, straddling him on the sofa. The fire was blazing, lighting her from behind.

"Maybe not the truth. But what they believe is true," she said. "It seems to have a tone. I never told anyone that because I thought it was magic."

"It is magic. Everything is," Barcus whispered.

She was working his tunic up slowly. Soon there would be nothing between them.

"I am done asking myself why this is happening or how," she said as his tunic came free and was over his head, joining her clothing on the floor.

"I love you, my Lord, my Equal. I always will. No matter what." With those words she reached down between them and guided him into her.

***

"I could get used to these fourth days," she said. She was spent, lying on his chest, sideways in bed. They had spent all afternoon there. A food tray, empty wine bottles and a cold empty teapot were all lost somewhere in the pillows.

"It will be dark soon," Barcus said, looking at the window.

"And then I will meet Stu? Where has he gone all day?" This thought made her nearly fly out of the bed. He watched her retrieve a basin and pitcher. She was never shy in her nakedness.

"It has been easy getting used to bathing," she noted. "I can remember going years without a good wash. You get accustomed to being filthy."

He watched her as she washed herself. When she was done, she washed him. It was very relaxing.

They dressed fully, and Barcus led her outside and around to the left where Par stood in the moonlight. It was a large, flat rocky place. Barcus saw in his HUD that the STU was initiating startup sequences. It wasn't a fast startup. But all the systems checks flew by quickly. It was a few more minutes before the Grav-foils came on-line.

The first indication that anything was happening was sound, a deep rumble that she could feel more than hear. In the moonlight, the ice began to bow and then all at once, fracture in a small explosion, like a thunder clap in the distance. Out of the lake rose a massive black insect-like shape. It was like the absence of light, it was so black, as black as Par and Ash. The only sounds were the great slabs of ice still crashing back down to the lake.

Several small wings fanned out and gently articulated. Mist rose up from these wings, as if the water was falling from it in the wrong direction.

Finally, everything became still.

Without a sound, the STU drifted toward them. Po realized that it was as big as a house and that it was going to settle in the flat just beyond them.

Silently, it flew directly over them and settled on five large legs as its carapace-like plates shifted and expanded and an opening the size of a barn door slid away.

Lights came up inside as Barcus advanced up the slight ramp, catching Po on her heels. She began to advance when Par also began to move.

"Par, please transfer all the 3D printer objects to your hold for transport. Add to inventory. We're going up."

"Barcus, wait," Em said. It was one of the rare times she spoke out loud instead of via his implants. "You need to know... I..." She paused and then appeared in his vision, as if she was standing there. "We were unable to...clean the decks."

Barcus froze with one foot on the ladder already.

"Thanks for reminding me, Em."

Po followed him up the ladder as she watched Par back up into a spot designed specifically for her. When she got to the top, she was not prepared for all the blood.

"I'm sorry, Barcus. But it was frozen before it was able to dry." It was a voice Po had not heard before. "All the cleaning bots had been removed and their spaces re-purposed during modifications."

Barcus was saying nothing. He was staring at the blood that looked all too fresh, even though it had shifted to brown. It did not help that the room was completely white. It was rounded and detail-free, like Par was sometimes.

Smoothly, the canopy seemed to disappear. It now looked like they were standing outside again, the stars and moon bright above. The floor became like a flat black pad set on the rocks outside.

Po could not stifle her gasp.

A man walked into their view from the shadows, but did not step onto the pad. They were all lit by some invisible light.

"Hello, my name is Po. You must be Stu," Po said, trying to remain calm, trying to break the moment.

"Hello, Po. It is nice to meet you in person at last," Stu said.

Barcus looked up at him now. He cocked his head to the side.

"Stu, you've changed," Barcus said.

"Yes, sir. It was a secondary mission priority. A full AI upgrade."

He was a handsome young man in his mid-thirties. He wore his hair and beard in traditional Tracker style and was dressed in that fashion as well.

Po looked down the ladder hatch to the cargo bay below. It looked like a hole into the ground to a cave. It wasn't cold. No wind touched her skin. She looked around again, trying to reconcile what she was seeing.

Interrupting, she demanded, pointing at Stu, "Barcus, is he a Keeper? You said you'd tell me everything. How is this NOT MAGIC?!"

Barcus was about to reply when Stu spoke first. "Po, have you ever seen a really good painting?" Stu knew she had. He had full scans of the hall she was raised in.

The question caught her up short. "Yes. I have."

"Could you paint one?" Stu asked simply.

Suddenly, the vista around them morphed to a mural, like the walls were painted and Stu was now a character in that painting. Rolling hills and trees with a high hall in the distance and grazing horses were all around. It was highly detailed, but still a painting.

Po's hand flew to her mouth.

Stu walked as close to her as her could, constrained by the canvas. "I am like a painting, Po. I have been created by brilliant minds and talented hands. But I am still a creation."

"This is the mural in Keeper Volk's private study. You are the tracker from that painting," Po said in awe.

Stu's definition faded from painting to real. Then the simulated countryside around them began to shift to the look of a tapestry, and then finally reality. "Did you know that the one that created me was a woman, a dear friend of Barcus?"

She noticed Stu glance at the blood. She turned to Barcus and clearly saw pain in his face.

"Imagine if you had to spend five years in here, in this tiny room," Stu said as the walls went white again.

"All this," he said as he spread his arms wide and it looked like they were back inside Foxden, "is a tool to keep men like Barcus sane and happy while they are forced to spend long days and years inside here." The scene faded to the simple white of the inside of the ship.

"I am a complex tool. Artfully rendered, complex, aware and even intelligent, but just a tool."

Po looked from Stu to Barcus.

"Do you feel like you are explaining fire to a three-year-old?" Po asked.

"No," Barcus said solemnly. "Well, maybe a five-year-old."

In a flash, without warning, she punched him hard in the ribs.

Barcus was surprised, uninjured, but he still affected a stagger back before saying, "See, you can learn."

She pounded his chest then, over the fully healed wound. Without turning or looking away from Barcus, she asked Stu, "Stu, do you have a mop or something that I can use to clean this up while Barcus is below, supervising the transfer of the materials we came for?"

"Yes, I have just the thing," Stu replied.

Barcus had a look of sadness and gratitude as Po led him to the hatch and he descended the ladder. The storage compartment revealed itself directly to the rear of the now completely white compartment. Stu was still there, as if he was standing just behind and to the left of the compartment. Po placed her hand on the wall in front of Stu. It seemed like there was a clear glass between her and the projection.

The compartment slid open. It was packed with containers of various kinds and types, but no mop, rags or bucket.

"There is a container that looks like this in that compartment," Stu said as he held it up close to her.

Slowly, she read out loud, "Bio Decontamination."

She found the aerosol canister and easily detached it from its holding.

"You seem to be taking this all in stride. Why is that?" Stu sounded genuinely curious.

She was staring at the can, avoiding Stu's stare, but after a small pause she spoke. "When the Telis Raptor got inside the Abbey," she paused, her throat caught, "I knew I was dead. Everyone knows that if you see one, it's the last thing you will ever see.

I lived. I knew every heartbeat after that was a gift and meant something. Right away, I knew that was true. I had to save Barcus. He almost died. To save him, I performed more magic than any Keeper I have ever seen. All of it, forbidden.

"It was that day I decided to take it all 'in stride', as you say. I like that term. I had already earned that anvil a hundred times. After that, it's like I just opened to every possibility, without question."

She was staring at the can, reading the instructions. She flipped the top open and turned to the nearest bloodstain before she continued.

"When he said he'd tell me everything, I knew he was going easy to not overwhelm me. It was a kindness, really."

She sprayed the nearest stain, got closer and sprayed again. The bloodstain began to dry and consume itself, leaving only a light dusting of what looked like fine gray ash.

"He tried to explain that the magic was not really magic at all. But to me, what you call it never mattered. It is understood or it isn't."

"Like the DeCon Spray?" Stu asked.

"Yes. I don't question or fear it any longer. It's a mystery to me how it works, but I can still use it."

She almost had all the blood removed. She sprayed the seat.

"Want to know what my favorite magic is?"

She looked up and Stu was smiling. He nodded.

"Binoculars. I even like saying the word."

She looked into her memory.

"If that isn't magic, I don't know what is."

She walked to the back of the compartment and turned to look at her handy work.

"Do you have a broom?"

"I can handle the rest. I can just over pressurize the cabin, then it will all evacuate when I crack the hatch."

Po secured the canister in its compartment. The door then slid closed, and the scene around her changed once again to the bright moonlit beach by the lake.

"Thank you for doing that. It would have been difficult for Barcus. He loved Chen very much. She died in his arms. It's one of the reasons he is still so angry."

She looked to the hatch.

"Angry? You call that angry?" she raised an eyebrow at Stu.

"Spilled red wine on a favorite rug would make a Keeper 'angry.' The fury in him is like the sun to a candle. Rumor says he has killed over a thousand hard mercenaries. I see him sometimes. His eyes are elsewhere and the look of hatred on his face... His jaw muscles nearly burst when they die. That face. There has never been such a face." She fell silent for a long minute.

"Can we chat on your Plate sometime? It's lonely at the bottom of the lake."

"I'd like that," Po replied.

"I think he's nearly done down there. It is a fourth day," Stu said.

"Good. Stu? It was nice meeting you."

"Care for him. He needs you. More than he knows," Stu said.

She was taken aback by the emotion in Stu's words as well as the content. She descended the ladder just as Barcus was securing the last of a dozen cases of various sizes inside The EM.

"Are you all right?" Barcus asked, straightening up.

"Yes. It's a lot to take in, but I am getting used to that around you."

A cold breeze moved her hair across her face. She was not used to it being out of the braid.

"Why does Stu have to stay at the bottom of the lake?" she asked.

"To hide." His reply earned him a puzzled look from her. He continued, "From the Keepers. They might see him from the sky."

"I have seen them fly over. But not often," she said, looking up at the sky.

"All it would take is once," Barcus said.

CHAPTER FORTY-TWO

Still Falling

"The Shuttle Transport Unit logs showed no indications of corruption or deletion. We speculate that the Em's activities were kept away from Stu. In fact, there is evidence this backup was stored on the STU's core."

--Solstice 31 Incident Investigation Testimony Transcript: Emergency Module Digital Forensics Report. Independent Tech Analysis Team.

<<<>>>

They closed up Foxden and left before first light, and they were back at The Abbey in the early morning.

The entire ride home, Barcus tried to explain as many of Par's capabilities as he could. He did not touch on the BUGs or the extent of his surveillance capabilities. He did cover the use of tactical maps, geo-location, communications and even demonstrated the weapons systems.

A huge elk with a massive rack didn't notice Em's approach. The 7.62mm round took it directly in the brain. Par lifted the beast easily, even though it must have weighed a thousand pounds.

Whitehall would have plenty of meat tonight.

"Call Olias and let him know," Barcus said.

***

They arrived via the north road to waving hands from the tower. The portcullis was on the rise even before they reached the stone bridge. Par did not enter The Abbey, but turned and opened the cargo ramp.

A half dozen men, led by Smith and Olias, were there by the time the ramp had descended.

"Hinges and tool handles as requested, and a few other things that might be useful." Barcus pointed to a medium sized trunk, set to one side. "Please take this one to the gatehouse."

"How was your day?" Smith inquired.

"It was lovely," Po replied as she looked at Barcus, before she went off to explain about the Elk.

Smith raised his eyebrow. "Did a bit of hunting on the day off?"

"Actually, we were lucky to get him on the way back. Par is an excellent hunter," Barcus said.

"Can we get Par to help Ash, bring the blocks back we need? It took him all night to bring the first three. Here, let me show you." Smith went up the tower stairs and didn't stop until he reached the top level, just beneath the roof.

Smith walked to the arch and looked down towards the eastern quad of The Abbey. They had dug down until they reached the white foamcrete of the Redoubt. Three stone blocks were already placed. Ash was supporting the level above, using a beam as a prop. Men scrambled to secure the new corner post, using ropes and tackle. The two levels above that had temporary posts were secured in many locations.

"We will repeat this process two more times, and then we will be able to repair the roof. Once the floors are in and the roof is above, that end is done. Then we can enclose it and begin to restore the interior rooms. We will need to decide what to do with this courtyard after all the rubble is removed."

"What's going on there?" Barcus pointed to a location with the ruined walls of the cathedral.

"They are clearing and sorting the blocks and beams that can be reused. No need to quarry it when we would have to clear it out anyway."

Barcus looked to the west and saw that the formal garden there had been completely cleared except for three huge, twisted, ornamental trees. The garden also had three obelisks set in an isosceles triangle and boulders set in an artful dry riverbed. A dozen people, men and women, were raking the dark soil and removing every rock as they chatted. Children were running back and forth as if collecting the stones into a wheel barrow was the greatest game ever invented.

"It's their fourth day," Smith said quietly. He was obviously enjoying the laughter.

He turned and looked at Barcus and then scanned the room to make sure they were alone.

"My Lord, I feel I must..."

Barcus cut him off. "Smith, please."

"Barcus, you bade me to always speak my mind. I shall, like it or no. These people are...in danger. I feel it, more now really, than when we were under Volk's heel."

"I know," Barcus replied, looking at the children chasing each other. Without his asking, the risk assessment window popped open in his HUD.

"The horses that populate the stables now, not all of them are from the villages that burned. I'm a smith. I have cared for many a High Tracker's horse, and more than one Keeper's horse."

"Yes. I know."

"Perhaps you don't know the sort of man the Lord High Keeper really is."

Smith looked out over The Abbey and even past the wall, to people in the distance who were clearing dead fall from the orchards.

"These people are children. Some of them will come to understand the truth. But most will go on thinking they have traded one anvil for another."

"They know what happened at Langforest Keep after we escaped. A few of the men were determined to stay behind and help you. Even now, I find it hard to believe."

Barcus hadn't known. "I am sorry they had to see that."

"They said you simply pointed at them as they laughed, and then their heads exploded. None that stood against you escaped. Further, in that chaos of moments, they said that you, Ash and Par hunted them all down, one at a time. You filled a barn with their bodies and even the dead horses, and you burned it as if it was soaked in oil."

He looked back out over The Abbey.

"Of course, I'm sure that half of it was either exaggeration or outright lies."

"It's true. I killed them all. I burned everything, but I salvaged some things - all of their weapons and one more Plate. That, above all, is what will get the High Keeper's attention, I fear. There were only four High Trackers with these men and no Keeper. The rest were just common thugs, mercenaries."

"There it is. Right there," Smith said, pointing at his chest.

"What?"

"Everyone believed the Keepers were all frauds. Volk certainly was. Cruel and powerful, but still a fraud. But you..." His voice faded.

"The things you can do. Ash and Par, they will do your bidding. It is said you killed a Telis Raptor alone. An adult male Telis Raptor! I have seen it, seen its tail blade. Hundreds of the High Keeper's men, maybe more, maybe a thousand. It's the only thing Olias won't talk about.

"Then there is Kat. You were alone with Kat for maybe ten minutes." Smith stared at him hard. "She should have died from that lashing. I don't think she will even have scars.

"And what have you done to Po?" Smith was clearly angry now.

"What do you mean?" Barcus asked.

"I never thought I would find a person in this whole world that hated the Keepers more than that girl." He pointed across The Abbey at the gatehouse. "And now I bloody think she has become one. The way she talks about you. No magic in the world is that powerful."

"Not in this world," Barcus said quietly.

"Po told me this last thing. But only after I swore never to repeat it." He swallowed heavily. "She said you were a...," he paused to swallow again, "a man from Earth." It was almost a confession.

Barcus didn't speak. He looked at the playing children below.

He nodded in admission.

"Barcus, you must never tell them this." Smith pointed to the people below.

"Let them believe they finally have a real Keeper to protect them. Don't confuse them with stories that will terrify them. They will believe you to be another Mad Monk."

"What do you know of the Mad Monk?" Barcus asked.

Smith shook his head, unable or unwilling to answer.

"None of them know what this place really is. Keep it that way," Smith said.

"What is it?" Barcus asked him.

"You really don't know?" Smith was incredulous.

"What are you saying?"

"This place is said to be built on the bones of the men of Earth. It's so haunted that the High Keeper cannot even see it from the sky. Had I known this was the place you would bring us, I may have refused. They must never know." Smith was adamant.

From below, a call in unison of a dozen men's voices went up: "Ready, steady, go!" And with a mighty coordinated lift of dozens of men using poles, props and block and tackles, the corner of the hanging floor was raised and the new beam, bound in iron, was shoved into place. Boys on ladders began to quickly hammer the nails that would secure it. A cheer went up when it was done. A great flurry of activity began then, of men passing up planking and tools, and the floor was closed up.

"In a few hours, the next level will be ready to secure. What do you say we lend a hand?" Barcus asked.

Smith stared at him a bit longer and then shook his head. "All right then. Let's get this done before supper. I hear it will be a special one." Smith moved to the stairs.

Barcus knew he was avoiding saying any more.

***

The next floor was levelled up in much the same way. Barcus was on a pole just like the rest of the men, and it went up without a snag. The new flooring went in so fast, it amazed Barcus. Looking up at the ruined roof, he wasn't sure they could do it at all. The beams looked more than a half meter across, and even though a good amount of the slate was missing from the roof, he had no idea how they would raise something so heavy. He had no idea why it had not completely fallen in decades ago.

After 60 or 70 props were in place, the noon break was called. They made their way to the communal hall for a lunch of stew and bread. Conversations were loud, and Barcus felt like just another person in the hall at the long tables.

Olias was sitting across from Barcus and was detailing the next salvage run. He was updating Barcus on the list of things they needed. "I have also organized two other teams to collect wandering livestock. Em has given us the locations of loose cattle, pigs, goats and even chickens." Olias pointed at a map he had spread out that he had painstakingly copied from his Plate with the areas they would look.

"Pardosa wants me to come with her, here and here and bring three others." He pointed on the map to two locations farther away than any other salvage operation so far.

"You have the current priority lists. Par keeps her own schedule. Smith needs her to bring some stone up from the quarry before you leave," Barcus requested.

Olias nodded his head saying in common, "It's already being done."

***

Barcus studied the survey map in his HUD. Fifty-seven small destroyed villages had been found. No further occupied villages had been located yet. The map had a layer that indicated the distribution of the BUGs over the survey area. It looked like a cloud, and another layer indicated aerial imagery where available.

He brought up the real-time imagery of the Salterferry Bridge. There was a gorge that was deep and about two hundred meters wide. The water was fast running rapids below. Each side of the bridge had a huge stone tower and the remnants of the burned bridge. Beyond, to the south, the road was cobblestone as far as he could see.

A window opened with a view of the east courtyard. Ash was off loading the last of the nine blocks from the quarry. Barcus smiled because he knew Em had picked the perfect time, while everyone was eating. Par said, "I can be ready to go in about thirty minutes. Ash can help with the upper level."

Par was gone when the crew returned after lunch. Ash was already up on the third floor, standing beneath the corner to be raised.

"Bring up a beam that Ash can use to reach the corner," Barcus said.

A pole that was as big around as Barcus's thigh was brought up. After each prop was manned, Ash took up the pole and placed it on the corner above.

Together in unison they chanted, "Ready, steady, go." Ash was holding the poll by the base and straightening out his legs. The roof went up a hand's breath. All the props were repositioned and set, and then Ash repeated the operation. It took about an hour to reach the desired height incrementally. The replacement timber was set in the corner and secured.

With the help of Ash, the blocks were set, and the additional supports were up in short order. Crews began working on each level to restore the floors to make them safe. A misstep on any of the levels would be very dangerous until the walls were closed up.

Barcus was on top of the wall now, looking at the condition of the slate roof. A dozen men and boys were already out on the slate inspecting it. Planks showed through in places, and individual pieces of slate continued to dislodge and slide down, and off the edge, to the ground 40 feet below. That area was cleared and marked off to ensure no one was hurt by falling slate.

Smith was out in the center of the huge expanse talking to a boy named Ansel, who was checking the slate nearest the edge where the most damage had occurred. There were large bare patches with the planking exposed.

"Now careful where you step. Some of the wood may be loose or rotted." Smith was speaking to the boy in common tongue. Barcus thought he understood.

Ansel approached the edge and turned before he knelt. He was very sure on the balls of his bare feet. His hands were on the slate, as he looked up the slope towards Barcus and Smith. "Sir, this whole section here..." The boy pointed up and to the right of where they were standing. "This section doesn't look right."

Barcus and Smith were focused on that section when it happened. There was a sharp cracking sound, and when they looked up, the boy was over the edge, hanging by an ankle that had broken through the roof.

Barcus was moving before Smith could even think. He belly-crawled fast to him.

On his belly, facing down slope, with his fingers clinging to the upper edge of a large slate tile, Barcus's face and right shoulder were over the edge next to Ansel. Barcus carefully reached down and grabbed the boy by his belt.

"Are you all right, Ansel?"

"Yes, my Lord. Except I think my ankle is broken." Ansel looked up at him, wincing then, away from the ground, four stories below.

"You know you are not supposed to call me that," Barcus said. The boy smiled through the pain. Barcus could hear Smith barking orders, calling for rope.

"Smith is getting us a rope. Don't worry, lad. I've got you."

"I appreciate that, sir. May I ask you a question while I have your attention?"

"You can ask me a question any time. Even now."

"Am I really going to learn to read?" Ansel didn't seem frightened at all now.

"If that's what you want. Yes. You'll love it. Come see me. I have just the book for you to borrow."

Then a rope appeared and almost hit Ansel in the face. He released Barcus's sleeve and grabbed it with both hands.

Then it happened.

An entire section of slate gave way. It came down like an avalanche. There was nothing Barcus could do as it all unfolded in slow motion. Except one thing. As the slate took him over the edge he released Ansel's belt.

Barcus turned to watch the boy, as he fell. At least Ansel held the rope and would be all right.

The last thing he heard before the darkness took him was an all too human, frightened, Em, screaming the word, "*Nooooooo!*" in his head.

CHAPTER FORTY-THREE

The Triage

"The Emergency Module was off the rails at that point. We believe now that this fall is what began the Solstice 31 Incident."

--*Solstice 31 Incident Investigation Testimony Transcript: Emergency Module Digital Forensics Report. Independent Tech Analysis Team.*

<<<>>>

Smith was the first to reach Barcus. He had slid down one of the rescue ropes they had tossed. He had burned his hand on the rope sliding down, but no one noticed until the next day.

Ash was there next, but Smith gestured him back. Ash ignored him and stood directly over them both just in time for another shower of slate to fall. The large tiles would have probably killed Smith and Barcus then if it had not been for Ash shielding them.

They gently unburied Barcus. They knew he was badly injured right away. He had landed flat on his back from a fall of just over 40 feet. He was breathing, but it was ragged. As they unburied him, they could see clearly that both of his legs were broken.

"Don't move him. Help is coming," Ash said in a calm, reassuring tone.

"Who is coming?" Smith asked, as Po nearly fell as she ran across the rubble, with a case marked with a large red cross.

She slid to a stop and paused only a second before she opened the case. Without prompting, she quickly affixed medical sensors in all the correct places. She put one on his forehead, one behind each ear and a ring on his right index finger. When her fingers came away bloody, she froze for a moment, but only a moment. She placed more sensors on his body after cutting his clothes away.

She withdrew her Plate and with shaking hands she asked, "What do I do?"

"There is a trauma kit here," Em said, and Po knew to hold the

Plate up so she could look through it to see the indicated item. She grabbed it and opened the small case.

There was a Nanite hypo there. She knew how to use that. The lessons had been very simple and clear. She injected the Nanites into his neck.

"Now what?" Smith asked. He had backed away. She seemed calm.

The Plate replied in Em's voice, "His injuries are too severe for field treatment. The Nanites will stabilize him, but we need to get him into the medical bay. The STU is already on the way. ETA 3 minutes 20 seconds."

"Stu is coming here?" Po nearly shouted the question.

"Yes. We need the medical bay. His skull is fractured, and his brain is already beginning to swell. He has broken ribs and a punctured lung. His spleen is ruptured, and he is bleeding internally. Secondarily, both legs are broken and ligaments are torn in both knees. He also has impact trauma from the slates hitting him. It's the head injury that's bad. We can only treat that in the Zero G med bay. Clear the rest of the slate off."

"Smith, there is a ship coming. It's big and black and it will scare the piss out of the people when they see it. You have to keep them from panicking," Po said in a rush.

"Two minutes. He will land just outside the main gate. Po, go with Ash to meet him. Ash knows what we need but doesn't have the hands for it. Smith, warn them."

They ran.

Lea arrived next. Cresting the mound of debris, she slipped down the rubble, as they ran. Em had no choice but to address her directly. "Lea, listen to me. Clear the rest of the stones off, but don't move him. I need you to remain calm."

Lea looked up at the monster crouched above her. She wiped her eyes on her sleeves and nodded her head. She had him completely cleared in less than a minute. She startled when she heard the sonic boom. The sky was blue, and it was like thunder. It rolled over her like a pressure wave. Dust fell from the structures around her.

She opened first one of his eyelids, then the other. They were fixed and dilated. She began to silently cry as she knew he was already dead, even though he was still faintly breathing. She had seen this kind of injury many times. It was always fatal.

The STU settled just beyond the bridge outside the main gate. The cargo door was already opening, and the lights were on full bright. Double doors slid open in the back of the hold. Em spoke as she held up her Plate. "The rescue gurney is here." The locker was highlighted in the Plate, and she retrieved it. It was extremely heavy as she dragged it from the locker, but it activated automatically. The entire rig simply floated.

She didn't wait to marvel. She pushed it before her at a run. The path down seemed to take forever. When she arrived, Lea was there with her face in her hands.

"No one dies this day," Po nearly growled. "I won't have it. Do you hear me, Barcus?"

Lea looked up when she heard Em's voice say, "Detaching the back board now. Lea, hold this." A blue plank detached from the top of the device as Po calmly placed it directly over Barcus, about face level. Lea took it, and it felt like it had no weight. As she drew it to her side, it began to reshape into a mold shaped like a man as if he was laying in it. Magic. She knew it was powerful magic.

The rescue gurney activated, and Barcus began to rise up towards it, never changing position.

"Brush the debris from beneath him, quickly." Em's tone was urgent.

Lea helped Po brush the floating rocks away. When they reached the edge of the gurney, they just fell. When they reached the edge of the anti-gravity field, created by the gurney, they fell. When Po gently brushed a larger rock from behind his head, she could feel the skull fracture. Her calm cracked for an instant, allowing a few tears to spill, but only for an instant.

"Lea, position the back board directly beneath him." When she did, it floated up to form perfectly with his body. He then rose up to be enveloped by the gurney. The surface activated, and vital signs appeared. It turned clear above his face.

"Back to the med bay. Hurry. Ash will bring the gurney," Em said.

It was only then, as Ash hurried away, that she looked up.

Every wall was lined with people. The tower was full. The perimeter of the crater was lined with silent, concerned faces. Even Smith was there, holding Ansel in his arms.

"I will see to Ansel. Go!" Lea said. Po closed the med kit and followed at a run.

***

Inside the STU, the medical bay unfolded. Ash was too tall to fit in there, so he got the gurney as close as he could. Po slid the gurney into the clearly marked "Zero G Medical Bay." The gurney ascended out of sight and the back board descended, became flat and covered the floor of the bay. A clear window closed, and a wind seemed to rise, clearing the grains of sand and dust. A dozen arms descended and began removing Barcus's clothes, cutting away some sections, loosening his belt and lowering it to a compartment with his pouches, knives and handgun. His pants and even his boots were cut off, revealing the horrific extent of his injuries.

Blood drifted from several wounds and was sucked away by vacuum arms. His knees were already black and swollen. Slate had cut him in many places. The bay focused on his head. Tiny arms moved with purpose. Tools deployed, and she watched as it quickly shaved his head with a mist and wind. It revealed his injury. Bloody pulp and an obvious dent.

Po was crying now as this "med bay" cared for him. It washed him and treated his minor wounds the same way she had treated his Telis wounds.

Smith was there. She had not noticed his approach.

"Em, what's happening?" She asked.

Em's voice seemed to come from all around them. "We have stabilized him. In a few minutes, we are going to realign the cranial bone structure so the Nanites can repair the bones. This kind of injury usually is handled by a full surgical facility, but we will make do. We have to relieve the pressure on his brain due to the subdural hematoma he has suffered."

One of the tiny hands held a tiny knife, and it cut his scalp all the way to the bone, just above the injury. Tiny silver fingers spread the flesh. Steam rose from the cuts, as if the knife had been hot.

In horror, Po watched another tiny hand select a drill. When she realized what it was about to do, she screamed. She pounded on the glass as she watched it drill into his skull. Suddenly, a spray of blood shot out around the tool, splashing the glass.

She stopped screaming and felt faint, but gritted her teeth and said, "Em, What's happening?"

"The pressure of the bleeding inside his head has been relieved. The Nanites are even now repairing the damaged blood vessels. The next step will begin in about four minutes. The bones will be realigned. Full continuous scans indicate his brain is bruised and he is in a coma."

"What is a coma, Em?" she whispered.

"It is a kind of sleep," Em said, kindness in her tone.

"Smith and I have seen this kind of sleep. It's called 'anvil slumber.' They just never wake."

"Come away now, Po. Let Stu work." Smith tried to guide her.

"No! I'll not leave him!" she yelled.

"But you're cold. You need to eat something, to rest."

"Stu, are you there?" Po said.

"Yes, Ma'am," Stu replied.

"Stu, this is Smith," Po said. "Please allow him open and close guest access. Please shut the main doors and moderate the temperature in the here. Is there a cot in the medical bay?"

"Yes, Ma'am." And a cot slid from the wall opposite the Zero G unit.

"All right. I will bring you some stew and blankets," Smith said, knowing she wasn't listening again. There were more knives and drills to watch. This time, they were working on his ribs. Em was explaining that they would drill a small hole in the ribs on either side of the breaks so that they could screw in a tool for leverage. The lung puncture was next most severe to be addressed. Smith exited via a small hatch that opened as he approached.

Po never noticed Olias in the corner, watching.

***

It was the longest night of Po's life. She watched as a great screw drilled into his skull and pulled out the bone to the correct position. Ribs were drilled and repositioned. Last of all was work on his legs. Tubes were attached to his arms and fluids flowed into him. A catheter was installed so fluids could flow out of him as well. Even his urine contained blood.

His legs were cut open all the way to the bones by the cruel little arms. Black pieces were inserted and attached with screws to shattered places. Bruises and swelling went from his toes to his hips. In the end, the tiny arms shaved his face and even cleaned the inside of the Zero G Bay. The last thing the tiny arms did was to cover him with a small towel. "For modesty," Em said.

"Now he'll rest. So should you," Em said.

The cot slid over until she was forced to sit on it. Then it rose until it was even in height to the Zero G bay. Obviously the cot was used for patients.

"Thank you, Em." Her forehead rested on a pillow touching the glass as the lights dimmed.

***

Olias had watched in horror for hours. Po had fallen asleep, but he felt like he would never sleep again. He felt his Plate vibrating. He drew it out.

"Are you all right?" Em whispered to him in common.

He shook his head no, unable to speak.

"I need you to be brave for me, Olias. Brave for him," she whispered. "I need you to do something for me." A small hatch clicked open to the right of the med bay, and a drawer slid out.

"Go to the drawer and take out two of the yellow boxes, the ones that are the size of your thumb." And image showed the items.

Olias stood and went to the drawer. Inside, there were several boxes of different colors. He wordlessly withdrew two of the yellow ones and went back to the corner. He tried to read the box.

HUD-INDS, Vid/Comms/1TB. V9.8.3

"I will show you how this works." The image on the Plate showed Em take a small yellow tube out of the box and hold it up.

Olias did the same.

"Turn it like this. Press the green button." In the image a bit of gel squeezed out onto the tip of the cylinder. "Don't touch the gel with your fingers. It will make them numb."

Olias did the same.

"Move your hair out of the way and touch it to your skin here."

The image showed a close-up of her pressing the gel end of the cylinder to the skin right behind her right ear.

Olias did the same and said, "I can't feel it."

"You are not supposed to. That's what the gel is for. After a few seconds, press it firmly against your skull like this." The image showed the cylinder press against her bone, and when she pressed hard enough, the button on the end depressed. She held it there for a moment.

Olias did it, followed her example on himself. Nothing seemed to happen.

"There is a small towelette in the box. Use it to wipe the gel off your skin like this." The image did it.

When Olias repeated this part, the towelette came away with a little blood on it.

"Olias, if you want to help Barcus, I need you to be strong and do the same procedure on Po. But don't wake her. She's been through so much already today."

"What is it?" He was trying to read the tube, but it made no sense.

"It's powerful magic. I will be able to explain it one day, I promise. It will save Barcus. Do you want to save Barcus, Olias?" she stated and questioned at the same time.

"Yes. More than anything," Olias answered.

"Po is sleeping now. It's the best time. Don't wake her if you want to save Barcus."

He opened the second box and looked at Po, fast asleep on the other side of the med bay.

***

Po awoke to the sound of murmuring voices.

On the other side of the bay, Ulric stood with a Plate in hand, pointing at displays on the med bay, talking quietly with Smith and Olias. The glass was not glass at all. It was, in fact, like a giant Plate. It was covered with images and words. A voice quietly spoke to her.

"How are you feeling?" Stu asked. His image was in the glass, as if he was standing behind her. She had a headache. It felt like a hangover. She was thirsty.

"How is he?" She ignored Stu's question.

"Most of his injuries are mending well. The soft tissues will be healed in a few days. The bones will take longer. His head injury is what concerns us most," Stu replied kindly.

"Won't the Nanites heal it?" she asked.

"The Nanites can repair the simple soft tissue infrastructure like muscles, blood vessels, skin and even bone to some extent, but much slower. They prevent infection and other complications. Doing massive repairs to major organs is far more complex. The damage to his lung, spleen and brain has been contained but will take a while. A simple med bay can only do so much. He needs a real hospital. But we don't have one, so for now, it is up to him."

CHAPTER FORTY-FOUR

Recouping

"Em stopped keeping logs after Olias injected the Deep Brain Implant Nanites into himself and Po. It was clear premeditation. All while Barcus lay unconscious."

--Solstice 31 Incident Investigation Testimony Transcript: Emergency Module Digital Forensics Report. Independent Tech Analysis Team.

"Is there anything to eat?"

Po woke from a dream. She thought she heard Barcus in the other room in the gatehouse. But she was still there next to him in the med bay.

"Is there?" Barcus whispered.

"What?" She sat up instantly.

"Is there anything to eat?" he whispered before his eyes closed again.

"Stu, are you seeing this? What is happening?" She was suddenly activating the medical screens like she was a modern doctor. Right away she could see that the Brain Activity Histogram (BAH) was alight with massive activity after fifteen days of minimal indications.

"He is dreaming, the dreams of normal sleep." Stu actually sounded relieved.

"This chart says it's been going on for almost three hours. Why didn't you wake me?"

Stu answered in a calming voice that sounded like he was smiling as he said it, "For the same reason you won't wake Smith, Ulric or Olias now. It's the middle of the night."

"He said he was hungry." These words made her composure crack. She burst into tears, completely uncontrolled, sobbing. Her hands held her face as her forehead leaned against the panel.

She was like this when Smith rushed in and saw her. "What has happened?"

Po ran to Smith and threw herself into his arms. "He woke up!" she choked out. "He's hungry! He's going to be all right!" Her tears turned to laughter.

Smith held her. "And so are you." He looked at her and took her face in his hands and kissed her forehead. "I'll go see who is in the kitchen."

Po watched as the med bay began removing tubes and sensors. Less than ten minutes later, Lea was there with a large mug of chicken broth and a tunic.

***

"Barcus, you have to wake up now." It was Em inside his HUD now. Drawing him back to the light. "You have slept long enough."

"What happened?" Barcus said as his eyes fluttered open, even though the light was painful. He was asking Em, but Po answered.

"You fell off the roof, you bloody fool! It's taken Stu fifteen days to sew your cursed carcass back together. If you were not mostly dead already, you would have been when I was done with you!" Po scolded.

"Is Ansel okay?"

This completely took the wind out of her sails. She was choking back tears again.

"Yes. Thanks to you." There was a long pause and the Zero G bay began to retract from around him until he found himself upright and then sitting up on the exam table.

Slowly, he dangled his feet over the side, and the table lowered until his feet were on the floor. He noticed Lea for the first time then. He also realized he was completely naked.

She was nonplussed as she handed him the tunic and tea. "I want you to sip some of this. No. I will hold the mug for you. Go slow." He had a few sips.

He tried to put the tunic on himself but was not up to the task. Po helped him. After a few minutes, he tried to stand but could not.

"I want to sleep in my own bed," Barcus said as they guided him back down onto the pallet. "We can arrange that, if Stu agrees," came her reply. Her hands flew across the controls and the Zero G gurney activated.

"Let's get you back to the gatehouse before it gets light." The gurney drifted silently through The Abbey by the light of a single lamp. The gatehouse was clean, and fresh sheets were on the bed even though Po had not been in there over two weeks. Barcus actually stood to undress, and turned to sit on the bed, out of breath.

She helped him drink a mug of water before lying down.

"You can have the side by the window," Po said to him.

Po took time to wash herself. She hadn't left his side in two weeks. When Po climbed in, he was already asleep. She slid beneath the covers on the near side next to him. Po slept deeply for the first time in weeks.

***

"*Barcus, wake up. It is well past noon, and there is a lot to do today.*" Em was there, standing at the foot of the bed. She was smiling.

"Status?" Barcus said it before he was fully aware of his surroundings.

Both Po and Barcus were in the bed, both naked. He tried not to move. Po was completely tucked under his arm with her head on his chest, her leg over his body just below his navel. A sheet covered their collective lower halves.

"What?" Po said sleepily.

"*You spoke out loud, jug head.*" Em was laughing. "*Look. Here is your status.*" A window opened up that showed a BUG view outside the gatehouse. "*Smith has pulled up a chair and has been keeping people away with his glare. The only one not intimidated enough to leave was Ansel. Now get your lazy ass up and show your ugly face.*"

He hugged Po a bit tighter, and her eyes opened. "Are you okay?" he asked.

"I'll be fine now. As long as you don't go roof climbing again," Po answered.

"I need to get up." He rolled toward her. "Help me."

Po got out of bed and stepped into her dress where she had let it fall. One button and she was dressed, and Barcus was smiling. Her hair was loose and wild.

She slid his tunic over his head and onto his arms.

"Help me up. There is something I need to do," he requested.

Leaning heavily on Po and various pieces of furniture, they made their way to the door. After taking a deep breath, he pulled open the door and leaned out enough to say. "Good morning, Smith. Can I have a word? Good morning, Ansel. Would you mind fetching a pitcher of fresh water for me?"

Barcus leaned back in heavily on Po as Ansel limped toward the kitchen. Smith entered and Po said, "Smith, a little help, please." The two carried him to the nearest overstuffed chair. He sat with a gasp. Po was suddenly worried.

"What's wrong?"

"The pain meds are wearing off. That's all. Em is compiling a detailed medical report, don't worry."

"Don't worry?!" Po was about to spin up again. He could see it.

"I'm sorry." He interrupted her, catching her hand and pulling her into his lap.

She said nothing more as Smith and Barcus talked.

"Immediately after the accident, Ulric stepped up," Smith said. "He actually claimed the role and title of the Keeper and told everyone to quit standing about groping, and get back to work. He said in clear terms that you were injured, but you would be fine. He wasn't paying them to stand about."

"He came in every day to the med bay, but never said anything. He kind of knew how the equipment worked," Po added.

"Turns out he was right," Smith finished. There was a soft knock at the door, and then Ansel came in. He set the pitcher on the table next to Barcus.

"Thirsty, my Lord?" Ansel caught his mistake, "I mean Barcus."

"Yes, thanks. Are you all right, Ansel? I presume you made it off the roof a bit slower than I did." Barcus could tell he was having a bit of trouble walking, as well as a little trouble with the high speech.

"I'm just fine, sir," he replied, handing him a mug of water. Barcus realized just how thirsty he was as he drank most of the cup.

"Easy, son. Take it slow to start," Smith said. Ansel refilled the mug, but Barcus left it on the table. Barcus noticed what he had called him instead of 'my Lord' and was pleased.

"Could you fetch Olias and Ulric for us, lad?" Smith asked him in common tongue, and he limped out. "The boy hurt his ankle badly in the accident. Getting it caught in the rafters is the only thing that saved him."

Po sat up from where she was leaning on his shoulder.

"You need to eat," she stated plainly, and she was up and moving. She found her boots and was finally "dressed proper" when she came out of the bedroom. Po went out, and Smith began to put a kettle on.

Barcus leaned his head back onto the soft chair as Smith continued.

"I can't say he stopped drinking all together, but he kept everyone moving. He was really great when the Trackers came."

"Trackers?"

"There were Trackers from the south here. They brought news and collected news."

"News?"

"They brought news of destroyed villages they had seen. There were also refugees. Survivors that spoke of raiders and demons and even monsters. But no, no one said a thing about Ash or Par. I think their reluctance to discuss it cemented the stories."

Just then, Ulric and Grady entered, followed by Olias.

Olias was beaming, saying nothing.

"Just when visitors start to show up, our gatesman decides he's a roofer. Did you have a nice vacation?" Ulric said.

"There will be lots of time for updates later," Smith said, standing.

"I just wanted to thank you. All of you. And let you see with your own eyes that I'm up. On the mend," Barcus said.

Ulric patted his shoulder. "Go easy, Barcus. No need to rush." Po shooed them away, once she returned with a bowl of pumpkin spiced porridge and a glass of milk.

"You cannot let these men overtax you, Barcus," Po said.

She made Barcus eat and then helped him back into bed.

Before he fell asleep, Em detailed his full medical report.

"You landed in the hard rubble. Both legs were badly damaged with bones broken and knees torn. There was extensive soft tissue damage. You broke your right hip, your right arm, six ribs, and three vertebrae in your neck. You also suffered head trauma with a fractured skull and concussion that resulted in a subdural hematoma. We needn't go into all the details of the gashes and all the blood that made it so very exciting.

"I called Stu. It took him only three minutes to arrive. Smith was smart enough to not move you, and we had you in the med bay in no time."

"Em says all your cranial implants were functioning normally. We don't know what that means. Ulric seemed to know," Po said.

"What else has happened in The Abbey?" He was getting drowsy now.

"New people have arrived, and a few have even left. Some, I am glad, are gone. Hugh Oatcake is gone. I'm glad because you might have killed him yourself. You would never stand the way he treated the women. It was the day after Caris Hooper was found on the rocks in the quarry. Smith thinks Hugh might have killed him. In all, about a half dozen men are gone. The ones that disagreed with your policies. I worry that they might say something."

Barcus was already asleep. He would not find out until much later what really happened to those men.

CHAPTER FORTY-FIVE

We Have a Car

"The EM eliminated all other narrative surveillance data after this point. All 1600 BUGs plus Par and Ash data. Wide gaps remain. Only the single narrative was preserved."

--Solstice 31 Incident Investigation Testimony Transcript: Emergency Module Digital Forensics Report. Independent Tech Analysis Team.

As the spring progressed, Barcus spent his days taking slow walks in the sun. Sometimes Ansel would come with him and practice his high tongue. Some days, like today, he would walk alone.

Smith had set up two new benches just outside the southern gate, one to each side of the entrance. They were much more comfortable than the old bench. Today, he was sitting alone when Ansel arrived, bringing him a mug of tea.

"Is there anything else you need, Barcus?"

"Thank you, no, Ansel." And with that, Ansel was off doing his part.

In the quiet of that spring morning, suddenly his HUD burst to life.

"Barcus, we have cracked the comms encryption. Data is flowing in now from the entire planet. All plates, SATs, ground stations and shuttle communications."

Maps were being filled in with cities and towns. A new window, depicting the satellite arrays surrounding the planet opened, followed by weather data, satellite camera imagery including thermal, chemical and even ground penetrating radar in some areas.

"Only one of the satellites is completely off-line. Thirty-one of them are still active and fully functioning. Five have various small issues. Not bad given the lack of maintenance. I also see the ID Transponders for all the shuttles on this planet. Various makes and models. Only fifteen active shuttles remain. This may be an opportunity. We can track them all. But they cannot track us."

"Stu, can you flesh out the map of this region for me please? Are there any villages remaining above the gorge?"

It only took Stu a few moments to reply.

"This is very interesting, Barcus." A window opened, showing a heavily forested area that included a single structure in the upper right corner.

"What am I looking at?" Barcus asked.

"This is the SAT view of The Abbey. The structure you see is the Lislehill Estate. Someone has very cleverly hidden The Abbey from the SATs."

"Are you sure?"

"This is the overlay of our own aerial recon." The Abbey and all the roads around it appeared in ghostly transparent vision. The roads, quarry, farms, vineyards and orchards were clearly seen, even though the forest came right up to the edge of The Abbey.

"I believe this is good news. The High Keeper will be unable to use his image analysts to discover where we are."

"There are many villages still occupied above the gorge. But many have been destroyed and continue to be destroyed." Stu zoomed in to a village that was on fire at the moment.

"I need to know where those troops are right away. Par and Ash, get ready for a road trip."

"Barcus, we may have overestimated these people."

"How so?"

"Apathy. It's the only term I can use. They use the network for weather monitoring, light comms and little else. They seem to have no control over the SAT systems or the automated defense missile systems. A quick inventory of the nodes showed minimal systems everywhere except this one location. The Citadel. A full data center exists there."

"Em, can you use this network?"

"I could, but not without alerting them. We do not want to become an active node on this network. They can geo-locate with these protocols too easily, just as we are."

A new SAT image window opened then. It was tagged "Foxden".

"I now believe that I could park near Whitehall and remain concealed beneath The Abbey coverage. The bottom of the quarry would work well. Lots of room, and you would have to be right on the edge to see me." Stu sounded excited. "I should be able to fly in quietly at night via Grav-foils and remain undetected."

***

Par had Ash mounted up that night. They were moving at speed towards the nearest group of mercenaries. It would take over a week to get there over land. Now that the STU could fly them there and insert them, they would be there that night. Once they reached a populated area, they would have to move quietly at night.

After dropping off Em and Ash, Stu returned and took up station in the quarry. Em remained uncomfortable with both Par and Ash so far away, but Barcus had hunting to do.

His campaign would last for weeks.

Repairs continued inside The Abbey. Gardens and fields were planted, the orchards were groomed and the vineyards were pruned. The beehives received some necessary maintenance, and new hives were established. All kinds of livestock were brought in, and a dog kennel was even revived.

They finally had cats.

More refugees trickled in. Most were Trackers or farmers because they were the ones best prepared to survive an attack in the villages. These Trackers, in turn, organized themselves to collect more refugees and survivors. They would all arrive via the southern gate in small groups or individually, finding Barcus sitting on a bench in the sun. He would introduce himself to them one at a time. He'd have a good look at them.

The cloud of security BUGs that surrounded The Abbey ensured that the bench was never vacant when a visitor came near. Since there was never any passing traffic, the BUGs would be tracking them for more than an hour before they approached. A few times, Trackers would approach and hide in the forest to observe. Barcus would allow it. He would monitor them as he was being observed. Barcus would let them watch him read or seem to stare into space until their patience wore thin and they would approach.

Only once did a lone High Tracker approach The Abbey. It was obvious he was determined to murder. He carried a crossbow, a weapon denied to normal Trackers. A BUG confirmed his intent and took an image of his face.

Barcus placed his book down on the bench as if he would be right back. Two minutes later, he appeared on the wall with his rifle. The thermal scope made it impossible for the High Tracker to hide. Olias organized a party to collect and dispose of the body.

For five weeks, Barcus convalesced in the sun as the leaves became full with spring and fields were planted. Po would watch his face as he stared into the distance, hatred on his face, etched in his jaw.

He would wake each morning early and make tea as Po still slept. He would climb the spiral stairs and walk the wall as the sun rose. He would hear singing coming from the kitchen each morning, as he quietly discussed the campaign with Em and Stu. Barcus had killed over 1,600 mercenaries and eight more Keepers, collecting ten more Plates, all while sitting on his bench.

On this glorious morning, he paused and decided to add the tower to his exercise routine. He saw the sunrise in clear skies as he watched Ash chased a Keeper through a forest in heavy rain in a HUD window. A small shuttle had been sent to save the Keeper. Fifty personal body guards were already dead or dying. With the Keeper screaming into his Plate for the pilot to save him, the pilot made a fatal error. Instead of prepping the ship for immediate takeoff, he grabbed his weapon, exited the craft and left the cockpit open.

The pilot had a plasma rifle. He was powering it up and heading to intercept the running Keeper in hopes of killing the demon that was chasing him. The trap worked exactly as Barcus had hoped.

As the pilot was raising the plasma rifle, the .50 cal bullet entered his chest just below his right armpit. His heart exploded as the bullet passed through it and out of the left side of his ribcage. The overpressure of the impact to his brain, killed him instantly. The head of the Keeper exploded with the next round. Ash collected his Plate and the pilot's helmet, leaving the bodies where they were.

The Plate disappeared from the network as it was placed in Par's

Faraday compartment. They would leave the helmet active for now.

The STU was dispatched to the site to collect the small shuttle. Ash and Par easily carried the small ship into the STU's cargo bay. It was called a "quad" - a four-seater. In less than five minutes, the STU was gone with his prize, with its Transponder removed but still transmitting where it was left.

Then Ash and Par waited, as Barcus watched...

As expected, by late afternoon another 30 mercenaries showed up to the spot where the helmet was resting unseen on a branch in a tree. The canopy above hid the fate that awaited this troop. Barcus watched the real-time imagery, just as he assumed the High Keeper was. Three more plasma rifles were collected in that effort. Ash had just retrieved the decoy helmet when Barcus issued an order.

"Get out of there! Maximum speed. Incoming!" Barcus called out.

Ash had just finished placing the helmet in Par's Faraday. They ran. There had been no need for Barcus to warn them. Em saw the shuttle coming and knew that it didn't contain troops.

The SAT image showed the largest cataloged shuttle veering off as a parachute opened just above the last known location of the helmet. In the time it took for the giant bomb to arrive and explode, Par and Ash got 1,000 meters away and were safely behind some rocky, tree-covered outcroppings.

The explosion left a crater 100 meters across, devoid of trees or life. The shock wave tore the leaves and some branches off the trees for another 300 meters in every direction.

Par and Ash waited for 24 hours for another team to arrive that they could ambush. But none came. Barcus had them on the move again the next day.

***

The STU brought the quad back to the quarry where Barcus could work on it. It was in pretty rough shape but easily serviceable. He was already making a fabrication list for Stu to print up. He'd start with the eighteen external body panels. The current ones were sheet metal that were dented and patched. The black fiber polymer panels in their place would act as armor on the little craft, making it more heat resistant and nearly frictionless in the atmosphere. It would also transform the craft visually, in case it was ever seen. Now it was black and sleek, as opposed to the older dented stainless look.

Over the next few days, Barcus, with the help of Olias and several others, rebuilt a large amount of the craft's simple internal thrust systems. Its software was also reviewed and updated. The navigation and comm systems were enhanced and integrated with EmNet.

The manuals Em obtained also revealed the purpose of the stone obelisks in The Abbey. They were landing and maintenance pilings.

As soon as these initial upgrades were finished, Barcus landed the quad in the abbot's garden on automatic. It worked perfectly.

CHAPTER FORTY-SIX

Redoubts

"Something else was happening, actively being hidden."

--Solstice 31 Incident Investigation Testimony Transcript: Emergency Module Digital Forensics Report. Independent Tech Analysis Team.

"Barcus, I think I have found something interesting," Stu said one morning as Barcus was taking his first sip of tea at the top of the tower. The walk up the tower was slower today. Stu had performed another knee operation two days ago, and Barcus was sorer than he expected.

"Show me."

"This is our new planetary map based on the comm traffic. Notice the even distribution of larger cities. To date, we have only seen villages and small towns. This matches the standard distribution of colony Redoubt deployment."

"Why is this interesting?" Barcus sipped his tea and flexed his sore back.

"The Abbey is located here." Another indicator displayed on the map. "This fits the routine deployment of Colony Redoubt Makers. This also means there may be additional abandoned Redoubts in these locations." More indicators displayed.

The closest node, the one that was further west and still above the gorge, was zoomed in. At first glance, the area looked wild and undeveloped.

Then he saw it.

There was a perfectly round hole in the ground, about 30 meters wide. It was overgrown with vines, and there was a tree trunk fallen across it at one edge, but it was there.

"The level of overgrowth indicates that it was abandoned hundreds of years ago and not revisited."

"I think it may be time to take out the new shuttle," Barcus grinned.

***

"Po, how would you like to go on a small field trip?" Barcus asked Po when he found her talking with Grady and Smith over breakfast later that morning.

"Where to?" She smiled.

Barcus knew the answer was always "yes."

"A potential salvage site. Another abandoned Redoubt."

"Is it flooded?" she asked.

"I don't think so. It's hard to tell." He paused. "I want to take the new shuttle."

Po's eyebrows went up and seemed to draw her up out of her seat. "I'll get my gear."

"Got any extra room in that thing? I always wanted to ride in one," Grady asked.

"Sure. We will head out in a quarter hour," Barcus said.

***

The PT-137 Quad was parked in the abbot's garden. The three, six foot tall obelisks were actually auto lander points for this type of shuttle. Barcus found the standard manual flight controls easy to manage, and were exactly the same as the first trainer he had flown as a kid. The landing autopilot was easy to get to use. It hovered and then set down on the three points in The Abbey garden. This had the added benefit of hiding it from the SATs as well as allowing service and maintenance.

When he had given the shuttle a thorough once over, he saw it was serviceable and functioning adequately. It had needed a lot of cleaning at the intakes. A standard maintenance routine there had been ignored for some reason. The intake blades had to all be replaced.

The shuttle carried no additional active location beacons. Em's diagnostics showed the antenna arrays, both primary and secondary, were missing due to some small impacts decades ago, and thus had been disabled. Stu would be able to fabricate new ones once the right raw materials were provided. They relied on the helmet's real-time transmitter for geo-location and comms now. Em had taken the helmet off-line and then later added it to her expanding closed network, EmNet.

Ulric wandered up while they were discussing their departure and schedule with Smith and Po. "I am ready to go!" Ulric said. He was sober, it seemed.

"I think you should stay here in case we are detained and have to walk back," Barcus said. "Keep your flock moving, as it were."

They all knew this undertone. Ever since his fall, Barcus always made sure the people of The Abbey were covered.

"Keep them shoveling the silt, as each level drains in the Redoubt below. At the rate we are growing, we will need the space." Barcus knew it was a dirty job. Ash could do it by himself but the twenty-man crew was working it now. Even still, the next time he was here from "the campaign," he would still have to power wash it when this level was clear. With mercs still above the gorge, Ash was always busy.

This was the first time Ulric wanted to leave The Abbey walls in weeks.

"Barcus, you seem to know a lot about shuttles," Ulric said.

"I actually know quite a lot," Barcus said.

"We should talk when you return," Ulric said.

He could tell Ulric wanted to discuss something in private later, so he left it at that.

The gull wings on the shuttle were up, and Grady got in the back with his ever-present backpack. Barcus got in the front left and Po in the front right.

The engines fired up as the doors descended. The high pitched, screaming whine of the turbines had been replace with a much quieter, smooth hum and sound of wind.

"How did you do that?" Po asked.

"I cleared the intakes, made some new parts and replaced the fuel in the cells with distilled water instead of straight rain water, all after cleaning out a hundred years of buildup." Barcus handed the helmet to Po. "Put this on." She did.

As the ship began to lift in a lazy spiral as part of the automated take off sequence, he explained the controls to Po and the peripheral HUD that was in the helmet. Barcus could see the same display.

"It spirals on ascent as a traffic safety scan. In cities where there was a garage full of these on the roof of every building, you really needed it," Barcus said.

"Here is where you enter the desired altitude, the distance from the ground. It will just hover there." Barcus selected 1,000 feet. None of the controls were in the metric system. He loved that. He didn't know if the pressure seals were still good, so he would keep it low.

"The controls are basic. Push this forward and it will go forward. To the left and it will go left. It can even go backwards. This is your power control. The more you apply, the higher or faster you will go. Your speed is indicated here. Now that the intakes and fuel cells are cleaned up, we will keep this number under 600 so we won't leave a vapor trail."

"Okay." Po said.

"Let's go." Barcus pushed the stick forward and added power.

Once they were under way he gradually increased their speed to 500 mph and increased the altitude to 3,000 feet.

Barcus let Po take the controls several times over the next hour, to Grady's chagrin. Po was getting the hang of it by the time they reached the Redoubt.

***

Barcus gently set the shuttle down in a clearing just north of the great hole. There was no comms chatter to reveal that they had been seen. Stu reported that new reports regarding political climates would be forthcoming.

Barcus knew that as the canopy opened, a small swarm of BUGs was already being deployed. As they readied their gear, the BUGs were descending the large opening.

It was better than he had hoped.

The Redoubt was completely intact. It was very dry inside, and any rain that may have gotten inside was easily drained away. He expected more debris.

Before they had completely unloaded, Barcus stopped them.

"I have an idea. Get back in."

They all piled back into the shuttle. Barcus hovered three meters above the ground and moved slowly over the hole. Even with the fallen tree, the shuttle easily fit down the mouth of the Redoubt. Once past the edge, the auto-landing sequence began, and the shuttle set down gently on pilings all the way on the lowest level. Leaves and birds filled the air as they powered down.

They were parked in an area that was obviously a hanger for about 30 shuttles of various sizes. As the gull wing doors swung open, the thing that was the most amazing was that there were lights on. Every level was illuminated.

This Redoubt was the same size as the one under The Abbey, but it was inverted. Instead of being oriented like a bowl, this one was a dome. The widest level was at the very bottom. Cobwebs were everywhere. Great machines stood in silent bays covered in cobwebs and bird nests and guano.

Many of the machines Barcus did not recognize, but he could tell the large ones were mining machines, based on the business ends of them.

"I think this is the Mining Redoubt. These great machines dug the raw materials for this and many of the other Redoubts." Barcus pointed to great tunnels that bore into the mountain in several places.

They explored and found workshops full of tools of all kinds, neatly put away as if their owners would return tomorrow. They found living quarters, barracks, computer rooms, command centers, officer suites, kitchens, mess halls, everything in orderly placement.

"What happened here?" Barcus said out loud. Em answered in his head.

"It appears that there was an orderly shutdown, but they never returned. Most of the large equipment is beyond repair, but there seems to be some solid state computer systems that have no reason to not function if we can power them up."

They had discovered that the only systems with power were the lights.

Barcus let Ulric know that they would be spending the night, as it would take more time for just the three of them to survey the Redoubt. By the time dusk came, they had done a quick search of only three levels when the light began to fade. With sunset, the lights also fell to black, leaving them in utter darkness.

Po and Grady used their Plates to create light. Barcus had his multi-tool, although his enhanced vision in his HUD meant he didn't need it.

Em spoke in his head, "*I believe I now understand the lights, Barcus. There are active solar collectors that power them when they are active, but the solar batteries are off-line."* Barcus's HUD displayed the usual location of the power banks, and they were quickly found. All the cells were bone dry.

They had discovered that most of the plumbing still worked, but the water that flowed was very brown. Several taps were available in the power cell room, and they were left running for over an hour before they ran clear.

Barcus showed them how the cells were all dry and only needed water to see if they still worked. It took almost six hours to fill them all.

"So why haven't the lights come on yet?" Olias asked.

"It will take days, perhaps weeks, to recharge them, if they ever work again. I also don't know how many solar collectors are active. I was hoping we'd find one to take back to The Abbey. I never expected to find all this."

***

The next day, they continued the search. They found a small hospital, an amphitheater, chem labs and fine instrument shops.

That night, the lights did not fade with the sun. The power control console was tiny and showed the small charge the batteries held. The needle on the ancient dial was out of the black and into the red, but it was holding steady.

"Em, I want a detailed report about the surrounding region. Include roads, villages, individual houses and even Tracker cabins. Tonight I want the STU to come under the cover of darkness and see if we can move that log. If we can, even the STU could land in here."

"Barcus, I believe I have found another Redoubt." Stu brought open another window.

Examining it he said, "Po and I will check it out tomorrow. It should only be 40 minutes away in the new shuttle."

"Also, the High Keeper is angry about the loss of another shuttle. The High Trackers are trying to tell him it was likely destroyed by the bomb. The helmet signal failed right when the bomb exploded. Many High Trackers were executed over the affair. This is all gathered from communications of Keepers that were somehow affected. The High Keeper himself keeps close his own counsel. He summons people. It's almost as if he doesn't trust his own comms."

***

That night, the STU showed up with Olias and 33 volunteers.

They brought extra provisions with the idea of setting up a long-term presence.

It took less than an hour to move the log from the hole. The STU was able to land in the bottom of the Redoubt easily. The next night, the power had gained additional ground but was still way into the red. Lights were on all night, however.

They also found the surface entrance from the inside. It was heavily overgrown.

Grady was left in charge of beginning the cleanup, with strict orders where to begin - the kitchen and the barracks. Olias insisted on going with Po and Barcus to the next Redoubt.

This trip took about an hour. Barcus continued to teach Po how to fly the simple shuttle. By the end of this trip, only manual take-offs and landings were an issue for her.

How does she pick these things up so fast?

They would have lots of time back at The Abbey to practice. Olias wanted to learn as well.

When they arrived at this hole, the evergreens around it had softened the edges of the opening, making it look like a small body of water below. Barcus opened the vent without explanation and deployed the BUGS, which descended into the hole and found this Redoubt completely empty.

Slowly, he descended the shuttle into the space, sending dust and leaves up in a great cloud. Turning on the shuttle's floodlights revealed the great space. In the center of the floor, there was a mound of bones and carcasses, as if a great monster had been tossing his leavings there.

For hundreds of years, game of all kind had fallen to their deaths from above. The Redoubt was so well concealed now, after hundreds of years, that running animals leapt over what they thought was a simple outcrop of rock into thin air.

Even the pilings used for auto-landing had been removed. A quick search showed empty shops, galleries, barracks and room after empty room stripped. The battery banks also were gone. All of the tree-like solar collectors were gone as well.

There were far less cobwebs here than in the last one. There was nothing but shallow corners to make them in, no nests to speak of, likely due to the constant smell of rotting meat that filled the stagnant air.

They decided not to spend the night. They took off before full dark because it was easier for Barcus to navigate out with a bit of light remaining.

On the way back, Barcus taught them about instrument flying at night.

It was full dark when they returned to the Mining Redoubt. Barcus allowed Po to take it in on autopilot. They descended smoothly through the glowing maw and down onto the very same pilings where they had departed.

Po beamed as she exited the shuttle.

***

Grady had overseen an amazing amount of cleanup while they were gone. The main atrium was now completely clear. The dust the shuttle kicked up looked like it was being swept away into huge vents that surrounded the great chamber, which made Barcus realize that the ventilation system was on-line.

"I believe as the basic systems begin to power up, more and more will automatically come on-line," Em reported. "In addition to ventilation, heat and humidity control has started up. They also say that there is hot water in the infirmary."

"The Infirmary?" Barcus asked.

"That's what the door calls it," Grady said.

"Why Grady, has no one mentioned that only Keepers can read?" Barcus smiled.

"By the way, the one thing we have not found here is an anvil," Grady said, ignoring him.

"Olias, I plan on returning to The Abbey with Po tonight. I want Stu to remain here for now. Let me know if you need anything else. Keep your Plate handy so I can get updates."

Grady wanted to go back himself. "I can't stand to be without the sky for much longer."

During the return flight, Po flew the entire way. She landed perfectly in the abbot's garden with the autopilot landing sequence.

They went directly to the pub for some of the excellent wine. It had been a long day. They sat at one of the new tables, talking about the joys of being able to fly a shuttle or a ship, when Ulric came up. He already had a mug of something, but seemed more sober than usual.

"I need to speak with you. May I sit?" Ulric asked formally, which was out of character. Barcus nodded.

"I have been lying to you," he stated.

CHAPTER FORTY-SEVEN

Ulric's Ship

"The Emergency Module was collecting assets. Preparing for something."

--Solstice 31 Incident Investigation Testimony Transcript: Emergency Module Digital Forensics Report. Independent Tech Analysis Team.

"What do you mean?" Barcus asked as he gestured for him to sit.

"I'm not really a Keeper," Ulric confessed.

Barcus and Po tried not to smile as they looked at each other.

"Why are you telling me this now?" Barcus asked.

"The sky fall last autumn was you. You are like me."

"Yes. He is a man of Earth," Po said quietly.

Ulric was horrified by the term. His eyes shot from Po to Barcus.

"Don't say that. Don't ever say that." Ulric was looking around to make sure no one heard it.

"Those Fuckers killed 2,000 of my people. Everyone I knew, everyone I loved, was on the ship. It was an unarmed survey ship. As soon as I am able, this man of Earth is going to make them pay. I don't care if I have to hunt down every Keeper there is. As soon as I gain control of all their systems, I will destroy this precious world they've made," Barcus growled.

He let it sink in.

"I already have their comms traffic. Soon I will be inside their mainframes and have all their secrets. Did you know they have a moon based, interstellar communications array?"

"What?"

"Em and Stu have discovered many things since cracking their comms," Barcus added.

"Yes, they have an old school communication antenna array that might be capable of talking to Earth. The signal will take years to get there, but at least then they will know what happened here. If they send a ship, by then I will have control of the orbital platforms, if they remain. It may take me decades to get home, but what the hell. I have nothing but time..."

"You have had the longevity treatments?" Ulric asked.

"Yes."

"How long will you live?"

"How long do any of us live? I will take their lives and their planet. And I will do it from my bench in the sun," Barcus growled.

Ulric's jaw clenched. "Will you let me help?"

Barcus raised an eyebrow.

"My ship has an EMP cannon," Ulric said.

"Really, why? After the last war, all the new tech has been made to be EMP resistant," Barcus said.

"Everything made AFTER the last war. Not like plasma rifles. Or these kind of computers. My ship may not even fly anymore. After that last hop, I have never tried again."

"Where is it? Let's have a look. I love the old Renalo class yachts, comfy," Barcus said.

"It's in an abandoned Redoubt. But not either of the ones you have found." He set his Plate down on the table and pointed. He indicated a spot that came up immediately in his HUD of one of the additional locations of potential Redoubts.

"When you said you had found the Mining Redoubt, I knew it wasn't this one. It lies in an area that does not have SAT coverage. It's destroyed and empty already. It is in an area of desolation."

"We could be there in about four hours," Po said. Barcus raised an eyebrow. She was right. How did she make that estimate so fast?

"Why are you telling me this now?" Barcus asked.

"I always thought I could become a Keeper and get close to the High Keeper. Close enough to kill him. But then I fell in love. We tried to build a life." He paused, "I started to travel with Grady. I hated what I'd seen. And loved it. I never thought to go to it again. You might be able to salvage it."

They sat in silence for a while. Listening to laughter around them. Finally Barcus spoke.

"Tomorrow we will go to the Mining Redoubt. We will collect some tools to take with us. Em is already compiling schematics and tool lists for a Renalo class yacht."

"I have something else to tell you. This place is haunted." He gestured with his mug and then took a deep pull but didn't continue.

***

The next day, Smith was left in charge. He took it in stride. Po asked Barcus, "Who do you think really runs things around here when you leave Keeper Ulric in charge?"

Ulric was late. Barcus sent Ansel to fetch him.

Ansel returned a few minutes later, blushing slightly. "He'll be along in a few minutes."

Stu came up then. "Barcus, I am now beginning a new phase of data infiltration. Before I begin, I wanted to get your permission. I have found not one, but twelve data centers so far, based on the comm traffic. The fastest way to gain access is to obtain a legitimate login and then work to escalate access once inside. I will take steps to conceal this access and eventually gain full admin authority."

"Do it. Keep me informed."

Barcus checked the AR72 before he stowed it in the trunk with the supplies for the trip. He had checked his handgun before he left the gatehouse that morning.

Ulric showed up disheveled, with two girls adjusting his garments as he moved. He was very self-conscious as he kissed them both, and they retreated holding hands.

***

Po got in and put on the helmet. The HUD came up straight away. She had already topped off the fuel and done a full preflight with Barcus.

"Manual or autopilot takeoff?" Po asked.

"Autopilot," was the response she heard in her ears. But she knew he had not moved his mouth. She shook her head and made no comment. Auto-ascend was initiated. The engines began a smooth hum, and they went up to 3,000 feet, slowly turning, providing a view in every direction.

"Make your way to this point, over the ocean and then proceed south. We will cut inland here and proceed to the coordinates. Ulric, are you strapped in?"

Barcus turned and saw that he was asleep.

Po flew the shuttle almost the entire way. They stopped on the way, on a washed stone beach in a deserted area for a leg stretch and the call of nature. They were still an hour from the target location and Ulric was still asleep. They woke him up by giving Po another lesson with the AR72 without its suppressor attached.

Ulric stumbled out of the shuttle and walked around to the opposite side to pee beside one of the landing skids. Shading his eyes, he looked up and watched Po screwing on the suppressor to the rifle's muzzle.

"Why the projectile weapons, anyway? I was expecting a LASER or plasma rifles." Ulric punctuated the comment with a coughing spree.

"The last war," Barcus answered.

When Ulric didn't respond with anything but confusion, Barcus continued. "The war was ended by returning to lower tech, less expensive, EMP resistant technology. Research in that area led to many advances. Low power, mechanical technologies were discovered to be EMP resistant. Par and Ash for example. They don't have motors or power plants. They have chemical processing units, mechanical fiber tech. It's like synthetic muscles. And like people, very EMP resistant. Par requires less power to walk than this flashlight consumes. Combat tactics were so dependent on particle, plasma and nuclear weapons they had no idea what to do when the options were all denied to them. They tried to shield their devices, but it was too late."

"Mechanical fiber, super-polymer armor and caseless ammunition turned out to be very stealth as well. It ended the war fast and decisively," Barcus said.

"There was another war?" Ulric said.

"Get back in the shuttle," Barcus said, shaking his head.

Po wanted to take off manually, and very nearly crashed them into the nearby cliff before Barcus took the stick.

After another twenty minutes of practice, they turned inland. The coast was low and very rocky, with no vegetation at all. Great cracks were everywhere. It looked impossible to navigate on foot. It was completely dead for miles in every direction.

"Those cracks are deceptively deep and filled with violent, tidal, salt water. It's as if the land was intentionally destroyed. The ship's name is the Sedna. It's in a ruin that is on the eastern face of a rocky outcropping. If you approach from the east, you can see it. But only from the east."

"How did you find it? Out here?" Barcus asked.

"I didn't, the pilot did. He never told me."

"That should be it just ahead," Po said.

Barcus took the controls and slowed on his approach. The sun was past noon, so the exposed part of the Redoubt was covered in shadow now. Slowly, they crossed into the shadows and the Redoubt's bones were revealed. An entire third of the dome was completely blown away. It was obvious that some kind of devastating explosion on the inside had blown this side of the Redoubt away.

"My god. What could do that to foamcrete?" Barcus asked.

"In the decades since I have been here, I have heard tales from Grady and other Trackers that the High Keeper once had a weapons research facility here. Away from prying eyes. There is no SAT coverage here. Why bother? I think it is a major reason why we managed to set down undetected."

They hovered low and then landed on a flat expanse of bleached stone. As the ship wound down its engines, they exited the small craft. They could see an edge of the round, thick ship.

It was once white, but was now dark gray on the top from decades of weather. The side facing out had actual windows that were dull mirrors looking across the desolation. These were on the main salon level, and the blast shield curtains were open. The blast shields were closed on the upper command deck.

They approached the starboard skid control panel, and it was dark and unresponsive. Barcus handed the AR to Po and said, "Keep watch while I access the manual hatch."

He moved around to the back of the skid and slowly moved up the ladder rungs that were built in there. The maintenance hatch at the top was not locked. The seals were still tight, but it opened inward easily enough. A small swarm of BUGs passed into the space quickly and confirmed that the space was as described in the schematics, but the headroom was tight here.

Po climbed up halfway and paused so she could safely hand up the rifle, then pass the tools up from Ulric.

Moving along to the end of the access way, Barcus lit his way with a flashlight from his pouch and opened the interior hatch. It swung stiffly into the main engineering bay. The air was dry and stale.

He was already at the engineering console by the time Ulric entered the space. "Wujcik handled the shutdown. He was a good engineer." There was a tone of regret in his voice.

Some lights came on at that point, and then a few more. A third of the panels began to power up. Barcus went from panel to panel, tapping screens and throwing toggles. A slight vibration could be felt in the air, and a few moments later, the air itself began to move as the life support came on-line.

Finally, he sat at the chief engineer's station. Curved screens, a meter high, surrounded 300 degrees around the station. More and more screens were coming to life. The lights came full on at that point.

"How does it look?" Ulric asked.

"What the hell kind of ship is this?" Barcus glared at him a moment before going back to work. "How long were you here before you set out?"

"Four, maybe five months."

"Your engineer was executing repairs that whole time. He was trying to make it space worthy again," Barcus said as he scanned through screens.

"Yes. But he failed. There were too many hull breaches." Ulric was staring at the past.

"How many people were on board when this damage happened?" Po asked.

"Seventy-one," Ulric said as he dug out a flask.

The front half of the engineering level came up on the display as a schematic, showing the rips in the hull inside a large bunk room.

"Were they in the barracks?" Barcus asked.

"The hold. Yes." Ulric turned and walked to a door marked LIFT. It opened and he stepped in. It closed behind him before he turned around.

As Barcus worked on the ship, Po began to explore. There was a corridor that opened into engineering on one side, the lift on the other, a wide ramp that looked like it opened to the back of the ship leading to wide overhead doors. She palmed the pad like she had seen Ulric do.

The door opened up. Some of the lights came on, mostly the ones at the edge of the room. The air smelled metallic and dusty. Damage was heavy and evident in this room. Minimal attempts to clean it up had been made. While engineering was spotless, this room was covered in old stains of some kind, torn debris scattered everywhere. Dry dust had found its way in over the decades.

She then realized that the stains must have been old blood. Footprints and drag streaks were now obvious. She backed out slowly and closed the door.

Barcus came out of engineering just then, saying, "We need to get to the command level."

They entered the elevator and selected Level 1. It opened on the back of the bridge. A command chair and three stations.

Barcus sat in the command chair, and it automatically slid up to the command consoles. Po was looking over his shoulder and actually recognized a few controls.

"Is it good?" Po asked.

"This may be the finest luxury yacht I have ever seen. It's old, but it is beautiful in its antiquity. Like this it will never hold up to FTL, but it will fly. I think. It will take a few hours for the reactors to warm up. There are some command codes I need for that. Where is Ulric?"

The blast shields were sliding back, letting in light and showing the desolate view as she said, "He must be in the middle level."

They went to the elevator and went down. They did not expect to see what they did when the door opened.

It was a beautiful salon.

The entire front of the room was floor to ceiling windows that looked out on the bleak landscape as if it were a beautiful painting. The rest was made of panels in deep rich teak and oak with beautifully crafted inlays. The furniture looked decadent and built in. Thirty people could be entertained in here easily. There was even a fireplace - a fireplace on a spaceship! There were paintings and even books, all secured as if it was an ancient sailing vessel. Po stood speechless before the wall of books.

Barcus went up to stand next to Ulric as he stared out the window.

"Slaves?" Barcus asked in a neutral tone.

"It was a group of colony prostitutes, 65 of them, all women, contract ownership only. The contracts were for seven years with option to renew. Guaranteed passage back to Earth, food and longevity treatments was the hook. Most knew they might never be free again, and they didn't care. It was worth gambling seven years for an extra 100 years. Only one survived. She was with me when we were hit. We were inside the Karazim, a Cobalt Class Destroyer when it achieved orbit. It managed to take out one orbital platform before being burned from the sky."

"They were in the forward...barracks," Barcus said.

Ulric emptied the cut crystal tumbler. Barcus could smell the bourbon.

"Can I interest you in a well-aged bourbon?" He moved to the bar.

"What I really need is the command code."

"JulietteBravoZeusArthur, no spaces, no biometrics, no special characters...no escape." He refilled his glass and started to run his hand along the wooden rail. His back was to them.

Barcus moved to the elevator and went back down to engineering with Po in tow.

The door closed and Barcus asked, "Do you think you could fly the shuttle all the way back to The Abbey by yourself?"

"If I auto-ascend and descend and then just follow Stu's map, I could. It's easier than steering a two horse cart, really."

"If I can get this off the ground, we should take it with us. It has...weapons."

Po wasn't going to press him. He was intent on his tasks again at the console. He entered the command code and obtained access to everything. The yacht was very heavily modified. Unfortunately, many of the weapons systems showed damage. No missiles were left. It looked like they were jettisoned, exlosive bolts had been activated. The engines themselves were not original spec. It took him a few minutes with Em's help to find the new schematics. The initiation sequence was there in detail. He began warming up the reactors.

Em now had access to every file and began ingesting and analyzing it. "Barcus, I can see why they were trying to repair it. The three FTL drives could have gotten them back into regular shipping lanes, and they could have been rescued. It was a good plan."

"What went wrong?" Barcus asked.

"Hull breach in ship stores. Reclamation systems damaged beyond repair. They ran out of water, even with rationing. They modified the ship's cargo loading tractor and took it overland. The logs end there."

"Can you control these systems now that you have access?" Barcus asked.

"No. I have only read-only access to files. There are no AI interfaces," Em replied.

***

Po and Barcus went to check on Ulric, and he was face down on a massive bed in the main stateroom. There was an empty bottle next to him.

Barcus said to Po, "Em has found why the Grav-plating won't come up. I need your help to reroute some power cables. It should not take long, if you don't mind crawlways."

Po didn't mind. In fact, she helped Barcus to run new cables to all the Grav-plates.

"We have a couple hours before the reactors are ready. Let's do a pre-flight check on the PT-137 Quad and get you some flying practice," Barcus suggested.

They did a lot of manual flying for the next hour. Po was very intent on learning.

"Has there ever been a woman pilot?" Barcus asked as they auto-landed.

"No. It's forbidden," she said, as she took off the helmet.

"You are in so much trouble now," Barcus smiled.

He looked at her, and she wasn't smiling. "Barcus, what are we doing?"

The question confused him.

"If it was just you and I, we could defy the anvil every day and I'd laugh about it. I had a long talk with Smith. He's worried."

She tried to look at him, but found it difficult.

"It's not just you and me and Olias trying to survive the winter. There are hundreds of people depending on you. All of them as weak as Ansel."

"What are we doing?" Barcus repeated. "What am I doing?"

Suddenly his look became intense.

"I am going to kill the High Keeper and bring down the Citadel block by block."

"But what about us?" she asked.

"You will become mighty." He looked at her. "Freedom." He said plainly.

"What if they don't want to be free?" she asked.

Barcus had no answer.

CHAPTER FORTY-EIGHT

The Sedna is Salvaged

"There was an agenda being run and everyone including Barcus followed without question."

--*Solstice 31 Incident Investigation Testimony Transcript: Emergency Module Digital Forensics Report. Independent Tech Analysis Team.*

Ulric never moved a muscle while they were gone. He was passed out drunk in the master stateroom.

As the reactors came on-line, Barcus could see the engineer's dismay in the logs prior to this event. The main reactor fuel was down to 6%. It explained why they were catching a ride with the Karazim. While that fuel would last for years here, it was nowhere near enough to get this back to Earth even if the FTL structural integrity wasn't compromised. Em had done a full analysis, and the Sedna would not see any interstellar flight without a full dry dock refit.

Barcus was ready to fly it. He was in the command chair. The main pilot seat. All systems were up, and the reactors were ready.

Unlike the STU, Renalo Class yachts had fixed position Grav-plates for takeoff and atmospheric flight. The reactors powered up the newly powered Plates, and the struts retracted. The Sedna drifted slowly out of the ruin and across the desolate plain on manual thrusters.

The controls were as smooth as butter, to Barcus. The interior of the ship had advanced inertial dampeners that Barcus did not realize were available on a ship this small. Aft cameras showed the dust blowing off the ship as it gained speed.

"Po, we are good to go," he said. A window in his HUD showed what she could see, and she had a small window with his face in it, thanks to Em.

"Auto-ascent initiated," Po said awkwardly from the pilot seat of the PT-137.

"You're doing fine, Po. Stick to the flight plan, and I will follow you," Barcus said over the comms.

He could see the small shuttle spiraling up in the aft display. It reached altitude, and soon it passed the larger ship. Barcus had never flown a ship this big with actual windows. Windows were not used in spaceships anymore. They were too easily damaged.

"Barcus, you can really see the damage from out here in the sun," Po said. "Lots of the...hull is ripped open with long gashes. And it looks like one of the...skids is still partially down. The center front one." Her words were gaining confidence.

"That is excellent information. The system shows all green lights." Po now knew what a green light meant. But now she knew it wasn't always right.

"Barcus?" It was Em this time on the open channel so Po could hear. "All the comms are down on this ship. None work. The main dish is gone, even though the display shows it stowed for FTL. I am concerned about all the false green status indicators."

"Barcus." It was Po.

"This is the best day of my life," She said. He was looking at her now. He couldn't see her face with the visor down, but he saw her wipe her cheeks from beneath the visor with her left hand.

"Magic, all of it. Do you believe me yet?" Her mouth was all he could see and her smile was wide.

***

The return trip was faster. The Sedna had very advanced navigation and sensor arrays. Once they were out over the water, they could move fast, without worries about being observed. When darkness fell, it auto-activated the night vision features of Po's helmet. Stu continued to monitor comms traffic easily because it wasn't really used very much.

Barcus noticed something odd on one of the status displays. "Em, do you see this?"

"Yes. Proximity to the Sedna has activated Ulric's HUD implant, once you brought everything up. He may be confused when he wakes up. He really should have gotten some sleep last night."

"Ulric has a HUD implant? What version? He must have been

wealthy to get one back then. Can you integrate it with the EmNet?"

"Yes," A minute later, "Done. Software upgrades in place. We will test it when he wakes."

The autopilot on the Sedna was not an autonomous AI like Stu, but it functioned well. It allowed Barcus and Em to go over system after system manually to discover why everything was indicating there were no problems. They found the reason why the board was always green, eventually.

The ship status board was driven by a continuous, verbose, system log, that was constantly monitored by another subsystem that drove the status board. It was being fed a historic log file in a continuous loop. It was easy enough to remedy by redirecting the subsystem to the correct log.

The moment the change was made, a full third of the status board went red, a klaxon began to howl, red emergency lighting engaged and the inertial dampeners went off-line with a lurch that almost tossed Barcus out of his chair.

"Barcus, what's wrong? The ship is drifting off course radically! You're falling!" Po said.

"I have just figured out what is wrong with the ship. Please stand by."

The autopilot had instantly disengaged when the log was redirected. With one hand on the flight controls, he started redirecting it back to the looped log file with the other.

Suddenly, the bridge door opened and Ulric tumbled into the room and yelled over the klaxon, "What the hell are you doing?"

Barcus didn't answer but simply pressed "enter" and the klaxon stopped, the lights all went green, the autopilot indicated it was available. He engaged it just as they were about to reach the shore. He had lost 2,000 feet in altitude.

"Barcus. Answer me!" Po demanded.

"We are sorted out now, Po. That was a very creative engineer you had there, Ulric."

Ulric was sitting at the center enginerring console in front, saying, "What the hell do you think you're doing? You can't just fly this thing without someone watching the logs! All the safety protocols have been disabled! You could be about to have a reactor core breach and you'd never know!"

Ulric was rapidly accessing unfamiliar control systems. Finally, he brought up a custom status panel that had the real status of the system, but no klaxons or overrides.

"Well?" Barcus said.

"The inertial dampener is overheating. We need to take it off-line. Nineteen percent of the Grav-panels are not functioning, but it looks like Wujcik rearranged them so all the failed ones are at the center. Fucking fuel is at 6%. DAMMIT! Six compartments have hull breaches, all comms are down and one of the skids is not retracted all the way."

"I saw the skid earlier. It's up most of the way," Po said.

Ulric's head spun around to look at Barcus. "What?"

"It's okay. The skid is up," Barcus repeated.

"The comms are down. Where is Po?" Ulric asked, incredulous.

"She is flying the shuttle back," Barcus replied.

"The fucking comms are not just down?! CORRECTION. They. Are. Gone!" Ulric shouted.

"Oh, your HUD is back on-line. All our comms are via the HUD now," Barcus said as if it was self-evident.

"My HUD works?" Ulric said.

"Yes. Makes a lot of things easier," Barcus said.

"Yes. Yes it does. Fuck. What is our ETA?" Ulric said.

"We should be back at The Abbey in about 70 minutes. Stu thinks we should land in the quarry. It will keep travelers from seeing it from a distance, and it will still be hidden from the SATs there," Barcus said.

"Barcus, excuse me. You have been detected." Stu played a transmission. It was in common tongue.

"A: Yes?

B: Anderson Wharf reporting, my Lord.

A: Yes.

B: Think it was a big one, sir. Kinda white in the moonlight. Sounded like a small though. Odd one that.

A: Will arrive in one hour. Out."

"I believe that the Keeper in Anderson Wharf was under orders to report any coastal sightings. The transmission originated 400 kilometers off the coast. There is nothing there, and no SAT coverage."

"We will proceed north and turn in as planned. There is no population there," Barcus said for everyone's benefit.

"Got it," Po added.

***

Just over an hour later, they landed the Sedna in the quarry and shut all the systems down after Stu backed up all the critical files for analysis. The reactors would take time to cool but would do it unattended. The generators were shut down as the battery systems from the four hour flight were now fully charged. As the ramp closed behind them, Ulric seemed to just realize that he had to walk up out of the quarry along the donkey path in the dark.

Barcus had a flashlight, and they made their way out in less than fifteen minutes.

Po had landed in the center of the road and was waiting for them. Barcus didn't mention the manual landing.

"Now what?" Po asked.

"Home. And I am hungry," Barcus said.

"And I need a drink," Ulric added.

"Let Smith know we will be back in a few minutes," Barcus said.

"Already did," Po replied as they climbed in.

Po auto-landed the shuttle as neat as could be in the pylon garden. Smith was there to meet them. Ansel was there as well, with a candle lantern. They moved up the stairs in the tower to the tavern.

"Everything go as planned?" Smith asked Barcus. He looked at Ulric to answer. He nodded an affirmative as Rose poured him a large mug of Hermitage.

"I would like to organize a cleaning crew to help me tomorrow. A crew that isn't squeamish," he said. Ulric was a bit abashed by this request.

"Would ten be enough? They all want to see the new ship. The third in our fleet," Smith said as he looked at Barcus.

They all sat in the booth. The light on the table showed the wince Barcus tried to hide.

"Is it in the quarry then?" Smith asked, and Ulric nodded again.

"Did you see the four Trackers I had watching for you? One of them beat you here by a few minutes. As long as it's there, they will ensure that no one approaches the quarry edge," Smith said.

"Well done. Ulric will issue them all Plates. We will not wait for runners again," Barcus said. Smith nodded and moved off.

Rose brought stew with bread and cheese for the three of them, with a smile. Ulric noticed that Saay and Kia were lurking across the way, until Ulric nodded to them and raised his mug. They drifted out and Ulric tucked into his meal .

They ate in silence.

Ulric soaked up the remains of his gravy with the last of his bread then stood. He left without another word.

Barcus stood slowly. Carefully.

"It's the bath for you," Po stated.

He knew better than to argue.

No one else ever used this room to bathe. Barcus had given up talking about it. Yet there always seemed to be fresh towels and tunics for him there. The fire was well tended and the bath the perfect temperature. The wing was repaired, and what was once the dangerous ledge was now a bright carpeted hall.

Po helped him undress and step into the tub before joining him.

"So. I hear you're a pilot. That must be exciting," Barcus teased.

"When can we go again?" Po was obviously trying not to sound eager.

"We need to check how Olias is doing in the morning. I need to have a closer look at Ulric's ship. But day after tomorrow is fourth day. We could fly to Foxden."

As Barcus soaked in the tub with his eyes closed, Em provided priority reports, silently.

Par and Ash were now twelve days away from The Abbey. No more indications that mercenaries remained above the gorge. Em sought and received permission for a night pickup by the STU at 0300. They would return to Whitehall, then the STU could take some more people to the Mining Redoubt to help Olias in the morning.

"*Barcus, I have been examining the Sedna's sensor data,*" stated Em. "*I have been trying to determine the gaps in SAT coverage in a more precise fashion. But the sensors have captured the SAT itself. It's damaged but still there.*

"How much nuclear material, and of what types do you think is contained in the warheads on the weapons platforms around this planet?" The question hung there. *"Also, I believe Ash could fit inside the lift on the Sedna."*

Status report after status report was detailed. One of the projects scanned by quickly, and Barcus paused it.

"Stu, the Map Fidelity project. Does it have Anderson Wharf?" Barcus asked out loud, sitting up. "What is off the coast there? Anything?" Barcus asked.

"Nothing at all," Stu replied.

"I want you to overlay transmission data from that area. You should be able to triangulate from the comm-sats that have line of sight even though they are not responsible for imagery in that area. Include historic data if available."

The image of the map had Plate transmission locations spattered all over the coast. But they were also concentrated in a single place off the coast, an island.

Zooming out, he saw there were vast empty areas to the west. No RF transmissions of any kind anywhere. For thousands of kilometers.

"I think I have found where you can practice flying." He opened his eyes and gathered her to him.

CHAPTER FORTY-NINE

The Visitor

"Em knew who it was."

--Solstice 31 Incident Investigation Testimony Transcript: Emergency Module Digital Forensics Report. Independent Tech Analysis Team.

Barcus had overdone it the day before.

He was very slow getting out of bed. He continued to marvel how deeply Po slept these days. He dressed quietly and went to the kitchen for a mug of tea. At this early hour all the "good mornings" were still being whispered, as usual.

When he reached the top of the tower, Em was there standing at the ramparts, like she used to when he was alone on the edge of sanity.

It was before the sun managed to reach the horizon. An extremely high altitude vapor trail was the only cloud illuminated in that late spring sky.

As the sun moved down the tower, he looked below at the roof that almost killed him. It was completed. That whole wing had been rebuilt while he was still in bed recovering. The crater below was filled in with the rubble and covered with topsoil. The gardens and fields were planted, the vineyards were pruned and goats trimmed the grass beneath the orchards while the dogs protected them. The cathedral walls had been demolished and new ones were forming. The opening to the Redoubt would be inside the new structure eventually once it had a roof.

Em knew not to bother him this early. But sometimes it could not be helped.

"Ash is already working in the Redoubt below. Catching up on his power washing. Par is out by the quarry. The STU is parked just beyond the north gate bridge, awaiting supplies and passengers. This group will bring the total to 81 at the Mining Redoubt.

"Olias is still at the Mining Redoubt and reports that the lights, ventilation and water are now all functional. Cleaning has been continuing at a very rapid pace, on the upper levels, mostly the residences, kitchens and the infirmary. Even the large refrigerators and freezers are back. We may want to consider relocating there. Olias has already expressed an interest in doing so."

"Wasn't he a starving boy two seconds ago?" Barcus laughed.

"You're the one that taught him. Some of them are even calling him 'milord.' He will be Keeper Olias in no time," Em said, smiling.

"I think we should move the hospital there. Train more people. The facility was designed to the correct scale. If it becomes fully powered, maybe we can even get the computers back up. It's so out of the way, they will be safe. No one will bother them there. I was originally going to strip it of everything useful to get this one up and running. But now I am thinking another sanctuary is a good idea. We'll find more."

"I came here to discuss Ulric. I think he is going mad." She was quite serious.

"How so?"

"The girls he sleeps with or doesn't sleep with. You know what I mean. They are there for more than just sex." Em paused and looked over the edge. "They keep him from hurting himself when he has nightmares. It's why he drinks so much."

"Tell me."

"His HUD is now active. I cannot help but wonder if it's malfunctioning. And why wasn't it active before? I presume that, because there was nothing to interface with, it had shut down completely.

"I also spoke to Grady. Well, Ash talks to Grady. He hates being in The Abbey, by the way. But he loves the oatmeal. He misses his family. But he can't leave Ulric for some unknown reason. He has a wife in Exeter."

"Grady? Really? Married?"

"Yes. Well, they don't really marry here. He carves flutes. You should hear him play."

Barcus sighed.

"What is on the agenda today?" Barcus asked, and a list displayed in his HUD. The top three all still involved cleaning. Cleaning Ulric's ship, cleaning the Mining Redoubt, cleaning the hermitage below.

"This morning you might want to inspect the front skid on the Sedna, but you have to be back here by lunch. We are expecting a visitor," she told him.

"Who?" Barcus asked.

"I have no idea. Outer perimeter BUGs picked him up on the road last night by his campfire. He looks like a well-equipped Tracker. Alone. He's not hiding. Doesn't have the look of a refugee. No forbidden weapons. He should be here midday."

***

The morning went well. The inspection uncovered a broken joint in the retraction gear. Based on the schematics they had, Barcus requested that Stu fabricate a new one. With the gear lowered and locked, it was easy to replace with the new tools. Barcus was back well before midday. He was done, physically, by then anyway.

Rose had just brought his lunch tray, as he sat on the bench when he first saw him, in the distance, on the road. He walked up without any rush, crossed the small bridge and spoke in formal high speech.

"Greetings. Would this happen to be Whitehall Abbey?"

"Yes it is. Can I offer you some water and rest? I'm Barcus, the gatesman. Would you care to share my lunch? Rose always brings me too much."

"Call me Ronan," the visitor said.

He leaned his unstrung bow and quivers against the wall and took off his pack to stretch.

In Barcus's HUD, a window opened saying, "WARNING: August Ronan is a senior Keeper in service directly to the Lord High Keeper. He is also a High Keeper in his own right. He is a member of the High Council of Keepers. Ash is moving to the wall directly above you."

"What brings you this far north? These are dangerous days on the road north of the gorge," Barcus said.

"I am looking for an unsettled Keeper named Ulric. Do you know him?" Ronan was very polite.

"Ulric is the Keeper of Whitehall, and quite well settled, actually. But he is not currently in residence. He is expected in a day or two."

Ulric was now listening to the conversation via his HUD. as well as Po and Smith on their Plates.

"Would you like to wait? We get so few visitors. We have extra beds," Barcus said.

"If I may, I will wait." Ronan bowed his head slightly to Barcus.

"Excellent. Keeper Ulric has rooms set aside above the stables. Visitors are not allowed to enter Whitehall proper without leave from the Keeper. I'm sorry, but it's all I have to offer. There are two stable boys that are also near there. If you need anything, they will be able to get it for you," Barcus said.

Ronan sat as if he was weary and reluctant to get up any time soon.

"What news do you have to share?" Barcus asked.

Ronan did graciously share the lunch. He told Barcus of the destroyed villages and that the Salterferry Bridge had been burned. He also told Barcus that there were demons behind the destruction and death, great black or hairy brown giants that eat the heads and burn the rest - men, women and children, even the High Keeper's men, that were sent to hunt them down.

"I know it sounds ridiculous. But it's what some of the survivors are saying. They head south, some do anyway, below the gorge, or north to Whitehall, and Keeper Ulric's protection," Ronan said.

"I have heard many variations. We have had refugees come," Barcus added. "People that return from somewhere to find their village gone. They arrive here with just the clothes on their backs. I think it's why Rose always brings me a whole pitcher of water and two cups. We even see rider-less horses. So many horses, smelling of smoke and fear."

"Is it not forbidden to live within a fortress?" Ronan carefully asked.

"We have been commanded by our Keeper. He is very troubled by these difficult days and rumors of demons. We have also been plagued by Telis Raptors," Barcus said. "It seemed a wise precaution."

Just then Ansel came running out, "Barcus!" He came up short, clearly surprised by Ronan.

"Ronan, this is my young friend, Ansel. He seems very excited about something. What is it Ansel?" Barcus asked.

"Pam had the baby. It's a boy!" Ansel exclaimed.

"That's wonderful, Ansel. Have you told Smith?" Ansel was

shaking his head before he finished asking. "Run and tell him, but then come straight back."

"You have a smith?" Ronan asked.

"Yes. But he mostly makes nails all day. If not him, then the boys are doing it," Barcus said. They could hear the Ding... ding ding rhythm of the hammer faintly over the wall.

Ronan spoke of events in Exeter for a while. Stories were long and detailed, but the names meant nothing to Barcus.

"What about you?" Ronan asked. "How did you become the gatekeeper?"

"To be honest, I fell off the roof last winter while we were making repairs. It almost killed me. Keeper Ulric helped put me back together. I am still recovering. But I can sit on a bench by the gate," Barcus said.

"What did you do before that? Carpenter?" Ronan asked conversationally.

"Bee keeper, actually," Barcus said. "Whitehall has a flourishing bee population that has gone unattended for decades. There is much to do," Barcus said.

"I have only been here above the gorge once before. I am enjoying the cool weather," Ronan said.

Ansel ran back out and skidded to a stop and said in common, "Found 'em!"

"Ansel, please show Ronan to his room when he is ready. The largest one, on this end, please. And fetch some fresh water for him so he can wash up if he'd like," Barcus said.

"Can I carry up your things, my Lord?" Ansel asked, pointing to his bow and pack.

"Thank you, Ansel. If you like," Ronan said.

Ronan remained sitting.

"It is just as well that Keeper Ulric isn't here now. I'm so tired." The words had weight of their own.

"I spend too much time in the cities of late. Not enough under the sky. This is the first time in years that I have gotten away on my own, like the old days," Ronan said.

"I always envied the life of a Tracker. So many of us do," Barcus said.

***

They sat in the sun and casually chatted the rest of the afternoon. Ronan was sincerely interested in bee keeping. Barcus seemed very well versed in the craft, having a window open and all the bee keeping lore available at hand, being fed to him in his HUD. Ronan spoke of casual knowledge of many things not usually associated with Trackers, from brewing, to barrel making, salt mining, bread baking, blacksmithing, to carving flutes, naming just a few.

Carving flutes caught his attention, but Barcus did not pursue it.

As the sun dipped below the trees, Ansel came out to tell Barcus dinner would be ready in few minutes. It was to be stew tonight.

"Would you like to join me for dinner? Or would you like to take it in your room?" Barcus asked, knowing Po, Ulric and Smith were still listening.

"That would be nice. I have enjoyed our talk of simple things." Ronan seemed a bit sad as he said this. A long silence held after that as the shadows grew long.

Inside his HUD, Barcus was notified that dinner was ready and the gatehouse prepared. The books were collected and placed in a trunk in the loft. Everyone in The Abbey knew of this visitor now, and was to lie low if asked what the story was.

Finally, Barcus stood and gestured Ronan to enter. He closed the small gate doors behind him and set the bar on the doors.

They entered the gatehouse to find the lamps already lit and a kettle on the fire hook.

Po entered a minute later, without a word, with a first tray with water, cups, bread, butter and honey. Ronan didn't even seem to see her.

Ronan seemed taller indoors. When he took off his long leather cloak and hung it on a peg, he was thinner than Barcus first thought. His clothes were clean and well maintained for a man so long on the road.

They took the two seats at the table and food was brought - steaming bowls of venison stew, with potatoes, onions and carrots. There was fresh bread and flavorful cheese. Cold water, wine and hot tea.

Ronan ate it all but made no compliments or complaints. As Po came in to clear the dishes away, Ronan finally seemed to notice her and spoke to her for the first time. "What is your name, child?"

She froze and stood still, eyes down to her feet. "My name is Po, my Lord."

"Where were you before Whitehall?" Ronan asked.

"Greenwarren, my Lord." Eyes downcast.

"What happened?" He was sincerely interested.

"I don't really know, my lord. There were men on horses, fire and screaming. Fern, the cook, said to hide and be quiet. After the killing began, I hid in the privy, and when I saw what was happening, the midden. When I heard violence coming closer, I went into the sewer."

"Did you see anything?" he asked.

"I stayed down there all night and most of the next day. When I finally came up, it was over. I ran. Eventually I found my way here, like so many others." Po trailed off.

"The story is the same again and again," Barcus added as Po, now silently dismissed, backed her way out.

Barcus was surprised that Ronan didn't ask additional questions. He didn't really seem interested in the topic.

As they moved to the armchairs, Barcus ventured, "If I may ask, why do you want to speak to Keeper Ulric? I may be able to provide you with information that could answer your question or smooth the audience. Keeper Ulric is...often easily distracted."

"It is a personal matter. I hope he knows where I can find a man named Grady Tolwood."

CHAPTER FIFTY

Invasion

"Even Em was surprised how this played out."

--Solstice 31 Incident Investigation Testimony Transcript: Emergency Module Digital Forensics Report. Independent Tech Analysis Team.

<<<>>>

Ronan's question still hung in the air when Barcus's HUD flooded with content.

"WARNING: The M79 Troop Transport Shuttle inbound at high speed. On a direct vector for the Lislehill Estate. ETA is 4 minutes. Barcus, its Transponder is off. It's running RF dark. It was detected by BUGs."

"Are you expecting company, Keeper Ronan?" Barcus asked coldly.

He didn't seem to notice that his question had been ignored.

"Not at all. In fact, after speaking to Ann and Pyke, I specifically had my pilot drop me off several days away, so I would not alarm or alert anyone where I was going," Ronan stated simply.

Barcus noted that he mentioned Ann before Pyke.

"When they were here, they spoke very highly of the Tracker they met. In discussions, I realized it was in fact Grady Tolwood. His wife is worried about him. I will soon be heading back to the Citadel, and I can get word to her as well as his brother."

"You walked for days to speak to Grady?" Barcus knew his tone carried more than he intended. "You? A High Keeper of the Council?"

"So you really do know who I am?" Ronan seemed amused. "How refreshing."

"Why is there a troop transport headed this way?" Barcus asked straight out.

"They have touched down, Barcus. One hundred and six men on horses are already headed this way."

"Troop transport?" Ronan seemed genuinely confused.

"Yes. There are apparently over a hundred men headed this way on horseback. Are you saying that you know nothing of this?" Barcus was not hiding his anger now.

Ronan surprised him by saying, "This is all my fault. The Lord High Keeper must have discovered I was here and alone. Forgive me. I don't know how. My Plate is off AND shielded."

"It's true Barcus. There is no RF from his Plate. I didn't even know he had one. The M79 has departed and is heading south. There are no Plates in possession of these troops. They look like mercs with one High Tracker. They are coming this way fast," Em said.

"Ansel! Tell Smith I want to see him right away." The door barely opened and Ansel poked his head out long enough to say, "Right away." And he was gone.

"Keeper Ronan, why are you here, really? Why did you send those Trackers here?"

He said nothing.

"Do you know why I didn't kill you on sight? It was something Smith said about you. After Ann and Pyke were gone. He said he met you once in the past, in Langforest Keep. He said you refused to eat any of Volk's food, when he saw how Volk treated his people. That you stormed out." Ronan met his gaze, unafraid.

"Will you tell me why the High Keeper's men are killing these people?" Barcus was standing now. Both hands were holding the edge of the table.

Ronan was not intimidated or defiant. He sighed and seemed to confess, "The people that live above the gorge cannot be ruled as he wishes. It's about control." He looked Barcus in the eyes. "There was an automated census three years ago. It records the size of the planet's population and their locations. Once again they passed the 'optimum' population size for the environment, his experiments, his domain." Ronan sighed. "North of the gorge has always been too far out of his control sphere for his experiments. It fixes his problems. Two hammers, one anvil. His breeding program. A control group was once a good idea. But now he has lost focus."

He sighed and paused.

"He doesn't even care that the mercenaries are dying. He is using the same mercenaries of his potential enemies. The weaker the population, the better it is in his eyes. They are disarmed, easier to control, to dominate. At least he isn't using plague this time."

"Plague?" Barcus asked.

"At one time long ago, he released a plague above the gorge. It was difficult to control, it did its job too well. But it left the villages intact. He wants them leveled now it seems." Ronan said. "How soon before they arrive?"

"Soon," Barcus answered. Smith came in at that point. He heard the last exchange.

"Smith. There will be over a hundred men here in an hour. Gather the people up. Take them below. Tell Ulric and Olias to keep them calm. Bar the gate and the door to the catacombs. You will know when it's time to come out."

"Barcus. You don't need to do this alone, son," Smith said, placing his scarred hand on his shoulder.

"I have seen the terrible things these men do. No more," Barcus growled.

Smith looked at Ronan, in the eyes, without fear. Ronan nodded. Smith moved back into The Abbey. They could hear the call go out.

***

They walked out of the gatehouse. Po was there. Her skirts were gathered again and tucked into her belt in the front. The AR was on a single point sling on her chest. She held it with both hands. Her right hand was on the pistol grip, index finger extended. She had her satchel of spare magazines.

She defiantly looked at Ronan, a look that would have meant the anvil in Exeter.

"I will be on top of the south tower with Ash," Po said.

"Do not open the gate until it's over." Barcus looked at Ronan. "He is coming with me." Barcus tilted his head at the Keeper.

She dropped the newly fabricated bar into place behind them.

"You are going to stay out there?" Ronan asked.

"Yes," Barcus growled.

"Par is in position," Em indicated.

"Can I speak to them before anything happens?" Ronan

requested.

"That is up to you. But, say the wrong thing, and I will burn you with the rest of them."

Ronan nodded as if to accept that fate.

***

Barcus and Ronan were sitting on the bench, watching the sunset, when the riders pounded up on the east road to collect just beyond the bridge. All four fires were lit on the corner braziers of the bridge. The air was silent. Even the birds had hushed. The horses' hard breathing was the loudest sound.

The leader was a High Tracker. He came forward, over the bridge, with five other riders, to stop directly in front of Barcus and Ronan. They stayed in their saddles.

"I might have known you were behind this, August." He used the High Keeper's first name with disdain.

"Hello, Donner. I'm amazed you'd risk yourself by coming north of the gorge these days," Ronan said.

"You think just because you sit on the Council that you are somehow immune to the simple realities of the Keeper's law. I would be willing to bet that they have an anvil in there, and a hammer. Your days of ignoring God's laws are over," Donner said.

Ronan sighed. "You have no idea what is about to happen to you, do you?"

"*Par standing by. Ash Standing by. Firing solution from the west. Stay close to the wall to avoid crossfire,*" Em reported in his head.

"You will know when it's time to go," Barcus said out loud, speaking to Em, Par and Po all at once.

"Go? Go where?" Donner asked, beginning to laugh as Barcus and Ronan began to stand.

"Donner, before this gets started, I need to ask you a question. You have spent enough time with the High Keeper, you have seen the subtle horrors he is making in the Citadel, you have seen the evil done to the people." The answer was already on Donner's smirking face, "Will you and your men stand with me when the time comes?"

Donner replied loud enough so all his men could hear, "I handpicked each of these men. While they each had blood on their hands and on their lips." Donner smiled.

"Go to hell," Barcus growled, drew his gun and shot him in the eye. The back of his head exploded, spraying blood into the faces of the men behind him.

Then it all happened at once.

Ash had jumped from the tower above, at the same time, landing on his feet in front of the gate with what seemed like a clap of thunder, before the echo of the gunshot was through.

Suddenly, while the riders stared at Ash in momentary shock, at the appearance of this rumored demon, ALL the men on horseback were suddenly bristling with arrows and crossbow bolts from their chests. Heads began to explode from suppressed AR gunfire. Ninety of them simply tumbled to the ground beside their horses, dead. Nine of them, not killed outright, tried to gallop off, only to catch a half dozen more shafts in their backs.

Ash ripped them from their saddles as he ran impossibly fast after them down the south road into the forest.

Barcus looked around and up to see the entire population of Whitehall on the wall above. Just as he saw the third volley fly, he was startled by a gunshot directly behind him. He turned to see Ronan pointing a stainless steel, heavy caliber revolver, with both hands, at one of the five lead escorts. He had been about to fire a crossbow at Barcus when Ronan dispatched him.

Men with axes spilled out of the gate then. They quickly ended any that remained moving.

It was over in 60 seconds.

***

Smith walked out of the gate to Barcus.

"I thought I asked you to take them below," Barcus asked, with eyebrow raised.

"You also said I'd know when it was time to come up," Smith said. "It was time."

Grady had been one of the men with axes. He walked up to Barcus and Ronan, wiping the blood from his ax with a rag. "I understand you wanted to speak to me, my Lord." Grady was very matter of fact, like cleaning blood from his ax was the same as drying a tea mug.

Ronan regained his composure. "It's good to see you again. Ann and Pyke send their kind regards."

Two riders that seemed to get clear and outrun Ash were dropped by Par's 10mm fire ripping them to pieces. The sound, like thunder, rolled over them and was ignored.

People began pouring out the south portal to lead the horses into The Abbey and the paddock. The horses were very well trained and never spooked during the fight. Two large wagons came out of the gate. The soldiers were being stripped of weapons, gear, provisions, pouches, belts and even cloaks if they were not too bloody. All of these items went into one wagon as bodies went into the other.

"Please return my greetings to them as well, if you live." Ronan saw Grady's muscles in his forearms clench as he awaited word from Barcus. Grady's eyes went to the revolver still in his hand, now pointed to the ground.

"It's your wife, Wex. And your brother. They are very worried. They expected you months ago. I owed your brother, Cyrus, a favor."

"And what is the favor?" Grady asked.

"I came to tell you that the High Keeper has taken Wex to the Citadel, to play the flute for him...and sing."

Grady stared at him in shock. Barcus didn't know what this meant. Without a word, he turned and walked into The Abbey.

Ronan studied Barcus's face in the fading light.

"I never thought I'd find someone that hated the Lord High Keeper as much as I do." Ronan turned and sat again on the bench, placing the gun in his lap. "You usually have to meet him to hate him so much."

"He killed everyone I loved. Everyone I knew," Barcus growled.

"So you ARE the man from Earth," he stated flatly.

Three of the women retrieving arrows and bolts nearby from the bodies froze for a moment at these words. Looking at one another, they continued working but did not move away.

"Yes. And I swear, I will be the demon under their beds. And perhaps yours," Barcus said though clenched teeth.

Looking into the distance, August said, "Thirty some years ago, something happened to the satellites over the East Isles." Ronan looked into the sky. "They lost communications, imagery, everything there. Since then, I have been collecting strong, smart and independent people there. In the beginning, it was to quietly revive some simple technology to make people's lives easier. Like better boat designs. I found the archives full of low tech innovations that would make my people's lives more comfortable, safer, without risking the anvil. Simple things like chimney designs, wood stoves, plumbing, better steel, medicines." He looked back to Barcus. He could tell Barcus was trying to decide what to do with him.

"I am not one of these." He gestured to the dead men. Ronan turned his revolver around and handed it to Barcus, grip first.

Po stepped up just then, with Ash right behind her as Ash said, "I like this Keeper. I will kill him last."

Ronan looked up at Ash and then suddenly laughed. It was infectious. Barcus soon followed along with Po.

"And you have a golem. Why am I surprised?" Ronan said.

"Where is Ulric?" Barcus asked out loud.

Po replied at the same time Em brought up a window in his HUD. "He is below with the children. He isn't afraid of the dark at least. He will stay there until this is done. He's telling those stories again. The ones the children beg for, and make their parents flinch."

Barcus could see the children were dragging him to the floor in a pile of arms and legs and laughter.

"Where is Smith?" The window switched views. He was back at his forge, shirt off, already glazed with sweat. Two boys worked the bellows as he stirred the coals. The sun was beginning to drop below the horizon.

They all moved in the gate to turn right, entering the paddock in front of the blacksmith shop.

"Well, if you are not going to kill me, I'd like to call my shuttle for a pickup. I'm getting too old to walk that far," Ronan said, as Smith drew a red hot iron out of the coals.

"Barcus..." Po was touching his arm, but looking at Smith ten yards away.

Barcus recognized the thing in Smith's hand. It was a branding iron. The same brand Po carried on her breast. He was tapping the red hot iron on the edge of the forge, dislodging tiny bits of charcoal.

Before anyone could move another step, without making a sound, Smith pressed the brand to his own chest. He held it there impossibly long.

Barcus stepped up, and took it from his hand.

Smith finally let go of the breath he was holding.

After a moment he stepped forward toward Ronan. "For generations, this mark meant we were slaves. They always knew they'd have to kill me before I allowed them to mark me." People were pausing to listen. "Now it means something else." There was pride in his eyes. His eyes shifted from Ronan to Barcus.

Barcus held his eyes for a full minute.

In one quick motion, he walked directly to the largest anvil, and taking the largest hammer in hand, Barcus destroyed the brand with a single devastating blow of the hammer.

Confirming it was flattened, he then tossed it into a barrel of water with a hiss.

"That is the last." Barcus looked up and everyone was silent.

CHAPTER FIFTY-ONE

Hume

"The AI was playing the long game. The deletions hid the true plan."

--Solstice 31 Incident Investigation Testimony Transcript: Emergency Module Digital Forensics Report. Independent Tech Analysis Team.

An hour later, it was as if nothing had happened at all. One of the inner courtyards had a central fire pit where people gathered, unable to sleep.

They spoke in quiet tones, as they drank beer or wine or sipped tea.

Barcus said quietly, "I wanted to spare them that burden, the dark business of killing. They didn't need to carry that weight."

Smith replied, "Interesting. That's exactly what they said about you."

"I still need to contact my people. I'm sorry. I am overdue for a check-in," Ronan said. "May I? It won't give away our position. I promise."

Barcus looked at Po. She nodded.

"Go ahead," he said.

He drew out a Plate. It was much smaller than the other Plates Barcus had seen.

"Checking in. I'm fine. Approach Sierra-Delta-Niner," was all that Ronan said.

"Barcus, his Plate is not on the global net. No geo-tag. No RF detected. Interesting," Em noted.

He put the Plate away and said, "There is someone I want you to meet." He was speaking to them all, but looking at Barcus.

***

It was only a few minutes later. *"Barcus, we have a craft coming this way at high speed and low altitude. ETA is less than two minutes. There is no ID*

Transponder. BUGs picked up the sounds in the dark," Em said, opening a tactical map. It was speeding toward Whitehall, directly along the road. "*Barcus, it's beneath the tree canopy. Only three meters off the deck.*"

"Something is coming in at high speed. Would you know anything about that?" Barcus asked. "Answer quickly before I destroy it."

Barcus was shown that Par was training her 10mm at the road, thermal tracking and automatic targeting was enabled.

"Hold fire. Please," Ronan said.

The smallest craft Barcus had seen thus far on this planet came in low and fast out of the tunnel made by the trees over the road. Em identified it as a modern AV-1201 Sportster, a small high performance two-seater, one person behind the other. They called them Hammerheads because of their shape and their center articulation. It had one turbine in the rear and two in the front. It circled Whitehall twice as it's turbines spun down and then hovered to land in the paddock at the far end. The entire craft was smaller than the wagons it parked in front of. By the lack of dust being kicked up, Barcus knew that it had modern anti-Grav tech.

As it settled down, the cowling hinged up slowly. A helmeted figure, clothed entirely in black, stepped out. The helmet stayed on, as it probably had some kind of night vision. It was a full face black mirror. The pilot was wearing a hooded cloak and tabard in addition to a standard black flight suit with a drop holster on the right side leg.

The pilot spoke as the turbines fell silent, "A Delta-Niner? Really?" It was a woman's voice.

She lowered the hood and then slowly took off her helmet. Her black hair, cropped very close, didn't even cover her ears. She was a small, beautiful, very dark skinned woman.

She took off a glove and extended her right hand to Barcus. "Sir, I'm Hume." Her teeth were bright white in contrast to her skin.

Barcus shook her hand, his mouth gaping.

"Hume, this is Barcus," Ronan said. "This is why I walked all this way," he explained to Hume, not Barcus.

"Valerie Hume. Lieutenant Valerie Hume!" Barcus said, recognizing her. Stunned.

She was wordlessly nodding.

He suddenly drew her into a hug that took her off her feet. She was tiny, just like Po. He spun her in the air as if she was a child.

"You remember me!" she laughed.

"You're alive?" he yelled, "I thought I was the only one. Are there others? My god, you're real!" He set her back on her feet. He touched her arms and shoulders, was finally holding the sides of her head, making sure she was real. "You have to tell me everything. I have so much to tell you," Barcus said.

Barcus turned to speak directly to Po. "Hume was with me on the Ventura. She was on the third shift command crew. The security chief."

Po said, "What's a Delta-Niner?"

Ronan replied, "It means, survivor found, alive."

"Have there been others? How did you find me?" Barcus was choking up. Po was the only one that noticed.

"I have someone that would like to speak to you." She reached into the cockpit and activated some controls. A small, tight-beamed, directional LASER based comm antenna deployed from her small ship and focused on the sky.

Barcus turned and reached for Po. "This is a friend from Earth," He whispered to her. She put her arm around his waist. He held her close, waiting for Hume.

"Barcus. You are saved." Po said, with an odd tone in her voice and an unfocused look in her eyes, "Barcus, I can see words, inside my eyes. Even if my eyes are closed."

Ulric walked up just then, "What's all this?" He was the first to say it, "Confirm."

A dialog popped up in Barcus's HUD that said, "A new network has requested protocol handshake. Confirm or deny?"

Just then, Po gave a huge flinch. She turned her head from side to side, blinking her eyes. She finally looked up at Barcus, saying, "I see the words. In my eyes. They say, 'A new network has requested protocol handshake. Confirm or deny?' what does this mean, Barcus?"

Barcus said. "Confirm." The dialog disappeared. He stared at her.

Barcus looked down at Ulric, then at her. She looked up at him as She said with wide eyes, "Confirm." Somehow she had a HUD. Barcus was staring at her trying to figure out exactly how that happened, when the comm channel opened.

"Barcus, is that you?" The voice over the HUD said. He looked back at Hume. It was obvious Po and Ulric could hear it too.

"Jimbo?" Barcus said.

"That's Captain Jimbo, asswipe! Barcus! You're not dead! How's it hanging, Bro?"

CHAPTER FIFTY-TWO

The Interim Report

"At this point we have decided to submit this as an interim report. The narrative attached is too important to await the full final report. The recovered backup of the Emergency Module, known as Em, has provided significant new insights. The HUD data it contains has confirmed that it was, in fact Lieutenant Valerie Hume and Captain James Worthington of the third shift command crew on the Ventura.

"Please note that it has been confirmed as Captain, not Commander Worthington. An automated field promotion had been initiated. This confirmed the death of Captain Alice Everett of the Ventura.

"Conclusions: This report invalidates the charges leveled against Roland Barcus regarding the destruction of the Ventura. It also calls into question assumptions regarding his role in the Solstice 31 Incident and the deaths of 110 million people on Earth two years later, on December 22, 2631.

"The Winter Solstice of 2631. The longest night in the history of Earth."

--*Solstice 31 Incident Investigation Testimony Transcript: Emergency Module Digital Forensics Interim Report. Independent Tech Analysis Team. March 9th, 2663.*

<<<>>>

ACKNOWLEDGMENTS

I have several people to thank for their help with this book. I will begin with my wife Brenda. Thank you for your patience as it appears I go deaf while I'm writing. Thank you for all your feedback and ideas. And thank you for caring for me all through that horrible year, encouraging me to write to forget my pain and my loss.

Thanks go to my son Gray and daughter Cady. Thank you for making me proud of you. Thanks for making it so easy to be your dad.

Thanks go to Kelly Lenz Carr, Dave Nelson, Karen Parent and Katherine Gotthardt for your help editing. I know it was a lot of heavy lifting.

Special thanks go to Mark Henshaw, Michelle Roman Higgins, Marko Kloos and Larry Correia for taking the time to answer my questions and give me advice about the craft, process and even fonts.

I'd like to thank my friends Tony, Rob, Nancy, Breda, Dave, Donna, Ginny, Jimbo, Roberta, my brother Carl and all the people at the Loudon Science Fiction Writers Group and Writers Eating DC for your help, support and inspiration.

Lastly, thanks go to Chris Schwartz. He gave me the first shove to write this book. He coined the term "Keeper", he introduced me to good bourbon, he inspired a favorite character and he gave me the most and best feedback to make this story better. Plus he always makes my wife smile. Brave he his…

ABOUT THE AUTHOR

Martin Wilsey is a writer, hunter, photographer, rabble rouser, father, friend, marksman, story teller, frightener of children, carnivore, engineer, fool, philosopher, cook and madman. He and his wife Brenda live in Virginia where, just to keep him off the streets, he works as a research scientist for a government funded think tank.

FOR MORE INFORMATION:

Blog: http://wilseymc.blogspot.com/

Web: http://www.baytirus.com/

Email: info@baytirus.com